PEN

T0176490

NATSUME SŌSEKI (in the Japanese order, surname first) is universally recognized to be Japan's greatest modern novelist. Born Natsume Kinnosuke in Edo in 1867, the year before the city was renamed Tokyo, he survived a lonely childhood, being traded between foster and biological parents, was deeply schooled in both the Chinese classics and English, and at the age of twenty-two chose from a Chinese source the defiantly playful pen name Sōseki ("Garglestone") to signify his sense of his own eccentricity. In 1893, Sōseki became the second graduate of (Tokyo) Imperial University's English Department and entered the graduate program, but in 1895 he abruptly took a position teaching English in a rural middle school. Though hoping to become a writer as early as the age of fourteen, Sōseki chose the more respectable path of English literature scholar, was sent to London by the Ministry of Education in 1900 for two years, and taught in his alma mater until 1907, when his early success as a part-time writer of stories and novels led him to accept a position as staff novelist for the *Asahi Shinbun* newspaper, in which he serialized the rest of his fourteen novels. Sōseki also published substantial works of literary theory and history (and contemplative essays, memoirs, lectures on the individual and society, etc.) and continued to think of himself as a scholar after his controversial resignation from the University. His works quickly lost any hint of academic artifice, however, relying initially on a freewheeling sense of humor, and then darkening as Sōseki wrestled with increasingly debilitating bouts of depression and illness. *Sanshirō*, his seventh novel, written in 1908, was the last in which the humor predominated. Sōseki wrote many Chinese poems and haiku as a form of escape from the stresses of the world he had created. He died in 1916 with his last—and longest—novel still unfinished. Each new generation of Japanese readers rediscovers Sōseki, and Western readers find in him a modern intellect doing battle in familiar territory, a truly original voice among those artists of the world who have most fully grasped the modern experience.

HARUKI MURAKAMI (in Western order) has written twelve novels, eight volumes of short stories, and over thirty books of nonfiction, while also translating well over thirty volumes of American fiction, poetry and nonfiction since his prizewinning debut in 1979 at the age of thirty. Known in the English-speaking world primarily for his novels *A Wild Sheep Chase*, *Hard-boiled Wonderland and the End of the World*, *Norwegian Wood*, *Dance Dance Dance*, *The Wind-up Bird Chronicle*, and *Kafka on the Shore*, Murakami has also published commentary on the 1995 Tokyo subway sarin gas attack in *Underground*, written a book of essays on the relationship of long-distance running to his fiction, *What I Talk About When I Talk About Running*, and edited a book of American, British and Irish fiction, *Birthday Stories*. His works have been translated into more than forty languages.

JAY RUBIN has translated Natsume Sōseki's novel *The Miner*, Akutagawa Ryūnosoke's *Rashōmon and Seventeen Other Stories* (Penguin, 2006), and Haruki Murakami's *Norwegian Wood*, *The Wind-up Bird Chronicle*, *after the quake*, and *After Dark*. He is the author of *Injurious to Public Morals: Writers and the Meiji State* and *Haruki Murakami and the Music of Words*, and the editor of *Modern Japanese Writers*. He began his study of Japanese at the University of Chicago, where he received his Ph.D. in 1970, and taught Japanese literature at the University of Washington and at Harvard University, where he is now an emeritus professor.

NATSUME SŌSEKI

Sanshirō: a Novel

With an Introduction by HARUKI MURAKAMI
Translated with Notes by JAY RUBIN

PENGUIN BOOKS

PENGUIN CLASSICS

Published by the Penguin Group
Penguin Books Ltd, 80 Strand, London WC2R ORL, England
Penguin Group (USA) Inc., 375 Hudson Street, New York, New York 10014, USA
Penguin Group (Canada), 90 Eglinton Avenue East, Suite 700, Toronto, Ontario, Canada M4P 2Y3
(a division of Pearson Penguin Canada Inc.)
Penguin Ireland, 25 St Stephen's Green, Dublin 2, Ireland
(a division of Penguin Books Ltd)
Penguin Group (Australia), 250 Camberwell Road, Camberwell, Victoria 3124, Australia
(a division of Pearson Australia Group Pty Ltd)
Penguin Books India Pvt Ltd, 11 Community Centre, Panchsheel Park, New Delhi – 110 017, India
Penguin Group (NZ), 67 Apollo Drive, Rosedale, Auckland 0632, New Zealand
(a division of Pearson New Zealand Ltd)
Penguin Books (South Africa) (Pty) Ltd, Block D, Rosebank Office Park, 181 Jan Smuts Avenue,
Parktown North, Gauteng 2193, South Africa

www.penguin.com

First published 1908–9
This translation first published in Penguin Classics 2009

027

Translation, Chronology, Further Reading and Notes copyright © Jay Rubin, 2009
Introduction copyright © Haruki Murakami, 2009
All rights reserved

The moral right of the translator and introducer has been asserted

Set in 10.25/12.25 pt PostScript Adobe Sabon
Typeset by Rowland Phototypesetting Ltd, Bury St Edmunds, Suffolk
Printed and bound in Great Britain by Clays Ltd, Elcograf S.p.A.

ISBN: 978-0-140-45562-5

www.greenpenguin.co.uk

Penguin Books is committed to a sustainable
future for our business, our readers and our planet.
This book is made from Forest Stewardship
Council™ certified paper.

Contents

Note on Japanese Name Order and Pronunciation

All Japanese names that appear after this page in the book are written in the Japanese order, surname first. The author is known in Japan as Natsume Sōseki, and the writer of the Introduction as Murakami Haruki. "Sōseki," however, is a traditional pen name (much like that of the seventeenth-century haiku poet, Matsuo Bashō), and it is by this, rather than the family name, that most Japanese and Western readers refer to the author. Sōseki's name has been given in the Japanese order but Murakami's in the Western order on the cover and title page because of their greater familiarity in the West and for convenience in cataloging.

Some guidelines to pronouncing Japanese names and terms:
All a's are long, as in "father," e is pronounced as in "bed," i sounds like "ee," and three-syllable names tend to have a stress on the first syllable. Thus, "Natsume" is pronounced "NAH-tsoo-meh" (three syllables) and "Sanshirō" is pronounced "SAHN-she-row." "Yojirō" sounds like "YO-jee-row." "Mineko" is "MEE-neh-ko." "Hirota" has a very slight stress in the middle: "Hee-ROW-tah."
Macrons have been included to indicate long syllables but have been eliminated from the place names Tōkyō, Kyōto, Ōsaka, Kōbe, Honshū, and Kyūshū, and from familiar words such as "shōji" and "Shintō."

Chronology

1854 *February*: Commodore Matthew Perry returns to Japan with gunboats to enforce previous year's demand from U.S. President Fillmore that Japan open its doors to trade. Tokugawa regime of warrior-bureaucrats, headquartered in city of Edo, agrees in writing to open the country, political unrest increases.

1854 or 1855: Widower with two daughters, Natsume Kohē Naokatsu (1817–97), an Edo *nanushi* (landowning merchant-class "headman" with local administrative and police powers), marries Fukuda Chie (1826–81), divorced daughter of a pawnbroker. Chie will give Naokatsu six more children between 1856 and 1867.

1867 *9 February*: Chie gives birth to her sixth child on day designated by astrological charts as "Elder Brother of Metal," which dooms the child to a life of thievery unless he is given a name with the character for "metal/gold/money" (*kin*) in it. Adding the male suffix "-nosuke" to "Kin," the Natsumes name the boy "Kinnosuke". Parents are embarrassed to have had a child at their advanced ages of forty-nine and forty (fifty and forty-two by Japanese count). Shortly after birth, Kinnosuke is sent to the relative of a Natsume family maid to nurse but is soon brought home by sixteen-year-old half-sister, who is scolded by father. A neighbor nurses the child.

1868 (1 year old) Tokugawa rule ends with the "restoration" of the emperor to a position of theoretical sovereignty. *3 September*: Edo is renamed Tokyo (Eastern Capital). *23 October*: the modernizing Meiji Period[1] (1868–1912)

begins. Naokatsu retains some authority under Meiji government and later holds various police positions, but family's
fortunes decline.

November: Kinnosuke adopted by Naokatsu's former
ward, Shiohara Masanosuke and wife Yasu. He remains
"Shiohara Kinnosuke" until 1888. Shioharas shower him
with love, nurture a fondness for traditional plebeian enter-
tainments, storytelling and comedy, by taking him to the
variety theater (see Chapter 3 of *Sanshirō*).

1874 (7) Shiohara marital turmoil. Kinnosuke changes hands,
homes, schools several times over next two years. Growing
consciousness of being traded like a piece of property will
emerge in novel *Michikusa* (*Grass on the Wayside*, 1915).

1876 (9) *April*: Shioharas divorce. *May*: Kinnosuke is returned
to the Natsume household, though still legally a Shiohara.
Learns from a maid that his "grandparents" are actually his
parents. Father stern, mother more loving.

1878 (11) Kinnosuke enters middle school, chooses course that
emphasizes Chinese studies instead of English, though this
invalidates him for entry into University Preparatory School.

1881 (14) Mother dies. Around this time, Kinnosuke leaves
middle school for a private academy of Chinese studies.
Enjoys Chinese literature, Japanese novels, thinks of becoming a writer, but elder brother scolds him for considering
such an unworthy profession. Beginning to think of pursuing
a university education.

1883 (16) Enters English academy, sells beloved Chinese books,
begins serious study for University Preparatory School
entrance exams.

1884 (17) Begins rooming-house life, returning to Natsume
home occasionally when ill.

September: Enters University Preparatory School Preparatory Course.

1885 (18) English schoolwork consistently signed "K.
Shiohara" until 4 January 1888.

1886 (19) *April*: Preparatory School renamed First Higher
Middle School. Pleurisy causes him to fail exam for advance-
ment to higher class. Shock of failure inspires him to go

to the head of his class and remain there until graduation. Teaching to support himself. Tokyo University renamed Imperial University; will remain the only Imperial University until 1897 when it is renamed Tokyo Imperial University after the founding of Kyoto Imperial University. Others added in 1907 (Tōhoku), 1910 (Kyushu), etc.

1887 (20) Two of three elder brothers die of tuberculosis. Suffers first of many eye diseases, acute trachoma. Considers studying architecture, but friend persuades him to change his mind.

September: University English Literature Department founded.

1888 (21) *28 January*: Name transferred from Shiohara to Natsume family registry upon large payment (¥170 down, ¥3 monthly, ¥240 total) by Naokatsu to Shiohara: legal name once again "Natsume."

September: Advances to regular course of First Higher Middle School, Faculty of Letters, more or less certain he will major in English literature. ("Middle" dropped from school name in 1894. This is the prestigious First Higher School or First National College where *Sanshirō*'s Professor Hirota teaches.)

1889 (22) *January*: Becomes friends with tubercular classmate and budding haiku poet Masaoka Shiki (1867–1902). Begins writing haiku, which remains a lifelong practice.

11 February: Minister of Education, Mori Arinori (1847–89), leaving home for ceremonial promulgation of new Meiji constitution, assassinated for supposed offenses against the national gods. *16 February*: Like *Sanshirō*'s Professor Hirota, Kinnosuke and classmates may have stood in formation at Mori Arinori's funeral. *May*: Speaks against mindless nationalism at student patriotic society. Writes a critique and nine poems—all in Chinese—for Shiki's hand-circulated literary anthology, using playful pen name "Sōseki" (Garglestone) for the first time. Identifies himself with the eccentric protagonist of a Chinese story who stubbornly insisted on the correctness of his all-too-obviously mistaken declaration, "I shall pillow my head on the stream and rinse my mouth out with stones."

1890 (23) *July*: Graduates from First Higher Middle School, but feeling depressed. *September*: Enters Imperial University English Literature Department with annual tuition advance of ¥85.

1891 (24) Outstanding record wins him a full scholarship, but Scottish instructor's insistence on rote-learning dulls his enthusiasm for English literature, which he will never love like Chinese. *July*: Deeply saddened by death of sister-in-law Tose (a secret love?) from complications of pregnancy. Boarding-house friend Tachibana Masaki becomes first graduate of English Literature Department (and later becomes customs official in Shanghai and Da-lien).

1892 (25) *April*: Changes official domicile to Hokkaidō, perhaps to avoid draft. *May*: Begins part-time teaching at private college (until 1895). Publishes several literary essays.

1893 (26) *July*: Becomes second graduate of Imperial University English Department, the only graduate that year. Enters graduate program, but has doubts about devoting himself to literary research, feeling he has been "deceived by English literature." *October*: Takes second part-time lectureship, in English, at Higher Normal School (annual salary ¥450), helping to support his father and half-sister Fusa.

1894 (27) Diagnosed with possible early stages of tuberculosis, afraid of meeting two brothers' fate, works to improve health, but plagued by depression.

   1 August: Sino-Japanese War begins.

   December–January: Seeks Zen enlightenment in Kamakura temple, befriends monks but leaves feeling he has failed.

1895 (28) *April*: Abruptly takes teaching position at middle school in Shiki's rural home town, Matsuyama. Hoping to save up for a trip to the West, but ¥80 monthly salary lasts only two weeks. *23–27 April*: Sino-Japanese War ends with demeaning treaty that will be avenged with the Russo-Japanese War of 1904–05. Long-distance negotiations for arranged marriage begin. Writing haiku, especially after Shiki comes to live with him in August. *October*: Feeling lonely after Shiki leaves for Tokyo. *December*: Visits Tokyo to meet Nakane Kyōko (1877–1963), daughter of Chief Secretary

of the House of Peers, at formal "interview" (*miai*). Decides
to marry.

1896 (29) Increasingly depressed by life in Matsuyama. *April*:
Resigns teaching post in Matsuyama, takes instructorship
(¥100/month) at Fifth National College in Kumamoto
(Sanshirō's alma mater). *June*: Kyōko and father come to
Kumamoto, wedding performed in Sōseki's rented house.
July: Promoted to professor.

   September: Terada Torahiko (1878–1935), the model for
Sanshirō's scientist, Nonomiya, enters the College. Lafcadio
Hearn (1850–1904) appointed lecturer in English literature
at Imperial University in Tokyo. Meanwhile, in Kumamoto,
Sōseki actively involved with student journal, class outings,
peaceful home life, writing haiku, Chinese verse, occasional
scholarly papers.

1897 (30) Father-in-law urges him to take a teaching post in
Tokyo, but he declines. *April*: Writes to Shiki that he wants
to quit teaching, spend all his time reading and writing literature. *29 June*: Naokatsu dies, but Kinnosuke continues supporting half-sister Fusa until 1915. *July*: Travels to Tokyo
with Kyōko, who experiences a miscarriage. *September*:
Returns to Kumamoto, Kyōko follows in October. Peaceful
life resumes, but letter from adoptive mother Yasu threatens
complications.

1898 (31) Writing Chinese verse, literary essays, guiding students in haiku composition. Kyōko suffers from attacks of
hysteria, attempts suicide in June or July, especially bad with
bouts of extreme morning sickness in autumn. *November/
December*: Publishes playful literary essay in Shiki and
friends' haiku magazine *Hototogisu* under the pen name
"Hechima Sensei" (Professor Loofah).

1899 (32) *31 May*: Daughter Fudeko born.

   August: Terada Torahiko leaves to study science at Tokyo
Imperial University. Good friends leaving Kumamoto for
Tokyo.

1900 (33) *April*: Appointed acting assistant principal. Kyōko
becomes pregnant with second child. *12 May*: Ordered by
Ministry of Education to spend two full years in England

studying the language at government expense (annual stipend
of ¥1,800 plus meager family support in his absence of ¥300
per year). Initially declines (neither the Ministry nor he had
any idea what he should do in England), but eventually
accepts. *July*: Sells or gives away all household goods, leaves
Kumamoto, depositing Kyōko and Fudeko with Tokyo in-
laws. *8 September*: Boards German ship for Genoa, arriving
19 October. *21 October*: Arrives in Paris by train. Visits
Louvre, World's Fair (Exposition Universelle). *28 October*:
Arrives in London without a clear purpose. Sees the sights.
November: Visits Cambridge, but concludes that government
stipend too low for study there. *November/December*:
Attends a class at University College, London. Lives in a
series of shabby rooming houses, mostly reading in his room,
but contracts with Shakespeare scholar William James Craig
(1843–1906) for weekly individual tutoring at 5 shillings per
hour (an arrangement that would continue until October
1901). No more formal study than this.

1901 (34) *27 January*: Second daughter, Tsuneko, born.
2 February: Views Queen Victoria's funeral cortège in Hyde
Park. Letters from this time express anger at Kyōko for
writing infrequently, and desire to teach at the First National
College in Tokyo upon his return to Japan instead of continuing to teach in Kumamoto. *May/June*: His informative letters
to Shiki are published in *Hototogisu* as "Letters from
London" and signed, haiku-style, "Sōseki."

    5 May–26 June: Chemist Ikeda Kikunae (1864–1936), later
inventor of MSG, introduced to Sōseki by a Fifth National
College colleague, takes temporary lodging in Sōseki's rooming house on his way back to Japan after a period of study
in Leipzig; Sōseki is so impressed by Ikeda's erudition and
cultivated intelligence that their long, intense conversations
stir him to engage in more substantial, systematic research.

    July: Changes rooming houses one last time, and for final
year and a half in London, spends practically all his time in
his room, reading and taking notes for what will be his
Bungakuron ("Theory of Literature", 1907). The strain and
isolation take a toll on his mental stability.

1902 (35) *30 January*: Anglo-Japanese Alliance signed, clearing the way for Japan to fight Russia over control of Korea; war fever builds slowly. The first "equal" military treaty between Japan and a Western power (in force until 1922), it causes great elation in Japan, but Sōseki derides it, comparing it to a poor man running around the village ringing bells and beating drums because he's bagged a rich wife (see *Sanshirō*, Chapter 6).

Autumn: Rumors of a mental breakdown reach Japan, putting University plans to hire him to work with Lafcadio Hearn on hold. Tries to calm his nerves by taking up cycling. *Late November*: Receives word that Shiki has died. *5 December*: Leaves London for return to Japan.

1903 (36) *24 January*: Arrives in Tokyo, finds father-in-law has lost his political appointment, and Kyōko and children living with him in near-poverty. Moves Kyōko and children into new rental house; must now partially support father-in-law. Friends have arranged part-time teaching positions for him: twenty hours of English at First National College (¥700/year) and six hours of literature at Tokyo Imperial University (¥800/year). Manages to resign from Kumamoto with doctor's certificate of mental problems. *April*: lectures begin. University students complain about his dry, analytical lectures after the more flamboyant style of predecessor Lafcadio Hearn (see Translator's Note). Disappointed with students' limited abilities, considers resigning. *June*: Publishes sardonic London memoir, "Bicycle Diary" ("Jitensha nikki"), in *Hototogisu*, signed "Sōseki." Nervous strain leads to over two months' separation from pregnant Kyōko. Fall lectures on literary theory and English literature well attended.

3 November: Third daughter, Eiko, born. He seeks diversion in painting and calligraphy. Newspapers calling for war against Russia.

1904 (37) *February*: Lectures to University faculty in the hilltop "Mansion" (see *Sanshirō*, Chapter 2) on his London theatre-going. Scholarly publications appear under "Natsume Kinnosuke." War fever leads to outbreak of Russo-Japanese War, inspires Sōseki (writing as "Natsume Sōseki") to publish jingoistic "new style" poem (*shintaishi*), "Jūgun-kō" ("Onward With the Troops"), extolling "swords that thirst for blood." *April*: Adds a third part-time teaching job, at Meiji University (¥30/month). Much creative writing toward the end of the year. Others publish anti-war sentiments toward end of year and are accused of harboring "dangerous thoughts."

1905 (38) New Year's issues of three magazines carry his work: the story "Wagahai wa neko de aru" ("I Am a Cat"), signed "Sōseki," essays "Rondon-tō" ("The Tower of London") and "Kārairu hakubutsukan" ("Carlyle Museum"), signed "Natsume Kinnosuke". Soon begins using "Natsume Sōseki" regularly. Sequels of "I Am a Cat" continue through August 1906, humor rising from high jinks and wordplay to genuine satire, scathing critique of war fever, darkening portrait of mustachioed, heavy-smoking depressive scholar protagonist.

May: Japan destroys Russia's Baltic fleet. Sōseki's explosive productivity continues. Torn between academic career and full-time writing. Short pieces from this time draw on Arthurian legends and London experience. A dozen young "disciples" begin to frequent the Natsume home.

September: New University student from Kyushu, German literature major Komiya Toyotaka (1884–1966), the model for Sanshirō, visits. Portsmouth Treaty seals Japan's victory in Russo-Japanese War.

October: First volume of *I Am a Cat* published.

15 December: Fourth daughter, Aiko, born.

1906 (39) *January*: Publishes "Shumi no iden" ("The Heredity of Taste"), harsh critique of Russo-Japanese war fever, horrific sacrifices of over 100,000 Japanese fighting men under "heroic" General Nogi Maresuke (1849–1912). *February*: Refuses academic committee work.

March: Shimazaki Tōson (1872–1943) publishes novel *Hakai (The Broken Commandment)*, beginning the rise of Japanese naturalism, the mainstream literary movement discussed in *Sanshirō* (Chapter 9); enthusiastically praised by Sōseki.

April: Simultaneously publishes tenth chapter of "Cat" and short novel *Botchan* ("Little Master"), based on Sōseki's year in Matsuyama but set against the Russo-Japanese War and ending in a rush of "righteous" violence. *May*: Suffering with chronic gastric catarrh; asks "disciple" to organize theoretical lectures for book publication. *August*: Eleventh and final chapter of *I Am a Cat* appears. *September*: Publishes "haiku novel," *Kusamakura* ("Pillow of Grass", or *The Three-Cornered World*) on the tension between modern life and poetic detachment. Father-in-law dies, reducing the number of relatives Sōseki must support. This and income from writing enable him to resign third job, at Meiji University, in October. Begins custom of welcoming visitors every Thursday after 3 p.m., initiating the Thursday Group. *November*: Middle volume of *I Am a Cat* published. Turns down invitation to join the *Yomiuri Shinbun* newspaper staff in charge of literature. Family moves into rental house in the University neighborhood: Nishikatamachi ten, block B, number 7 (cf. Professor Hirota's Nishikatamachi ten, block F, number three).

1907 (40) *January*: Publishes short novel, *Nowaki* ("Autumn Wind") in *Hototogisu*, much ranting against the rich, called by some the best novel of 1907. 24 *February*: *Asahi Shinbun* newspaper inquires if he might consider becoming a staff novelist. Negotiations continue until 15 March (government sponsorship of foreign study obligates him to teach until this month). ¥200 monthly salary higher than editor-in-chief's, book royalties are his to keep, all fiction to be serialized in the *Asahi*. Submits resignations to University and College, joins the newspaper officially in April. The news causes a sensation, but Sōseki insists that working for a newspaper is neither more nor less a trade than working for a university. *May*: Advertisement for his first professional novel, *Gubijinsō* ("The Poppy"), appears, inspires feverish marketing of "Poppy" robes and "Poppy" rings. Volume of University lectures, *Bungakuron* ("Theory of Literature") appears under the name "Natsume Kinnosuke."

5 *June*: First son, Jun'ichi, born. Government becoming

concerned about corrupting effects of individualistic literature on compliant populace, Prime Minister invites writers
to a gathering, but Sōseki declines. Serialization of *The Poppy*
begins in *Asahi Shinbun*, continues through October.
Warmly received by public, less so by critics. Overwritten
and moralistic, it disappointed even Sōseki, who soon wanted
to kill off his overwrought heroine. Final volume of *I Am a
Cat* published.

September: Angrily moves out of Nishikatamachi house
when landlord raises the rent.

November/December: writing next novel.

1908 (41) *1 January*: Naturalist movement coalescing in all the
major journals, prompts government to increase censorship
of "dangerous thoughts" in literature. Serialization of *Kōfu*
(*The Miner*) begins, continues until 6 April to universally
negative reviews. Abstract, phantasmagorical, written in a
simple style in contrast with *The Poppy*'s jewel-encrusted
language, too radically modernist for most readers. General
disappointment with Sōseki; 1906 was "his year," but 1907
showed his decline, his lack of seriousness as compared with
the naturalists, say critics. *July*: Linked stories, "Yume jūya"
(*Ten Nights of Dream*), serialized. *1 September*: serialization
of *Sanshirō* begins, continues until 9 December; it is warmly
received, and has significant element of humor.

October: Government announces a "campaign of national
mobilization" to stem the tide of "dangerous thought" such
as socialism, naturalism, anarchism, individualism, etc.

17 December: Birth of second son, Shinroku.

1909 (42) *1 January*: Literary journals discuss rumors of
impending establishment of a government-sponsored literary
academy. *19 January*: Attends Minister of Education's party
for literary men, opposes idea of an official academy of literature as a form of control. *March*: Publishes *Bungaku hyōron*
("Criticism of Literature"), a compendium of University lecture notes on topics in English literature, signed "Natsume
Sōseki." Former foster father, Shiohara, begins pressuring
him for money; unpleasant negotiations continue through
November. *May*: *Sanshirō* published in book form. Readers

of *Taiyō* magazine choose Sōseki as the best writer to serve
on a government literary academy, if established; he rejects
the award. National Diet issues first Press Law, strengthening
government's control of literature. Censorship and protests
increase. *27 June*: Serialization of *Sore kara* (*And Then*)
begins, continuing until 14 October. Protagonist more intelligent and internalized than Sanshirō, much darker view of
human and international relations, awareness of police as
ominous presence: the first of Sōseki's late novels. *August*:
Attack of acute gastric catarrh. *2 September*: Leaves for tour
of Manchuria and Korea until 17 October. *21 October–
30 December*: Serializes "Man-Kan tokoro-dokoro"
("Travels in Manchuria and Korea"), a victor's eye view of
the land wrested from Russian control, cut short at year's
end (nothing on Korea). *25 November*: Inaugurates weekly
"Bungei-ran" (Literary Column) in *Asahi Shinbun*, featuring
wide variety of writers. *28 November*: Pays Shiohara ¥100
to end their relationship.

1910 (43) *1 March–12 June*: Serialization of *Mon* ('The Gate'),
dark culmination of trilogy that began with *Sanshirō*; protagonist fails to find comfort in religion.

   2 March: Fifth daughter, Hinako, born. *June–February*:
Suffering with stomach ulcers, nearly dies at Shuzenji Hot
Spring on 24–25 August, hospitalized until February 1911.

   June–January: Government crushes leftist political and
literary activity in trumped-up "High Treason Incident,"
execution of prominent socialists; decade-long "winter
years" of socialism begin.

   September–December: Writing poetry and memoirs;
painting.

1911 (44) *February–April*: Spars publicly with Ministry of
Education over honorary Doctorate of Letters; Sōseki refuses
to accept it, Ministry refuses to take it back. *18–20 May*:
Publishes three-part critique of Ministry of Education's
new "academy," the Committee on Literature, and its goal
to encourage the production of "wholesome" literature.
11 August: Leaves Tokyo on four-lecture tour for Osaka
Asahi Shinbun (includes "Gendai Nihon no kaika" ("The

Civilization of Modern-day Japan")) but hospitalized for ulcers after final lecture on 18th, unable to return to Tokyo until 14 September. Hemorrhoid surgery; treatment into following year. *12 October*: Personnel problems lead to end of *Asahi* Literary Column. *1 November*: Sōseki tenders pro-forma resignation but remains on *Asahi* staff.

29 November: Sudden death of daughter Hinako (at twenty months). Memorializes his sorrow in next novel.

1912 (45) *1 January*: Begins serializing *Higan-sugi made* (*To the Spring Equinox and Beyond*), until 29 April; episodic parody of detective story notable for "Rainy Day" chapter on sudden death of small daughter. Stomach ailments, nervous tension.

30 July: Meiji emperor dies; name of period changed from Meiji to Taishō. *13 September*: Cannon fire in imperial palace signals massive funeral of Emperor Meiji; General Nogi Maresuke commits ritual disembowelment, following the emperor in death.

26 September–2 October: Hospitalized for second hemorrhoid surgery. *6 December*: Begins serialization of *Kōjin* (*The Wayfarer*); unfocused, interrupted by health problems.

1913 (46) January–June: Period of intense depression. *March–May*: flare-up of ulcers. *7 April*: Last installment of *Kōjin* until September. In bed at home until late May. *Summer*: Unsuccessful attempt at oil painting. *16 September*: Serialization of *Kōjin* resumes, completed 15 November with intense portrait of intellectual who sees only possible release from breakdown in human communication in faith, madness or death. Watercolor painting.

1914 (47) *20 April*: Serialization of masterpiece *Kokoro* begins, until 11 August; set against end of Meiji period, protagonist's struggle with ego ends in death. *June*: Transfers official domicile from Hokkaidō to Tokyo.

15 July: Dines with Raphael von Koeber, who plans to return to Germany. *28 July*: Outbreak of First World War, Koeber trapped in Japan. Enjoying calligraphy and ink painting.

September–October: Fourth flare-up of ulcers. Painting to pass the time. Creates original binding design for *Kokoro*, which becomes maiden publication of Iwanami Shoten, Japan's soon-to-be premier publisher and authoritative publisher of Sōseki's posthumous Complete Works. *25 November*: Lecture, "Watakushi no kojinshugi" ("My Individualism").

1915 (48) *January–February*: Serializes memoir "Garasudo no uchi" (*Inside My Glass Doors*). *March–April*: Fifth flare-up of ulcers while traveling to Kyoto with friends; Fusa dies in March. *3 June–10 September*: Serializes *Michikusa* (*Grass on the Wayside*), overtly autobiographical novel on childhood adoption, aftermath, becoming a writer. *November*: Resting at hot springs. Begins reading Dostoevsky with mounting interest.

December: First visit to Sōseki's home by budding writer Akutagawa Ryūnosuke (1892–1927), author of *Rashōmon and Seventeen Other Stories* (Penguin, 2006), who joins the Thursday Group and becomes one of Sōseki's "disciples." Apparent rheumatism making writing painful.

1916 (49) *January*: Serializes "Tentōroku" ("A Record of Affirmation"), reflections on the current war in Europe as a battle between German militarism and British individual freedom, declaring his gratitude for life and his determination to use the time he has left as well as he can. *19 February*: Lavishly praises Akutagawa's maiden work, "Hana" ("The Nose"). *Mid-April*: New diagnosis reveals that his "rheumatism" is actually diabetes; treatment continues until July. *7–16 May*: Bedridden with stomach pain, begins writing last novel, *Meian* (*Light and Darkness*), serialization begins 26 May: modern life and marriage as a battlefield of egos. By August he is writing one unpleasant installment of *Meian* in the morning, and spending afternoons on comforting traditional pastimes (watercolor painting, calligraphy, Chinese poetry).

Early November: Speaks to Thursday Group about phrase *sokuten kyoshi* ("follow heaven, abandon the self"), possibly just a slogan for successful calligraphy, sincerity of expression in writing, or the ultimate answer to the pain of modern life, as seen in works as early as *I Am a Cat*.

22 November: Final ulcer flare-up begins, ending on *9 December* with death. A national event. Funeral services presided over by Zen priest friend who failed to guide him to enlightenment in 1894. Ashes buried in Zōshigaya Cemetery.

14 December: Final installment of unfinished *Meian* appears.

1918–19 Iwanami Shoten publishes first of many *Sōseki zenshū* (Complete Works of Sōseki), in 14 volumes, with colorful binding Sōseki designed for *Kokoro*. Disciple Komiya Toyotaka, the model for Sanshirō, participates in editing, becomes major editor of later editions and Sōseki biographer.

1984–2004 Sōseki replaces Itō Hirobumi (1841–1909), the Restoration leader and autocrat he mocked in *I Am a Cat*, on the face of the ¥1000 bill.

NOTE

1. *Meiji Period*: On Japanese era names, see the article headed "nengō" in *Japan: An Illustrated Encyclopedia*, 2 vols (Tokyo: Kodansha Ltd., 1993) vol. 2, p. 1073.

Introduction

The (Generally) Sweet Smell of Youth

I confess, I became seriously interested in the works of Natsume Sōseki only after I had reached adulthood. Between my university graduation and the time of my marriage, I hardly looked at anything of his—which is not exactly accurate, come to think of it, because I was already married before I graduated from the university. But the main thing about that time in my life is that I was poor.

Why didn't I bother to read Sōseki before then? I really can't remember, but perhaps the biggest reason is that, from my early teens, I was obsessed with foreign fiction and simply never bothered to read Japanese novels. Another reason might be that I had not been much moved by the Sōseki novels we read in school (the problem there being with the choice of works, perhaps). Then again, during the turbulent 1960s, when I was in my teens, the reading of Sōseki was not fashionable: it won you no admiration or praise. That was the age of revolution and counter-culture, the time of Che Guevara and Jimi Hendrix. Nowadays, of course, Natsume Sōseki is *the* representative modern Japanese novelist, a figure of truly national stature, but his works were not all that warmly received back then, I think— at least not amongst the younger generation.

I got married in 1972 to a university classmate of mine (who remains my wife to this day). She graduated before I did and went to work as a proofreader under contract to a publishing company. I took a series of part-time jobs while attending the university a few days a week to earn the remaining credits I needed to graduate—clerking in a record store, waiting on tables, that sort of thing. And when I had time, I did

housework—laundry, cooking, cleaning, shopping, taking care
of the cats. I was a kind of house-husband. It was a hard way
to live, but I didn't mind it too much, except for the fact that
we didn't have enough money to buy books.

We were, as I said, poor, or perhaps I should say that we
were trying hard not to spend money. We were planning to
open a little jazz club. For us, leading secure lives by taking
respectable jobs with respectable companies was simply not an
option. It didn't interest us. And so the two of us worked hard
and saved our money. If we couldn't afford a gas stove, we
made it through the cold nights by sleeping with our cats, all
huddled together. If the alarm clock broke, we couldn't buy a
new one. But we were young and healthy and eager, and we
had a goal.

Not being able to buy books, though: that was hard. Far
from buying them, we often found ourselves having to sell some
of the books we owned just to make ends meet. In those days
(not so much anymore), I absolutely devoured books. I would
hurry from one book to the next as if in a race with time. I felt
it was the only way I could go on living, which is why not being
able to buy new books was as painful and constricting to me
as not being able to breathe fresh air.

Soon I found myself having to reread my books. And when I
had no more books left to read a second time, I started reading
the books that remained in my wife's bookcase. She had
majored in Japanese literature, so she owned quite a number of
books I had never read. Among them were two sets of "Complete Works" that piqued my curiosity: one belonging to the
poet Miyazawa Kenji (1896–1933) and the other the Complete
Works of Natsume Sōseki. My wife had originally planned to
write her graduation thesis on Miyazawa Kenji. She saved her
money and bought the complete works, but somewhere along
the way she gave up on writing about Miyazawa (I'm not sure
why) and switched to Sōseki. A friend of hers had used the
Sōseki set to write a graduation thesis and no longer needed
the books, so my wife was able to buy them cheaply. It was the
height of practicality. She also owned a number of books by the
novelist Tanizaki Jun'ichirō (1886–1965), the eleventh-century

classic *The Tale of Genji*, and the publisher Iwanami's *World Literature for Boys and Girls*. These were all very different from my own literary tastes, but at least there was no overlap—none at all.

Since I had nothing else to read, I turned to these books in my spare time, though without much enthusiasm. Miyazawa Kenji, I have to say in all honesty, did not do much for me, nor could I see—in those days, at least—anything to like about *The Tale of Genji*. Sōseki and Tanizaki, though, were not so bad. And so it came about that the novels of Sōseki and Tanizaki always bring back to me scenes from my life as a poverty-stricken newly-wed at the age of twenty-two. Our place was cold indoors, and the water in the kitchen sink was usually frozen on winter mornings. The alarm clock was broken, so if I wanted to know the time I had to go peek at the clock out in front of the tobacco shop at the bottom of the hill (I still smoked back then). We had a large window facing south, so at least there was plenty of sunshine coming in, but the National Railways' Chūō Line ran by just below the window, which made it horribly noisy (on a par with Dan Aykroyd's apartment next to the elevated railway in the movie *Blues Brothers*). When there was a strike and the National Railways stopped running for twenty-four hours, most people were greatly inconvenienced, but it gave us pure relief. We used to have long freight trains running by until the sun came up.

This, then, was the setting in which I read Sōseki's works, which is why, for me, they are permeated with memories of reading while stretched out in the sunshine and hearing the roar of passing express trains. Of course the sun wasn't always pouring in, but that is the impression that remains the strongest. The cats would lie next to me, sleeping. I didn't read all of Sōseki's works at the time but chose the most important ones, some of which I liked better than others. My favorite novels were the three that compose his so-called "first trilogy," *Sanshirō*, *Sore kara* (*And Then*), and *Mon* ("The Gate"). I especially remember the strong sense of identification I felt with *Mon*, the story of a young married couple living in far-from-ideal circumstances.

For me, Sōseki's apparently most popular novel, *Kokoro*, left something to be desired, and while I did enjoy the late works so widely praised for their psychological insight, I could never fully identify with the deep anguish of the modern intellectual depicted in them. "What's the point of going on and on about this?" I would often feel. In that sense, I'm probably a bit removed from the "mainstream" Sōseki reader. There is no doubt, however, that the "Sōseki experience" I had at that time, belated though it was, remains firmly rooted within me to this day, and that, whenever I have a chance to reread Sōseki's novels, I am always struck by how fine they are. Sōseki is always the name that first comes to mind when someone asks me who my favorite Japanese author is.

By the time I had my "Sōseki experience," the student movement was already past its most ferocious peak, and the mood was heading swiftly toward something more tranquil. The university campuses were still full of huge signboards scrawled with political slogans, but the possibility of revolution had simply evaporated (not that it was there to begin with, of course), and hopes for reform were swiftly fading. The banners of idealism had mostly been furled. Janis Joplin, Jimi Hendrix, and Jim Morrison were dead. In this somewhat listless, dead-end atmosphere, the worlds of writers like Sōseki and Tanizaki may have been taking on a new meaning once again. We could almost feel it in the skin. Or at least, that is how it seems to me looking back from my current vantage point. In any case, this was my first genuine encounter with Sōseki.

In terms of my own feeling, *Sanshirō* was the right novel to be reading on a sunny veranda. Confused though he may be, the protagonist generally has his eyes trained on the future. His face is tilted slightly upward, and broad skies open up before him. This is the kind of impression the book gives. And in fact, the novel's characters are constantly looking at the sky, descriptions of which figure prominently in the narrative.

Novels like this are rare among Sōseki's works—or perhaps I should say they are virtually non-existent. Most of his protagonists face real-life contradictions. They experience anguish over how they ought to live, and are confronted with real-life decisions that are being forced upon them. They struggle earnestly to find where they stand amid the competing demands of the pre-modern and the modern, between love and morality, between the West and Japan. They don't seem to have the freedom to spend time gazing up at the sky. Instead, the characters who appear in Sōseki's other novels all seem to be looking at the ground as they walk. The protagonists of the late novels, especially, appear to the reader to be suffering with severe stomach pains just as the author himself actually did (though, strangely enough, Sōseki's pen never lost its natural quality of humor).

The protagonist of *Sanshirō*, however, is different. He, too, is unable to find his proper place amid dislocated circumstances, but he never fully confronts those circumstances as a problem within himself. Instead, he accepts them in a relatively natural way, with a young man's particular kind of nonchalant resignation, as something entirely external to himself. "Oh, well, that's how it goes," he seems to say. Stomach pain has not yet entered his world. I think that *Sanshirō* is a personal favorite of mine because it depicts this natural functioning of the young protagonist's psyche in an utterly mellifluous style. Sanshirō watches life sweeping him along the same way he looks at clouds sailing through the sky. The free movement of his gaze draws us in almost before we know it, and we forget to view him critically.

Of course, such a carefree, detached style of life cannot go on forever. The person may stand back and declare "I have decided nothing," but this only remains possible during one short—and possibly happy—stage of life. Eventually, like it or not, one must bear the burdens of responsibility, and once that happens, the cloud-gazing must come to an end. This is what happens to Daisuke, the protagonist of Sōseki's next novel, *And Then*, and with even greater severity to Sōsuke, the protagonist of the following work, "The Gate". Together, the books comprise a trilogy, which Sōseki completed as serialized newspaper novels in the short space of three years, depicting with absolute mastery the youth—and the end of youth—of young intellectuals living in the Meiji era. We could probably call the three novels "The Growing Up Trilogy." Sōseki's own growth as a writer during those three years was almost shockingly swift, like a movie on fast-forward.

But let me get back to *Sanshirō*. The protagonist of this novel is still in the pre-dawn of life. He is unaware of the burdens he will eventually have to bear, and this lack of awareness is precisely what makes him Sanshirō: a young man who still has the time to look up at the sky and gaze at the clouds in all innocence. We see here not anguish but omens of anguish to come, of suffering that still has no concrete form. Sōseki is in no hurry in this novel. He is not pushing Sanshirō from behind, urging him to move ahead, forcing him toward anguish or defeat before his time. He neither criticizes him nor praises him. Sōseki merely allows Sanshirō to be Sanshirō, and he paints him as he is, with free and leisurely strokes, and here is where we see the author Sōseki in all his greatness.

When I first read *Sanshirō* at the age of twenty-two, I, too, had little sense of the burdens to come. I was newly married, still a student. However poor my daily existence might be, however noisy the trains rushing by, I was still sprawling in the sunshine with two soft, warm cats sleeping nearby.

I grew up in a quiet suburb near the city of Kobe and went to Tokyo at the age of eighteen when I entered Waseda University. Originally I had no strong desire to go to Tokyo and was planning to take the relaxed route by attending a local college, but at the very last moment I started to feel I would like to leave home and test myself—to live alone for the first time in my life. I packed my stuff and said goodbye to my girlfriend. Having sent the larger packages on ahead to my dormitory, I was carrying one bag with me when I boarded the recently-built Shinkansen "bullet" train from Osaka station. In my pocket was a paperback copy of John Updike's *The Music School*. The cover of that book remains seared in my brain as part of that special time. (Updike died a matter of days before I wrote this Introduction, I am sorry to say.)

I was doing the same thing we see Sanshirō doing at the opening of the novel, going to Tokyo from the provinces to enter a university, though of course the details were very different. *Sanshirō* was written in 1908, and I went to Tokyo in 1968, exactly sixty years later. Travelling from Kobe to Tokyo at that time took fifteen or twenty hours on a steam train. For me, on the electrically powered Shinkansen, it took only four. Traveling from distant Kyushu to Tokyo, Sanshirō spent two nights on the road. In other words, we grew up in very different environments. The social standing of university students was different as well. Anyone entering a university in Sanshirō's day was treated with respect, but it was nothing special in my day. The educational systems were also different. Sanshirō has just graduated from a "higher school" (*kōtōgakkō*), which was more like a modern-day liberal arts college, and he is already twenty-two (in Western terms) when he enters the university for more focused study, whereas I was only eighteen. Perhaps there was not so great a difference between us, however, in our excitement at going to a strange big city and beginning a new life.

Needless to say, the kind of erotic encounter that Sanshirō experienced on his trip to Tokyo did not happen to me on the Shinkansen. He stayed overnight in an inn, after all, while I spent only four hours on the bullet train. To tell the truth, however, something a little bit like Sanshirō's experience did happen to me. To save money on the fare, I took the slower bullet train, the Kodama, which made more stops along the way than the usual Hikari, and at one of those stops—Shizuoka, I think—a young woman got on and sat down next to me. The car was practically empty, and it would have been easy for her to occupy a two-person seat all to herself, but she nevertheless decided to sit by me. She was a nice-looking woman in her early twenties—no more than twenty-five, I'd say—not exactly a beauty, but attractive enough. Not surprisingly, having her sit next to me like that made me rather tense.

Once she had settled in, she started talking to me with friendly smiles. Where did I come from? Where was I going? She spoke in a very open, straightforward way, and I answered her questions as honestly as I could. I told her I was from Kobe and going to enter a university in Tokyo, that I would take a major in literature, that I liked to read books, that I would be living in a dormitory in the Mejiro neighborhood, that I was an only child, and so on and so forth. I don't really remember the details. Even at the time my head was not that clear, and my answers just seemed to spill out.

In any case, this young older woman remained seated next to me all the way to Tokyo. We talked the whole time, and I recall that she bought me some kind of drink. We stepped down to the platform when the train reached Tokyo. "Good luck in school, work hard," she said to me, and with a wave of the hand, she was gone. That was the end of that. I have no idea why she chose to sit next to me on that nearly empty train. Maybe she just wanted someone to talk to and figured a kid like me would pose no threat (I'm pretty sure that was it). Or maybe she had a younger brother close to my age. Whatever her reason, she left me standing on the platform at Tokyo Station with a strange, almost buoyant sort of feeling. So this was the start of my new life in Tokyo, tinged from the outset with the faint scent of something female, a young woman's wonderful fragrance, like a sign of things to come. Unquestionably, such smells would help determine the course of my life from that point forward.

I have read *Sanshirō* several times now, and each time I am reminded of that period in my life. Always the book revives in me that strange sensation I felt upon going to Tokyo and sensing that I was slowly but surely separating from the streets of my home town, from my life as a typical suburban teenage boy, from the security my parents had given me, from the girlfriend I had left behind, and from the values I had known until then. But what had I gained—and what would I gain—to take their place? Of that I could not be sure. Indeed, I had no certainty that there even existed real things that *could* take their place. I felt both an exhilarating sense of freedom and a terrifying sense of loneliness, like a trapeze artist who has let go of one trapeze before he is sure that the next one is there for him to grab.

What makes *Sanshirō* such an outstanding work of fiction, it seems to me, may well be the way its protagonist, Sanshirō, never openly displays this clash between his excitement and his terror. It certainly isn't there on the surface—in the form of modern novelistic "psychological complications." In his story, Sanshirō is always an observer. He accepts everything and lets it all pass through him. He does at times make judgments about good and bad, about his likes and dislikes, and he sometimes even offers his impressions with a degree of eloquence, but always in the form of "tentative rulings." He uses far more psychic energy in *seeing* than in *thinking*. He is not so much deciding things as gathering materials for decisions to be made later. His footwork is hardly the lightest; indeed, he can be clumsy, but at the same time he is not hobbled. Sōseki succeeds beautifully in investing this innocent—but still fundamentally intellectual and, in his own way, richly endowed—provincial with a free and open point of view.

This freedom and openness, coupled with a kind of danger lurking in the background, are simultaneously characteristic of the adolescence of Sanshirō the individual and, perhaps, of the adolescence of Japan itself, that turn-of-the-century period known as "mid-to-late Meiji." In the youthful Sanshirō's footwork and gaze we may be able to see elements in common with a young nation undergoing a growth spurt, its pulse heightened after having cast off the old feudal system, breathing deeply of the newly introduced air of Western culture, and questioning its future direction and goals. But neither in the footwork nor in the gaze do we find a strong consistency. Things happen to be in balance for the moment, but no one can predict how events might cause them to falter.

One character, however, does seem to sense the danger to come. Professor Hirota, the odd fellow whom Sanshirō chances to meet on the Tokyo-bound train and who will become a mentor to him, offers a harsh assessment of Japan's fate. Japan might swagger like a first-class power following its victory in the Russo-Japanese War (in 1905, just three years before the novel was written), but as a country, he says, it still has shallow roots. What do the Japanese have to boast of abroad? Mount

Fuji? It's nothing but a natural object that has been there for all time. The Japanese didn't make it. Japan may give the impression of having modernized, the Professor points out, but it's all on the surface. Psychologically, the country still has one foot deeply thrust into the pre-modern world.

Sanshirō is not especially patriotic, but the strange man's words offend him, and he tries his best to defend the country: "But still," he protests, "Japan will start developing from now on at least." To which the man replies curtly, "Japan is going to perish." Sanshirō is shocked, but at the same time he has to admire the man. Yes, he thinks, Tokyo people are different. No one in his home island of Kyushu (an especially conservative region) would dare to say anything so outrageous. "Japan is going to perish." But Sanshirō never thinks to ask, "Why?"

You have to look at the world from a broader perspective, the Professor admonishes Sanshirō, and, even more importantly, you have to look hard at yourself. Perhaps he is being deliberately provocative, but his words become a kind of prophesy that hangs over the story—a warning—with regard to both Japan's latent fragility and, simultaneously, the limits of the psyche of one young Meiji intellectual named Sanshirō.

Sanshirō is treated to another, more direct, prophesy with regard to the erotic side of things. It is delivered by the woman he meets on the train and with whom, on their stopover in Nagoya, he happens to share a room. As they part the next morning, she gives him a knowing look and says, "You're quite a coward, aren't you?", both mocking and reproaching him for having failed to take any initiative with her during their night together. Sanshirō feels "as if he were being flung onto the platform" when he hears this. He flushes red to the tips of his ears and stays that way for a very long time; he knows that what stopped him from touching her in the night was not morality but a sheer lack of courage. Her feminine intuition enables the woman to jab at his greatest weakness.

As strongly as he is capable of doing, Sanshirō takes the two shocking prophesies or warnings to heart as he plunges into his new life in Tokyo. In this sense, his train trip from Kyushu to

Tokyo is the first in a series of rites of passage for Sanshirō. In terms of myth, the prophesies comprise the first two important motifs for the innocent prince who enters the forest. Will Sanshirō successfully overcome the prophesies or warnings on his journey to maturity? Will the young hero of this coming-of-age myth forge his way into the deep, unknown forest, do battle with his shadow, and take for himself at least part of the treasure of wisdom that awaits him there?

No easy answers await the reader of *Sanshirō*, a novel that contains only the palest hint of mythical elements. The protagonist himself gives little sign of being poised to do battle with someone or to take something into his own hands. Indeed, he still has no idea what might be out there for him to take. Making such a person the hero of a myth would be virtually impossible. In this sense, *Sanshirō* is rather different from a typical modern European *Bildungsroman*, in which a young person—usually, like Sanshirō, an unspoiled young man or woman from the provinces—encounters many obstacles, endures many wounds and defeats, internalizes new psychic and erotic values, matures as a human being, and passes through the gates to a broader society, now a fully fledged "citizen," as in Romain Rolland's *Jean-Christophe* or Flaubert's *L'Éducation sentimentale*.

Compared with such novels, the course of Sanshirō's growth seems to have little straight-line continuity. He does experience his stumbles, and his expectations are undercut, but though things fail to go as he might wish, the story never really clarifies whether such experiences amount to defeat for him—or whether, indeed, a clear standard exists in Sanshirō's own mind as to what would constitute "defeat." To confront a situation thrust before him, to experience anguish from it, to demand answers from it: such a posture is wholly lacking in Sanshirō. If something unexpected occurs, Sanshirō merely feels surprised or moved or baffled or impressed.

In Tokyo, Sanshirō re-encounters Professor Hirota, the man he chanced to meet on the train, and he comes to regard him as a kind of mentor. There is little hint, however, that Sanshirō feels anything like a resolve to learn something important from the older man as someone who has preceded him to a (seem-ingly) superior state in life. He simply observes the Professor the same way he would watch a majestic cloud sailing through the sky. He does a similar thing with his small circle of acquaint-ances, viewing them as he would particularly beautiful or inter-esting clouds. He is more or less drawn to the Professor's lifestyle, but it never occurs to him to take him as a role model. He falls in love with one member of his circle of his own age, the beautiful and intelligent Mineko (and she seems attracted to Sanshirō's radiant innocence), but he takes no positive steps to make her his own. With regard to both psyche and eros, he always keeps himself in a warm zone of comfort. Never once does he corner himself with logic.

Perhaps Sanshirō harbors too little longing for maturity for a young man, and it may well be that he lacks any conception of what constitutes a "citizen." From a Western point of view, his stance may appear all too immature and irresponsible, both individually and socially. He is already twenty-two (twenty-three by Japanese numbering), and as a Meiji period student at Tokyo Imperial University, he is a member of the super-elite, one of those groomed to shoulder the burdens of the nation. How can such a character stay this way, arms folded, vacillat-ing, unable to choose a path through life? If a foreign reader were to press me with such questions, I would probably have little choice but to answer, "You may be right." And yet, quite honestly, that arms-folded, lukewarm life stance of Sanshirō's that wraps logical and ethical complications in the softest poss-ible emotional cloak is strangely comfortable for me and prob-ably for most Japanese readers.

It may be possible, in that sense, to define *Sanshirō* as a novel of growth without maturity. The innocent Sanshirō enters a new world, and he moves toward becoming an adult by meeting new people and having new experiences, but it is doubtful that he ever grows to the point of entering society as a "mature citizen" in the European sense. Nor is there any strong expectation in the society that surrounds him that he will do such a thing, for Japanese society had slipped sideways from a feudal system into the authoritarian emperor system that held sway until the Second World War without experiencing the maturation of a middle-class citizenry. This is something I feel very strongly.

Western "modernity" in that sense had not yet taken root in Meiji Japan, nor, perhaps, is it all that firmly rooted even in our own day. The concept of the "mature citizen" does not seem to hold much importance among us now, for better or worse (not that anyone can say for sure what is "better" and "worse"). This may be precisely why *Sanshirō* has become a perennial classic for the Japanese, attracting over the years a steady stream of readers who identify with it strongly. Such thoughts come to mind almost inevitably as I read the novel.

As an avid reader and outstanding scholar of English literature, Sōseki must surely have had a clear concept of the Western *Bildungsroman*, and his storytelling shows the obvious influence of Jane Austen. He willingly adopted such Western novel forms as models and modified them in his own way. In fact, with his profound knowledge of two cultures, he may have been the perfect writer to perform such a feat: Sōseki was deeply versed in English literature, and several of his compositions in the *Complete Works* display considerable mastery of the language, but he also wrote haiku through most of his adult life and was highly educated in the Chinese classics.

As a result, in *Sanshirō*, despite its Western framework, cause and effect become confused here and there, the metaphysical and the physical are jumbled together, and affirmation and negation are nearly indistinguishable at times. This is the author's conscious choice, of course, and Sōseki keeps the story progressing smoothly while supporting this fundamental fuzziness by bringing into play his uniquely sophisticated sense of humor, his free-ranging style, the sheer rightness of his descriptions, and above all the simple honesty of his protagonist's character.

Sōseki has long been known as a Japanese "national author," and I would not dispute that designation. Into the format of the modern Western novel, he smoothly and very accurately transplanted the many forms and functions of the Japanese psyche he observed around him, and which we can easily recognize even now. He did so with great sincerity and, as a result, with great success.

Sanshirō is the only full-length novel that Sōseki wrote that focuses on the coming of age of a young man. One such novel may have been enough for him to write in his lifetime, but he had to write at least one. It thus occupies a special place among Sōseki's works. Virtually all novelists have such a work. In my own case, it is *Norwegian Wood* (1987). I don't especially want to reread it, nor do I have any desire to write another one like it, but I feel that in completing it, I was able to take a great step forward, that the existence of that work provides a solid backing for what I produced later. That feeling is important to me, and I imagine (based on my own experience if nothing else) that Sōseki must have felt the same way about *Sanshirō*.

I look forward to seeing how readers abroad receive Sōseki—and especially *Sanshirō*—in this highly accurate and lively translation. I will be happy if you enjoy the book. It is a personal favorite of mine, and I suspect you will find that, no matter where in the world you are, and no matter what the particular shape and direction of your adolescence, the special fragrance of that important stage in life we all pass through is just about the same.

Murakami Haruki

Further Reading

SŌSEKI'S WORKS IN ENGLISH TRANSLATION
(arranged chronologically)

Wagahai wa neko de aru (1905–06), translated by Aiko Itō and Graeme Wilson as *I Am a Cat*, 3 vols (Rutland and Tokyo: Charles E. Tuttle Co., 1972, 1979, 1986).

"Rondon tō" (1905), translated and introduced by Damian Flanagan in the collection *The Tower of London* (London: Peter Owen, 2005). (Also contains short selections from 1901–09.)

"Koto no sorane" (1905): see "Yume jūya."

"Shumi no iden" (1906): see "Yume jūya."

Botchan (1906), translated by J. Cohn as *Botchan* (Tokyo: Kodansha International, 2005).

Kusamakura (1906), translated by Alan Turney as *The Three Cornered World* (London: Peter Owen, 1965). Also translated by Meredith McKinney as *Kusamakura* (London and New York: Penguin Classics, 2008).

"Nihyakutōka" (1906), translated by Sammy I. Tsunematsu as *210th Day* (Boston and Tokyo: Tuttle Publishing, 2002).

Bungakuron (1907), partial translation in *Theory of Literature and Other Critical Writings*, edited by Michael Bourdaghs, Atsuko Ueda and Joseph A. Murphy (New York: Columbia University Press, 2009).

Kōfu (1908), translated, and with an Afterword, by Jay Rubin as *The Miner* (Stanford University Press, 1988).

"Yume jūya" (1908), "Koto no sorane" (1905), "Shumi no

iden" (1906), translated by Aiko Itō and Graeme Wilson as *Ten Nights of Dream, Hearing Things, The Heredity of Taste* (Rutland and Tokyo: Charles E. Tuttle Co., 1974).

Sanshirō (1908), translated by Jay Rubin as *Sanshiro* (Seattle: The University of Washington Press, 1977). Distributed by the Center for Japanese Studies, University of Michigan, Ann Arbor, Michigan.

Sore kara (1909), translated by Norma Moore Field as *And Then* (Baton Rouge: Louisiana State University Press, 1978). Distributed by the Center for Japanese Studies, University of Michigan, Ann Arbor, Michigan.

"Man-Kan tokoro-dokoro" (1909), translated as "Travels in Manchuria and Korea" by Inger Sigrun Brodey and Sammy I. Tsunematsu in their *Rediscovering Natsume Sōseki* (Folkestone, Kent: Global Oriental, 2000).

Mon (1910), translated by Francis Mathy as *Mon* (London: Peter Owen, 1972).

"Gendai Nihon no kaika" (1911), translated by Jay Rubin as "The Civilization of Modern-day Japan," in Edwin McClellan (tr.), *Kokoro, A Novel, and Selected Essays* (Lanham: Madison Books, 1992).

Higan-sugi made (1912), translated by Kingo Ochiai and Sanford Goldstein as *To the Spring Equinox and Beyond* (Rutland and Tokyo: Charles E. Tuttle Co., 1985).

Kōjin (1913), translated by Beongcheon Yu as *The Wayfarer* (Detroit: Wayne State University Press, 1967).

Kokoro (1914), translated by Edwin McClellan as *Kokoro* (Chicago: Henry Regnery, 1957). Also in *Kokoro, A Novel, and Selected Essays* (Lanham: Madison Books, 1992).

"Watakushi no kojinshugi" (1914), translated by Jay Rubin as "My Individualism," in Edwin McClellan (tr.), *Kokoro, A Novel, and Selected Essays* (Lanham: Madison Books, 1992).

"Garasudo no uchi" (1915), translated by Sammy I. Tsunematsu, with an Introduction and Afterword by Marvin Marcus, as *Inside My Glass Doors* (Boston: Tuttle Publishing, 2002).

Michikusa (1915), translated by Edwin McClellan as *Grass on the Wayside* (Chicago: University of Chicago Press, 1969).

Meian (1916), translated by V. H. Viglielmo as *Light and Darkness* (London: Peter Owen, 1971).

STUDIES OF SŌSEKI

Doi Takeo, *The Psychological World of Natsume Sōseki*, translated by William Jefferson Tyler (Cambridge: Harvard University Press, 1976).

Fujii, James A., *Complicit Fictions: The Subject in the Modern Japanese Prose Narrative* (Berkeley: University of California Press, 1993).

Gessel, Van C., *Three Modern Novelists: Sōseki, Tanizaki, Kawabata* (Tokyo: Kodansha International, 1993).

Hibbett, Howard, "Natsume Sōseki and the Psychological Novel," in Donald H. Shively (ed.), *Tradition and Modernization in Japanese Culture* (Princeton University Press, 1971), pp. 305–46.

Iijima, Takehisa and James M. Vardaman, Jr. (eds), *The World of Natsume Sōseki* (Tokyo: Kinseido Ltd., 1987).

Keene, Donald, "Natsume Sōseki," in *Dawn to the West: A History of Japanese Literature*, Volume 3 (New York: Columbia University Press, 1984–98), pp. 305–54.

Marcus, Marvin, *Reflections in a Glass Door: Memory and Melancholy in the Personal Writings of Natsume Sōseki* (Honolulu: University of Hawai'i Press, 2009).

Matsui Sakuko, *Natsume Sōseki as a Critic of English Literature* (Tokyo: Centre for East Asian Cultural Studies, 1975).

Matsuo, Takayoshi, "A Note on the Political Thought of Natsume Sōseki in his Later Years," in Bernard Silberman and H. D. Harootunian (eds), *Japan in Crisis* (Princeton, NJ: Princeton University Press, 1974), pp. 67–85.

McClellan, Edwin, *Two Japanese Novelists: Sōseki and Tōson* (Chicago: University of Chicago Press, 1969).

——, "The Implications of Sōseki's *Kokoro*," *Monumenta Nipponica*, vol. 14 (1958–9), pp. 356–70.

Masao Miyoshi, *Accomplices of Silence* (Berkeley: University of California Press, 1974).

Rubin, Jay, *Injurious to Public Morals: Writers and the Meiji State* (Seattle: University of Washington Press, 1984). (On Sōseki's resignation from the University, rejection of the Doctorate of Letters and critique of the Committee on Literature, etc.)

Sakaki, Atsuko, *Recontextualizing Texts: Narrative Performance in Modern Japanese Fiction* (Cambridge: Harvard University Press, 1999). (See especially "The Debates on *Kokoro*: A Cornerstone," pp. 29–53.)

Washburn, Dennis, "Translating Mount Fuji," in *Translating Mount Fuji: Modern Japanese Fiction and the Ethics of Identity* (New York: Columbia University Press, 2007), pp. 71–106.

Yiu, Angela, *Chaos and Order in the Works of Natsume Sōseki* (Honolulu: University of Hawai'i Press, 1998).

Yu, Beongcheon, *Natsume Sōseki* (New York: Twayne Publishers, 1969).

Translator's Note

Sanshirō is a novel about a young man from the sleepy country-side who opens his eyes to the modern world of the city and to the women who are that world's most alluring—and frighten-ing—denizens. The opening phrases of the book, "He drifted off, and when he opened his eyes the woman . . ." are thus powerfully symbolic of Sanshirō's journey as a whole, but they are securely anchored in the practical realities of travel in 1908, when the novel was serialized from 1 September to 29 December in the pages of the *Asahi Shinbun* newspaper. By the time we see him on an evening train, Sanshirō might well have been dozing because he would have been on the road for some thirty-one hours, with another twenty-six to go. (Travelers in 2008 could complete Sanshirō's entire itinerary in under six hours by connecting to one of Japan's famous bullet trains.)[1]

When he stops in Nagoya for his second night on the road, Sanshirō writes in the hotel registry that he lives in "Masaki Village, Miyako County, Fukuoka Prefecture," an address in Japan's southern main island, Kyushu, of which only the name of the village is fictional. It is based on the home of Sōseki's "disciple," Komiya Toyotaka (1884–1966), who came from the village of Saigawa.[2] The train station nearest to Komiya's home has been named Higashi-Saigawa Sanshirō to com-memorate its connection with the now classic novel. Toyotsu, an actual town a few minutes away on the same line, is where Sanshirō occasionally went to the bank, as mentioned in Chapter 8. Like the name Masaki Village, however, most of *Sanshirō* is pure fiction, and Sōseki felt perfectly free to stipulate that the train to Nagoya was due in at 9.30 even though the "real" train was scheduled to arrive at 10.39, to mention only one of many divergences from fact that have been noted by Japanese scholars.[3]

The novel's Tokyo setting is also quite real, and the layout of the University of Tokyo's central campus in Hongō—the hospital, the athletic field, the faculty center on the hill above the pond—remains much as it was in Sōseki's day, though few of the buildings described by Sōseki in such detail survived the devastating 1923 earthquake. The pond is now known as "Sanshirō Pond." *Sanshirō* is one of Sōseki's most beloved novels, both for its nostalgic view of student life and its panorama of Meiji-period Tokyo—or at least the University district. Edward Seidensticker wrote that "Sanshirō lives in Hongō, and does not have a very exciting time of it . . . students had to go to [the neighboring] Kanda [Ward] for almost everything, from school supplies to Kabuki . . . Hongō was dominated by more austere sorts, professors and intellectuals and the young men of the future."[4] Indeed, when Sanshirō and his friend Yojirō go out for a good time, they board the streetcar to leave the neighborhood. Sanshirō does a lot of walking throughout the city, and many place names are briefly mentioned in the course of his rambles, but only a few significant ones are annotated in the translation.

The action of the novel begins in early September and ends some time after the New Year, and most references to actual people and events suggest that the old year is 1907. The Literary Society's drama performance near the end, for example, is clearly based on one that Sōseki attended on 22 November 1907, and the storyteller En'yū, who died in November 1907, is discussed in the present tense. The off-track betting system that allowed Yojirō to lose money on a horse race in November was outlawed in October 1908 but was still perfectly legal in 1907. The few details that date indisputably from 1908 are relatively unimportant.[5]

Verisimilitude has nothing to do with the sub-plot involving the University students' campaign to hire a Japanese professor of foreign literature. The botched plan is a major source of humor in the novel, but it masks some bitter experience for

Sōseki in the academic world and it gestures toward some intriguing parallels between the lives of Sōseki and his predecessor on the Tokyo Imperial University English faculty, Lafcadio Hearn (1850–1904).

Hearn had been dead for four years by the time Sōseki wrote *Sanshirō* in 1908. Sanshirō and his friend Yojirō are walking by the University pond when Yojirō mentions "how the late Professor Koizumi Yakumo [Hearn's Japanese name] had always disliked the faculty room. After his lectures he would walk around the pond." Of Greek-Irish descent, Lafcadio Hearn made his reputation as a journalist in the United States until 1890, when, at the age of thirty-nine, he went to Japan, married a Japanese woman, and became world-famous for his imaginative writings on Japan, most notably his beautifully wrought retellings (and occasional inventions) of Japanese folktales. Hearn never felt fully accepted in Japan, however, and he was only able to achieve Japanese citizenship—with the name Koizumi Yakumo—in 1896, the year he began teaching at the University. From 1891 to 1894, he had taught at Sanshirō's alma mater, the Fifth National College in Kumamoto, where Sōseki taught as a full professor from 1896 to 1900.

As popular as he was with students in both Kumamoto and the University, Hearn was never more than a hired hand, a lecturer, and although his literary fame and his good relationship with the University president earned him twice the lecturer's usual 200-yen monthly salary, he had to be reappointed from year to year. Especially now that he was a fully fledged Japanese citizen, he felt he deserved a professorial appointment. Instead, his position became increasingly insecure when the University president died in 1900 and was replaced by a man who was far more conscious of Hearn's lack of academic credentials than he was impressed by his literary reputation. Hearn's foreign colleagues at the University also made him uncomfortable. Two were devout Catholics, and made it clear they resented his abandonment of Christianity—and perhaps resented both his marriage to a Japanese woman and the worldwide fame of his exoticist writings as well. He heard the philosophy lecturer Raphael von Koeber (1848–1923) declare that all heretics should be burned alive to save their souls and that the world should be ruled by the Catholic Church, after which he never again set foot in the faculty room. (Koeber was also a very popular lecturer; Sōseki had attended an aesthetics lecture of his in 1896 and socialized with him in later years.) Instead, he would go out to the pond during class breaks with his native Japanese smoking paraphernalia in a bag, sit on a rock and smoke his long, slim *kiseru* pipe.[6]

Things came to a head for Hearn in November 1902, when he requested a year's leave to accept an invitation to lecture on Japanese culture at Cornell University. Annoyed at Hearn's expectation of special treatment, the strongly nationalistic president, Inoue Tetsujirō (1855–1944), rejected his request and resolved to augment the English teaching staff with a native Japanese professor. The administration immediately began considering a plan to reduce Hearn's weekly classroom hours from twelve to eight and use the savings to hire a Japanese instructor to share teaching duties with Hearn. The best candidate for that position, they determined, was Natsume Kinnosuke (i.e. Sōseki), who was then studying in London on a government stipend. The one problem with that plan was that rumors had been reaching Tokyo that Natsume might be having mental problems, so they decided to wait for him to return, and they sought Hearn's advice on the matter. Hearn, of course, was already steaming over the Cornell debacle, and he absolutely refused to take reduced teaching hours with lower pay.

Sōseki was on his way back to Japan when a letter arrived at Hearn's home on 15 January 1903, expressing President Inoue's regret that the University would be unable to continue his contract beyond 31 March. Word of Hearn's resignation reached students at the end of February, and a heated campaign erupted to retain him. Some of the English students at a meeting on 2 March called for a mass resignation from the University if the administration moved to suppress the campaign (a position that did not receive unanimous support). A few student representatives visited Hearn at his home on 8 March and were allowed to read Inoue's letter. Hearn was almost inaudible when he delivered his last lecture the next day, and he never came back to the University. Shocked at this sudden development, President Inoue visited Hearn and offered to let him stay with reduced hours, but Hearn would not hear of it. The break was final.

Far from being the object of a student movement to force the administration to bring a Japanese professor into the faculty, then, Sōseki arrived at the University with the administration's backing and with the students dead set against him. His first class, on the morning of 21 April 1903, only confirmed their antipathy. He called on individual students to read aloud and translate from *Silas Marner* and found himself correcting one error after another. Hearn had never trained them to look at texts closely and had even ingrained in the students an attitude of contempt for the learning of English for utilitarian purposes, providing inspirational lectures instead of requiring effort on their part in grammar, composition and conversation. They hated this new instructor for correcting their pronunciation and embarrassing them as if they were middle-school students. Who was this stiff-necked intruder with the plebeian name of Kinnosuke and a few essays in a haiku magazine who presumed to replace the world-famous Hearn? Natsume's afternoon lecture, a theory of English literature with more psychology than literature in it, only made things worse. The students felt that his objective, Western-style analysis, in contrast to Hearn's more emotive "Japanese" approach, was like taking a scalpel to things of rare beauty. Some students walked out and never came back. One First National College student, scolded by Sōseki for his poor performance, committed suicide that May, and Sōseki was not entirely convinced, despite assurances from others, that his scolding had not been the immediate cause. He blamed himself, too, for the large number of students who failed his University spring examinations (including Osanai Kaoru (1881–1928), who would later become one of the leading figures in modern Japanese drama), and he offered his resignation, which was not accepted.

Yojirō's campaign to make Hirota a University professor, then, is in effect a reversal—and a parody—of the situation that pertained when Sōseki began to teach at Tokyo Imperial University. Subsequent events also had their ironical implications. That

fall, Sōseki's lectures on Shakespeare transformed him from the
least popular to the most popular lecturer in the Faculty of
Letters. As for Hearn, once his break with the University was
complete, he was dealt a final blow in the form of a letter from
Cornell withdrawing their invitation because the city of Ithaca
and the university campus were experiencing a typhoid epi-
demic that eventually killed eighty-five people. Hearn took one
final teaching position, at the less prestigious, private Waseda
University, beginning in March 1904, but he died from a heart
attack in September at the age of fifty-four and was buried in
Tokyo's Zōshigaya Cemetery.[7]

Meanwhile Sōseki, who had been scolded by his brother for
wanting to be a writer in his mid-teens, and who had fantasized
at thirty about leaving academe for the writer's life, would
shock the public in 1907 by resigning from the nation's most
prestigious educational institution to become a newspaper staff
novelist. He continued to think of himself as a scholar, however,
and he surrounded himself with a dozen young "disciples,"
some of them former students, as he produced a prodigious
stream of publications (including two sizeable tomes of literary
theory and criticism based on his University lectures) before
joining Hearn in Zōshigaya Cemetery in 1916.

This translation is based primarily on the virtually identical
texts of *Sanshirō* in volume 5 of the 29-volume *Sōseki zenshū*
(Complete Works), published by Iwanami shoten in 1993–9,
with annotations by Yoshida Hiroo, and in volume 26 of the
60-volume *Nihon kindai bungaku taikei* (Shōgakkan: 1969–74),
annotated by Shigematsu Yasuo. Most of the annotations are
taken from these copiously annotated editions without individual attribution. The Iwanami text is unusual in that it indi-
cates the breaks between newspaper installments, and though
the present translation does not go so far as to number each
section, the breaks are indicated here with the symbol *.

The choices made in the translation of three very common
words are worth noting: *kage* (shadow), *mori* (forest), and *onna*
(woman).

Focusing as it does on a generally innocent young man, *Sanshirō* is a work with much radiant imagery, but it does have its shadows, hinting at disillusionment to come. Sōseki often uses the word *kage*, which can also mean "image" or "reflection" or "the hidden side" of an object, to convey these dark hints almost subliminally. The English text employs the word "shadow" somewhat more frequently than strictly idiomatic translation would require.[8]

Mori usually means "woods" or "forest," and as such it is often as richly symbolic as any forest in a Grimm Brothers' fairytale, but it can also mean "a grove where a Shinto shrine is located," and when it appears in *Sanshirō* as the surname of the assassinated Minister of Education, Mori Arinori (1847–89), it is also an important element in one character's deepest memories. Ironically, Mori was a renowned modernizer who once suggested that English should be made Japan's national language, and he was murdered for having supposedly violated the sanctity of a nationally revered Shinto shrine.

Onna can mean a woman of any age, and in *Sanshirō* it refers to the dangerous woman on the train, to that woman as a mother, to Sanshirō's own mother, to the lovely young women in Tokyo who figure so prominently in Sanshirō's new world, and to the pretty little girl of twelve or thirteen glimpsed in a funeral procession by Professor Hirota twenty years before. Mineko, the young woman loved by Sanshirō, removes herself from the progress of his life when she becomes enshrined in a painting, unchanged, as "Woman in Forest" (*mori no onna*). The little girl whose image was burned into the brain of Professor Hirota, after which he went on changing with the passage of time, was someone he saw first in the funeral procession for Mori Arinori, and then in the forest of his dream, which makes her also an unchanging *mori no onna*.

I felt some urgency about translating *Sanshirō* when I first read it in my early thirties, thinking that its youthful appeal might not outlast my own youth. Students I recommended it to always loved it, and my own enthusiasm for the novel has only grown over the years. I have probably spent more time reworking it for this edition, in my mid-sixties, than I did for the original translation, which was published by the University of Washington Press in 1977 and made available to students until 2009 by the Center for Japanese Studies at the University of Michigan. Much of the pleasure this time around came from consulting with Professor Maeda Shōsaku, a linguist with insatiable curiosity about the English translation of Japanese literary texts. Other friends who have read and commented on the manuscript include Ted Goossen, Lindeth Vasey, Shibata Motoyuki, Shibata Hitomi and, as always, my wife Rakuko. My first translation of *Sanshirō* was dedicated jointly to my young son, Gen, and his grandmother, my mother Frances or "Baba." Let this version be dedicated to the memory of Baba and to my own wonderful grandchildren—Makena, Kaia, and my daughter Hana's new baby, Kai.

NOTES

1.   Sanshirō comes from Kyushu, the southernmost of Japan's four main islands, and is taking a 730-mile, 3-day trip to Tokyo, spending almost 40 hours on the train, plus two stopovers. After the first 50 miles (covered in about 2½ hours by train), he would have taken a 15-minute steam ferry connection from the port of Moji on the northeastern corner of Kyushu to Shimonoseki on the southwestern tip of the main island, Honshu (tunnels were not completed until 1942 and 1944), and continued on by a San'yō Line train to Tokyo, with stops at Hiroshima (175 miles from home), Kobe (365 miles, where the line becomes the Tōkaidō), Osaka (385 miles), Kyoto (410 miles) and Nagoya (500 miles). When we first meet him, Sanshirō is on the Kyoto–Nagoya leg of his trip and is about to spend his second night on the road. A 29-hour "Extreme Express" [*saikyūkō*] from Shimonoseki to Tokyo was available at the time of the novel, but this would not have matched Sanshirō's itinerary, most notably his all-important stopover in Nagoya. A likely itinerary was this: depart Saigawa on local Kyushu train at 11.12 a.m., arrive Yukuhashi 11.36; depart Yukuhashi 12.06, arrive Kokura 13.08; depart Kokura 13.16, arrive Moji 13.43; ferry 13.45–14.00; San'yō Line train #42 depart Shimonoseki 14.40, arrive Kyoto

(end of line) 8.58 the next day. Tour Kyoto. Tōkaidō Line train
#36 depart Kyoto 16.58, arrive Nagoya (end of line, still 230
miles from Tokyo) 22.39. Overnight in Nagoya. 8.00 a.m. train
#24 from Nagoya, arrive Tokyo 20.06; Professor Hirota's
presence on this train is never explained.

2. In 2006, Saigawa became part of the town of Miyako-machi.
The area is still rural and remote, and rail service is limited to a
small line, the Heisei–Chikuhō Railway, which runs only one or
two one-car trains an hour.

3. See Takagi Fumio, "Sanshirō no jōkyō," in Tamai Takayuki et.
al. (eds), *Sōseki sakuhin-ron shūsei 5: Sanshirō* (Tokyo: Ōfūsha,
1991), pp. 149–160. My re-creation of Sanshirō's itinerary is
based partly on this source and largely on Tezuka Takemasa
(ed.), *Kisha- kisen ryokō annai*, No. 164 (May 1908), pp. 36–40,
72–5, courtesy of Kōtsū kagaku hakubutsukan (Modern Trans-
portation Museum), Osaka, kindly obtained for me on a blazing
summer day in 2008 by Professor Maeda Shōsaku.

4. Edward Seidensticker, *Low City, High City* (New York: Knopf,
1983), p. 243.

5. See *Nihon kindai bungaku taikei*, 60 vols (Tokyo: Shōgakkan,
1969–74), vol. 26, pp. 106 n5, 197 n17, 198 n1, and 576 n 87.

6. Etō Jun, *Sōseki to sono jidai: Dai-ni-bu* (Tokyo: Shinchōsha,
1970), pp. 242–3. On *kiseru*, see note 26 to the main text.

7. Ibid., pp. 243–8.

8. For a more detailed discussion of this and other elements of the
book's visual imagery, see my "Sanshirō and Sōseki: A Critical
Essay" in the earlier version of this translation, as published by
the University of Washington Press (1977), Perigee Books (1982),
and the Center for Japanese Studies at the University of Michigan
(2002), pp. 213–48.

SANSHIRŌ

I

He drifted off, and when he opened his eyes the woman was still there. Now she was talking to the old man seated next to her—the farmer from two stations back. Sanshirō remembered him. The old man had given a wild shout and come bounding onto the train at the last second. Then he had stripped to the waist, revealing the moxibustion scars[1] all over his back. Sanshirō had watched him wipe the sweat off, straighten his kimono, and sit down beside the woman.

Sanshirō and the woman had boarded this train in Kyoto, and she immediately caught his eye. She was very dark, almost black. The ferry had brought him from Kyushu the day before, and as the train drew closer to Hiroshima, then Osaka and Kyoto, he had watched the complexions of the local women turning lighter and lighter, and before he knew it he was homesick.[2] When she entered the car, he felt he had gained an ally of the opposite sex. She was a Kyushu-color woman.

She was the color of Miwata Omitsu. At home, he had always found Omitsu an annoying girl, and he had been glad to leave her behind. But now he saw that a woman like Omitsu could be very nice after all.

The features of this woman, however, were far superior to Omitsu's. Her mouth was firm, her eyes bright. She lacked Omitsu's enormous forehead. There was something pleasant about the way everything fitted together, and he found himself glancing at her every few minutes. Several times their eyes met. He had a good long look at her when the old man took his seat. She smiled and made room, and soon after that Sanshirō drifted off.

The woman and the old man must have struck up a conversation while he was sleeping. Awake now, Sanshirō listened to them.

Hiroshima was not the place to buy toys, she was saying. They were much cheaper and better in Kyoto. She had to make a brief stop in Kyoto in any case and bought some toys near the Tako-Yakushi Temple. She was happy for this long-delayed return to her native village where her children were staying, but she was concerned about having to live with her parents now that the money was no longer coming from her husband. He was a laborer at the Kure Navy Yard near Hiroshima, but had gone to Port Arthur during the War.[3]

He came back for a while when the War ended, but left again for Da-lien because he thought he could make more money there. His letters came regularly at first, and money arrived every month, but there had been neither word nor money for the past six months. She knew she could trust him, but she herself could no longer manage to live in Hiroshima without work. At least until she learned what had become of him, she would have to go home to her parents.

The old man did not seem to know about the Tako-Yakushi Temple or care about toys. He responded mechanically at first. But the mention of Port Arthur brought a sudden show of compassion. His own son was drafted into the Army and died over there, he said. What was the point of war, anyway? If there were prosperity afterward, that would be one thing, but people lost their sons and prices went up; it was so stupid. When there was peace, men didn't have to go off to foreign countries to make money. It was all because of the War. In any case, he said, trying to comfort her, the most important thing was to have faith. Her husband was alive and working, and he would come home soon. At the next stop the old man wished her well and stepped briskly from the car.

*

Four other passengers followed the old man out, and only one got in. Far from crowded to begin with, the car now seemed deserted. The sun had gone down: maybe that had something to do with it. Station workers were tramping along the roof of the train, inserting lighted oil lamps into holders from above. As though reminded of the time, Sanshirō started to eat the box lunch he had bought at the last station.

The train started up again. It had been running for perhaps two minutes when the woman rose from her seat and glided past Sanshirō to the door of the car. The color of her obi caught his eye now for the first time. He watched her go out, the head of a boiled sweetfish in his mouth. He sunk his teeth into it over and over and thought, she's gone to the toilet.

Before long, she was back. Now he could see her from the front. He was working on the last of his dinner. He looked down and dug away at it with his chopsticks. He took two, three bulging mouthfuls of rice, and still it seemed she had not come back to her seat. Could she be standing in the aisle? He glanced up and there she was, facing him. But the moment he raised his eyes, the woman started to move. Instead of passing by Sanshirō and returning to her seat, however, she turned into the booth ahead of his and poked her head out of the window. She was having a long, quiet look. He saw how her side locks fluttered in the rush of wind. Then, with all his strength, Sanshirō hurled the empty wooden lunchbox from his window. A narrow panel was all that separated Sanshirō's window from the woman's. As soon as he released the box into the wind, the lid appeared to shoot back against the train in a flash of white, and he realized what a stupid thing he had done. He glanced toward the woman, but her face was still outside the window. Then she calmly drew her head in and dabbed at her forehead with a print handkerchief. The safest thing would be to apologize.

"I'm sorry."

"That's all right."

She was still wiping her face. There was nothing more for him to say, and she fell silent as well, poking her head out of the window again. He could see in the feeble light of the oil lamps that the three or four other passengers all had sleepy faces. No one was talking. The only sound was the ongoing roar of the train. Sanshirō closed his eyes.

"Do you think we'll be getting to Nagoya soon?"

It was the woman's voice. He opened his eyes and was startled to find her leaning over him, her face close to his.

"I wonder," he answered, but he had no idea. This was his first trip to Tokyo.

"Do you think we'll be late?"

"Probably."

"I get off at Nagoya. How about you?"

"Yes, I do too."

This train only went as far as Nagoya. Their remarks could not have been more ordinary. The woman sat down diagonally opposite Sanshirō. For a while again the only sound was that of the train.

At the next station, the woman spoke to him once more. She hated to bother him, she said, but would he please help her find an inn when they reached Nagoya? She felt uneasy about doing it alone. He thought her request reasonable enough, but he was not eager to comply. She was a stranger, after all, a woman. He hesitated as long as he could, but did not have the courage to refuse outright. He made a few vague noises. Soon the train reached Nagoya.

*

His large wicker trunk would be no problem: it had been checked all the way to Tokyo. He passed through the ticket gate carrying only a small canvas bag and his umbrella. He was wearing the summer cap of his college[4] but had torn the school patch off to indicate that he had graduated. The color was still new in just that one spot, though it showed only in daylight. With the woman following close behind, he felt somewhat embarrassed about the cap, but she was with him now and there was nothing he could do. To her, of course, the cap would be just another battered old hat.

Due at 9.30, the train had arrived forty minutes late. It was after ten o'clock, but the summer streets were noisy and crowded as though the night had just begun. Several inns stood across from the station, but Sanshirō thought they were a little rich for him—three-story buildings with electric lights.[5] He walked past them without a glance. He had never been here before and had no idea where he was going. He simply headed for the darker streets, the woman following in silence. Two houses down a nearly deserted backstreet he saw the sign for an inn. It was dirty and faded, just the thing for him and this woman.

"How about that place?" he asked, glancing back at her.

"Fine," she said.

He strode in through the gate. They were greeted effusively at the door and shown to a room—White Plum No. 4. It all happened too quickly for him to protest that they were not together.

They sat opposite each other, staring into space, while the maid went to prepare tea. She came in with a tray and announced that the bath was ready. Sanshirō no longer had the courage to tell her that the woman was not with him. Instead, he picked up a towel and, excusing himself, went to the bath. It was at the end of the corridor, next to the toilet. The room was poorly lit and dirty. Sanshirō undressed, then jumped into the tub and gave some thought to what was happening. He was splashing around in the hot water, thinking what a difficult situation he had gotten himself into, when there were footsteps in the corridor. Someone went into the toilet. A few minutes later the person came out. There was the sound of hands being washed. Then the bathroom door creaked open halfway.

"Want me to scrub your back?" the woman asked from the doorway.

"No, thank you," Sanshirō answered loudly. But she did not go away. Instead, she came inside and began undoing her obi. She was obviously planning to bathe with him. It didn't seem to embarrass her at all. Sanshirō leapt from the tub. He dried himself hastily and went back to the room. He was sitting on a floor cushion, not a little shaken, when the maid came in with the register.

Sanshirō took it from her and wrote, "*Name:* Ogawa Sanshirō. *Age:* 23. *Occupation:* Student. *Address:* Masaki Village, Miyako County, Fukuoka Prefecture."[6] He filled in his portion honestly, but when it came to the woman's he was lost. He should have waited for her to finish bathing, but now it was too late. The maid was waiting. There was nothing he could do. "*Name:* Ogawa Hana. *Age:* 23. *Address:* As above," he wrote and gave back the register. Then he started fanning himself furiously.

At last the woman came back to the room. "Sorry I chased you out," she said.

"Not at all," Sanshirō replied. He took a notebook from his bag and started a diary entry. There was nothing for him to write about. He would have plenty to write about if only she weren't there.

"Excuse me, I'll be right back," the woman said and left the room. Now, writing was out of the question. Where could she have gone to?

*

The maid came in to put down the bedding. She brought only a single wide mattress. Sanshirō told her they must have two mattresses, but she would not listen. The room was too small, the mosquito net too narrow, she said. And it was too much bother, she might have added. Finally she said she would ask the clerk about it when he came back and then bring another mattress. She stubbornly insisted upon hanging the single mosquito net and stuffing the mattress inside it.

Soon the woman came back. She apologized for taking so long. She started doing something in the shadows behind the mosquito net and eventually produced a clanking sound— probably from one of the children's toys. Then she seemed to be rewrapping her bundle, after which she announced that she would be going to bed. Sanshirō barely answered her. He sat on the doorsill, fanning himself. It occurred to him that he might best spend the night doing just that. But the mosquitoes were buzzing all around him. It would be unbearable outside the net. He stood up and took a muslin undershirt and underpants from his bag, slipped them on, and tied a dark blue sash around his waist. Then, holding two towels in his hand, he entered the net. The woman was still fanning herself on the far corner of the mattress.

"Sorry, but I'm very finicky. I don't like sleeping on strange mattresses. I'm going to make a kind of flea guard, but don't let it bother you."

He rolled his side of the sheet toward the side where the woman lay, making a long, white partition down the center of the bed. The woman turned the other way. Sanshirō spread the towels end to end along his side of the mattress, then fitted his body into this long, narrow space. That night, not a hand nor a foot ventured out beyond Sanshirō's narrow bed of towels. He spoke not a word to the woman. And she, having turned to the wall, never moved.

The long night ended. The woman washed her face and knelt at the low breakfast table, smiling. "Did you have any fleas last night?"

"No, thank you for asking," Sanshirō said gravely. He looked down and thrust his chopsticks into a small cup of sweet beans.

They paid and left the inn. It was only when they reached the station that the woman told him where she was going. She would be taking the Kansai Line to Yokkaichi. Sanshirō's train pulled in a moment later. The woman would have a brief wait for hers. She accompanied Sanshirō to the ticket gate. "I'm sorry to have put you to so much trouble," she said, bowing politely. "Goodbye, and have a pleasant trip."

Bag and umbrella in one hand, Sanshirō took off his hat with the other and said only, "Goodbye."

The woman gave him a long, steady look, and when she spoke it was with the utmost calm. "You're quite a coward, aren't you?" A knowing smile crossed her face.

Sanshirō felt as if he were being flung onto the platform. It was even worse after he boarded the train; his ears started to burn. He sat very still, making himself as small as possible. Finally, the conductor's whistle reverberated from one end of the station to the other, and the train began to move. Sanshirō leaned cautiously toward the open window and looked out. The woman had long since disappeared. The large clock was all that caught his eye. He edged back into his seat. The car was crowded, but no one seemed to be paying any attention to

him. Only the man seated diagonally opposite him glanced at
Sanshirō as he sat down again.

*

Sanshirō felt vaguely embarrassed when the man looked at him.
He thought he might distract himself with a book. But when
he opened his bag, he found the two towels stuffed in at the
top. He shoved them aside and pulled out the first thing his
hand chanced upon in the bottom of the bag. It was a collection
of Bacon's essays, a book he found unintelligible. The volume's
flimsy paper binding was an insult to Bacon. Sanshirō had been
unlucky enough to come up with the one book in the bag he
had no intention of reading on the train. It was in there only
because he had failed to pack it in the trunk and had tossed it
into the bag with two or three others at the last minute. He
opened Bacon's essays at page twenty-three. He would not be
able to read anything now, and he was certainly in no mood
for Bacon, but he reverently opened the book at page twenty-
three and let his eyes survey its entire surface. In the presence
of page twenty-three, he might try to review the events of the
night before.

What was that woman, really? Were there other women like
her in the world? Could a woman be like that, so calm and
confident? Was she uneducated? Reckless? Or simply innocent?
This he would never know because he had not tried to go as
far as he could with her. He should have done it. He should
have tried to go a little farther. But he was afraid. She called
him a coward when they parted, and it shocked him, as though
a twenty-three-year-old weakness had been revealed at a single
blow. No one, not even his mother, could have struck home so
unerringly.

These thoughts only made him feel worse. He might as well
have been given a thrashing by some stupid little nobody.
He almost wanted to apologize to page twenty-three of Bacon.
He should never have fallen apart like that. His education
counted for nothing here. It was all a matter of character. He
should have done better. But if women were always going to
behave that way, then he, as an educated man, would have no

other way to react—which meant that he would have to steer clear of them. It was a gutless way to live, and much too constraining, as though he had been born some kind of cripple. And yet . . .

Sanshirō shook off these ruminations and turned to thoughts of a different world. He was going to Tokyo. He would enter the University. He would meet famous scholars, associate with students of taste and breeding, do research in the library, write books. Society would acclaim him, his mother would be overjoyed. Once he had cheered himself with such derelict dreams of the future, there was no need for Sanshirō to go on burying his face in page twenty-three. He straightened up. The man diagonally opposite was looking at him again. This time Sanshirō looked back.

The man had a thick mustache on a long, thin face, and there was something about him reminiscent of a Shinto priest. The one exception was his nose, so very straight it looked Western. Sanshirō, who was looking with the eyes of a student, always took such men to be schoolteachers. The man wore a youthful summer kimono of a blue-and-white splashed pattern, a more sedate white under-kimono, and navy blue split-toed socks. This outfit led Sanshirō to conclude that he was a middle-school teacher—and thus of no interest to anyone with the great future he himself had in store. He must be forty, after all—beyond any future development.

*

The man smoked one cigarette after another. The way he sat with his arms folded, blowing long streams of smoke from his nostrils, he seemed completely at ease. But then he was constantly leaving his seat to go to the toilet or something. He would often stretch when he stood up, looking thoroughly bored, and yet he showed no interest in the newspaper that the passenger next to him had set aside. His curiosity aroused, Sanshirō closed Bacon's essays. He considered taking out another book, perhaps a novel, and reading that in earnest, but finding it would have been too much bother. He would have preferred to read the newspaper, but its owner was sound asleep. He reached across and, with his hand on the paper, made a point of asking the man with the mustache, "Is anyone reading this?"

"No, no one," he said, looking sure of himself. "Go ahead."

This left Sanshirō, with the paper in his hand, feeling ill at ease. The newspaper contained little worth reading. He skimmed through it in a minute or two and returned it, properly folded, to the seat opposite. As he did so, he nodded to the man with the mustache. The man returned his nod and asked, "Are you a college student?"

Sanshirō was pleased that the man had noticed the dark spot on his cap. "Yes," he answered.

"From Tokyo?"

"No, Kumamoto.[7] But—" he began to explain, then stopped. There was no need to say that he was now a University student, he decided.

The man answered simply, "Oh, I see," and continued puffing on his cigarette. He was not going to ask Sanshirō why a Kumamoto student would be going to Tokyo at this time of year. Perhaps he had no interest in Kumamoto students. Just then the man across from Sanshirō said, "Ah, of course." That he was still sleeping, there could be no doubt. He was not just sitting there talking to himself. The man with the mustache looked at Sanshirō and grinned.

Sanshirō took the opportunity to ask, "And where are you going?"

"Tokyo," was all the man said, stretching out the syllables. Somehow, he no longer seemed like a middle-school teacher. Still, if he was traveling third class he was obviously no one special. Sanshirō let the conversation lapse. Every now and then the man, arms folded, would tap out a rhythm on the floor with the front lift of his wooden clog. He seemed very bored, but his was a boredom that betrayed no desire to engage in conversation.

When the train reached Toyohashi the sleeping man bolted up and left the car, rubbing his eyes. Amazing how he could wake himself at the right time like that, thought Sanshirō.

Concerned lest the man, still dazed with sleep, had alighted at the wrong station, Sanshirō watched him from the train window. But no, he passed through the ticket gate without incident and went off like anyone in full possession of his faculties. Reassured, Sanshirō changed to the seat opposite. Now he was sitting next to the man with the mustache. The man moved across to Sanshirō's former seat. He poked his head out the window and bought some peaches.

When he was seated next to Sanshirō again, he placed the fruit between them and said, "Please help yourself."

Sanshirō thanked him and ate a peach. The man seemed to enjoy them very much. He ate several with great abandon and urged Sanshirō to eat more. Sanshirō ate another one. The eating continued, and soon the two of them were talking like old friends.

*

The man remarked that he could well understand why the Taoists had chosen the peach as the fruit of immortality. Mountain ascetics were supposed to live forever on some ethereal essence, and peaches probably came closer to that than anything else. They had a mystifying sort of taste. The pit was interesting too, with its crude shape and all those holes. Sanshirō had never heard this particular view before. Here was a man who said some pretty inane things, he decided. The man spoke of the poet Shiki's[8] great liking for fruit. His appetite for it was enormous. On one occasion he ate sixteen large persimmons, but they had no effect on him. He himself could never match Shiki, the man concluded.

Sanshirō listened, smiling, but the only subject that interested him was Shiki. He was hoping to move the conversation a little more in that direction, when the man said, "You know, our hands reach out by themselves for the things we like. There's no way to stop them. A pig doesn't have hands, so his snout reaches out instead. I've heard that if you tie a pig down and put food in front of him, the tip of his snout will grow until it reaches the food. Desire is a frightening thing." He was grinning, but Sanshirō could not tell from the way he spoke whether he was serious or joking. "It's lucky for us we're not pigs," he went on. "Think what would happen if our noses kept stretching toward all the things we wanted. By now they'd be so long we couldn't board a train."

Sanshirō laughed out loud. The man, however, remained strangely quiet.

"Life is a dangerous business, you know. There was a man called Leonardo da Vinci who injected arsenic into the trunk of a peach tree. He was testing to see if the poison would circulate to the fruit, but somebody ate one and died. You'd better watch out—life can be dangerous." As he spoke, he wrapped the chewed-over peach pits and skins in the newspaper and tossed them out the window.

This time Sanshirō did not feel like laughing either. Somewhat intimidated by the mention of Leonardo da Vinci, he had suddenly thought of the woman. He felt oddly uncomfortable and wanted to withdraw from the conversation, but the man was oblivious to his silence. "Where are you going in Tokyo?" he asked.

"I've never been there before, I really don't know my way around. I thought I might stay at the Fukuoka students' dormitory for the time being."

"Then you're through with Kumamoto?"

"Yes, I've just graduated."

"Well, well," the man said, offering neither congratulations nor compliments. "I suppose you'll be entering the University now," he added, as though it were the most commonplace thing one could do.

This left Sanshirō a little dissatisfied. His "Yes" was barely enough to maintain the civilities.

"Which Faculty?" the man asked.

"I was in the First Division—Law and Letters."

"I mean in the University. Will you be in Law?"

"No, Letters."

"Well, well," he said again.

Each time he heard this "Well, well," Sanshirō found his curiosity aroused. Either the man was in so exalted a position that he could walk all over people, or else the University meant nothing to him. Unable to decide which was true, Sanshirō did not know how to behave with the man.

                                    *

As if by prearrangement, they both bought meals from the platform vendors in Hamamatsu. The train showed no sign of moving even after they had finished eating. Sanshirō noticed four or five Westerners strolling back and forth past the train window. One pair was probably a married couple; they were holding hands in spite of the hot weather. Dressed entirely in white, the woman was very beautiful. Sanshirō had never seen more than half a dozen foreigners in the course of his lifetime. Two of them were his teachers in college, and unfortunately one of those was a hunchback. He knew one woman, a missionary. She had a pointed face like a smelt or a barracuda. Foreigners as colorful and attractive as these were not only something quite new for Sanshirō, they seemed to be of a higher class. He stared at them, entranced. Arrogance from people like this was understandable. He went so far as to imagine himself traveling to the West and feeling insignificant among them. When the couple passed his window he tried hard to listen to their conversation, but he could make out none of it. Their pronunciation was nothing like that of his Kumamoto teachers.

Just then the man with the mustache leaned over Sanshirō's shoulder. "Aren't we ever going to get out of here?" He glanced at the foreign couple, who had just walked by. "Beautiful," he murmured, releasing a languorous little yawn. Sanshirō realized what a country boy he must appear; he drew his head in and returned to his seat. The man sat down after him. "Westerners are very beautiful, aren't they?" he said.

Sanshirō could think of nothing to say in reply. He nodded and smiled.

"We Japanese are sad-looking things next to them. We can beat the Russians, we can become a 'first-class power,' but it doesn't make any difference. We still have the same faces, the same feeble little bodies. Just look at the houses we live in, the gardens we build around them. They're just what you'd expect from faces like this. —Oh yes, this is your first trip to Tokyo,

isn't it? You've never seen Mount Fuji. We go by it a little
farther on. Have a look. It's the finest thing Japan has to offer,
the only thing we have to boast about. The trouble is, of course,
it's just a natural object. It's been sitting there for all time. We
didn't make it." He grinned broadly once again.

Sanshirō had never expected to meet anyone like this after
Japan's victory in the Russo-Japanese War. The man was almost
not Japanese, he felt.

"But still," Sanshirō argued, "Japan will start developing
from now on at least."

"Japan is going to perish," the man replied coolly.

Anyone who dared say such a thing in Kumamoto would
have been beaten on the spot, perhaps even arrested for treason.
Sanshirō had grown up in an atmosphere that gave his mind
no room at all for inserting an idea like this. Could the man be
toying with him, taking advantage of his youth? The man was
still grinning, but he spoke with complete detachment. Sanshirō
did not know what to make of him. He decided to say nothing.

But then the man said, "Tokyo is bigger than Kumamoto.
And Japan is bigger than Tokyo. And even bigger than
Japan . . ." He paused and looked at Sanshirō, who was listening intently now. "Even bigger than Japan is the inside of
your head. Don't ever surrender yourself—not to Japan, not to
anything. You may think that what you're doing is for the sake
of the nation, but let something take possession of you like
that, and all you do is bring it down."

When he heard this, Sanshirō felt he was truly no longer in
Kumamoto. And he realized, too, what a coward he had been
there.

Sanshirō arrived in Tokyo that same evening. The man with
the mustache never did tell Sanshirō his name. Nor did Sanshirō
venture to ask it; there were bound to be men like this everywhere in Tokyo.

2

Tokyo was full of things that startled Sanshirō. First, the ringing of the streetcar bells startled him, and then the huge numbers of people that got on and off between rings. Next to startle him was Marunouchi, the busy commercial center of the city. What startled him most of all was Tokyo itself, for no matter how far he went, it never ended. Everywhere he walked there were piles of lumber, heaps of rock, new homes set back from the street, depressing old storehouses half demolished in front of them. Everything looked as if it were being destroyed, and at the same time everything looked as if it were under construction. The sheer movement of it all was terrible.

And Sanshirō was utterly startled. The shock he felt was identical in quality and degree to that of the most ordinary country boy who stands in the midst of the capital for the first time. His education could no more prevent this shock than might some store-bought remedy. He felt a large portion of his self-confidence simply disappear, and it made him miserable.

If this violent activity was what they called the real world, then his life up to now had been nowhere in touch with it. He had been straddling the fence—and had fallen asleep there![9] All right, then, could he end his napping today and contribute his share of activity? Not likely. He stood in the center of activity now, but his life as a student was the same as before. He had merely been set down in a new position from which to observe the activity all around him. The world was in an uproar; he watched it, but he could not join it. His own world and the real world were aligned on a single plane, but nowhere did they touch. The real world would move on in its uproar and leave him behind. The thought filled him with a great unease.

Sanshirō stood and watched the activity of the streetcars and the trains, of people in white and people in black, and this was how he felt. Behind the student life, however, lay the world of ideas with its own activity, and of this Sanshirō was still unaware. Meiji[10] thought had been reliving three hundred years of Western history in the space of forty.

Sanshirō was feeling very much alone and hemmed in by the restless city when a letter came from his mother. The first since his arrival in Tokyo, it was full of news. The rice crop was excellent this year, she began. He must take good care of himself and watch out for Tokyo people, none of whom could be trusted. He need not worry about money; his school expenses would arrive at the end of every month. The cousin of Katsuta Masa was a University graduate now working in some place called the Faculty of Science; Sanshirō ought to go visit him and ask for his kindness in the future. His mother had apparently left out the man's name at first. In the margin it said, "Mr. Nonomiya Sōhachi." There were a few other items in the margin. Saku's gray horse had died all of a sudden, and Saku was feeling very bad. Miwata Omitsu had given them some sweetfish. His mother would have liked to send him a few, but they would have spoiled on the way to Tokyo, so she had eaten them. And so on.

Sanshirō felt as though his mother's letter had arrived from the musty past. He concluded, with a twinge of conscience, that he had no time to waste reading such stuff. He read it through again, nevertheless. After all, if he was in touch with the real world now, the only point of contact was his mother, an old-fashioned lady in an old-fashioned country town. Aside from her, there was the woman he had met on the train. He had hardly been "in touch" with her, however. It had been too brief and intense, a bolt of lightning from the real world.

Sanshirō concluded that he would do as his mother said and visit Nonomiya Sōhachi.

*

The next day was hotter than usual. The University was closed
for the summer, which meant that he was not likely to find
Nonomiya there. But his mother had not included Nonomiya's
home address. He thought he might go over to the campus by
way of finding out where Nonomiya lived. At four o'clock that
afternoon he walked past the First National College and entered
the University's Yayoi-chō gate. The unpaved road leading up
to the gate lay under a thick blanket of dust. It bore the imprint
of shoes and sandals and wooden clogs and countless tracks
left by rickshaws and bicycles. It was a narrow, stifling street,
after which the University grounds, with its many trees, came
as a relief.

The first door he tried was locked. He walked around to the
rear of the building, but still had no success. He took one last
push on a side door and found it open. A janitor was napping
inside where two corridors intersected. Sanshirō stated his
business, but the man just sat there, staring off at the Ueno
woods to revive himself. Then, snapping out of it, he
announced, "He might be here," and disappeared into the
depths of the hushed building. He came back some moments
later and said to Sanshirō, as if to an old friend, "He's here.
C'mon." Sanshirō followed him around a corner and down
a concrete incline. The world darkened suddenly. He was
momentarily blinded, as in the glare of the hot sun, but his eyes
began to adjust soon enough. He was in a cellar. The air was
cooler down here. A door stood open on the left, and from the
door a face emerged. Its broad forehead and large eyes suggested an affinity with Buddhism. The face's owner wore a suit
coat over a cotton crepe undershirt. The coat was stained in
several places. The man was tall, his thin frame just right for
the hot weather. He bowed, keeping his head and back in a
perfectly straight line.

"Over here," he said and turned away, taking his face into
the room. Sanshirō approached the door and looked inside.
Nonomiya was already seated. "Over here," he said again.

"Here" was a small platform, a plank atop four square legs.
Sanshirō sat on it and introduced himself, adding that he hoped
he could turn to Nonomiya for advice or help, should the

occasion arise. Nonomiya listened, responding now and then
with a "Yes, yes" that reminded Sanshirō somewhat of the man
with the peaches on the train. Once he had dispensed with the
preliminaries, Sanshirō ran out of things to say. Nonomiya also
stopped his "Yes, yes."

Sanshirō began to look around. A long, heavy oak table
stood in the center of the room. Some kind of complicated
machine covered with thick wires sat on top of it, and next to
the machine was a large glass bowl full of water. There was
also a file, a knife and a discarded necktie. Last of all he noticed
a three-foot granite block in the far corner. It had an intricate-
looking machine on top about the size of a tin can. He noticed
two holes in the can's side. They shone like the eyes of a boa
constrictor.

"See how they shine?" Nonomiya said, smiling. "I set everything up like this during the day and I come back when traffic
and other activity dies down at night. Then it's dark and quiet
down here and I look at those things like eyes through the
telescope. It's an experiment on the pressure exerted by a beam
of light.[11] I've been working on it since the New Year, but the
instruments are hard to handle and I still don't have the results
I want. It's not so bad in summer, but those winter nights are
unbearable. I can hardly stand the cold, even with an overcoat
and scarf."

This all came as a shock to Sanshirō, and he struggled to
grasp what kind of pressure a beam of light could have and
what function such pressure could possibly serve.

*

"Take a look," Nonomiya suggested. Just for fun, Sanshirō
walked over to the telescope, which stood several yards from
the granite block. He applied his right eye to the eyepiece, but
he could see nothing.

"How's that? Can you see?" Nonomiya asked.

"Not a thing."

"Ah, the lens cap is on."

Nonomiya left his chair and took something off the end of
the telescope. There was nothing to see but the scale of a ruler

inside a bright area with hazy outlines. The figure "2" appeared
at the bottom. Again Nonomiya asked, "How's that?"

"I can see a '2.'"

"Watch how it moves," he said and walked around behind
the machine, where he started to fiddle with something.

Soon the scale began to move inside the bright area. The "2"
disappeared and a "3" took its place. Then a "4" appeared,
and a "5." It went all the way to "10," after which it started
to move backward. The "10" disappeared, the "9" disappeared, then "8" changed to "7," "7" to "6," and so on
until it stopped at "1."

"How's that?" Nonomiya asked. Shocked again, Sanshirō
took his eye from the telescope. He could see no point in asking
what the scale meant.

He thanked Nonomiya and left the cellar. Up again where
people came and went, he found the world still blazing. Hot as
it was, he took a deep breath. The sun, now sinking in the west,
illuminated the broad slope at an angle. The windows of the
Engineering buildings flanking the top of the slope were spark-
ling as if on fire. Pale red flames of burning sun swept back
from the horizon into the sky's deep clarity, and their fever
seemed to rush down upon him. Sanshirō turned left and
entered the woods, whose back, like his, lay half in darkness,
half in the streaming rays of the setting sun. He walked beneath
a canopy of black-green leaves, the openings between them
dyed red. On the trunk of a large zelkova tree a cicada was
singing. Sanshirō came to the edge of the University pond and
squatted down.

It was extraordinarily quiet. Not even the noise of the streetcars penetrated this far. One streetcar line was to have run past
the Red Gate, but the University had protested and it had gone
through Koishikawa instead. Squatting by the pond, Sanshirō
recalled that he had read about this incident in the Kyushu
papers. If it refused to let streetcars pass by it, the University
must be far removed from society.

He had entered its precincts and found Nonomiya there, a
man who spent the better half of a year underground, experimenting with the pressure of light. Nonomiya's clothing was

plain, so plain that on the street Sanshirō would have taken
him for an electrician. Yet he had to admire him: Nonomiya
pursued his research cheerfully, tirelessly, his life centered on a
hole in the ground. One thing was clear, however: the scale in
the telescope could move all it liked, and it would still have
nothing to do with the real world. Perhaps Nonomiya hoped
to avoid contact with the real world as long as he lived. A
person could come to feel that way quite naturally, no doubt,
breathing this quiet atmosphere. And he, too, Sanshirō wondered, perhaps he too ought to lead a life like this, undistracted,
unconnected with the living world.

He stared at the surface of the pond. The reflection of many
trees seemed to reach to the bottom, and down deeper than the
trees, the blue sky. No longer was he thinking of streetcars, or
Tokyo, or Japan. A sense of something far-off and remote
had come to take their place. The feeling lasted but a moment,
when loneliness began to spread across its surface like a veil of
clouds. The solitude was complete, as if he were sitting alone
in Nonomiya's cellar. At school in Kumamoto, he had climbed
to the top of nearby Tatsuta Mountain, a place still more silent
than this; he had lain by himself in the playing field when it
was carpeted in evening primrose; he had often felt the pleasure
of forgetting all about the world of men. But never before had
he known this sense of isolation.

Could it be because he had seen Tokyo's violent activity? Or
perhaps—and at the thought of the woman on the train, Sanshirō turned red. Yes, the real world was something he needed.
But it was dangerous and unapproachable. He decided to hurry
back to his room and write a letter to his mother.

*

Sanshirō looked up. There were two women standing on a low
hill to the left overlooking the pond. The bank opposite theirs
lay beneath a high cliff surmounted by a grove of trees. Behind
the trees stood a Gothic-style building of bright red brick. By
now the sun had dropped low enough to cast its light from
behind all this, directly at the women. From his low, shadowy
place by the water's edge, the top of the hill looked very bright.

One of the women, uncomfortable in the glare, held up a stiff, round fan to shade her eyes. He could not see her face, but the youthful colors of her kimono and obi shone brilliantly. She wore sandals, their thongs too narrow to show color at this distance, but revealing white split-toed socks at the hem of the kimono. The older woman was dressed entirely in white. She did not try to shade her eyes, but instead knit her brow as she looked into the grove atop the cliff. There the old trees hunched over the pond, stretching their branches far down to the water. The one with the fan stood just ahead of the woman in white, who held back a step from the edge. Together their figures made a line oblique to Sanshirō's line of vision.

The sight gave him an impression of pretty colors, nothing more. A country boy, he could not have explained what was pretty about them. His only thought at the moment was that the woman in white must be a nurse, and when the thought had passed, he continued watching them, entranced.

The one in white began to move, but in a manner that suggested no will or purpose, as though her legs had begun to walk without her knowing it. The young woman with the fan was moving now too, he saw. They were coming down the slope, both, as if by agreement, walking in that manner devoid of purpose. He continued watching them.

At the bottom of the path was a stone footbridge. If they did not cross it, they would go straight ahead to the Science building. If they did, they would continue along the bank toward Sanshirō. They crossed the bridge.

The young one no longer held her fan up. Her left hand pressed a small, white flower to her face. She came toward him with her eyes down, inhaling the fragrance of the flower. Six feet from Sanshirō she stopped short. "What kind of tree is this?" she asked, looking up. A large oak thrust out its dense, round burden of leaves above her, casting an unbroken shadow to the water's edge.

"This is an oak tree," the nurse said, as if to a child.

"Oh? Doesn't it have any acorns?" Her eyes came down from the tree to the flower, glancing at Sanshirō as they moved. Sanshirō was fully conscious of the instant her deep, black eyes were upon him. The impression of color vanished, to be replaced by something inexplicable, something very like his feeling when the woman on the train called him a coward. He was frightened.

They walked past Sanshirō, and the young woman dropped her white flower in front of him. He watched them walk away, the nurse ahead, the young one behind. He could see her obi now, dyed in bright colors except for a frond of autumn grass in the white of the cloth. In her hair she wore a pure white rose. It shone brilliantly against the black hair, in the shadow of the tree.

Sanshirō was in a daze. Squatting by the water, he began to see that there was something wrong, some terrible contradiction—but where was it ? In the young woman and the atmosphere of the University? In the colors and the way she looked at him? In his thinking of the woman on the train when he saw this one? Was it that his plans for the future had two conflicting courses? Or that he had experienced fear from a sight that had also given him great pleasure? This young man from the country could not be sure. He knew only that somewhere there was a contradiction.

He picked up the flower that lay before him and brought it to his nose. It had no fragrance to speak of. He threw it into the pond, where it floated. Just then someone called his name.

*

Sanshirō turned his head. The tall figure of Nonomiya stood on the other side of the bridge.

"So you're still here," Nonomiya said.

Sanshirō stood up and, without answering, took a few lethargic steps toward Nonomiya. "I guess so," he said at last when he was standing on the bridge.

Nonomiya showed no surprise at his abstracted state. "Enjoying the cool?" he asked.

"I guess so," Sanshirō said again.

After looking at the water for a moment, Nonomiya began to feel around in his right-hand pocket. An envelope protruded from the pocket, the writing on it apparently a woman's. Unable to find what he was looking for, Nonomiya let his hand dangle at his side again. "The instruments are a little funny today," he said. "No experiment tonight. I was going to take a walk through Hongō[12] on the way home. Would you like to come along?"

Sanshirō accepted with pleasure. They climbed to the top of the hill where the two women had been standing. Nonomiya paused to look at the red building through the green of the trees, and at the pond far below the cliff. "Nice view from here, don't you think? See how just the corner of that building sticks out a little? From the trees. See? Nice, isn't it? Had you noticed what a fine piece of architecture it is? The Engineering buildings aren't bad either, but this is better."

Nonomiya's appreciation for architecture came as a surprise to Sanshirō. He himself had no idea which of the two was better. Now it was Sanshirō who replied only, "Yes, yes."

"And the—shall I say—the *effect* of the trees and the water. It's nothing special, but after all this *is* the middle of Tokyo. Very quiet, don't you think? The academic life demands a place like this. Tokyo is so damned noisy these days." Walking on, he pointed to the building on the left. "Over here is 'The Mansion,'[13] where the faculty meet. Somehow, they manage to do things without my help. All I have to do is continue my life in the cellar. Research goes on at such a mad pace nowadays, you can't let up for a minute or you're left behind. My work must look like some kind of joke to other people, but I can see it from the inside, and I know my mind is working furiously— maybe a lot harder than all those streetcars running around out there. That's why I don't go away, even in the summer. I hate to lose the time."

Nonomiya looked up at the broad sky. A meager gleam was all that remained of the sun's light. A long wisp of cloud hung across the sky at an angle, like the mark of a stiff brush on the tranquil layer of blue. "Do you know what that is?" Nonomiya asked. Sanshirō looked up at the translucent cloud. "It's all snowflakes. From down here, it doesn't look like it's moving, but it is, and with greater velocity than a hurricane. —Have you read Ruskin?"

Sanshirō mumbled that he had not. Nonomiya said only, "I see." A moment later he went on, "This sky would make an interesting painting, don't you think? I ought to tell Haraguchi about it. He's a painter, you know."

Sanshirō did not know.

*

They walked down the hill past the playing field and stopped in front of a large bronze bust. "DR. ERWIN BAELZ, PROFESSOR DER MEDIZIN, 1876–1902," the inscription read.

"How do you like this?" Nonomiya asked, and again Sanshirō could think of nothing to say.

They left through the side gate and walked alongside Karatachi Temple to the busy avenue. The streetcars never stopped coming.

"Don't you hate those things? They're so noisy!" said Nonomiya.

Sanshirō not only hated them, he was frightened of them. But he said only, "Yes," to which Nonomiya responded, "I do, too." He did not seem the least bit bothered by them, however.

"I don't know how to transfer by myself," he continued. "The conductor has to help me. They've built so damned many lines the past few years, the more 'convenient' it gets, the more confused I get. It's like my research." He smiled.

The school year was just beginning. They passed many students on the street wearing new college caps. Nonomiya looked at them with evident delight. "A lot of new ones," he said. "Young people are so full of life! By the way, how old are you?"

Sanshirō gave the age he had written in the hotel register.

"You're seven years younger than I am. A man can do a lot in seven years. But time really does fly, you know. Seven years is nothing."

Sanshirō could not decide which was true.

They approached an intersection where many bookstores and magazine shops stood on either side of the street. A few shops were swarming with people, all of whom were reading magazines. They would come and go, but never buy anything.

"Not an honest man among them." Nonomiya smiled and paused to thumb through the latest issue of the *Sun*.

They came to the intersection, where two gift shops stood on opposite sides of the street to the left. The nearer one handled imported goods, the far one Japanese. Streetcars turning the corner thundered between them, bells ringing. The dense traffic made it almost impossible to cross, but Nonomiya pointed to the shop on the other side and announced, "I'm going to buy something over there at the Kaneyasu." He dashed across between rings of the streetcar bells, with Sanshirō close behind. He went in alone, however. Waiting outside, Sanshirō looked at the display window. The rows of combs and hair ornaments behind the glass aroused his curiosity. What could Nonomiya be looking for in there? He went inside. Nonomiya dangled a ribbon in front of him as delicate and transparent as cicada wings. "How do you like it?" he asked.

Sanshirō considered buying something for Miwata Omitsu in return for the fish, but he decided against it. Omitsu was sure to convince herself that he had something more in mind than gratitude.

Nonomiya treated Sanshirō to dinner at a Western restaurant in Masago-chō. This restaurant had the best food in Hongō, Nonomiya said, but Sanshirō knew only that it tasted like Western cooking. Still, he ate everything he was served.

They parted in front of the restaurant. Sanshirō was careful to return to his Oiwake lodgings by way of the familiar intersection, where he turned left. He wanted to buy some wooden clogs, but in the first shop he peeked into there was a girl in stark white makeup sitting beneath an incandescent gas lamp. She looked like some kind of grotesque creature made of plaster. Repelled, he headed straight home. All the way back he thought about the complexion of the young woman he had seen by the University pond. It was a tawny, foxlike shade, the translucent color of a lightly toasted rice cake, its texture incredibly fine. That was the only way for a woman's skin to be.

3

The academic year began on 11 September. Sanshirō dutifully went to the Law and Letters building at 10:30. He found the lecture schedule posted up in front of the building, but not a single student. He copied the times of his lectures into his notebook, then went on to the administration office, where the administrative staff, at least, were present.

"When do classes begin?" he asked.

"On 11 September," they answered as if stating the obvious.

"But none of the rooms I looked into had any classes going on."

"No, because the professors aren't there."

That was it, of course. Sanshirō left the office. He walked around to the rear of the building and looked up through the large zelkova tree into the high, cloudless sky. It seemed brighter than the usual sky. Down a hill with low bamboo shrubs, he came to the edge of the pond and squatted down once again near the oak tree. He kept looking at the hill and wishing the young woman would come again, but there was no one. He knew he was asking too much, but he went on crouching there anyway. The boom of the noon gun[14] startled him, and he went back to his room.

The next day Sanshirō went to school at precisely eight o'clock. Entering the main gate, he noticed first of all the twin rows of gingko trees that lined the broad walk before him. Where the trees gave out ahead, the walk turned into a gentle downward slope, and of the Science building below the slope, only part of the second story could be seen. Far behind the Science building, the Ueno woods sparkled in the morning sun, the sun itself a backdrop to the woods. The great depth of the scene delighted him.

On the right-hand side of the walk, where the row of gingkos began, stood the Law and Letters building. On the left, and somewhat farther down the walk, was Natural History. The two buildings were architecturally identical, with high arched windows surmounted by prominent triangular gables. A narrow stone border ran between the red brick and the black roof, rising to a peak at each gable. The bluish stone was a tasteful complement to the almost too-red brick just below it. The tall windows and high triangles were repeated at several points.

Sanshirō's newfound appreciation for the buildings was owing entirely to Nonomiya, but this morning he felt that his view of them had been his own from the start—especially the interestingly asymmetrical way Natural History was set back a little way from the gate instead of being in a line with Law and Letters. This was an original discovery that he would have to mention to Nonomiya.

The library, too, Sanshirō found impressive. It was set just to the right of Law and Letters, and its main wing ran a good fifty yards farther out toward the gate. He could not be sure, but it looked as though it might be the same type of architecture as the others. And those five or six big hemp palms planted against the red wall were a very nice touch.

The Faculty of Engineering far off to the left might have been based on some medieval Western castle. It was a perfect square. Even the windows were square. The corners and the doorway were rounded, however, along with some towerlike things that were probably meant to resemble castle turrets. It was a solid structure, as a castle ought to be, unlike the Law and Letters building, which looked ready to topple over. It looked like a squat sumo wrestler.

He surveyed all that lay before him, called to mind the many other buildings excluded from his view, and experienced the whole with a sense of grandeur. "This is how the Seat of Learning ought to be. This is what makes it all possible—the study, the research. What a magnificent place!" He felt as if he were already a famous scholar.

Once inside the classroom, however, Sanshirō waited in vain for the professor to appear, even after the bell had rung. But then, no students came, either. The next hour was the same. Sanshirō left the classroom incensed. Just in case, he walked around the pond twice before returning to his room.

*

Classes finally started some ten days later. As he waited with the others for the professor to come to the first lecture, Sanshirō was moved to reverence. Surely, he imagined, this was how a Shinto priest must feel as he dons his robes to perform a sacred ritual. Now he knew what it was to be struck with the majesty of academe. But this was only the beginning, for when the bell rang and fifteen minutes went by with still no sign of the professor, the suspense added all the more to his veneration. Soon the door opened and a dignified old man, a foreigner, walked in and began to lecture in fluent English. First Sanshirō learned that the word "answer" came from the Anglo-Saxon "*andswaru*." Then he learned the name of the village where Sir Walter Scott had gone to grammar school. He carefully recorded both facts in his notebook.

Next Sanshirō went to the lecture on literary theory. The professor entered the classroom and paused to look at the blackboard, where someone had written "*Geschehen*" and "*Nachbild*." "Hm, German," he said, laughing as he obliterated them with an eraser. This destroyed some of the respect with which Sanshirō had until then regarded the German language. The professor went on to list twenty definitions of literature that had been formulated by men of letters down through the ages. These, too, Sanshirō recorded carefully in his notebook.

After noon, Sanshirō went to the main lecture hall. Seventy or eighty other students were there, and the professor spoke in a declamatory style. "A single boom of the cannon shattered the dreams of Uraga,"[15] he began, the subject of Japan's opening to the West immediately arousing Sanshirō's interest. Finally, however, the mention of a great many German philosophers' names made the talk extremely difficult. He looked at his desk top, into which someone had deftly engraved the words, "Flunk

Out." The person had obviously devoted quite a bit of time to this. The skill with which he had carved the characters into the hard oaken plank bespoke no amateur talent; this was a grimly rendered feat. The student next to Sanshirō seemed to be taking notes with admirable diligence. Sanshirō peered across at his notebook to find that he was not taking notes at all but drawing a caricature of the professor. As soon as Sanshirō glanced at his notebook, the student displayed his work. It was skillfully done, but Sanshirō could not make sense of the caption beneath it: "Cuckoo in the far-off heavens."

Sanshirō felt tired after the lecture. He stood at a second-story window, chin on hand, looking at the school grounds within the main gate. There was a large pine tree, a cherry tree, and a broad gravel lane running between them, nothing more. But the very fact that little had been done to the area made it all the more pleasant to look at. According to Nonomiya, the place had not always been so nice. Once, a teacher of his had been riding around here on horseback. This was years ago, during the teacher's own student days. The horse, a bad-tempered one, dragged him under a tree. His hat became entangled in a pine branch, and the lifts of his wooden clogs caught in the stirrups. The barbers emerged en masse from the shop across the street to enjoy the spectacle. Several interested parties back then had pooled their funds to have a stable built on campus. They bought three horses and hired a riding master, but the man turned out to be a great drunkard and ended up selling a white horse, the best of the three, and drinking away the money. The old horse was said to have been sent to Japan by Napoleon III.[16] No, that could never be, thought Sanshirō, but he had to admit that things had been pretty easy-going in the old days.

At this point the student who had been drawing the caricature walked up to him. "These university lectures are so damned boring," he said. Sanshirō offered some vague reply. In fact he was quite unable to determine whether they were boring or not. But from this time on, he found himself on speaking terms with the student.

*

Sanshirō was in a low sort of mood by then, too fed up with things in general even for a walk around the pond. He went straight back to his lodgings. He reread his lecture notes after supper, but this neither cheered nor depressed him. He wrote a jumbled letter to his mother.[17] —The term had started. He would be going to campus every day. The University was really big and the buildings were really beautiful. There was a pond in the middle of the campus. He enjoyed walking around it. He was finally used to riding the streetcars. He wanted to buy her something, but he didn't know what. She should let him know if there was anything she wanted. The price of this year's rice would be going up soon, and she ought to hold off selling it a little longer. She should not be too friendly toward Miwata Omitsu. There were plenty of people here in Tokyo—many men, but many women too.

When he had finished the letter, Sanshirō started reading an English book. Six or seven pages were all he could take. What good would it do to read one book? He spread his bedding on the matted floor and crawled under the covers, but it was no use, he stayed awake. He should see a doctor right away if he came down with insomnia, he was thinking as he fell asleep.

Sanshirō went to the University at the usual time the next day. Between classes he heard students talking about where some of this year's graduates had gone to work, and how much they were being paid. Two who had yet to find jobs were supposedly competing for a post in one of the government-run schools. Sanshirō felt something heavy and oppressive, as though the distant future were closing in on him, but he forgot about it soon enough. More interesting were the remarks on Shōnosuke's latest doings.[18] He stopped a classmate in the hall, another student from Kumamoto, to find out who this Shōnosuke could be. The student told him that she was a ballad singer in the variety theater, went on to describe the theater's signboard and where it was located in Hongō, and invited Sanshirō to accompany him there on Saturday night. Sanshirō was much impressed until the fellow added that his own first exposure to the theater had been the night before.

Sanshirō thought he would like to go and see Shōnosuke for himself.

He was about to return to his rooming house for lunch when the student who had done the caricature walked up to him. The fellow dragged Sanshirō off to the main street of Hongō and ordered him a dish of rice and curry at a place called the Yodomiken, which was a fruit store at the front and a small restaurant at the back. The building was new. The student pointed at the façade and said it was in the art nouveau style. Sanshirō was amazed to learn that there was an art nouveau style in architecture. On the way back, the fellow showed him the Aokidō café, another place frequented by students. They entered the Red Gate together and strolled around the pond. The student told Sanshirō how the late Professor Koizumi Yakumo[19] had always disliked the faculty room. After his lectures he would walk around the pond. The young man spoke as if he himself had studied with Professor Koizumi. Sanshirō asked why the Professor never mixed with the other teachers.

"It's so obvious. You've heard their lectures. Not one of them knows how to talk."

Sanshirō was shocked at his cool delivery of this harsh criticism. The fellow's name was Sasaki Yojirō. He said he had just started taking courses at the University as a special student after graduating from a private college. He invited Sanshirō to visit him some time. The address was No. 5, Higashikatamachi, care of Hirota. Was it a rooming house? Sanshirō asked. "Not on your life. Professor Hirota teaches at the First National College."

*

For a while after that Sanshirō attended classes faithfully, but he felt that something was missing. Sometimes he would go to lectures beyond his course requirements, but the feeling persisted. He started sitting in on courses that had nothing whatever to do with his field of specialization. Most of these he would attend no more than two or three times, and in no case did he stay with a course for a full month. Nevertheless, he averaged forty hours a week. Even for Sanshirō, a hard-working student, this was a little too much. He felt himself under constant pressure, but whatever was missing stayed that way. The fun had disappeared.

One day he mentioned his dissatisfaction to Sasaki Yojirō. When he heard that Sanshirō was attending classes for forty hours a week, Yojirō's eyes popped. "You idiot! Do you think it would 'satisfy' you to eat the slop they serve at your rooming house ten times a day?"

"What should I do?" Sanshirō pleaded.

"Ride the streetcar," Yojirō said.

Sanshirō tried without success to find Yojirō's hidden meaning. "You mean a real streetcar?" he asked.

Yojirō laughed out loud. "Get on the streetcar and ride around Tokyo ten or fifteen times. After a while it'll just happen—you'll become satisfied."

"Why?"

"Why? Well, look at it this way. Your head is alive, but if you seal it up inside dead classes, you're lost. Take it outside and get the wind into it. Riding the streetcar is not the only way to get satisfaction, of course, but it's the first step, and the easiest."

That evening Yojirō dragged Sanshirō out to ride the streetcar. They boarded at Yonchōme[20] and went to Shinbashi. At Shinbashi they turned back and went as far as Nihonbashi. Yojirō led Sanshirō from the streetcar and asked, "How's that?"

Next they turned into a narrow side street and entered a restaurant called Hiranoya, where they had dinner and drank sake. The waitresses all spoke in the Kyoto dialect, which gave the place a rich, heavy atmosphere. Outside, the red-faced Yojirō asked again, "How's that?"

Next, Yojirō said he would take Sanshirō to an authentic variety theater. They turned into another narrow side street and entered a place called Kiharadana. They heard a storyteller whose name was Kosan.[21] When they came out after ten o'clock, Yojirō asked once again, "How's that?"

Sanshirō could not say he felt satisfied, but neither was he totally unsatisfied. Yojirō then launched into a discourse on

Kosan. Kosan was a genius. Artists of his caliber were a rarity. He seemed common enough because you thought you could hear him whenever you liked, which was doing him a disservice. It was our great good fortune to be alive at the same time as Kosan. If we had been born a little earlier or a little later, we could never have heard him perform. En'yū was good too, but his style was different. When En'yū played a jester, you enjoyed it because it was En'yū as a jester. Kosan in the same part was enjoyable because he became a character quite separate from Kosan himself. If you were to hide the En'yū part of a character that En'yū was playing, the character would disappear. You could hide the Kosan part of Kosan's character and the character would still be there as lively as ever. That was what made Kosan great.

"How's that?" Yojirō asked.

Sanshirō had not in fact appreciated Kosan. Nor had he ever heard this "En'yū" person perform. He could say nothing either for or against Yojirō's theory. He was, however, quite impressed with the comparison that Yojirō had made, so shrewd one might call it literary.

When they parted in front of the College, Sanshirō said, "Thanks, that was very satisfying."

"The only thing that will satisfy you from now on," said Yojirō, "is the library." He turned the corner into Higashikata-machi. This final remark made Sanshirō realize for the first time that he could go to the library.

*

From the following day, Sanshirō cut his forty hours of class time nearly in half and started going to the library. It was a big, long building with a high ceiling and many windows on both sides. Of the stacks, only the doorway was visible. From outside it seemed there must be all kinds of books in there. As he stood looking, someone would emerge from the stack entrance every few minutes with two or three thick volumes in his arms and turn left into the faculty reading room. One man took a volume from the shelf, spread it open and, still standing, proceeded to look something up. Sanshirō envied them. He wanted to go into the recesses of the library. He wanted to climb up to the second floor, the third floor, far above the streets of Hongō, amid the smell of paper, without a living thing nearby—and read. But faced with the question of what to read, he had no clear idea. It did seem that there ought to be many things inside that he would want to read.

As a first-year student, Sanshirō was not allowed to enter the stacks. He had to use the card catalogue. Stooped over the cabinet, he went through one card after another. No matter how many titles he flipped past, a new one took its place. Finally his shoulders started to ache. He straightened up for a moment and surveyed his surroundings. The library was silent, as a library is supposed to be. In the reading room there were many people. He saw those at the far end as a black blur of heads, their features indistinguishable. Beyond the high windows he could see a few trees and a patch of sky. The sounds of the city came from afar. Standing there, Sanshirō thought to himself how very quiet was the scholarly life, and profound. Then he went back to his room.

The following day, Sanshirō ended his daydreaming and borrowed a book as soon as he entered the library. It was a poor choice, however, and he returned it immediately. The next one he borrowed was too difficult and he returned it also. He took out at least eight or nine books a day like this. Some of them he even read a little. He was surprised to find that every volume he took out had been read at least once. They all had pencil markings. In pursuit of an unread book, he took out a novel by someone called Aphra Behn. This one would be untouched, he was sure—until he opened it. Again he found the careful pencil markings. This was more than he could bear. Just then a marching band passed by outside and put him in a walking mood. He went out to the street and ended up at the Aokidō.

There were two groups of students in the café and a man sitting alone in the far corner, drinking tea. Glimpsed in profile, he looked very much like the one who had eaten all those peaches on the train to Tokyo. He did not notice Sanshirō. With an unhurried air, he would take a sip of tea and follow it with a puff on his cigarette. Instead of the light summer kimono, he now wore a suit, which did not make him any more impressive to look at. Perhaps his white dress shirt put him a cut above Nonomiya-of-the-light-pressure. The more Sanshirō looked, the more certain he felt that this was the peach man himself. Now that he was attending lectures at the University, the things the man had said to him on the train had suddenly come to seem very meaningful. He wanted to approach and say hello, but could find no opening. The man kept looking straight ahead, sipping and puffing.

Sanshirō continued to stare at the man's profile. Then, draining his glass of wine, he dashed outside and hurried back to the library.

*

Thanks to the wine and to a kind of mental excitement, Sanshirō enjoyed his studies that day as never before. This made him happy. He had been absorbed in reading for two hours when he realized it was time to leave. Gathering his things, he flipped open the cover of the one volume he had yet to read that day and found something wildly scribbled in pencil across the entire flyleaf.

"When Hegel lectured on philosophy at the University of Berlin, he had not the slightest intention of selling his philosophy. His were not lectures that simply expounded the Truth, they were the lectures of a man who embodied the Truth, lectures not of the tongue but of the heart. When Truth and the individual are joined together in a pure union, that which the man expounds, that which he speaks, is not a lecture for the sake of lecturing, but a lecture for the sake of the Way. Only when it attains to this is a philosophical lecture worth hearing. He who plays with the Truth on the tip of his tongue leaves nothing but an empty record on dead paper in dead ink, a thing without significance ... Swallowing my anger, swallowing my tears, I read this book now for the sake of an examination—for my daily bread. You must never forget how I clutch my throbbing head and curse the examination system for all eternity!"

The writer had not signed his name, of course. Sanshirō found himself smiling at the end. And yet, in one way or another, he felt enlightened. This was something true not only of philosophy, but of literature as well. He turned the page to find still more.

"The students who flocked to Berlin to hear Hegel's lectures"—this fellow was obviously a great admirer of Hegel—"were not driven by ambition. They did not intend to exploit the lectures to qualify themselves for making a living. No, they came because their hearts were pure. They knew only that a philosopher called Hegel transmitted from his lectern the ultimate universal Truth and, their quest for Truth a pressing need, they sought at his feet to resolve their disquieting doubts. And when they listened to Hegel with pure hearts, they were able to determine their future, to remake their personal destiny. What magnificent conceit it is for you, a Japanese University student, to equate yourself with them, you and your kind who go to lectures with empty heads, who graduate and leave the University with empty heads! You are nothing but typewriters, greedy typewriters. Whatever you do or think or say is finally unrelated to the urgent life force of a changing society. And that is how you shall always be: empty-headed until death! Empty-headed until death!"

This put Sanshirō into a deeply meditative mood until someone tapped him on the shoulder. It was Yojirō. Notwithstanding the advice he dispensed on the importance of the library, Yojirō was a hard man to find here.

"Nonomiya Sōhachi was looking for you," he said. Sanshirō had never imagined that Yojirō knew Nonomiya. Did he mean Nonomiya of the Faculty of Science? He did. Sanshirō left his books and hurried out to the newspaper area, but he did not see Nonomiya. He went to the front door, but Nonomiya was not there, either. He walked down the stone stairway and stretched to see in all directions, but found no trace of Nonomiya. He gave up and went back. Yojirō was standing by his seat, pointing at the discourse on Hegel.

"He really let himself go," he whispered. "Must be one of the old-time graduates. Those guys were wild men but kind of interesting, too. Just like this." Yojirō grinned. He seemed very pleased with the piece.

"I couldn't find Nonomiya."

"That's funny, he was at the door a minute ago."

"Do you think he wanted to see me about something?"

"Maybe so."

They left the library together. Yojirō told Sanshirō how he knew Nonomiya. The scientist had once been a student of Professor Hirota, in whose house Yojirō himself was now living, and he often came to visit. He was a devoted scholar and had published a good deal. Everyone in his field was acquainted with the name of Nonomiya, even in the West.

Recalling the story of Nonomiya's teacher, Sanshirō asked if Professor Hirota was the one with the mean-tempered horse. It might well have been him, Yojirō laughed. The Professor was not above such things.

*

The next day happened to be a Sunday, which meant that Sanshirō would not be able to find Nonomiya on campus. He kept wondering, though, what Nonomiya could have wanted with him the day before, until it finally occurred to him that a visit to Nonomiya's new house would be the perfect excuse for finding out.

Sanshirō hatched his plan in the morning, but what with reading the newspaper and dawdling, he was still at home at noon. He was on his way out after lunch when the friend from Kumamoto put in a rare appearance. By the time the friend left, it was after four o'clock—a little late, but Sanshirō decided to go anyway.

Nonomiya's house was far away. He had moved out to Ōkubo several days before. By commuter train, however, it was an easy trip, and the house would not be hard to find. It was supposed to be near the station. But Sanshirō had been making terrible mistakes on the streetcar ever since his outing with Yojirō. Once, he got on at Hongō Yonchōme to go to the Commercial College in Kanda, went past his stop all the way to Kudan, from there to Iidabashi, where he transferred at last to the Sotobori Line, went from Ochanomizu to Kandabashi and, unaware that he had missed his stop again, hurried down Kamakuragashi to Sukiyabashi. After that he felt leery of streetcars. The Kōbu Electric Line, however, was just a single stretch of track, and he took it with an easy heart.

Getting off at Ōkubo, he walked along Nakahyakunin Street away from the Toyama Military Academy. Just across the tracks he turned into a narrow lane. From there it was an easy climb to a sparse bamboo grove with a house at both its near and far ends. Nonomiya's was the nearer one. The modest front gate stood at an angle that had nothing to do with the direction of the road. The house, too, proved oddly placed. The gate and the entrance must have been added later. A fine hedge shielded the kitchen end of the house, while the garden itself had no enclosure at all. Only a single large bush clover, grown taller than a man, partially concealed the veranda. Nonomiya had brought a chair onto the veranda and was sitting there, reading a foreign magazine.

"Over here," he said when he noticed Sanshirō, as in the cellar of the Science building. Sanshirō hesitated: should he walk straight in through the garden or use the front door?

"Over here," Nonomiya said again. Sanshirō went in through the garden. Nonomiya was sitting outside his study, a comfortable eight-mat room. Many of his books were in foreign languages. He left his chair and sat on the matted floor near Sanshirō, who began with small talk. What a quiet place this was, a surprisingly quick trip from the University. How was the experiment with the telescope going? Then he said, "I heard you were looking for me yesterday. Was it anything important?"

"No, nothing at all," he said, looking apologetic.

"Oh, I see."

"Did you come all the way out here just for that?"

"No, not exactly."

"Well, I did receive a present from your mother. Her note thanks me for looking after you. It was such a nice gift I thought I would like to thank you for it, too."

"Oh, I see. She sent you something?"

"Yes, some kind of red fish pickled in sake lees."

"Oh, it must be *hime-ichi*." That was nothing for her to send him! But Nonomiya asked all about it. Sanshirō's explanation concentrated on the cooking of the *hime-ichi*. It was broiled together with the lees, but you had to remove the lees the second before you transferred it to the plate or the flavor would be lost.

In the course of this dialogue on *hime-ichi* the sun went down. Sanshirō was about to take his leave when a telegram arrived. Nonomiya opened and read it. "Oh, no," he muttered to himself.

*

Sanshirō could not act unconcerned, but neither did he want to pry. He said only, "Is something the matter?"

"No, it's not important." Nonomiya showed the telegram to Sanshirō. "Come at once," it said.

"Will you be going out now?"

"I suppose so. My sister's in the University Hospital. She's the one who wants me to 'come at once.'" He was perfectly calm, unlike Sanshirō, who found the news disturbing. Nonomiya's sister, her illness, the University Hospital, and the young woman he had seen by the pond all coalesced in Sanshirō's mind.

"It must be very serious, then."

"No, I'm sure she's all right. My mother is taking care of her. If she were really sick, the quickest way to let me know would be for my mother to run out here on the train. No, Yoshiko is just playing games, I'm sure, the silly thing. She does it all the time. I haven't been to see her since I moved out here, and she was probably expecting me today because it's Sunday. That's the answer." He cocked his head to one side thoughtfully.

"Still, you really ought to go, don't you think? What if it were serious?"

"I can't imagine such a sudden change in four or five days, but I suppose you're right. Maybe I'll go."

"That would be best, I'm sure."

This decided, Nonomiya had a favor to ask of Sanshirō. If

by any chance his sister's condition really had taken a turn for
the worse, he could not come back tonight, which meant the
maid would have to stay alone in the house. She was very timid,
however, and the neighborhood was not as safe as it should
be. Fortunately, Sanshirō was here. If it wouldn't interfere with
tomorrow's classes, could he spend the night? Of course
Nonomiya would return immediately if there were nothing to
the telegram. Had he known this was going to happen he could
have asked Sasaki to stay, but now there was no time for that.
He realized he was asking more than he had any right to of
such a new acquaintance, but . . .

Sanshirō was not a man who required such lengthy expla-
nations. He consented immediately.

Nonomiya left both his guest and his dinner. To the maid he
announced only that he would not be eating, and to Sanshirō
he said, "Sorry, but you can eat without me." A moment after
he had gone out, his voice boomed through the dark bush
clover, "Read any of my books you like. There's nothing much
good, but have a look. I've got a few novels, too . . ." and he
vanished. When Sanshirō thanked him from the veranda, he
could still discern each bamboo shaft in the sparse little grove.

A few minutes later he was seated cross-legged on the matted
floor of the study, eating dinner from a small lacquered table
the maid had set out for him. Nonomiya's *hime-ichi* was there.
He liked the way it smelled of home, but the rest of the meal
was not as good. Kneeling nearby to serve him, the maid was a
timid-looking creature, as Nonomiya had said.

*

When he had finished eating, the maid withdrew to the kitchen.
Alone finally, Sanshirō could relax—and begin worrying about
Nonomiya's sister. She was on her deathbed . . . Nonomiya had
been too late . . . She was undoubtedly the young woman he
had seen by the pond. He recalled her as she looked that day:
her face, her eyes, her clothing. He placed her in a hospital bed,
stood Nonomiya by her side, and had them say a word or two
to each other. But the scene needed more than a brother. Before
he knew it, Sanshirō had taken the brother's place and was

caring for her tenderly. Just then a train thundered past below
the bamboo grove. Owing to the condition of the floor joists,
possibly, or the nature of the soil, the room seemed to shake
a little.

Sanshirō turned from his lovely patient and looked around
the room. This was a nice old house, the pillars glossy with age.
The doors did not slide smoothly, however, and the ceiling was
black with soot. Only the oil lamp shone with the glow of
modernity. It was of the same order of things as Nonomiya
himself. A modern scholar, he nevertheless chose to rent an old
house like this and live within view of a feudal-age bamboo
grove. Of course, he was free to live in any kind of place he
liked. But what a pity if economic necessity had forced him
into exile in the suburbs! Despite his scholarly renown, the
University paid him only fifty-five yen a month,[22] which was
probably why he taught at a private college. He could hardly
afford to keep his sister in the hospital. Maybe that was why
he had moved to Ōkubo.

The night had just begun, but a stillness had descended on
the suburbs. Insects murmured in the garden. Alone, Sanshirō
felt the melancholy of early autumn.

A voice cried in the distance, "Oh, oh, it won't be long now."
It seemed to come from the rear of the house, but he could not
be certain. It was too far away and had ended too quickly. But
this single cry had sounded to Sanshirō like a true soliloquy,
the solitary utterance of one who has been abandoned by all,
who seeks an answer from no one. An eerie feeling came over
him. Another train echoed in the distance. He heard it drawing
nearer, and when it passed below the bamboo grove, its roar
was fully twice the volume of the earlier train's. Sanshirō went
on sitting there vacantly as long as the room continued to
tremble, but in a flash he brought together the cry he had heard
and the roar of the train. A shock ran through him when he
saw what a frightening connection he had made.

He found it impossible to sit still. A tingle of horror was
running down his spine to the soles of his feet. He stood and
went to the toilet, where he looked from the window at the
clear, star-filled night. The roadbed beneath the embankment

was still as death, but he went on staring into the darkness, nose thrust between the bamboo lattices.

Some men came down the tracks from the station holding paper lanterns. Judging from the voices, there were three or four of them. Past the crossing, the glow of the lanterns disappeared behind the embankment, and only voices were left when they passed below the bamboo grove. Sanshirō could hear them distinctly.

"A little farther down."

The footsteps drew away into the distance. Sanshirō went back through the study to the garden and stepped into his wooden clogs. He scrambled down the six-foot embankment and started after the lanterns.

*

He had gone only a few yards when someone else jumped down from the embankment. The man spoke to him.

"Someone was hit by a train, don't you think?"

Sanshirō tried to say something, but his voice would not come. The man's black shadow went on ahead. This must be Nonomiya's neighbor from the house at the other end of the bamboo grove, Sanshirō decided, following after him. Another fifty yards down the track, he came to where the lanterns and the men had stopped. The men stood mute, holding the lanterns high. Sanshirō looked down without a word. In the circle of light lay part of a corpse. The train had made a clean tear from the right shoulder, beneath the breast, to the left hip, and it had gone on, leaving this diagonal torso in its path. The face was untouched. It was a young woman.

Sanshirō would always remember the way he felt at that moment. He started to turn on his heels but could hardly move his legs. When he crawled up the embankment and entered the room, his heart started pounding. He called the maid to ask for water. She seemed to know nothing, fortunately. A short time afterward there was some sort of commotion in the neighbor's house. He was back, thought Sanshirō. Presently a din arose below the embankment, and when that ended, everything was silent again, almost unbearably so.

Sanshirō could still see the face of the young woman and hear her impotent cry. When he thought of the cruel fate that must lurk within them both, he sensed that the roots of life, which appear to us so sturdy, work loose before we know it and float off into the darkness. Sanshirō was terrified. It had happened in that moment when the train roared past. Until then she had been alive.

Sanshirō recalled how the man eating the peaches on the train had said to him, "You'd better watch out—life can be dangerous." For all his talk of danger, the man was annoyingly self-possessed. Perhaps one could be like that if he stood in a position so free of danger that he could afford to warn others against it. This might be a source of amusement for those men who, while part of the world, watched it from a place apart. Yes, for certain, the man was one of them. It was obvious from the way he ate those peaches, the way he sipped his tea and puffed on his cigarette, looking always straight ahead. The man was a critic. Sanshirō tried out the word "critic" with this unusual meaning, and he was pleased with himself. Indeed, he went so far as to wonder if he, too, should live as a critic some day. The ghastly face of the dead woman could inspire such thoughts.

Sanshirō looked at the desk in the corner of the room, at the chair in front of the desk, at the bookcase beside the chair, at the foreign books neatly lined up in the bookcase, and he reflected that the owner of this quiet study was as safe and happy as that critic. There was no question of crushing a woman under a train to study the pressure of light. Nonomiya's sister was ill, but he had not caused her illness, she had contracted it on her own. His mind flew thus from one thing to the next, and soon eleven o'clock had come. There would be no more trains from the city. Sanshirō started worrying again: perhaps Nonomiya was not coming back because his sister was truly ill. At that point a telegram arrived. "Sister well. See you in a.m."

Sanshirō went to bed relieved, but his dreams were full of danger. The woman who had killed herself was involved with Nonomiya, and he had not come home because he knew what she was up to. The telegram had simply been a way to put

Sanshirō's mind at ease. The part about the sister was a lie; she had died at the very moment the woman threw herself under the train. And the sister was none other than the young woman he had seen near the pond.

He awoke unusually early the next morning.

*

He smoked a cigarette, staring at the rumpled bedding where he had slept in strange surroundings. Last night was like a dream. He went to the veranda and looked up at the sky beyond the low-hanging eaves. It was a fine day, the world a clear, fresh color. He finished breakfast, drank his tea, and was reading a newspaper in a chair on the veranda when Nonomiya came back as promised.

"I heard there was a suicide on the tracks last night," he said. They must have told him at the station. Sanshirō related his experience in detail. "How interesting!" Nonomiya responded. "You don't get a chance like that very often. Too bad I wasn't here. They've gotten rid of the body, I suppose. I probably couldn't see anything if I went for a look now."

"Probably not," Sanshirō answered simply, but Nonomiya's coolness shocked him. He ascribed this insensitivity to the difference between night and day, youthfully unaware that a man who experiments on the pressure of light reveals that characteristic attitude in all situations, even one like this.

Sanshirō changed the subject to Nonomiya's sister. It was just as he had suspected, Nonomiya said, there was nothing wrong with her. Disappointed that he had not visited her for several days, she had tricked him into coming just to dispel her boredom. She was angry that he had been "so cruel" as to stay at home on a Sunday. "She's such a little idiot." He seemed to mean exactly what he said: how stupid she was to waste the time of a man as busy as himself! Sanshirō, however, could not see it that way. If the man's sister wanted him to come so badly that she would send a telegram, he should not mind using up a Sunday evening or two for her. Time spent with people was real time, while the many days Nonomiya spent experimenting in the cellar should be considered leisure time distant from human life. If he were Nonomiya, it would make him happy to have his studies interrupted by his younger sister. By now Sanshirō had forgotten about the suicide.

He had slept poorly last night, Nonomiya said, and his head was unclear. Fortunately, this was the day he did not go to the University, but went instead to teach at a private school in Waseda in the afternoon. He would sleep until then.

"Were you up late?" Sanshirō asked.

Nonomiya said that his old College professor, a man named Hirota, had chosen that day to visit his sister at the hospital, and they were all up talking until after the last train had gone. He would have spent the night at Hirota's but his sister had peevishly insisted that he stay at the hospital. The place was so cramped and uncomfortable he couldn't sleep. What a silly little fool she was. Nonomiya started in on his sister again. Sanshirō found this comical. He thought of saying a word or two in her defense, but he felt uneasy in the role and decided against it.

Instead he asked about Hirota. By now Sanshirō had heard the name three or four times and in his mind had given it not only to the peach professor and the professor at the Aokidō, but also to the one with the mean-tempered horse. Nonomiya said that the man on horseback had indeed been Hirota. Then Hirota *must* have been the man on the train, Sanshirō concluded—though it did seem a little far-fetched.

When it was time for Sanshirō to leave, Nonomiya asked if he would deliver a kimono to the University Hospital before noon. This made Sanshirō very happy.

*

He was wearing his new four-cornered University cap and liked the idea of being seen with it in the Hospital. He left Nonomiya's, beaming.

Leaving the train at Ochanomizu Station, he hired a rickshaw—something the usual Sanshirō would never do. The Law and Letters bell began to ring just as his rickshaw man was charging in through the Red Gate. He would ordinarily be walking into Classroom 8 now with his notebook and bottle of ink, but it wouldn't hurt to miss a lecture or two. He had the man deliver him straight to the front door of the Hospital's Aoyama Wing.

Through the door, down the hall, right at the second intersection, left at the end of the hall, and there it was, the second room on the right. NONOMIYA YOSHIKO, said the black-lacquered nameplate. Having read it, he went on standing in front of the door. Fresh from the country, where all you had to do was walk in, Sanshirō was not sophisticated enough to knock on the door.

"In this room is Nonomiya's sister. Her name is Yoshiko," he thought. He wanted very much to see the face on the other side of the door, but he hated the thought of being disappointed. It bothered him that the face in his mind bore no resemblance whatever to Nonomiya Sōhachi.

A nurse was coming toward him, the sound of her straw sandals closing in from the rear. Sanshirō went ahead and pushed the door open halfway, coming face to face with the young woman inside, his hand still gripping the doorknob.

She had large eyes, a narrow nose, and thin lips. Her broad forehead and sharp chin gave the impression of a large, wide-mouthed bowl. This was all he took in of her features, but the expression that flickered across them for that instant was something he had never seen before. He noticed the rich, black hair combed back from the pale forehead and falling naturally past the shoulders. The morning sunlight streamed in from the eastern window behind her, and where the hair and sunlight touched she wore a violet-flaming, living halo. The face and forehead were in deep shadow, pale in darkness. The eyes had a far-off look. A high cloud never moves in the depths of the sky, and yet it must. But the movement is like a slow crumbling. She looked at Sanshirō with eyes like this.

He found in her a union of languid melancholy and unconcealed vivacity. This sense of union was for him a most precious fragment of human life and a great discovery. Still gripping the doorknob, his face protruding into the room from the shadows behind the door, Sanshirō gave himself up to the moment.

"Please come in."

She sounded as though she had been expecting him. There was a calm in her voice unusual in a woman meeting a man for the first time. She could hardly engage him this way unless she was a pure child or a woman who had known men to the full. But she was not being unduly familiar; they were old friends from the start. She smiled at him, moving the spare flesh of her cheeks, and her pallor took on a reassuring warmth. Sanshirō's feet brought him into the room, and through this young man's mind flitted the shadow of his mother at home far away.

*

When the door closed behind him and he stood facing forward at last, Sanshirō was greeted by a woman in her fifties. She had apparently left her seat and stood waiting for him to come around from the other side of the door. "Mr. Ogawa?"

Good, he did not have to speak first. The woman looked like Nonomiya and also like her daughter. That was all he noticed about her. He handed her the bundle with which he had been entrusted. She took it and thanked him. Offering him her own chair, she went around to the far side of the bed.

The mattress, he saw, was covered in pure white. The quilt, too, was pure white and folded halfway down at an angle. Yoshiko sat on the edge of the bed so as to avoid the thickness of the fold. The window was at her back. Her feet did not touch the floor. She held a pair of knitting needles. A ball of yarn rolled under the bed, and a long, red line ran to it from her hands. Sanshirō considered retrieving the ball of yarn for her, but she seemed unconcerned with it. He restrained himself.

From her side of the bed, the mother thanked him profusely for last night. She knew how busy he must be. Not at all, Sanshirō replied, he had been doing nothing in any case. Yoshiko remained silent during the exchange, but as soon as it ended she asked, "Did you see the suicide?"

There was a newspaper in the corner of the room. "Yes," he said.

"Was it very frightening?" she asked, looking at Sanshirō with her head cocked to one side. Her neck was long, like her brother's. He stared at the bend of the neck without answering, partly because the question had been too simple and partly because he forgot to answer it. She seemed to notice what he was doing and quickly straightened her neck. Her pale cheeks reddened slightly. Sanshirō decided it was time to go.

He said goodbye and left the room. Turning the last corner, he saw the bright square of the entrance at the end of the long corridor and, standing just inside, where reflections of green spilled in upon the floor, the young woman from the pond. Startled, he broke the swift rhythm of his gait. The dark shadow of the woman, painted on a transparent canvas of air, moved forward then by a step. Sanshirō, too, moved forward, as though drawn in her direction. The two moved closer, destined to pass somewhere along the narrow corridor. Suddenly she looked back. In the bright space out front there was only the floating green of early autumn. Nothing entered the square in response to her backward glance, nor did anything there anticipate it. Sanshirō used the moment to register her stance and clothing in his mind.

He had no idea what the color of her kimono should be called. It was like the shadowy reflection of evergreens in the University pond. Vivid stripes ran the length of it from top to bottom. In their course they moved in waves, drawing together, moving apart, overlapping in broad bands, separating into twin lines. A wide obi cut across the irregular but unchaotic pattern a third of the way from the top. The obi had a warmth to it, perhaps because it contained yellow.

Her right shoulder moved back when she turned, while her left hand, resting on her hip, moved forward. In the hand was a handkerchief. The cloth below the fingers splayed out softly: it must be silk. Everything below the hips remained facing forward.

*

She soon turned toward him again. Eyes downcast, she moved two steps in Sanshirō's direction, then suddenly raised her head and looked directly at him. Her eyes were well shaped, the outer corners chiseled deep and long into the face, the flesh of the lids softly creased. The eyes were alive, beneath brows of remarkable blackness. He could see her beautiful teeth now as well. The contrast between her teeth and the color of her skin was, for Sanshirō, something unforgettable.

Today she wore a trace of white powder. It was not in such poor taste, however, as to hide the skin beneath. With its glow of color, the smooth flesh looked as though it would be unaffected by strong sunlight, and she had given it but the slightest touch of powder. The face did not shine. The flesh— the cheek, the jaw—was firm, with no more than necessary on the bone. And yet the face overall was soft. The very bone, it seemed, and not the flesh, was soft. It was a face that gave a sense of great depth.

She bowed to him. Sanshirō was less startled by this courtesy from a stranger than by the grace with which it was performed. She dropped forward from the waist, as softly as a piece of paper floating on the wind, and very quickly. Then, arriving at a certain angle, she stopped, easily, precisely. This was not something she had been taught.

"Pardon me . . ."

The voice emerged from between the white rows of teeth. It was crisp but had a near-aristocratic ease. This was hardly a voice for asking whether acorns had formed on an oak tree in midsummer, but Sanshirō lacked the composure to notice such a thing.

"Yes?" He stopped short.

"Do you know where room fifteen would be?"

Sanshirō had just left room fifteen. "Miss Nonomiya's room?"

"Yes . . ."

"You turn at that corner, go to the end of the hall, then left, and it's the second room on the right."

"Turn at that corner?" She pointed with a slender finger.

"Yes, that corner, just ahead."

"Thank you very much."

She walked on. Sanshirō stood watching her from behind. She reached the corner and, on the point of turning, looked back. Caught off-guard, he blushed. She smiled and asked with a look, was this the corner? He found himself nodding. Her shadow moved right and disappeared into the whiteness of the wall.

Sanshirō wandered out of the front door. He took five or six steps, wondering if she had mistaken him for a medical student when she asked for Yoshiko's room. Then it came to him. Damn it, he should have shown her the way!

He did not have the courage to retrace his steps now. Resigned, he took a few more paces, and this time drew up short. An image of her hair ribbon flashed through his mind. In color and texture it was exactly like the one Nonomiya had bought at the Kaneyasu. His legs grew suddenly heavy. He was dragging himself past the library toward the main gate when Yojirō appeared from nowhere and called out to him, "Hey, Sanshirō, you should have come to class today. It was a lecture on how Italians eat macaroni." He walked up and clapped him on the shoulder.

They continued on together a short way. Nearing the main gate Sanshirō asked, "Do women wear thin ribbons in their hair even at this time of year? I thought they were just for very hot weather."

Yojirō laughed out loud. "You'd better ask Professor O. about that. He's an expert on everything." Yojirō refused to take him seriously.

At the main gate Sanshirō said he was feeling ill, and wouldn't be attending his lectures today. Yojirō hurried back to class as if to say that he had wasted his time coming this far with Sanshirō.

4

Sanshirō's spirit was restless. Lecturers spoke to him from afar. On bad days he would fail to write down their most essential points, and at the worst of times he felt he was listening with ears rented from a stranger. It was all so stupid. He turned to Yojirō in despair. How dull the lectures were these days, he would say. Yojirō's answer was always the same.

"Of *course* the lectures are dull! You're a country boy, so you've been sticking with it all this time, hoping for big things. What stupidity! Their lectures have been like this since the beginning of time. No sense feeling disappointed now."

"That's not it, exactly . . ." Sanshirō would try to explain himself. His painful slowness of speech was comically mismatched with Yojirō's patter. They repeated this dialogue two or three times, and before Sanshirō knew it half a month had gone by. His ears gradually came to seem his own again.

Now it was Yojirō who turned to Sanshirō. "You have an odd look these days. That's the face of a man who's tired of life—a *fin de siècle* face."

In response to this critique, Sanshirō answered as before, "That's not it, exactly . . ." Phrases like *fin de siècle* had no power to please him, so little had he breathed the air of artificiality. Nor could he use them yet as toys, so little did he know of certain circles. But "tired of life"—that was a phrase he rather liked. Come to think of it, perhaps he had been feeling tired lately. His diarrhea could not be the only cause. But neither was his view of life so modish that he could display a greatly wearied countenance. And so this conversation ended without further development.

Soon autumn was at its height, the season when the appetite quickens and a young man of twenty-three can in no way be tired of life. Sanshirō went out often. He walked around the University pond a lot, but nothing ever came of it. He passed the University Hospital often, but encountered only ordinary human beings. He went to Nonomiya's cellar to ask about his sister and found that she had left the hospital. He thought of mentioning the young woman he had seen in the doorway, but Nonomiya seemed busy and he restrained himself. There was no hurry; he could find out all about her when next he visited Ōkubo.

Restless, he walked up one street and down another. Tabata, Dōkanyama, the graveyard in Somei, Sugamo Prison, the Goko-kuji Temple—Sanshirō walked as far as the Yakushi in Arai. From there, he decided to walk by way of Ōkubo and visit Nonomiya at home, but he took the wrong street near the Ochiai crematorium and ended up at Takata. He took the train home from Mejiro. On the way, he ate most of the chestnuts he had bought as a gift for Nonomiya, and the next day Yojirō came and finished off what was left.

Sanshirō was restless, but it was a light, airy restlessness, and the more he felt it, the happier it made him. He had concentrated too hard on the lectures until he could barely hear them well enough to take notes, but now he listened only moderately well and there was no problem. He thought about all sorts of things during the lectures. It no longer worried him if he missed a little. The other students did the same, he noticed, Yojirō included. This was probably good enough.

Now and then, as his thoughts wandered, the ribbon came to mind. That bothered him, ruined his mood. He thought of rushing out to Ōkubo. But thanks to the associative links of the imagination and to the stimulus of the outside world, the feeling soon vanished. For the most part he was carefree. He was dreaming. The visit to Ōkubo never happened.

*

Rambling about the city as usual one afternoon, Sanshirō turned left at the top of Dangozaka and came out to the broad avenue in Sendagi Hayashi-chō. These days, ideal autumn weather made the skies of Tokyo look as deep as those back home in the country. Just to think that one was living beneath skies like this was enough to clear the mind. Walking out to open fields made everything perfect. The senses unwound and the spirit became as broad as the heavens. For all that, the body took on a new firmness. This was not the irresponsible balminess of spring. Gazing at the hedges on either side of him, Sanshirō inhaled Tokyo's autumn fragrance for the first time in his life.

The chrysanthemum doll show had opened at the bottom of Dangozaka[23] two or three days earlier. Sanshirō had noticed a few banners as he turned left at the top of the slope. Now he could hear only the distant shouts, the beating of drums and clanging of bells. The rhythms floated slowly uphill and, when they had dispersed themselves completely into the clear autumn air, they turned at last into exceedingly tenuous waves. The waves stirred by those waves moved on as far as Sanshirō's eardrums and came to rest. All that remained of the noise was a pleasant sensation.

Just then two men appeared from a side street. One of them called out to Sanshirō. There was a note of restraint in Yojirō's voice today. But then, he had someone with him. The sight of Yojirō's companion confirmed for Sanshirō what he had long suspected: the man drinking tea at the Aokidō was indeed Hirota. Sanshirō had had some strange connection with this man ever since the peaches. The man had become fixed in his memory with particular tenacity when, drinking tea and smoking cigarettes, he caused Sanshirō to flee from the Aokidō to the library. As always, the man's face looked to him like a Shinto priest's with a Western nose attached. He wore the same summer suit he was wearing the last time, but he did not look cold.

Sanshirō hoped to find some appropriate civility, but too much time had intervened; he did not know what to say. He simply removed his hat and bowed. This was too polite for Yojirō, but rather too curt for Hirota—a middle path that was appropriate to neither.

Yojirō took care of the introductions simply. "This is a class-mate of mine," he said. "He's just arrived in Tokyo from Kumamoto." He had to go and blurt out Sanshirō's rustic background. To Sanshirō he said, "This is Professor Hirota. Of the College."

"Never mind, we know each other," Professor Hirota said.

This brought an odd look from Yojirō, but instead of bother-ing to pursue the matter, he asked Sanshirō, "Do you know of any houses for rent in the neighborhood? We want a nice, big one with a room for a student houseboy."

"Houses? I don't . . . yes, I do."

"Where? We don't want anything run-down."

"Don't worry, it's very nice. It has a big stone gate out front."

"Good, where is it? A stone gate, Professor! Wonderful, let's take it."

"No stone gates," said the Professor.

"No stone gates? Why not?"

"I said no, that's all."

"But they're so impressive! Just think, we could look like a new baron!"[24]

Yojirō was serious, Hirota grinning. Finally the serious side prevailed; they would at least look at the place. Sanshirō led the way.

*

They retraced their steps to a back street. Half a block north was a lane that appeared to end in a cul-de-sac. Sanshirō went in first. At the far end was a gardener's front yard. They stopped several paces from the entrance. Two good-sized granite columns stood on the right, supporting an iron gate. This was it, said Sanshirō. And in fact a sign showed the house to be for rent.

"Look at this monster, will you!" said Yojirō, pushing hard against the iron gate. It was locked. "Wait a minute," he said, "I'll go and ask." He dashed into the gardener's. Left alone, Hirota and Sanshirō started a conversation.

"How do you like Tokyo?"

"Well . . ."

"Just a big, dirty place, isn't it?"

"Well . . ."

"I'm sure you haven't found anything here that compares with Mount Fuji."

Sanshirō had completely forgotten about Mount Fuji. Come to think of it, the mountain as he had first seen it from the train window, with Professor Hirota's commentary, was something noble. There was no way to compare it with the chaotic jumble of the world inside his head now, and he was ashamed of himself for having let that first impression slip away. Just then Hirota flung an unexpected question at him. "Have you ever tried to translate Mount Fuji?"

"Translate . . . ?"

"It's fun. Whenever you translate nature it turns into something human. 'Noble,' say, or 'great,' or 'heroic.'"

Sanshirō saw what he meant by "translate."

"It always gives you a word having to do with character. Nature can't influence the character of someone who can't translate nature into character."

Sanshirō waited quietly for the rest, but Hirota was finished. He looked into the gardener's and muttered as if to himself, "What is Sasaki doing in there? He's taking so long."

"Shall I go see?" Sanshirō asked.

"No, don't bother. Sasaki wouldn't come out just because somebody went looking for him. We might as well wait here."

He squatted down by the hedge and began sketching in the dirt with a pebble. Here was a man who took life easily! In this he went as far as Yojirō, but in the opposite direction.

Just then Yojirō shouted from the other side of the gardener's pine trees, "Professor Hirota!"

The Professor went on sketching something. It appeared to be a lighthouse. When he did not answer, Yojirō was forced to come out.

"Professor, come and look at this place. It's really nice. The gardener here owns it. I could have him open the gate, but it would be quicker to go through the back."

They went around through the gardener's and walked from

room to room opening the storm doors. It was a good, middle-
class house. The rent would be forty yen, with a three-month
deposit. They came outside again.

"Why bother looking at a house that good?" Hirota said.

"Why not? What's wrong with just looking?" Yojirō
answered.

"You know we're not going to take the place."

"But I *was* going to take it. It's just that he wouldn't give it
to us for twenty-five yen."

Hirota said only, "Of course he wouldn't."

Yojirō then launched into the history of the stone gate. Until
recently it had stood at the mansion of one of the gardener's
clients. They had given it to him when they rebuilt their house
and he had brought it straight here. Yojirō, true to form, had
been doing some odd research.

*

On the main thoroughfare again, they walked down the slope
at Dōzaka toward Tabata. By the time they reached the bottom
of the hill, the three were simply walking; they had forgotten
about looking for houses. Yojirō, however, would make an
occasional remark about the stone gate. To bring it from
Kōjimachi to Sendagi had cost five yen, he said. The gardener
must be pretty rich. Who was going to pay forty yen to rent a
house in such a location? Yojirō did all the talking, concluding
that the rent was sure to go down when no one took the
house. They ought to bargain with the gardener again when
that happened. Hirota seemed not to share his view of the
situation.

"Think of all the time you wasted talking nonsense with that
fellow. You should have found out what you had to and come
out."

"Was I in there such a long time? I saw you drawing some
kind of picture, Professor. I'm not the only easy-going one."

"Maybe you're a little better at it than I am."

"What was that picture, anyhow?"

Hirota did not answer. Sanshirō spoke up, a serious expression on his face. "It was a lighthouse, wasn't it?"

The artist and Yojirō laughed aloud.

"A lighthouse—how bizarre! You were drawing Nonomiya Sōhachi, then, right?"

"What do you mean?"

"Nonomiya shines in far-off foreign countries, but down at the base of the lighthouse,[25] in Japan, he's pitch dark, no one knows who he is. He shuts himself up in that cellar and gets a miserable little salary. They don't pay him what he's worth. It breaks my heart just to look at him."

"The best you can do, Sasaki, is throw a little light around where you sit—maybe two or three feet in all directions. You're like a paper lantern."

Having been compared to an outmoded domestic implement, Yojirō turned suddenly to Sanshirō and asked, "When were you born, Ogawa? What year of Meiji?"

Sanshirō said simply, "I'm twenty-three."

"I thought so: Meiji 18.[26] Professor, I hate things like that— paper lanterns, and those slim pipes[27] they used to smoke when Tokyo was still Edo. Maybe it's because I was born after Meiji 15 but, I don't know, old-fashioned things like that bother me. How about you, Ogawa?"

"I don't mind them especially."

"No, of course not, you've just arrived from the wilds of Kyushu. Your mind is still back in Meiji Zero."

Neither Sanshirō nor Hirota had anything to say to this.

A little farther on they came to an old temple, next to which a cedar grove had been cleared away and the earth leveled to make room for a blue-painted Western-style house. Professor Hirota stood looking back and forth between the temple and the painted building. "What an *anachronism*," he said, using the English word. "Both the material and spiritual worlds of Japan are like this. You two know the lighthouse in Kudan, I'm sure." Again the subject of lighthouses. "That's an old, old thing. You can find it in the *Illustrated Guide to Edo Attractions*."

"Oh come on, Professor, the Kudan lighthouse may have been around a while, but it's not in the *Edo Guide*. That would make it a hundred years old!"

Professor Hirota laughed. He had been thinking of a print
series on Tokyo attractions, he said. He then expounded on the
construction of a modern brick building like the Military Club
next to a survivor from another age like the lighthouse. The
two of them together looked absurd, but no one noticed. It
just didn't bother anyone. This was representative of Japanese
society.

Both young men said "I see" and left it at that. A few hundred
yards past the temple, they came to a large, black gate. Yojirō
suggested they go through it and cut across to Dōkanyama.
The others wondered if that was all right. Of course, he insisted,
this was the suburban villa of the Satake Lords: *everybody* cut
through here. They went in and walked through a grove of tall
bamboo, coming out to the shore of an old pond. At that
point a watchman appeared and cursed at them for trespassing.
Yojirō offered his cringing apologies.

They came to Yanaka and continued on through Nezu. Sanshirō reached his Hongō lodgings as the sun was going down.
He could not recall the last time he had spent such a carefree
afternoon.

*

Yojirō was not at school the next day. Sanshirō thought he
might come to campus after lunch, but he did not. Neither
could he find him in the library.

Sanshirō went to the joint lecture for all literature students
from five to six o'clock. It was too dark for taking notes, too
early to turn on the lights. This was the hour when the depths
of the great zelkova tree outside the high, narrow windows
began to turn black. Inside the hall, the faces of the students
and the lecturer were equally indistinct, which made everything
somehow mystical, like eating a bean jam bun in the dark. He
found it strangely pleasant that he could not understand the
lecture. As he listened, cheek in hand, his senses became dulled,
and he began to drift off. This was the very thing, he felt, that
made lectures worthwhile. Just then the lights snapped on, and
everything gained a measure of clarity. He suddenly wanted to
go home and eat. The Professor, too, grasped the mood and

improvised an ending for his talk. Sanshirō walked quickly
back to Oiwake.

He changed his clothes and sat down before the low table
that had been brought to his room. Next to his cup of steamed
custard was a letter. The seal told him that it came from his
mother. Inexcusably, he hadn't given a thought to his mother
for the past two weeks or more. What with the *anachronisms*,
the character of Mount Fuji, and the mystical lecture, not even
the young woman had crossed his mind since yesterday. This
gave him great satisfaction. He would read his mother's letter
afterward, at his leisure, but first he ate dinner and had a cigarette. The sight of the smoke reminded him of today's lecture.

At that point Yojirō dropped in. Sanshirō asked why he had
not come to classes. He was far too busy with house-hunting,
Yojirō said.

"Are you in such a hurry to move?"

"Such a hurry? We were supposed to have moved last month
but they let us stay until the Emperor's Birthday, the day after
tomorrow. We've got to find a place tomorrow, no matter
what. Don't you know of anything?"

If he was going to be so rushed today, how could he have
wasted the whole day yesterday? That house-hunting had been
indistinguishable from a casual stroll. This was almost more
than Sanshirō could fathom. Yojirō insisted it was because the
Professor had come along.

"It was a mistake for him to get involved in looking for
houses. He's never done it before. There must have been something wrong with him yesterday. It was his fault we got yelled
at like that in the Satake villa. That was embarrassing as hell.
—Are you sure you don't know of some place?"

He was suddenly talking about houses again. This actually
did appear to be his sole reason for coming. Sanshirō pressed
for a few details on why they had to move. Their damned
extortionist of a landlord made him furious the way he kept
raising the rent, Yojirō said, and he had announced their intention to leave. So it was Yojirō's responsibility.

"I went all the way to Ōkubo today but couldn't find anything
there, either. As long as I was in Ōkubo I stopped in to see

Yoshiko. She's still looking washed out, sorry to say—one of those anemic beauties. Her mother sends her regards to you. The neighborhood has been quiet ever since you were there—no suicides or anything."

Yojirō flew from one thing to another. Never very good at sticking to the point, he was especially agitated today over the house-hunting problem. When each new topic was exhausted he would ask, as a refrain, whether Sanshirō knew of a place. Finally, Sanshirō burst out laughing.

*

Soon Yojirō's buttocks were settling ever more comfortably on the matted floor, and he began amusing himself with Chinese literary references.[28] "How does that poem go . . . ? 'Autumn is here, let us read by the lamplight.'" For no very good reason, the conversation turned to Professor Hirota.

Sanshirō asked, "What is the Professor's given name?"

"'Chō.' It's written with an unusual character." He drew the strokes in the air. "I wonder if it's even in the dictionary. It's supposed to mean some kind of bitter-tasting fruit the Chinese call a 'sheep-peach.' They pinned a weird one on him."

"You say he's a professor at the College?"

"That he is. From once upon a time to this very moment. Isn't that something? They say ten years can shoot by like a day, but he's been at it a good twelve or thirteen years."

"Does he have any kids?"

"Kids? He's a bachelor."

This came as a surprise to Sanshirō. Was it possible to remain single so long? "Why isn't he married?"

"That's what makes the Professor the Professor. You wouldn't know it, but he's a great theorist. He doesn't have to get married to know that a wife would be no good for him. He says his theory proves it beforehand. It's ridiculous. That's why he's so full of contradictions. He's always saying what an eyesore Tokyo is, but when he sees a nice stone gate it scares him to death. 'No stone gates,' he says, or, 'It's too good for us.'"

"Well then, maybe he ought to get married as an experiment."

"He might actually like it, who knows?"

"He talks about how dirty Tokyo is and how ugly the Japanese are, but has he ever been abroad?"

"Are you kidding? Professor Hirota? He's like that because his mind is more highly developed than anything in the actual world. One thing he does do is study the West in photographs. He's got tons of them—the Arc de Triomphe in Paris, the Houses of Parliament in London—and he measures Japan against them! Of *course* Japan looks bad in comparison. Meanwhile, he can live in a shack and not give a damn. It's weird."

"I met him in the third-class carriage."

"He must have been complaining how filthy it was."

"No, he didn't say much about that."

"Anyhow, Professor Hirota is a philosopher, you know."

"Is that what he teaches?"

"No, in school he only teaches English, but what's interesting about him is that the man himself is made of philosophy."

"Has he written any books?"

"Not one. He writes an essay now and then, but there's never any response to them. It can't go on like this. What's the good if nobody knows about him? He called me a paper lantern, but the Professor himself is a great darkness."

"He ought to try to get out in the world and make a name for himself."

"Make a name for himself? He can't do anything for himself. He couldn't eat three meals a day if he didn't have me around."

Sanshirō laughed out loud as if to say that Yojirō was talking nonsense.

"It's true. It's pitiful how little he does. I'm the one who orders the maid to do things the way he likes them. But never mind all that. I'm planning to really get moving and find him a position at the University."

Yojirō meant it. Sanshirō was shocked. But that made no difference to Yojirō, who went on, leaving Sanshirō's shock intact. He concluded with a request. "Be sure to come and help us move." He sounded as if the new house had been decided on long before.

*

It was nearly ten o'clock by the time Yojirō went home. Seated on the floor alone now, Sanshirō felt a vague chill. He noticed that the window by his desk was still not shuttered for the night. Sliding back the shoji, he found the moon in the night sky. A *hinoki* cypress fire-tree stood outside his window. This tree bothered him whenever he caught sight of it, and especially so tonight when the bluish light of the moon gave the edges of its black silhouette a smoky look. He closed the shutters, thinking how odd it was to have the autumn moon on the seasonless evergreen.

He crawled into bed without further delay. More a rambler in the groves of academe than a serious student, Sanshirō read comparatively little. One pastime he enjoyed, however, was to savor repeatedly the memorable scenes he encountered. This gave life greater depth, he felt. Now would ordinarily be the time of day for him to enjoy recalling such moments as when the lights snapped on during the mystical lecture. First, though, he had his mother's letter to deal with.

Shinzō had given her some honey, she wrote, and she was drinking a little each night, mixed with spirits. Shinzō was a tenant farmer of theirs who brought twenty bales of rice each winter as his annual rent. He was an exceptionally honest fellow but very hot-tempered, and he would beat his wife with a piece of kindling every now and then. Sanshirō recalled how Shinzō first came to keep bees five years earlier. He discovered a swarm of two or three hundred clinging to an oak tree behind his house and took every one of them alive in a big rice funnel sprayed with sake. He put them in a box, cut a hole for the bees to go in and out, and set it on a rock in a sunny place. The bees gradually multiplied, and one hive was no longer enough. He made another, and soon two were no longer enough. He made yet another and went on increasing them this way until he had more than half a dozen hives. He would take one down from its rock each year and cut out the honeycombs "for the bees' sake," as he put it. Every summer when Sanshirō was home from school, Shinzō invariably promised to give them some honey but never brought any. Apparently his memory had improved this year, and he had fulfilled his long-standing promise.

Heitarō had asked her to come and see the stone he had put up on his father's grave, the letter continued. It was made of granite, and it stood in the very center of Heitarō's yard, where not a tree or a blade of grass grew on the red earth. Heitarō was quite proud of the granite slab. Just to cut it out of the mountain had taken him several days, and the engraver had charged him ten yen. A farmer wouldn't realize the value of the stone, Heitarō said, but young master Sanshirō was in the University, and he would be sure to appreciate it. Heitarō wanted her to ask him about it in her next letter and have him say a few kind words about this stone that he had made for his father at a cost of ten yen. Sanshirō chuckled over this one. It was generating a lot more heat than the stone gate in Sendagi.

His mother went on to ask him for a photograph of himself in his student uniform. He would be sure to have one taken for her some time, he thought, and moved on to the next item. As he had feared, it was about Miwata Omitsu. Omitsu's mother had come to see his mother recently and suggested that Sanshirō marry her daughter when he graduated from the University. His mother noted that Omitsu was a pretty girl with a nice disposition, their family owned a good deal of rice land, and considering the two families' long-standing relationship, it should work out well for both sides. She added two postscripts: "It would certainly make Omitsu happy, too." "I don't want you to marry a Tokyo girl. I don't understand those people."

Sanshirō rolled up the letter and returned it to its envelope. He placed it by his pillow and closed his eyes. Some mice began to scurry around in the ceiling, but they quieted down eventually.

*

Three worlds took shape for Sanshirō. One of them was far away and had the fragrance of the past, of what Yojirō called the years before Meiji 15. Everything there was tranquil, yes, but everything was sleepy, too. It would not be difficult for him to go back, of course. He need only go. But he would not want to do that except as a last resort. It was, after all, a place of retreat, and in it he had sealed up the discarded past. He felt a twinge of remorse to think that he had buried his dear mother there as well. Only when her letters came did he linger a while in this world, warm with nostalgia.

In his second world stood a mossy brick building. It had a reading room so vast that, standing in one corner, he could not make out the features of people in the other. There were books shelved so high they could not be reached without a ladder, books blackened with the rubbing of hands, the oil of fingers, books whose titles shone with gold. There was sheepskin, cowhide, paper of two hundred years ago, and piled on all of these, dust. It was precious dust, dust that took twenty, even thirty years to accumulate, silent dust enough to conquer the silent passage of time.

He saw the human shadows flitting through his second world. Most of them had unkempt beards. Some walked along looking at the sky, others looking at the ground. All wore shabby clothing. All lived in poverty. And all were serene. Closed in on every side by streetcars, they freely breathed the air of peace. The men in this world were unfortunate, for they knew nothing of the real world. But they were fortunate as well, for they had fled the Burning House of worldly suffering.[29] Professor Hirota was in this second world. So, too, was Nonomiya. Sanshirō stood where he could understand the air of this world more or less. He could leave it whenever he wished. But to do so, to relinquish a taste he had finally begun to savor, was something he was loath to do.

Sanshirō's third world was as radiant and fluid as spring, a world of electric lights, of silver spoons, of cheers and laughter, of glasses bubbling over with champagne. And crowning everything were beautiful women. Sanshirō had spoken to one of them, he had seen another twice. This world was for him the most profound. This world was just in front of him, but it was unapproachable, like a shaft of lightning in the farthest heavens. Sanshirō gazed at it from afar and found it baffling. He seemed to possess the qualifications to be a master of some part of this world; without him, a void would open up in it. This world should have wanted to fill that void and develop to perfection, but for some reason it closed itself to him and blocked the route by which he might gain free access.

Lying in bed, Sanshirō set his three worlds in a row and compared them, each to the others. Then he mixed the three together and from the mixture obtained a conclusion. The best thing would be to bring his mother from the country, marry a beautiful woman, and devote himself to learning. It was a mediocre conclusion. But a lot of thinking had gone into it, and from the point of view of the thinker himself, who could adjust his evaluation of the conclusion according to the effort he had expended in arriving at it, it was not so mediocre.

The only drawback to this scheme was that it made a mere wife the sole representative of the entire vast world number three. There were plenty of beautiful women. They could be translated in any number of ways. (Sanshirō tried out the word "translate" as he had learned it from Professor Hirota.) And in so far as they could be translated into words relating to character, Sanshirō would have to come into contact with as many beautiful women as possible in order to enlarge the scope of the influence derived from those translations and to perfect his own individuality. To content himself with knowing only a wife would be like going out of his way to ensure the incomplete development of his ego.

Sanshirō carried the argument this far, when it occurred to him that his thinking had been "corrupted a little" by Professor Hirota. For in fact he was not so dissatisfied as all that with his one-woman scheme.

*

The next day's lectures were as boring as ever, but with the atmosphere of the classroom still distant from the mundane, he succeeded by three in the afternoon in becoming a fully fledged citizen of world number two, and when he ran into Yojirō near the Oiwake police box, Sanshirō bore himself with an air of greatness.

"Ha ha ha ha ha! Oh, ho ho ho ho ho!"

Thanks to Yojirō, the bearing of greatness crumbled to bits. Even the officer at the police box was looking at him with a faint smile.

"What's that for?"

"What do you mean, 'What's that for?' Walk a little more like an ordinary human being. That's *romantische Ironie* if I've ever seen it!"

Sanshirō did not understand this foreign term. Instead of pursuing it he asked, "Did you find a house?"

"I was just at your place to tell you about that. We move tomorrow. Come and help."

"Where is it?"

"Nishikatamachi ten, block F, number three. Get there by nine o'clock, will you, and clean the place up. We'll be there later. All right? Make it nine o'clock. Block F, number three. See you there."

Yojirō hurried away and Sanshirō hurried on home. He went back to the library that evening to look up *romantische Ironie*. It was a term first used by the German philosopher Schlegel, he found, and apparently it was some kind of theory to the effect that a genius ought to spend the whole day hanging around, without purpose or effort. Relieved, Sanshirō returned to his room and went to sleep.

The next day was 3 November, the Emperor's Birthday. Despite the holiday, Sanshirō rose at the usual hour and set off as if going to campus. He had promised to help Yojirō. He went to Nishikatamachi ten and found block F, number three, halfway down an oddly narrow street. It was an old house. Instead of the usual stone-floored foyer, a single Western room jutted out from the front of the house. This room formed an L with the matted Japanese parlor, behind which was a smaller sitting room, also matted. Beyond the sitting room was the kitchen, and beyond that the maid's room. The house also had a second story of uncertain size.

He had been asked to clean up, but he saw nothing in special need of cleaning. The place was not clean, of course, but nothing struck him as having to be thrown out. If you were determined to get rid of something, the mats and paper doors could possibly stand replacement, but that was all. He slid back the storm doors and sat on the veranda, looking at the garden.

There was a large crepe myrtle. It was rooted, however, in the neighbor's yard and merely leaned most of its trunk over the cedar fence, taking up space on this side. There was a large cherry tree. It, to be sure, was growing on this side of the fence, but half its branches had fled the garden for the street and would soon obstruct the telephone lines. There was a single large chrysanthemum. Perhaps it was a winter variety, though, for it had no blossoms. There was nothing else. It was a pitiful sort of garden. The soil, however, level and of a very fine consistency, was quite beautiful. Sanshirō looked at it for some time. This was, in fact, a garden made for looking at the soil.

Soon a bell sounded, opening the holiday ceremonies at the College. It must be nine o'clock, Sanshirō thought. At last it occurred to him that he should not be sitting there doing nothing. Perhaps he could sweep up the leaves that had fallen from the cherry tree. But there was no broom. He sat down again on the veranda. Perhaps two minutes had gone by when, without a sound, the garden gate opened and, to Sanshirō's amazement, the young woman from the pond stepped in.

*

Two sides of the garden were enclosed by a hedge. The square bit of land did not quite come to twenty feet on one side. When he saw the young woman from the pond standing within this narrow enclosure, Sanshirō had a momentary insight: one should always view a flower cut, in a vase.

Sanshirō moved away from his seat on the veranda. The young woman moved away from the gate.

"Pardon me," she began, bowing. As before, she floated forward from the waist. But her face did not move down. Even while she was bowing, she stared straight at Sanshirō. Her throat seemed to extend toward him, and at the same time her eyes flashed into his.

A few days before, Sanshirō's aesthetics instructor had shown the class some portraits by Greuze. Using an English term, he had explained that all women painted by this artist wore richly *voluptuous* expressions. Voluptuous! There was no other way to describe her eyes at that moment. They were trying to tell him something, something voluptuous, something that appealed directly to the senses. But their plea pierced the bone

of the senses and reached the marrow. It went beyond bearable
sweetness and became a violent stimulus. Far from sweet, it
was excruciating. This was not, to be sure, cheap coquetry.
There was a cruelty in her glance that made the one it fell
on wish to play the coquette. Nor did she bear the slightest
resemblance to a portrait by Greuze. Her eyes were small, half
the size of those in his paintings.

"Would this be Professor Hirota's new house by any
chance?"

"Uh-huh. This is it." Sanshirō's tone of voice and manner
were very brusque in comparison to hers. He was aware of this,
but he knew no other way to answer her.

"Has he not moved in yet?" She expressed herself clearly,
without letting her voice trail off the way so many women did.

"No, not yet. He should be here soon."

She hesitated for a moment. In one hand she held a large
basket. Sanshirō found the material of her kimono unfamiliar
again today. He was aware, at least, that it did not gleam as the
others had. The fabric looked almost bumpy and had some
kind of stripes or pattern, a most haphazard design.

A leaf would drop now and then from the cherry tree above.
One settled on the lid of the basket. Hardly had it come to rest
than it was blown away. The wind embraced the woman. The
woman stood in the midst of autumn.

"And you are . . . ?" she asked when the wind had moved on
to the neighboring garden.

"They wanted me to come and clean up," he said, then
realized with some amusement that she had found him sitting
and daydreaming. She smiled, too, as she spoke to him.

"Perhaps I ought to wait here with you . . . ?" It pleased him
that she seemed to be asking his permission to stay.

"Well," he replied, which, to his way of thinking, was meant
to serve as a shorter "Well, please do," but she did not move.
All he could do was ask her the same thing she had asked him.
"And you are . . . ?" She set her basket on the veranda and
handed him a name card from the folds of her obi.

*

"Satomi Mineko," it said. She lived in Hongō, Masago-chō, just a short walk from there down one hill and up the next. She sat on the edge of the veranda while Sanshirō was reading her card.

When he had put the card into the sleeve of his kimono, he looked up and said, "We've met before. Do you remember?"

"I think so. Once, in the hospital . . ." She returned his glance.

"And once before that."

"By the pond," she answered immediately. She had seen him, then, and she remembered. Sanshirō ran out of things to say. She closed the subject with an apology.

"I'm afraid I was very rude."

"No, not at all," he replied.

The exchange was executed with the greatest concision. They began looking at the cherry tree. A few worm-eaten leaves still clung to its branches. The Professor's belongings were taking a very long time to arrive.

"Did you want to see the Professor about something?" Sanshirō asked without warning. She had been gazing intently at the withered upper branches of the tall cherry tree, but now she spun around to look at him. Oh, you're terrible, you startled me, her expression seemed to say, but her reply carried no hint of accusation.

"They asked me to help, too."

Sanshirō noticed a layer of sand on the veranda where she was sitting. "Look at all the sand here. Your kimono is going to get dirty."

"Oh, yes," she said, glancing to either side. She did not move. After their brief survey of the veranda, her eyes turned to Sanshirō. "Have you cleaned up?" She was smiling. Sanshirō found something in her smile that told him they could be friends.

"No, not yet."

"Why don't we start helping them now? We can work together."

Sanshirō stood up at once. She did not move. Where were the broom and duster? she asked. There weren't any—he had come empty-handed; perhaps he should go and buy some? That would be a waste, she insisted; better borrow them from a neighbor. He went next door. When he came hurrying back with the borrowed broom and duster—and bucket and rags, too—she was in the same place on the veranda, looking up at the high branches of the cherry tree.

"Oh, you found them?" she said.

Sanshirō had the broom on his shoulder and the bucket dangling from his right hand. "Here they are," he replied, stating the obvious.

She stood up on the sandy wooden deck. Each step she took in her white stockings left a slender footprint. She produced a white apron from the sleeve of her kimono and tied it on at the waist. The apron had a lacy border. It was far too pretty for doing housework. She picked the broom up.

"Let's sweep first," she said, slipping her right arm from the kimono sleeve, which she then draped over her shoulder. Bare past the elbow, the arm was lovely. A beautiful under-kimono showed at the edge of the raised sleeve. Sanshirō, who had been watching entranced, darted around to the kitchen door, his bucket rattling.

*

Mineko swept the wooden floors, and Sanshirō wiped them after her. Sanshirō beat the floor mats clean while Mineko dusted the shoji. By the time the job was finished, the two were well on the way to becoming friends.

Sanshirō went to the kitchen to change the water in the bucket, and Mineko went upstairs with the duster and broom.

"Could you come up here a minute?" she called to him.

"What is it?" he said, approaching the foot of the stairs, bucket in hand. It was dark where she stood. He could see nothing but her apron, stark white. He climbed up a few steps with the bucket. She remained very still. Sanshirō climbed two more steps. Their faces came to within a foot of each other in the shadows.

"What is it?"

"I don't know, it's so dark."

"Why's that?"

"I don't know, it just *is*."

He decided not to pursue the matter. Slipping by Mineko, he continued up the stairs. He set the bucket down on the second-story veranda and started to open the storm doors. Indeed there was a problem: he did not know how to work the bolt. Soon Mineko came up.

"Can't you open it?" She went to the other side. "It's over here." Without a word, Sanshirō moved toward her. His hand was about to touch hers when he stumbled against the bucket with a loud thump. He managed to open one of the shutters at last, and a strong burst of sunlight flooded into the room. It was dazzling. The two looked at each other and laughed.

They opened the rear window as well. It had a bamboo lattice, through which they could look down on the landlord's garden. There were chickens down there. Mineko started sweeping again. Sanshirō bent down on all fours and began wiping the floor after her.

"My goodness!" she exclaimed, looking down at him with the broom in her hands.

When she was done, Mineko dropped the broom on the floor mats and went to the rear window, where she stood looking out. Sanshirō was soon finished with his wiping. He plopped the damp rags into the bucket and joined Mineko at the window.

"What are you looking at?"

"Guess."

"The chickens?"

"No."

"That big tree?"

"No."

"I don't know, then. What?"

"I've been watching those white clouds."

He saw what she meant. White clouds were moving across the broad sky. They sailed steadily onward like thick, shining wads of cotton against the endlessly clear blue. The wind appeared to be blowing with tremendous force. It tore at the ends of the clouds until they were thin enough for the blue background to show through. Sometimes they would become frayed in clumps and form bunches of soft, white needles.

Mineko pointed to this and said, "They look like ostrich-feather boas, don't you think?"

Sanshirō did not know the word "boa," and he said so. Again Mineko exclaimed, "My goodness!" but she was quick to offer him a detailed explanation.

"Oh, I've seen plenty of those," he said. He went on to tell her, as Nonomiya had told him, that the clouds were made of snowflakes and that they would have to be traveling with greater than hurricane velocity to look so fast from down here.

"Oh, really?" Mineko looked at him. "That takes all the fun out of it," she declared in a manner that would permit no disagreement.

"How does it do that?"

"Because, it just does. A cloud should be a cloud. Otherwise, it's not worth watching in the distance like this."

"It isn't?"

"What do you mean? Don't you care if it's made of snow?"

"You like to look at things up high, don't you?"

"Yes."

Mineko went on looking at the sky through the bamboo lattice. White clouds sailed past, one after another.

*

Soon there came the far-off sound of a wagon. The way the ground was rumbling, the wagon had obviously just turned off the quiet back street and was drawing nearer.

"They're here," said Sanshirō.

"They're early," said Mineko, pausing to listen intently, as though the sound of the moving wagon had something to do with the white clouds' movement across the sky. The wagon drew relentlessly nearer through the placid autumn. Finally it reached the gate and stopped.

Sanshirō left Mineko and bounded down the stairs. He reached the front door just as Yojirō came in through the gate. Yojirō was the first to speak.

"You got here early."

"Well, *you* got here late!" Sanshirō answered, quite the opposite of Mineko.

"Late? Maybe so. I did it all in one trip, and there was just me. The only help I had was the maid and the porter."

"How about the Professor?"

"He's at school for the ceremonies."

While they were talking, the porter began to unload the wagon. The maid came in, too. She and the man were to handle the kitchen things while Yojirō and Sanshirō brought the books to the Western room. There were lots of books, and putting them in the shelves would be a major undertaking.

"Didn't Satomi Mineko get here yet?"

"Yes, she did."

"Where is she?"

"Upstairs."

"What's she doing up there?"

"How should I know? She's up there."

"Look, I'm serious."

A book in his hand, Yojirō walked down the hall to the foot of the stairway and called out in his usual tone of voice, "Mineko! Come and help us straighten out the books, will you?"

"I'll be right down." Mineko calmly started down the stairs, broom and duster in hand.

"What have you been doing?" Yojirō grumbled from below, trying to hurry her.

"Cleaning the upstairs," she answered from above.

Too impatient to wait for Mineko, Yojirō walked ahead of her to the doorway of the Western room, where the porter had deposited several piles of books. Sanshirō was squatting among them, his back to Yojirō. He had become absorbed in reading.

"My goodness, look at all the books. What are we supposed to do with them?"

Sanshirō, still squatting, looked around when he heard Mineko's voice. He wore a big grin.

"What do you *think* we're supposed to do with them?" Yojirō snapped. "We just move them inside and put them away. Anyhow, it won't be too bad. The Professor should be here soon to give us a hand. —Ogawa, get up and get to work. If you're so interested in that book, borrow it later and read it on your own time."

Mineko and Sanshirō sorted books at the doorway and handed them in to Yojirō, who arranged them on the shelves.

"Not so wild, please. There should be another volume to go with this one." Yojirō brandished a slim, green book.

"No, that's the only one," said Mineko.

"It can't be."

"Here it is!" Sanshirō said.

"Oh, let's see." Mineko leaned close to Sanshirō to see the book he had found. "*History of Intellectual Development.*[30] That's it!"

"Of course it is. Come on, let's have it."

*

The three of them put in half an hour of concentrated effort, by which time Yojirō had stopped his nagging. One minute he was hard at work, and the next he was seated cross-legged on the floor, facing the bookcases. Mineko nudged Sanshirō, who smiled and called out to him, "Hey Yojirō, what's going on?"

"Oh, nothing. It's maddening, though. What does the Professor think he's going to do with all these useless books? He should sell them and buy stocks or something and really make some money. What's the use?" he sighed without budging from his cross-legged position.

Sanshirō and Mineko looked at each other and smiled. As long as the brains of this operation was not functioning, they could relax a bit, too. Sanshirō began flipping through a book of poems. Mineko opened a large picture book on her lap. The maid and the porter had a noisy argument going in the kitchen.

"Look at this," Mineko said softly. Sanshirō leaned over her to look down at the album. He caught the scent of cologne in her hair.

It was a picture of a mermaid, naked and in a sitting position, with her fishtail curled around behind her. She faced forward combing her hair, holding the overflowing tresses in one hand. The sea stretched away in the background.

Sanshirō's and Mineko's heads touched, and together they whispered, "A mermaid."

Still cross-legged on the floor, Yojirō seemed to snap out of his mood. "What is it? What are you looking at?" he asked, coming out to the hallway. The three of them, heads together, examined the picture book a page at a time. The critical remarks were many and varied, and based on nothing much.

At that point Professor Hirota arrived from the Emperor's Birthday ceremonies wearing a frock coat. They set the picture book aside to welcome him. He wanted the books, at least, to be taken care of right away, he said, which inspired another serious effort. With the Professor here, they would have to work more seriously, and an hour later the books were out of the hallway and on the shelves. The four of them stood in a row to inspect the neatly arranged volumes.

"We'll get the other stuff put away tomorrow," Yojirō said, all but instructing Hirota to be satisfied with what they had done.

"You have so many books," said Mineko.

"Have you read them all?" Sanshirō asked as though he had a real need to ascertain this fact for his own future reference.

"Hardly! Sasaki here might do it, but not me."

Yojirō scratched his head. Sanshirō explained that he had a serious purpose in asking the question. He had been reading books from the University library in recent weeks, and he found that every book he looked at had been read by someone before him. Once, as a test, he had taken out a novel by someone named Aphra Behn, and even that had marks in it. What was the limit to the breadth of one's reading?

"Aphra Behn? I've read her stuff," said Hirota. Sanshirō was amazed.

"That's astounding," said Yojirō. "You read books that no one else ever reads, Professor."

Laughing, Hirota walked into the parlor, probably to change his clothes. Mineko followed him out. Left to themselves now, Yojirō said to Sanshirō, "That's why I call him the Great Darkness. He reads everything, but he doesn't give off any light. I wish he would read something a little more fashionable and make himself a little more conspicuous."

Yojirō was not being critical of the Professor. He spoke with true feeling. Sanshirō stared at the bookcases. Mineko called out to them from the parlor, "Come and have some lunch, you two."

*

They walked down the hall and found Mineko's basket, uncovered, in the middle of the parlor floor, full of sandwiches. Mineko sat next to it, distributing the contents onto four plates.

"How nice. You didn't forget to bring lunch," said Yojirō.

"No, you were very specific about that."

"Did you buy the basket, too?"

"No, I didn't."

"You had this thing in the house?"

"That's right."

"It's huge. Your rickshaw man must have helped you with it. As long as you brought him, you should have kept him here to work for a while."

"He was on an errand today. Besides, the basket isn't all that big. A woman can handle it."

"*You* can handle it. Any other young lady would have left it at home."

"Really? Perhaps I should have."

Mineko continued to arrange the plates of food while she carried on this dialogue with Yojirō. She responded without hesitation, but unhurriedly, with the utmost calm, and hardly ever looking at Yojirō. Sanshirō was filled with admiration for her.

The maid brought tea from the kitchen. Sitting around the basket, the four began to eat their sandwiches. No one spoke for a time. Then Yojirō addressed Professor Hirota.

"Professor, about that writer you mentioned before, somebody-or-other Behn, was it?"

"Aphra Behn, you mean?"

"Who is Aphra Behn?"

"She was a famous English novelist. Seventeenth century."

"Seventeenth century? That's old stuff, nothing the magazines would want."

"It's old all right. But she was the first professional woman novelist. That's why she's famous."

"So she's famous, but I still don't know anything about her. What did she write?"

"The only thing I've read is a novel called *Oroonoko*. You must have come across that title in her complete works, Ogawa?"

Sanshirō had no recollection whatever.

It was the story of Oroonoko, said the Professor, an African prince who was tricked by an English sea captain, sold as a slave and made to suffer great hardships. It was believed to be the author's actual eyewitness account.

"That's quite a story," said Yojirō. "How about it, Mineko? Why don't you write something like *Oroonoko*?"

"I wouldn't mind, but I've never been an 'actual eyewitness' to anything."

"If it's an African hero you need, you've got Ogawa here, the Kyushu black man."

"You're terrible," she said as if in defense of Sanshirō, but then she turned to him and asked, "May I write about you?"

When he looked into her eyes, Sanshirō recalled the moment when she had appeared with her basket at the garden gate this morning. He felt a wave of intoxication come over him, but it was more paralyzing than pleasurable. For him to have answered "Oh yes, please do" would have been out of the question.

*

Professor Hirota began to smoke, as usual. Yojirō remarked that what the Professor blew from his nose was the smoke of philosophy. And in fact the smoke did emerge in a somewhat unusual manner. Two thick shafts slipped slowly from his nostrils. One shoulder blade against the sliding paper door, Yojirō stared at the pillars of smoke in silence. Sanshirō's eyes wandered out to the garden.

This was hardly the moving of a household. It looked more like a tea party. The conversation, too, was appropriately light. Only Mineko kept busy. In the shadows behind Professor Hirota, she started folding the suit that she had apparently helped him out of earlier. Sanshirō admired the poise with which she undertook even such dreary feminine tasks.

"About *Oroonoko*," the Professor said, interrupting the stream of smoke, "I don't want you to make another of your careless mistakes, so let me just say this."

"I would be appreciative of any instruction," Yojirō said with the utmost propriety.

"A man named Southerne wrote a play based on the novel, and the play had the same title. You mustn't confuse the two."

"No, of course not."

Mineko, still folding the suit, glanced at Yojirō.

"There was a famous line in the play, 'Pity's akin to love.'" The Professor stopped here and produced great quantities of philosophical smoke.

Now Sanshirō joined in. "It sounds like a line you might come across in Japan."

The others agreed with him, but no one could recall having heard such a line in Japanese. Perhaps they should try to translate it? But the results were inconclusive. Finally Yojirō voiced a characteristic opinion.

"The only way we're going to translate this is to make it like a line from a popular song. That's the kind of thing it is, after all." Everyone decided to cede full translation rights to Yojirō. He mulled over the problem for a while. Then he said, "It may be a little forced, but how about this? 'When I say that you're a poor little thing, it only means I'm crazy about you.'"

"Terrible! Terrible!" the Professor cried, scowling. "It's the cheapest thing I've ever heard!" He really did seem to find it offensively cheap, which brought a burst of laughter from Sanshirō and Mineko. They were still laughing when the garden gate creaked open and Nonomiya walked in.

"Is everything put away?" he asked, approaching the veranda and peering in at everyone in the parlor.

"Oh, no, there's still a lot to be done," said Yojirō, jumping at the opportunity.

"Let's have him help a little!" Mineko chimed in.

Grinning, Nonomiya said, "You seem to be having quite a time. What's going on?" He spun around and sat on the veranda with his back to the room.

"The Professor was just scolding me for a translation I did."

"A translation? What kind of translation?"

"It's nothing, really. 'When I say that you're a poor little thing, it only means I'm crazy about you.'"

"Wha-a-at?" Nonomiya turned to face them at an angle. "I don't get it."

"Neither do we," said the Professor.

"What is the original supposed to be?"

Mineko repeated the phrase for him: "Pity's akin to love." Her English pronunciation was clear and lovely.

Nonomiya stood up from the veranda, took a few strides into the garden, and spun around, facing the room. "Not a bad translation at all, I'd say."

Sanshirō could not help observing Nonomiya and the direction of his gaze.

*

Mineko went out to the kitchen. She washed a cup, filled it with fresh tea, and brought it to the edge of the veranda. Inviting Nonomiya to drink, she sat down near him.

"How is Yoshiko?" she asked.

"Physically, at least, she's recovered." Nonomiya resumed his seat and drank the tea. Then he turned toward the Professor. "I went to all the trouble of moving out to Ōkubo, Professor, and now it seems I'll have to come back to live in this area."

"Why is that?"

"It's my sister. She says she doesn't want to walk through the drill field at Toyamanohara on the way to and from school. And she feels lonely at night waiting for me to come home when I'm experimenting late. She's all right now while my mother's here, but my mother will be going back to the country soon and she'll only have the maid. They're both a couple of cowards. They won't be able to stand it alone in the house. What a lot of trouble!" He sighed, smiling, then looked at Mineko. "Take an extra lodger?"

"Fine, anytime at all."

"Which Nonomiya will that be?" Yojirō interjected. "Sōhachi or Yoshiko?"

"I'll take either one," Mineko replied.

Only Sanshirō kept quiet. Hirota, on a serious note, asked, "And what about you, Sōhachi? What do you plan to do?"

"As long as my sister is settled, I don't mind living in a room for a while. Otherwise, we'll have to move to another house. I'm thinking of putting her into a dormitory or something— someplace I can visit all the time or she can leave to see me whenever she wants. She's still a child, after all."

"Well, that settles it—Mineko's is obviously the only place!" Yojirō was offering his opinions again.

Ignoring Yojirō, Hirota said, "She could stay upstairs here, but I'm afraid this fellow Sasaki is there."

"Oh please, Professor, let Sasaki keep his upstairs room!" Yojirō pleaded for himself.

Laughing, Nonomiya said, "We'll manage somehow. I do have my hands full with her, though—all grown up and still a little idiot. She even wants me to take her to see the chrysanthemum dolls at Dangozaka."

"What's wrong with that?" said Mineko. "I'd like to see them myself."

"Well come along, then."

"I'd love to. You come too, Sanshirō."

"All right, I will."

"And Yojirō."

"Chrysanthemum dolls? No, thanks. I'd go to the moving pictures[31] before I'd do that."

"The chrysanthemum dolls are a fine thing," Professor Hirota began. "I doubt there's anything so artificial in any other country. Everyone ought to see once in his life that such completely artificial creations actually exist. No one would go to Dangozaka to see them, I'm sure, if the dolls looked like ordinary people. If it's ordinary people you're after, you can find four or five of them in any house. You don't have to go all the way to Dangozaka."

"A theory all your own, Professor," Yojirō offered his critical opinion.

"I always used to fall for those things when I was a student of the Professor's," said Nonomiya.

"You come with us, too, Professor," Mineko said finally. Hirota said nothing. Everyone else laughed aloud.

The old woman in the kitchen called out for someone to come. Yojirō shouted back and left the room. Sanshirō stayed where he was.

"Well, it's about time for me to be leaving," Nonomiya said, standing up.

"So soon? You were supposed to be helping us," Mineko said.

"Oh, Sōhachi, can you wait a little while on that business we talked about?" Hirota said.

"Yes, of course," Nonomiya answered and went out through the garden.

As his shadow disappeared beyond the gate, Mineko seemed to recall something. "Oh, yes!" she murmured and, stepping into her wooden clogs below the veranda, she ran after him. They stood talking in the lane.

Sanshirō remained seated, silent.

5

He walked in through the gate. The bush clover he had noticed on his last visit, grown taller than a man, now wore a mass of autumn foliage that cast a black shadow at its base. The shadow crept along the ground and disappeared into the house. It also seemed to climb up the hidden sides of the densely overlapping leaves, so strong was the sunlight striking their outer surfaces. Some nandinas stood beside the garden wash basin outside the lavatory. These, like the bush clover, were unusually tall. Their three fragile plumes stood close together, leaves stretching above the lavatory window.

The veranda was partially visible between the bush clover and the nandinas. It ran away at an angle that took off from the nandinas. The shadow of the bush clover struck the house at the far end of the veranda, although the bush itself was the first thing inside the gate. Yoshiko sat in the shadow of the bush clover, on the edge of the veranda.

Sanshirō approached until he was almost touching the bush clover. Yoshiko stood up, her feet resting on the broad, flat stepping-stone in the garden. Only now did Sanshirō realize with a shock how tall she was.

"Come in."

Again, she spoke as if she had been waiting for him, which reminded him of that day at the hospital. He walked past the bush clover as far as the veranda.

"Please sit down."

He sat on the edge of the veranda as ordered, his shoes resting on the garden stone. Yoshiko brought out a cushion for him.

"Here, sit on this."

Again he did as he was told. He had yet to speak since entering the gate. This simple girl merely said to him what was on her mind without, it seemed, expecting any answer from him. Sanshirō felt that he was in the presence of an innocent young queen. He need only obey her commands. Flattery was out of the question. A sycophantic word from him, and everything would be cheapened. Better to do her bidding like a mute slave. The childlike Yoshiko was treating him like a child, but he felt no injury to his self-respect.

"Did you want to see my brother?"

Sanshirō had not come to see Nonomiya. Neither had he not come to see him. Sanshirō did not really know why he had come.

"Is he still at the University?"

"Yes. He always comes home late at night."

Sanshirō was quite aware of this. He did not know what to say. Then he noticed a box of paint and brushes on the veranda. Also a half-finished watercolor.

"Do you paint?"

"Yes, just for fun."

"Who is your teacher?"

"I don't have one. I'm not that good."

"May I look?"

"At this? It's not finished yet." She handed the painting to Sanshirō. It was to be a picture of the garden. Only the sky, the neighbor's persimmon tree, and the bush clover were done. The persimmons were too red.

"Pretty good," he said.

"This?" said Yoshiko with a start. There was nothing forced in her reaction, as there had been in Sanshirō's compliment.

It was too late now for him to make light of what he had said or to insist that he had meant it. Either way, Yoshiko would be contemptuous of him. He went on looking at the picture, blushing inwardly.

*

Turning toward the parlor, he found it empty and still. There was no sign of anyone in the sitting room or the kitchen. "Has your mother gone home to the country?"

"Not yet. She should be leaving soon, though."

"Is she here now?"

"She's out shopping."

"Are you really going to move in with the Satomis?"

"Why?"

"No reason—just that they were talking about it the other day at Professor Hirota's."

"We haven't decided yet. Maybe I will, though."

Sanshirō now had part of what he was looking for. "Have the Satomis and Nonomiyas always been close?"

"Yes, old friends."

Did she mean that Satomi Mineko and Nonomiya Sōhachi were just "friends"? There was something odd in that, but he could not pry any further. "I heard that Professor Hirota used to be Sōhachi's teacher."

"That's right."

Yoshiko's answer brought the topic to a dead end.

"Would you prefer to live with Mineko?"

"Me? I guess so. But I'd hate to be any trouble for her brother."

"She has a brother?"

"Yes, he graduated the same year as my brother."

"Is he a scientist, too?"

"No, he took his degree in Law. Mineko had another brother who was a good friend of Professor Hirota's, but he died young. Now she has only Kyōsuke."

"How about her mother and father?"

"No," she answered with a little smile, as if to say that it was comical to imagine Mineko with parents. They must have died quite some time ago. Yoshiko probably had no recollection of them at all.

"So that's how Mineko knows the Professor?"

"Yes. The brother who died was supposedly very close to the Professor. And Mineko likes English. I'm sure she goes there a lot to study with him."

"Does she come here, too?"

Yoshiko had started painting again at some point in the conversation. She did not allow Sanshirō's presence to interfere with her work, but she could still answer his questions.

"Mineko?" she asked, adding some shadow to the thatched roof beneath the persimmon tree. "I made it a little too black, didn't I?" She held the picture up for Sanshirō.

This time he answered honestly. "Yes, a little."

Yoshiko wet her brush and started to wash out the black area. "She does." Sanshirō had his answer at last.

"Often?"

"Yes, often." She was still facing her picture. The conversation had become a good deal easier for Sanshirō once Yoshiko started the painting.

*

He watched in silence as she concentrated on washing out the black shadow beneath the thatched roof. But she used too much water, and her brushwork was inept. The black stuff streamed off in all directions, and the bright red persimmons turned the color of the tart, shade-dried kind. Yoshiko's brush hand came to rest. She held the paper out at arm's length and leaned her head back, looking at the picture from as far away as possible. Finally she murmured, "Oh well, it's ruined." It really was ruined beyond denial. Sanshirō felt sorry for her.

"You ought to forget about this one and start a new one."

Facing the picture, Yoshiko looked at him out of the corner of her eye. The eye was large and moist. Sanshirō felt increasingly sorry for her. And then she burst out laughing.

"How stupid, wasting two whole hours like this!" She painted several thick stripes lengthwise and breadthwise across the picture and slammed down the lid of the paintbox.

"Enough!" she said, standing. "Come inside, I'll make you some tea." Sanshirō did not move. It was too much trouble to take his shoes off. Yoshiko's belated offer of tea left him greatly amused. Not that he was laughing at her for performing her feminine duties in her own good time, but the sudden "I'll make you some tea" struck him with a kind of irrepressible delight. This was not how one felt in approaching a member of the opposite sex.

He heard voices in the sitting room. The maid was there after all. Eventually the door slid back and Yoshiko emerged carrying a tea set. Seeing her face from the front, he thought it the most feminine of feminine faces.

Yoshiko poured the tea and set it between them on the veranda. She knelt opposite him on the matted floor of the parlor. Sanshirō had been thinking of leaving, but now that he was sitting near her, it no longer mattered. He had rushed out of the hospital that day, having stared at her and made her blush, but today he was all right. The tea was a good opportunity for them to start talking again across the width of the veranda.

After they had exchanged a few remarks, Yoshiko asked him an odd question: did he like her brother Sōhachi? At first it sounded like something a naïve little girl might ask, but what she had in mind was a bit more profound. Academics, she said, look at everything as objects of study, and so their emotions dry up. But if you look at things with feeling, you never want to study them because everything comes down to love or hate. Unfortunately, as a scientist, her brother could not help viewing her as an object of study, which was unkind of him, because the more he studied his sister, the more his love for her would decrease. Great scholar though he was, however, Nonomiya still showed great love for his sister. Conclusion: he must be the best person in all of Japan.

Sanshirō felt that her argument was perfectly reasonable and, at the same time, it was missing something. Just what it was missing, though, his muddled brain would not tell him, and he presented no open critique. He blushed to think that, in failing to offer a lucid critique of the remarks of a mere girl, he made such a feeble showing as a man. He realized, too, that one had to take these Tokyo schoolgirls seriously.

Filled with a new respect for Yoshiko, Sanshirō returned to his rooming house. There he found a postcard waiting for him. "Please come to Professor Hirota's tomorrow. We leave for the chrysanthemum doll show at one o'clock. Mineko." Her writing looked familiar. He had seen it on the envelope in Nonomiya's pocket. He read the card over and over again.

*

The next day was Sunday. After lunch Sanshirō went straight to Nishikatamachi wearing a new uniform and well-shined shoes. He walked down the quiet lane to Professor Hirota's. From inside he heard the voices of a man and a woman.

The garden of the Professor's house lay just within the front gate to the left. One could enter the garden gate and approach the veranda without walking through the house. Sanshirō had been just about to slip the bolt, which was visible through a gap in the photinia hedge, when he became aware of the voices in the garden. They belonged to Nonomiya and Mineko.

"Then you just fall to earth and die." This was Nonomiya.

"I think it's worth dying for," Mineko replied.

"Of course, anyone that reckless would deserve to fall down and die."

"What a cruel thing to say."

At this point Sanshirō opened the gate. Standing in the center of the garden, the talkers looked his way. Nonomiya offered him an ordinary "Hello, there" and a nod. He wore a new brown fedora.

"When did the postcard come?" Mineko asked Sanshirō, bringing the conversation with Nonomiya to an abrupt end.

The master of the house was seated on the edge of the veranda, dressed in a suit and emitting his customary streams of philosophy. He had a foreign magazine in his hand. Yoshiko stood next to him, leaning back with her hands on the veranda and staring at the thick straw sandals on her outstretched feet. Obviously, everyone had been waiting for him.

Hirota threw his magazine aside. "Let's get going, then. Congratulations, you've finally dragged me out of the house."

"What an awful chore this must be for you," said Nonomiya, going out with him. The two women looked at each other and shared a private laugh. They walked out of the garden in single file.

"How tall you are," Mineko said from behind.

"A bean pole," Yoshiko replied simply. When they came side by side at the front gate, she explained, "That's why I wear sandals whenever I can."

Sanshirō was starting out of the garden after them when a

shoji on the second story clattered open and Yojirō emerged at the handrail.

"You going?" he asked.

"Yes. Are you?"

"No, what's the point? A lot of stupid, fixed-up flowers."

"Oh, come on. What's the point of staying at home?"

"I'm writing an essay, a major essay. I don't have time for stuff like that."

With a startled laugh, Sanshirō hurried after the others. They were two-thirds of the way down the lane toward the street. When he caught sight of them in silhouette beneath the sky's expanse, Sanshirō felt that his present life was becoming a thing of far deeper significance than his life in Kumamoto had been. Worlds number two and three were both represented in this group image. One half was dark and gloomy, the other as bright as a field of flowers. The two were in perfect harmony in Sanshirō's mind. And Sanshirō himself was being woven into the fabric almost before he knew it. But there was something unsettled about the design that made him feel anxious. As he walked along, it occurred to him that the immediate cause of this anxiety was the topic of Nonomiya's conversation with Mineko in the garden. He wanted to ferret it out as a way of dispelling his anxiety.

The four of them had reached the corner. They stopped and looked back toward him. Mineko held her hand to her brow.

*

Sanshirō caught up with them in less than a minute, but no one said a thing. They merely started walking again. After a while, Mineko spoke to Nonomiya. "You *would* say something like that. You're a scientist." It seemed to be a continuation of their talk in the garden.

"That has nothing to do with it. If you want to fly, you have to think up a device that is capable of flying. It's as simple as that. You have to use your mind first, don't you see?"

"Maybe that would be enough for someone who didn't want to fly very high."

"It would *have* to be enough for him. Otherwise, he'd just get killed."

"So the best thing is to play it safe and stay on the ground. What a bore."

Instead of answering, Nonomiya turned to Hirota. "Lots of women are poets," he said, smiling.

"And the trouble with men," Hirota said, "is that they can never quite become pure poets."

Nonomiya said nothing in response to this odd remark. Mineko and Yoshiko started their own conversation. Sanshirō could finally ask his question. "What were you two just talking about?"

"Oh, nothing," Nonomiya said. "Flying machines."

Sanshirō felt as if he were hearing the punch line of a comic story.

No one said much after that. Lengthy conversations were impossible now in any case amid the weekend crowds. A beggar was kneeling on the ground outside the Ōgannon Temple. Forehead pressed to the earth, he poured forth a stream of loud entreaties. He would raise his face at intervals to reveal a white smudge of sand on his forehead. No one looked at him. Sanshirō and his four companions also passed him by, unconcerned. When they had left him several yards behind, Professor Hirota suddenly turned and spoke to Sanshirō. "Did you give that beggar anything?"

"No," Sanshirō answered, looking back. The beggar, hands pressed together beneath his white forehead, was persisting with his loud cries.

"He doesn't really inspire you to give him anything, does he?" Yoshiko put in.

"What do you mean?" Her brother looked at her, but his tone of voice was not reproachful. His expression was, if anything, cool and detached.

Mineko offered her critique. "The way he keeps on ranting, it doesn't have any effect."

"That's not it," said Hirota. "He's in the wrong place. There are too many people going by. If they came across him on a deserted mountain top, everyone would feel like giving him something."

"Yes, but he could wait all day without a soul coming by," Nonomiya said with a chuckle.

Listening to the others' critiques of the beggar, Sanshirō felt that some damage was being done to the moral precepts he had cultivated thus far. Not only had it never crossed his mind to toss the beggar money, however: he had actually found it unpleasant to walk past the man. He had to admit that the others were being truer to themselves than he was. They were people of the city who lived beneath heavens that were broad enough to enable them to be true to themselves.

*

The farther they walked, the more people they encountered. Soon they came across a lost child, a little girl of perhaps seven. She swept aimlessly back and forth beneath the sleeves of the throng. "Grandma, Grandma," she called out in tears. Everyone who saw her seemed touched. A few stopped to look. "The poor little thing," someone said. But no one took her in hand. The little girl attracted the attention and sympathy of everyone around her, but still she had to keep crying loudly in search of her grandmother. It was a strange phenomenon.

"She's in the wrong place, too, I suppose," Nonomiya said, keeping his eye on the shifting shadow of the little girl.

"Everyone figures a policeman is bound to take care of her sooner or later, so they avoid the responsibility," Professor Hirota explained.

"If she comes near me, I'll take her to the police box," Yoshiko said.

"So why don't you just go get her and take her over?" her brother suggested.

"I don't want to go chasing after her."

"Why not?"

"I don't know—there are so many people here. I don't have to be the one."

"That's it," Hirota said, "avoiding the responsibility."

"She's in the wrong place after all," Nonomiya said. The two men laughed.

At the top of Dangozaka, they found a swarm of people by

the police box. The lost child was finally in the hands of the police.

"You can relax now," Mineko turned and said to Yoshiko.

"Oh, I'm so glad."

Viewed from the top, the slope of Dangozaka curved to the right. The narrow street looked like the pointed end of a sword. The two-story buildings on the right obscured the lower half of the high exhibition sheds on the left. Higher up beyond the sheds flew a number of tall banners. People seemed to be plunging down into the valley below. Those who were plunging down and those who were crawling up came together in a chaotic jumble that clogged the street and gave what must have been the lowest part of the valley a grotesque sort of movement, a fitful squirming that quickly tired the eye.

Standing atop the slope, Professor Hirota exclaimed, "This is horrible!" He was obviously ready to go home. All but pushing him from behind, they walked down the hill. Toward the bottom, where the slope began to curve and level out, there were large, reed-thatched exhibition sheds lining either side and towering over the narrow street. They were enough to make the sky itself look cramped. Everything was so tightly packed together the street was darkened. Amidst all this the ticket takers at the shed doors were shouting at the top of their lungs. So utterly remote from normal voices were their cries, they prompted a critique from Professor Hirota: "Those are no human sounds. They're the voices of the chrysanthemum dolls."

They entered a shed on the left. The first tableau was a scene from a Kabuki play showing the attack of the Soga Brothers.[32] All of the dolls, from the lowly Gorō and Jūrō to the great Yoritomo himself, wore equally gorgeous costumes fashioned from chrysanthemums. The faces, hands, and feet, however, were carved of wood. The next was a snow scene with a young woman in agony. She, too, was a wooden doll covered with clothing made entirely of chrysanthemums.

Yoshiko gave her full attention to the dolls. Hirota and Nonomiya became involved in another discussion. They were saying that these chrysanthemums were cultivated differently, or some such thing, when a few other spectators came between them and Sanshirō, and he moved several feet ahead. Mineko had already gone ahead of Sanshirō. Most of the crowd was composed of local shopkeepers and their families. There seemed to be few educated people here. Standing in this crowd, Mineko turned around and craned in Nonomiya's direction. Nonomiya was pointing across the bamboo railing toward the roots of a chrysanthemum, heatedly explaining something. Mineko turned away and, pushed along by the other spectators, headed for the far exit. Sanshirō forced his way through the crowd in pursuit of her, leaving the others behind.

*

"Mineko!" he called when he had at last caught up with her. She reached for the green bamboo railing and turned her head the slightest bit to look at him. She said nothing. Beyond the railing was a scene depicting the Yōrō waterfall.[33] A round-faced young man with an axe in his belt was crouching at the basin of the waterfall, holding a gourd scoop. Sanshirō was nearly oblivious to what lay beyond the railing when he looked at Mineko.

"Is something wrong?" The words slipped out. Still she said nothing. She let her black eyes settle languorously on Sanshirō's forehead. He found in the soft crease of her eyelids some unfathomable meaning, and in that meaning a fatigue of the spirit, a slackness of the flesh, an appeal close to suffering. Sanshirō forgot that he was waiting for an answer from her and relinquished everything to her eyelids and eyes.

"I want to leave this place," Mineko said.

The eyes and eyelids seemed to be drawing closer together. The nearer they came to each other, the more strongly the feeling took root in his heart that he must leave this place for her sake. Almost at the moment this feeling reached its height, she turned away with a swing of the head. Withdrawing her hand from the railing, she stepped toward the exit, Sanshirō following close behind.

When he caught up with her outside, Mineko hung her head and placed her right hand against her forehead. The crowd swirled around them. Sanshirō leaned close to her. "Is something wrong?" he whispered.

She began to walk through the crowd in the direction of Yanaka. Sanshirō, of course, went with her. They had gone half a block when she came to a halt in the middle of the crowd. "Where are we now?"

"On the way to Tennōji in Yanaka. Exactly the opposite direction from home."

"Oh? I don't feel well . . ."

Standing in the street, Sanshirō felt painfully helpless. He tried to think of something.

"Isn't there some quiet place we could go?" Mineko asked.

In the lowest part of the valley, where Yanaka and Sendagi met, there was a little stream, the Ogawa. If they followed it through the neighborhood to the left, they would soon come out to an open field. The stream flowed straight north. Sanshirō thought about the many walks he had taken, often on the far side, just as often on the near. Mineko was standing now beside a stone bridge that crossed the Ogawa. This was where it flowed out to Nezu after cutting across Yanaka.

"Can you walk another block or so?"

"Yes, I can."

They crossed the bridge and turned left, walking several yards to the end of a kind of alleyway that led to someone's house. Just before they reached the gate, a wooden bridge took them back across the stream. They continued upstream along the bank to a broad field where there were no more passers-by.

Out in the tranquil autumn, Sanshirō became suddenly talkative. "How do you feel? What is it, a headache? It must have been the crowd. There were some pretty low-class men in the doll shed—did one of them do something?"

Mineko did not speak. After some moments, she raised her eyes from the moving water and looked at Sanshirō. The flesh of her eyelids was taut again. This reassured him somewhat.

"Thank you, I feel much better now."

"Shall we rest a while?"

"Yes, let's."

"Can you walk a little farther?"

"I think so."

"Good. There's a much nicer place over there where we can sit down."

"All right."

*

A hundred yards upstream they came to another bridge. It was an old plank, perhaps a foot wide, that had been thrown across the stream. Sanshirō strode over and Mineko came after him. He turned and waited for her. She walked as easily here as anywhere, it seemed to him. She moved ahead in even strides with none of that affectedly feminine tiptoeing. There would be no point in offering her his hand.

They saw a thatched roof farther on. The entire wall below the roof was red. Moving closer, they found the color was that of red peppers hung up to dry. Mineko stopped walking when they were close enough to make this out. "How lovely," she said, sitting down on the narrow band of grass that bordered the stream. What little grass there was had lost its summer greenness. Mineko showed no concern that she might soil her bright kimono.

"Can you walk on a little farther?" Sanshirō urged, still standing.

"Don't worry, this is fine."

"You're not feeling better?"

"I'm just tired."

Sanshirō relented and sat on the dirty patch of grass several feet away from Mineko. The stream ran by just below them. It was shallow now that the water level had fallen with the coming of autumn, shallow enough for a wagtail to fly over and perch on a jutting rock. Sanshirō gazed long into the clear water. It gradually began to turn muddy. A farmer upstream, he saw, was washing radishes. Mineko was looking into the distance. A broad field lay on the other side of the stream, beyond the field some woods, and above the woods stretched the sky. The color of the sky was changing little by little.

Streaks of color began to trail across its monotonous clarity. The deep, transparent blue background grew slowly more diffuse, and a heavy, white pall of cloud came to overlay it. The overlay began to melt and stream away, but so languidly that it was impossible to distinguish where background ended and cloud began. And over all of this drifted a soft hint of yellow.

"The sky was so clear before," said Mineko. "Now the color is all muddied."

Sanshirō took his eyes from the stream and looked up. This was not the first time he had seen a sky like this, but it was the first time he had heard the sky described as "muddied." And she was right, he saw. There was no other way to describe this color. Before he could say anything in reply, however, Mineko spoke again.

"It's so heavy! It looks like *marble*," she said, using the English word. She was looking up high, eyes narrowed. Then she moved her narrowed eyes slowly, until they were turned upon Sanshirō. "It does look like *marble*, don't you think?"

Sanshirō had no choice but to agree. "Yes, it looks like *marble*."

Mineko fell silent. After some minutes, it was Sanshirō who spoke.

"Under a sky like this, the heart becomes heavy, but the senses become light."

"What do you mean by that?" Mineko asked.

Sanshirō had not meant much of anything by it. Instead of answering her question he said, "It's a comforting, dreamy sort of sky."

"It seems as if it's about to move, but then it never does."

Mineko began watching another far-off cloud.

*

Every now and then, they would hear the cries of the chrysanthemum doll ticket-takers welcoming customers.

"What loud voices they have."

"It's amazing they can shout like that all day long," Sanshirō said. He suddenly recalled the three companions they had left behind. He started to say something, but Mineko replied to him first.

"It's their business—just like the beggar at the Ōgannon Temple."

"They're in the wrong place, then?" Sanshirō brought forth an unaccustomed flash of wit and enjoyed a good laugh at his own joke. Hirota's comment on the beggar had struck him as very funny.

"The Professor is always saying things like that, you know," Mineko said softly, almost as if she were talking to herself. Then she added with sudden life, "We could be *very* successful beggars sitting here like this!" Now it was her turn to laugh at her own humor.

"Nonomiya was right, though. We could wait here forever without anyone coming along."

"All the better, don't you think?" she shot back, but continued, "We're beggars who don't beg, after all." It sounded as if she had added this to elucidate the first remark.

Just then a stranger appeared. He had emerged from the shadows of the house where the red peppers were drying and at some point had crossed to the other side of the stream. Now he moved steadily in their direction. He wore a suit and had a mustache, and he seemed to be about Professor Hirota's age. When he came opposite, he jerked his head around and glared directly at them with a look of unmistakable loathing. Sanshirō found it difficult to go on sitting there. The man eventually passed them by, walking off with his back to them. Sanshirō watched the man's receding shadow and said, as if it had just occurred to him, "I'm sure Professor Hirota and Nonomiya have been looking for us."

"Don't worry," Mineko responded coolly. "We're big boys and girls. It won't matter that we're lost."

"But we *are* lost, and I'm sure they'll try to find us," he insisted.

Mineko's coolness only increased. "All the better for someone who likes to avoid responsibility."

"Who do you mean? Professor Hirota?"

Mineko did not answer.

"Nonomiya?"

Still she did not answer.

"Are you feeling better now? We ought to go back," he said, starting up.

Mineko looked at him. He sat on the grass again. It was then that Sanshirō knew somewhere deep inside: this woman was too much for him. He felt, too, a vague sense of humiliation accompanying the awareness that he had been seen through.

Still looking at him, Mineko said, "Lost child."

He did not respond.

"Do you know how to translate that into English?"

The question was too unexpected. Sanshirō could answer neither that he knew nor that he did not know.

"Shall I tell you?"

"Please."

" 'Stray sheep.' Do you understand?"

*

Sanshirō never knew what to say at times like this. He could only regret, when the moment had passed and his mind began to function clearly, that he had failed to say one thing or another. Nor was he superficial enough to anticipate such regret and spit out some makeshift response with forced assurance. And so he kept silent, feeling all the while that to do so was the height of stupidity.

He thought he understood the meaning of "stray sheep," but then, perhaps he did not. More than the words themselves, however, it was the meaning of the woman who had used them that eluded him. He looked at her helplessly and said nothing. She, in turn, became serious.

"Do I seem so forward to you?" Her tone suggested a desire to vindicate herself. He had not been prepared for this. Until now she had been hidden in a mist that he had hoped would clear. Her words cleared the mist, and she emerged, distinctly, a woman. If only it had never happened!

Sanshirō wanted to change her attitude toward him back to what it had been before—a thing full of meaning, neither clear nor clouded, like the sky stretched out above them. But this was not to be accomplished, he knew, with a few words of flattery.

"Well, then, let's go back," she said without warning. There was no trace of bitterness in her voice. Her tone was subdued, as if she had resigned herself to being someone of no interest to Sanshirō.

The sky changed again, and a wind blew from the distance. The sun darkened, and the broad field looked coldly desolate. Sanshirō suddenly felt how the damp earth had chilled his flesh. He could hardly believe that he had continued sitting in such a place. Had he been alone, he would have gone somewhere else long ago. Mineko, too—but perhaps Mineko was a woman who would sit alone in a place like this.

"It's turned cold. We ought to stand up, at least. A chill could make you sick. Are you all right now?"

"Yes, I'm all right." Her reply was unambiguous. She stood up quickly, murmuring—almost intoning to herself—as she did so, "Stray sheep." Sanshirō, of course, said nothing in reply.

Pointing in the direction from which the man in the suit had come, Mineko said that she would like to go past the red peppers if there was a road there. They walked toward the house with the thatched roof and found a path behind it. They had covered half its length when he asked, "Will Yoshiko be coming to live with you?"

Mineko gave him a crooked little smile and replied to his question with one of her own. "Why do you ask?"

Before he could answer, they came to a mud puddle, a brimming four-foot stretch of the path, in the middle of which someone had set a stepping stone. Sanshirō hopped across without the aid of the stone, then turned to watch Mineko. She set her right foot on the stone, but it was unsteady. She rocked back and forth, preparing to spring across. Sanshirō held out his hand.

"Here. Hold on."

"No, I'm all right." She was smiling. As long as Sanshirō held his hand out, Mineko stayed where she was. When he withdrew it, she shifted all her weight to her right leg and swung her left leg across. Determined not to muddy her feet, however, she jumped too hard and lost her balance. She fell forward against Sanshirō, her hands grasping his arms.

"Stray sheep," she murmured. Sanshirō could feel her breath against him.

6

The bell rang and the instructor left the room. Sanshirō shook the ink from his pen and was closing his notebook when Yojirō turned to him.

"Hey, let me see that, will you? I missed a few things."

Yojirō drew the notebook over and peered into it. The page was covered with the words "Stray sheep."

"What's this?"

"I got tired of taking notes and started scribbling."

"Pay more attention next time, will you? He was saying something about Kant's transcendental idealism versus Berkeley's transcendental realism, wasn't he?"

"Something like that."

"You weren't listening?"

"No."

"You really are a 'stray sheep.' Oh, well . . ."

Yojirō stood up with his notebook and started away from his desk. "Come with me," he said to Sanshirō, who followed him out of the classroom. They went downstairs and out to the front lawn. A large cherry tree stood there. The two sat down beneath it.

This place became a field of clover in the early summer. When Yojirō had first arrived with his application for admission to the University, he had seen two students lying under the tree. One said to the other, "If they'd let me sing the oral exam, I'd have plenty of answers for them." The second began to sing softly:

> Oh, give me a professor
> Who knows what life's about.
> So when I take a test on love,
> I'll pass without a doubt.

Ever since that day, Yojirō had been fond of this spot under the cherry tree, and whenever he had something to tell Sanshirō he would bring him here. When Sanshirō heard the story, he understood why Yojirō had translated "Pity's akin to love" like a popular song. Today, however, Yojirō was unusually serious. He sat cross-legged on the grass and pulled out a magazine entitled *Literary Review*, which he handed to Sanshirō open and rotated in his direction.

"What do you think of this?" he asked.

The open page carried the heading "The Great Darkness" in large letters. The author had signed himself "A. Propagule."[34] Sanshirō recognized "The Great Darkness" as the phrase Yojirō always used for Professor Hirota, but he had never heard of this "A. Propagule"—if there was such a person. He looked at Yojirō before venturing a reply. Yojirō said nothing, but instead thrust his flat face toward Sanshirō, pressing his right index finger against the tip of his nose. He held this pose for some time. A student across the way started grinning at them. Yojirō noticed him and took his finger from his nose.

"It's me," he said. "I'm the one who wrote it." Now Sanshirō understood.

"Is this what you were writing when we went to see the chrysanthemum dolls?"

"Don't be stupid. That was just a few days ago. They can't print stuff that fast. The one I wrote that day will come out next month. This one I wrote a long time ago. You can guess what it's about from the title."

"Professor Hirota?"

"Of course. First I'll arouse public opinion, then take care of the groundwork for the Professor to get into the University . . ."

"Is this such an influential magazine?" Sanshirō had never heard of it before.

"No, that's the trouble," Yojirō replied.

Sanshirō could not help smiling. "What's the circulation?"

Yojirō avoided a direct answer. "Anyhow, it's better than not writing at all," he insisted.

*

Yojirō explained that he had a long-standing connection with the magazine, that he wrote something for nearly every issue when he could find the time, but that he changed his pseudonym with each article and, as a result, aside from two or three of the student editors, no one knew who he was. Yojirō's lack of renown came as no surprise: this was practically the first that Sanshirō himself had heard of Yojirō's literary associations. He failed to see the point, however, of Yojirō's using a playful pseudonym like "A. Propagule" and publishing his "major essays" in secret. When Sanshirō was imprudent enough as to inquire if he were writing to make some spare cash, Yojirō's eyes nearly popped.

"Only somebody who has just emerged from the wilds of Kyushu and doesn't know anything about the major literary trends would ask a question like that. No one with a brain in his head can stand here in the center of the intellectual world and be indifferent to the violent upheavals going on before his eyes. We young men are the ones who hold today's literary power in our hands, so we have to take the initiative to make every word, every phrase, count. The literary world is undergoing a spectacular revolution. Everything is moving in a new direction, and we must not be left behind. We have to make the new trends go the way we want them to, or it's not worth being alive. The way they throw the word 'literature' around, you'd think it was garbage, but that's just the 'literature' you hear about in places like the University. What we mean by literature, the new literature, is a great mirror of life itself. The new literature will have to influence the movement of the whole of Japanese society. And in fact it is doing just that while they're all asleep and dreaming. It's awe-inspiring."

Sanshirō listened in silence. He thought Yojirō was laying it on a bit thick, but he was certainly intense enough, and he spoke with the utmost solemnity. Sanshirō was moved. "If that's the spirit in your work, I suppose you don't even think about getting paid for it."

"Now there you're wrong. I try to get as much as I can. Of course, the magazine doesn't sell, so they haven't paid me yet. We really have to figure out a way to sell more. Do you have any ideas?" Now he was asking for Sanshirō's advice. The level of discourse had suddenly descended to practical matters. Sanshirō found this very odd, but it didn't seem to bother Yojirō. The school bell started clanging. "Anyhow, take this copy and read my essay. Great title, don't you think? It's bound to shock people. If you don't shock them, they won't read you, damn them."

They went inside to the classroom and took their seats. Soon the professor came. They started taking notes, but "The Great Darkness" had aroused Sanshirō's curiosity. He placed the open *Literary Review* beside his notebook and began to read the essay as unobtrusively as possible during pauses in his note-taking. Fortunately the professor was nearsighted and totally absorbed in his own lecture. Sanshirō's delinquency was of no concern to him. Very sure of himself now, Sanshirō proceeded to alternate between taking notes and reading the essay until, in his one-man pursuit of a feat that was meant for two, he succeeded in thoroughly losing track of both "The Great Darkness" and the lecture. The only clear impression he retained was a passage of Yojirō's: "How many aeons did nature expend in fashioning a precious jewel? And how many aeons did the jewel lie gleaming in the earth until fate brought it forth?" The rest simply passed him by. He did, however, manage to get through the hour without once writing the words "Stray sheep."

*

As soon as the lecture ended, Yojirō turned to Sanshirō. "How did you like it?"

When Sanshirō answered that he had not actually read the essay yet, Yojirō berated him for not knowing how to use his time. "Be sure to read it." Sanshirō promised to do so at home. By then it was lunchtime. They walked out through the gate together.

"You'll be going tonight, won't you?" Yojirō asked, halting at the corner of the side street leading to home in Nishikatama-chi. Sanshirō had forgotten—the class dinner was tonight. Yes, he said at last, he would be going. "Stop by for me, will you? There's something I want to talk to you about." Yojirō had a penholder tucked behind his ear—perhaps a little too self-consciously. Sanshirō agreed to stop by.

He took a bath and went up to his room feeling refreshed. There was a postcard on his desk. The sender had drawn a picture on one side of the card. It showed a little stream with shaggy grass on its banks and two sheep lying at the edge of the grass. Across the stream stood a large man with a walking stick. He had a ferocious-looking face modeled closely on the devil in Western paintings. Lest there be any doubt, he had been labeled "Devil" in a phonetic rendering of the English word. The card's only return address, written in tiny script, was "Lost Child." Sanshirō knew who that was, and it thrilled him that she had put two stray sheep in the picture, suggesting that he was the other one. Mineko had included him from the beginning, it seemed. Now at last he understood what she had meant by "Stray sheep."

He thought about reading "The Great Darkness," as he had promised Yojirō, but he was not in the mood for it. He kept looking at the postcard. The drawing had a comic quality that was not to be found even in Aesop. It looked innocent, but at the same time witty and unconventional. And there was something behind it all that moved Sanshirō's heart. In terms of technique as well, it was a thoroughly admirable job. Each detail had been rendered clearly. Yoshiko's persimmon tree was not to be compared with it—or so it appeared to Sanshirō.

Eventually he started in on "The Great Darkness." He could not concentrate at first, but the essay began to draw him in after two or three pages, and before he knew it he was moving five pages, six pages ahead until he had effortlessly taken care of the essay's full twenty-seven-page length. Only when he read the final sentence did he realize that he had come to the end. He took his eyes from the magazine and thought to himself, "Ah, now I've read it."

But in the next instant, when he asked himself what it was he had read, there was nothing. There was so much nothing, it was funny. He felt only that he had enjoyed a big, exciting read. Sanshirō was struck with admiration for Yojirō's literary skill.

The essay began with an attack on contemporary men of letters and ended with extravagant praise for Professor Hirota. It was particularly severe on the foreigners teaching foreign literature at the University. The University should immediately appoint a suitable Japanese to teach courses worthy of its greatness, or else the institution that was supposed to be the pinnacle of academe would be no better than an Edo temple grammar school—a great brick mummy. To be sure, the situation could not be helped if there were no suitable men, but here was Professor Hirota, a man who had taught in the College for ten long years, content with low pay and obscurity, but a true scholar nonetheless. Here was a man who deserved a professorial post at the University, who would contribute to the new trends in the scholarly world and relate to the vital forces of society. Boiled down, this was all the essay had to say, but this little bit had been stretched out to twenty-seven pages of extraordinarily reasonable-sounding prose and brilliant aphorisms.

Among the many entertaining passages were pronouncements like these: "Only old men pride themselves on baldness." "Venus was born from the waves, but men of vision are not born from the University." "If the University has only Ph.Ds to boast of, then the beach at Tago-no-ura[35] has only jellyfish." But the essay had nothing else to offer. In one especially strange passage, after likening Professor Hirota to a great darkness, Yojirō compared other scholars to paper lanterns that can do no more than glow feebly on a two-foot space around themselves, precisely as the Professor had said of him. He also noted, as he had that day, that objects such as paper lanterns and slim pipes were relics of a bygone age, "of no use whatever to us young men."

*

Sanshirō thought about Yojirō's essay and concluded that it had much vitality; he wrote as if he were—all by himself—a representative of the new Japan, and this mood swept the reader along. But the thing was totally without substance, like a battle without a base of operations. Worse, it could be interpreted as a piece of political chicanery. But Sanshirō, a country boy, could not formulate his suspicions so precisely. He merely felt, once he had read the essay and considered his reactions, that something about it dissatisfied him. He picked up Mineko's postcard again and looked at the two sheep and the devil. He found everything about it pleasing, which only served to increase his dissatisfaction with Yojirō's piece. He stopped thinking about the essay after that and turned his attention to writing a reply to Mineko. Unfortunately, he did not know how to draw. He would compose something literary. It would have to be something worthy of the postcard. But such excellent phrases did not come easily to mind. He dawdled away the time until after four.

Changing into formal wear, Sanshirō left for Nishikatamachi to pick up Yojirō. He went in through the back door to find Professor Hirota eating dinner at a small table on the matted floor of the sitting room. Yojirō knelt respectfully nearby, serving him and asking, "How do you like them, Professor?"

The Professor's cheek was bulging with what appeared to be a hard object. On the table was a dish holding ten red, black, burnt things, each about the size of a pocket watch.

Sanshirō knelt on the mats and bowed. The Professor went on struggling with the thing in his mouth.

Yojirō plucked one of the objects from the plate with chopsticks and held it out to Sanshirō. "Here, have a taste." Balancing it on his palm, Sanshirō saw that it was a dried clam broiled in soy sauce.

"Big, aren't they?" he said.

"You bet they are!" Yojirō agreed. "And these are no ordinary clams, either. They're idiot clams."

"What in the world . . . ?"

"You know. When they die, their shells open and this long red neck comes out—like an idiot with his tongue hanging out."

"Why are you eating such weird things?"

"What do you mean, 'weird'? They're good. Try one. I made

a special trip to get them for the Professor. He's never had any before."

"A special trip? Where did you have to go for them?"

"Downtown. Nihonbashi."

Sanshirō found this all very comical—rather different from the tone of the essay he had just been reading.

Again Yojirō asked, "How do you like them, Professor?"

"They're tough."

"Maybe so, but they're good. You've got to chew them well to get the flavor."

"If you chewed them that long, your teeth would wear out. Why did you buy such old-fashioned things?"

"Shouldn't I have? Maybe they're no good for you, Professor. They're better suited to Satomi Mineko."

"Why is that?" Sanshirō asked.

"She's so calm and patient, she would just go on chewing until the flavor came out."

"She's calm, all right," said the Professor, "but wild, too."

"It's true she is wild. There's something of the Ibsen woman about her."

"With Ibsen women, it's all out in the open. Mineko is wild deep inside. Of course, I don't mean wild in the ordinary sense. Take Nonomiya's sister: she has this kind of wild look at first glance, but in the end she's very feminine. It's an odd business."

"So with Mineko the wildness is directed inward, then?"

Sanshirō listened to the others' evaluations of Mineko without saying anything. He could not agree with either. To begin with, he found the use of "wild" to describe Mineko incomprehensible.

*

Eventually Yojirō left the room and returned wearing the same kind of formal outfit that Sanshirō had on—the dark coat, the split skirt. "We'll be going now," he said to the Professor, who merely sipped his tea in silence.

They went out. By now it was quite dark. They were only a few steps beyond the front gate when Sanshirō spoke up. "The Professor called Mineko 'wild,' didn't he?"

"Yes, he's like that. Given the time and place, he'll say anything that comes into his head. It's really a joke when he starts in on women. What he knows about them probably adds up to zero. How the hell can you understand women if you've never been in *love*!" Yojirō spat out the English word.

"Yes, but you agreed with him."

"Right. I said she's wild. Why?"

"What's wild about her?"

"It's not any one thing. All modern women are wild, not just Mineko."

"You said she's like an Ibsen character, didn't you?"

"I did."

"Which character did you have in mind?"

"Well . . . she's just like an Ibsen character, that's all."

Sanshirō was not convinced, but he decided not to pursue the matter. They had walked a short way in silence when Yojirō said, "Mineko is not the only one like an Ibsen character. All women are like that nowadays. And not just women. Any man who's had a whiff of the new atmosphere has something of Ibsen about him. People just don't *act* freely the way Ibsen's characters do. Inside, though, something is usually bothering them."

"Nothing is bothering me."

"You're just kidding yourself. There's not a society anywhere without its flaws, right?"

"I guess not."

"Well, then, every creature living in a society is going to feel dissatisfied about something. Ibsen's characters have been the clearest in their perception of the flaws in the modern social system. We'll all be like that before long."

"Do you believe that?"

"I'm not the only one. All men of intelligence can see it."

"Does the Professor think so, too?"

"The Professor? I don't know about him."

"But it stands to reason. He said Mineko is calm and at the same time wild, didn't he? If you interpret that, it means she can stay calm because she's able to go along in harmony with her surroundings, but since she's dissatisfied with something, she's wild underneath it all. Don't you see?"

"I do now. What a mind he has! When it comes to things like this, the Professor *is* great, after all."

Sanshirō had been hoping to advance the discussion a little more in the direction of Mineko's character, but with his gush of praise for the Professor, Yojirō had changed the subject.

"The thing I wanted to talk to you about was—Oh, before I get to that, did you read 'The Great Darkness'? What I have to say won't make much sense unless you've read it."

"I read it at home after I left you."

"How did you like it?"

"What did the Professor have to say?"

"The Professor? He doesn't know a thing about it."

"Well, I did enjoy it, but, I don't know, it's like drinking beer when you want to eat. It doesn't fill you up."

"That's fine. So long as it was exciting, that's all that matters. That's why I used a pseudonym. I'm still in the preparatory stage, after all. I'll keep it this way for now and come out with my real name when the time is right. Anyhow, enough of that. Here's what I wanted to tell you."

*

At tonight's gathering, Yojirō was going to bemoan the inactivity of the Department of Literature, and Sanshirō would have to join him. Since the inactivity was a known fact, others were certain to support them, and together they would devise a plan to correct the situation. Yojirō would suggest that a Japanese professor be brought into the Department without delay. Everyone would agree with him, of course, because it was so obvious. Then the question would arise of who would be a suitable candidate, and Yojirō would bring up Professor Hirota's name. Sanshirō must then back him up with his wholehearted praise of the Professor. Otherwise, someone who knew that Yojirō lived with the Professor might raise doubts. Yojirō didn't care what anyone might think about him personally, but he did not want to cause the Professor any embarrassment. Everything would go well, of course, since there were several others in on the scheme, but the more supporters they had the better. For that reason, it was important for Sanshirō to speak. In the event they reached a consensus, they would choose a representative to see the Dean and the President of the University. Things might not go that far tonight, but that was all right, too. They would play it by ear.

Yojirō spoke with a singular eloquence. Regrettably, however, it was a slippery eloquence, and it lacked weight. At times it sounded as if he were delivering a deadly serious lecture on a joke. Essentially, though, his cause was a good one, and Sanshirō expressed his general approval. Only Yojirō's somewhat devious methods bothered him, he said. This brought Yojirō to a halt in the middle of the street. They were standing now in front of the Morikawa-chō shrine gate.

"To you it looks like I'm being devious, but all I'm doing is using human ingenuity beforehand to keep the natural order of things from going astray. That's entirely different from hatching foolish schemes that go against nature. So what if I'm being devious? Devious methods aren't bad. Only bad methods are bad."

Sanshirō could say nothing to this. He thought he had objections to raise, but he could not verbalize them. The only things in Yojirō's speech that had made a clear impression on him were the ones that had never occurred to him before. Those were the parts that won his admiration.

"That's one way to look at it," he answered vaguely, and the two walked on again side by side. The field of view broadened suddenly when they entered the University gate. The buildings stood out here and there as large, black shapes. Where the roof lines gave out, the luminous sky began. The stars were out in enormous numbers.

"Look how beautiful the sky is," Sanshirō said. They took a few more paces, looking up.

"Hey, Sanshirō."

"What?" Sanshirō thought this would be a continuation of their conversation.

"How do you feel when you look at a sky like this?"

It was an unusual question coming from Yojirō. Sanshirō had any number of stock answers he could give him—eternity, infinity—but he was sure they would only invite Yojirō's laughter, so he kept them to himself.

"We're so damned useless. Maybe I'll give up this stupid campaign tomorrow. Writing 'The Great Darkness' won't do any good."

"What's this, all of a sudden?"

"Looking at this sky does it. Sanshirō, have you ever fallen for a woman?"

Sanshirō could not answer him immediately.

"Women are terrifying," said Yojirō.

"I know," said Sanshirō.

Yojirō burst out laughing. The night-time quiet made it sound awfully loud. "What do *you* know about women?"

Sanshirō hung his head.

"It's going to be a nice day again tomorrow, just what they need for the track meet. You ought to go. There'll be lots of good-looking women there."

The two walked through the darkness to the student assembly hall. Electric lights were burning brightly inside.

*

They walked along the wooden porch and turned into the dining room. Several others had arrived before them and gathered into groups. There were three separate groups of different sizes. A few individuals who chose not to join them were silently reading the hall's newspapers and magazines. There were conversations going on everywhere—more conversations than groups, it seemed—but the room was relatively calm and quiet. The greater release of energy was in the billows of tobacco smoke.

More and more students arrived. Their black shadows would materialize out of the darkness on the porch, then light up one by one and enter the room. At times, five or six shadows in a row would light up like this. Soon everyone was there. Yojirō was running back and forth through the smoke. Wherever he went he discussed something in hushed tones. Sanshirō watched him and thought, "The campaign is starting."

A little later, the student organizer called for everyone to find a seat. The tables had been set beforehand. The students flocked to the tables, in no order whatever, and the dinner started.

In Kumamoto, Sanshirō had drunk only red sake, a cheap local brew.[36] That was all Kumamoto students ever drank, and no one questioned the custom. If they went out to eat, it would be at the local beef house. Some suspected that the beef in that particular restaurant might be horse meat. The students would lift the meat from the plate and slap it against the wall. If it fell, it was supposedly beef; if it stuck, it was horse meat—like magic. For Sanshirō, this gentlemanly gathering of students was a unique occasion. He manipulated his knife and fork with great pleasure. And when those were at rest he consumed large quantities of beer.

"The food here is terrible, isn't it?" the student next to Sanshirō said to him. He was a soft-spoken young man with extremely close-cropped hair and gold-rimmed glasses.

"I suppose so," Sanshirō replied. With Yojirō he would have answered honestly that the food tasted excellent to a country boy like himself. But in this case he feared that an honest answer might be taken for sarcasm.

The student then asked Sanshirō, "Where did you go to college?"

"Kumamoto."

"Oh, really? My cousin went there. He says it's a terrible place."

"Yes, barbaric."

Loud voices suddenly echoed from the far side of the room. Sanshirō looked over to see Yojirō holding forth to his immediate neighbors. Every now and then he would say something like "*De te fabula*."[37] Sanshirō had no idea what this meant, but each time Yojirō said it his listeners would burst out laughing. He grew increasingly ebullient. "*De te fabula*, we young men of the new age . . ." The student sitting diagonally opposite Sanshirō, a light-complexioned, genteel-looking fellow, rested his knife a moment to look at Yojirō's group. Then he smiled and said, chuckling at his own French, "*Il a le diable au corps*." Yojirō and his cohorts seemed not to have heard this;

at that moment all four raised their beer glasses in an exultant toast.

"He certainly is a lively one," the young man with the gold-rimmed glasses said to Sanshirō.

"Yes, he does a lot of talking."

"He once treated me to a plate of rice and curry at the Yodomiken. I had never seen him before. He just walked up and dragged me over there." He laughed. Sanshirō realized that he was not the only one that Yojirō had treated to rice and curry at the Yodomiken.

*

Soon coffee was served. One of the students stood up. Yojirō started clapping wildly, and the others joined in.

The one who stood up wore a new black student uniform and had already grown himself a mustache. He was extremely tall—a man made for standing up in front of others. He began to deliver a speech.

"That we have gathered together here tonight to partake of an evening's merriment in the name of friendship is in itself a cause for pleasure. It occurs to me, however, that the significance of this gathering is not merely social, that it may well produce something having far greater influence, and so I rise to address you now. This dinner began with beer and is ending with coffee. It is a thoroughly ordinary dinner. But the nearly forty men who drink this beer and coffee are by no means ordinary. And what is more, in the interval between our starting the beer and finishing the coffee, we have achieved an awareness of the expansion of our destiny.

"The call for political freedom took place long ago. The call for freedom of speech is also a thing of the past. Freedom is not a word to be used exclusively for phenomena such as these which are so easily given outward manifestation. I believe that we young men of the new age have encountered the moment in time when we must call for that great freedom, the freedom of the mind.

"We young men can no longer endure the oppression of the old Japan. Simultaneously, we live in circumstances that compel us to announce to the world that we young men can no longer endure the new oppression from the West. In society, and in literature as well, the new oppression from the West is just as painful to us, the young men of the new age, as is the oppression of the old Japan.

"All of us here are engaged in the study of Western literature. A study of literature, however, is always and ever a study. It is fundamentally different from bowing at the feet of that literature. We do not study Western literature in order to surrender ourselves to it, but to emancipate minds that have already surrendered to it. We possess the confidence and determination never to study any literature, however coercively it may be pressed upon us, that does not coincide with this purpose.

"It is in our possession of this confidence and this determination that we differ from ordinary men. Literature is neither technique nor business. It is a motive force of society, a force that is more in touch with the fundamental principles of human life. This is why we study literature. This is why we possess the aforementioned confidence and determination. This is why we anticipate from tonight's gathering an effect of more than common importance.

"Society is in violent motion. This is equally true of literature, which is a product of society. In order to avail ourselves of this motive energy, and to guide literature in conformity with our ideals, we insignificant individuals must band together and fulfill, develop, and expand our destiny. In that this evening's beer and coffee have carried this hidden purpose a step ahead, it is precious beer and coffee, a hundred times more precious than ordinary beer and coffee."

When the speech ended, the assembled students all cheered enthusiastically. Sanshirō was among the most enthusiastic. Then Yojirō sprang to his feet.

"*De te fabula!* Who gives a damn how many words Shakespeare used or how many white hairs Ibsen had? We don't have to worry about 'surrendering ourselves' to stupid lectures like that. But it's the University that suffers. We've got to bring in a man who can satisfy the youth of the new age. Foreigners can't do it. First of all, they have no authority in the University."

Again the room was filled with cheers. Then everyone was laughing, and the man next to Yojirō shouted, "A toast to *de te fabula!*" The student who had spoken earlier immediately seconded the idea. But there was no beer left. Yojirō ran out to the kitchen. The waiters brought sake. When all had drunk, someone shouted, "Another toast. This time to 'The Great Darkness'!" Those around Yojirō burst into raucous laughter. Yojirō scratched his head.

When the dinner ended and the young men all dispersed into the darkness, Sanshirō asked Yojirō, "What is *de te fabula*?"

"It's Greek," he said without elaborating, and Sanshirō let it go at that. The two walked home beneath the beautiful sky.

*

Next day, as expected, the weather was fine. It had been an unusually mild year, and today was especially warm. Sanshirō went to the public bath in the morning. It was nearly empty since men of leisure were then in short supply. In the changing room, he noticed a large poster for the Mitsukoshi fabric store. It featured a drawing of a pretty woman who looked something like Mineko. On closer inspection he saw that the eyes were different, and he could not tell how straight the teeth were. Of Mineko's features, it had been her eyes and her teeth that had most startled Sanshirō. Yojirō was of the opinion that she was slightly buck-toothed, which explained why her teeth were always showing, but Sanshirō did not believe it . . .

His mind thus occupied as he soaked in the bath, Sanshirō finally emerged without really washing himself. The awareness that he was a youth of the new age had been strengthened suddenly the night before, but nothing else had been strengthened; physically, he was still the same. On weekends, he relaxed far more completely than anyone else. Today, he would go to the track meet after lunch.

Sanshirō had never been fond of sports. He had gone rabbit hunting a few times at home. And once he was the flagman for a college boat race. That time he was the target of a great outcry when he mixed up the red and green flags. Of course, the professor in charge of the pistol for the final race had failed to fire it. Or, rather, he fired it but it didn't go off, and this confused Sanshirō. He stayed away from athletic contests after that. Today's, however, was the first track meet to be held since his arrival in Tokyo, and he meant to see it. Yojirō, too, had urged him to go. According to Yojirō, it was the women, rather than the meet itself, that were worth seeing. One of those women would be Nonomiya's sister. And with Nonomiya's sister would be Mineko. He wanted to go over and say "Hello" or something.

Sanshirō went out after lunch. The entrance to the meet was at the south end of the playing field. There the Rising Sun and the English flag were displayed crosswise. He understood what the Rising Sun was doing there, but why the English flag? Maybe it was for the Anglo-Japanese Alliance.[38] But he could not see any connection between the Anglo-Japanese Alliance and the University track meet.

The playing field was a grass rectangle. Much of its color had faded with the deepening of autumn. The spectators' area was on the west side, bounded at the rear by an artificial hill, in the front by the playing field fence, and arranged in such a way that everyone was herded into it. Too small for the crowd that had come, the place was packed. At least he did not feel cold, though, thanks to the good weather. He did see a fair number of overcoats, but there were also women holding parasols.

Sanshirō was disappointed to find that the ladies' seats were separate from the rest and unapproachable for ordinary human beings; also, that there were a lot of important-looking men here in frock coats, which made him appear less impressive than he might have wished. Ogawa Sanshirō, youth of the new age, had shrunk a little in stature. He did not fail to survey the ladies' section, however, through the spaces between the men. His view from the side was not a good one, but the sight was lovely nonetheless. All of the ladies were decked out for the occasion and, viewed from a distance, all had beautiful faces. But this meant that no one stood out as more beautiful than anyone else. The whole had its beauty as a whole, a beauty by which women subdue men, not by which one woman outdoes another. This, too, came as a disappointment to Sanshirō. But

if he looked closely, he thought, Mineko and Yoshiko should
be there. He discovered them eventually in the front row next
to the fence.

*

Now that he knew where to look, Sanshirō was enjoying the
satisfaction of having accomplished this much when five or six
men flew before his eyes. It was the end of the 200-meter race.
The finish line was directly in front of Mineko and Yoshiko—
just under their noses, in fact—and in watching them Sanshirō
could not avoid having these young gladiators enter his field of
vision. Soon the five or six increased to twelve or thirteen, all
of them out of breath. Sanshirō compared the attitude of these
students with his own, and the difference shocked him. Whatever possessed them to go galloping along like that? But the
ladies were watching with great enthusiasm, and Mineko and
Yoshiko more so than any. Sanshirō suddenly wanted to start
galloping.

The man who had just won the race was standing in purple
shorts, facing the women's section. Sanshirō took a good look
at him and thought he resembled the student who had spoken
at the gathering last night. Anyone as tall as that would naturally come in first. The timer wrote "25.74 seconds" on the
blackboard. When he was done, he threw the chalk down and
turned toward the stands. It was Nonomiya. He wore a black
frock coat with an official's badge on the chest. Sanshirō had
never seen him so handsomely dressed. Nonomiya took out a
handkerchief and slapped it two or three times against his
sleeve, then left the blackboard and cut across the lawn to
where Mineko and Yoshiko were sitting. Leaning over the low
fence, he stretched his neck into the ladies' section and started
talking. Mineko stood up and walked over to him. They seemed
to be talking back and forth across the fence. Mineko suddenly
turned around, smiling delightedly. From his distant vantage
point, Sanshirō kept close watch on the two of them. Next,
Yoshiko stood and approached the fence. Now the two had
become three. On the lawn, the shot put competition was
starting.

Probably nothing required as much strength as putting the shot. Neither was there anything else that, in proportion to the strength it required, was such a bore. All it involved was, literally, putting the shot. It had nothing to do with skill. Standing by the fence, Nonomiya glanced at the proceedings and smiled. Then it seemed to have occurred to him that he could be obstructing the view; he left the fence and retreated to the lawn. The two women returned to their seats. The shot was being put every now and then. Sanshirō had almost no idea how far the things were supposed to go. He felt stupid, but he went on standing there nevertheless. Finally, the event seemed to have been concluded. Nonomiya wrote "11.38 meters" on the blackboard.

There was another running event, then the broad jump, and next the hammer throw. With the beginning of the hammer throw, Sanshirō's patience gave out. People should go ahead and hold all the athletic meets they liked. They simply shouldn't expect other people to watch them. Convinced that these female spectators' ardor was terribly misplaced, Sanshirō slipped away from the playing field and came out to the artificial hill behind the seats. A cloth partition stood in his way. Retracing his steps, he turned right and walked a short distance along a gravel-topped area where he encountered a few others who had escaped from the meet. Some were finely dressed ladies. He turned right again and climbed a path to the top of a steep rise. Where the path gave out, there was a large boulder. He sat down on it and looked at the pond beneath the rock wall. The crowd let out a roar in the playing field below.

Sanshirō spent a blank five minutes sitting atop the boulder. Soon he felt the urge to move again and stood, pivoting on the balls of his feet. Through the pale red maple leaves at the skirt of the hill, he caught a glimpse of Mineko and Yoshiko walking by.

*

Sanshirō stood at the top, looking down at the two of them. They emerged from the network of branches to an open, sunny patch. If he said nothing, they would pass him by. Perhaps he ought to shout? But they were too far away. He took several swift paces down the grassy hillside, and one of them happened to glance in his direction. This brought him to a halt. He did not like the idea of ingratiating himself with them. He was still somewhat annoyed about the track meet.

"Oh! Look who's there!" Yoshiko exclaimed, smiling. This young woman could be depended upon, it seemed, to greet the most commonplace sight with eyes full of wonder. It was not hard to imagine, though, that she would encounter the extra-ordinary with a look of fulfilled expectations. And so there was not the slightest discomfort in meeting her; the mood was always relaxed. Standing there, it occurred to him that this was due entirely to those big, always moist, black eyes of hers.

Mineko also came to a halt. She looked at Sanshirō, but today for once her eyes were not trying to tell him anything. She might as well have been looking up at a tall tree. In his heart, Sanshirō felt he had seen a lamp go out. He went on standing where he was. Mineko, too, remained still.

"Why aren't you at the track meet?" Yoshiko asked from below.

"I was there until a minute ago, but I got bored and came here." Yoshiko turned to look at Mineko, but Mineko's expression did not change. "How come you two left? I saw how fascinated you were," he said, too loudly to conceal a hint of reproach. Mineko smiled a little now for the first time. The meaning of her smile was not clear to Sanshirō. He moved two paces closer to them. "Are you going home now?" Neither of them answered him. He took two more steps in their direction. "Are you going somewhere?"

"Well, just . . ." Mineko said softly. He could not hear her clearly. Finally he came the rest of the way down the hill until he was standing in front of them. He simply stood there, however, without pressing for a destination. The crowd let out a roar in the field.

"It's the high jump!" Yoshiko said. "I wonder how high that one was?"

Mineko gave only another little smile. Sanshirō, too, remained silent. He had no intention of remarking on the high jump.

Mineko asked, "Is there something interesting up there?"

Atop the hill there was only the boulder and the rock wall. She should know there was nothing interesting up there.

"Nothing at all."

"Oh?" she answered, as though there were some doubt in her mind.

"Let's go up and see," Yoshiko suggested eagerly.

"Haven't you been here before?" Mineko asked, unmoved.

"Oh, come on!"

Yoshiko went up first, and the others followed. Stepping to the edge of the grass, Yoshiko turned and said with some exaggeration, "It's a sheer cliff!" adding, "It's just the kind of place Sappho could have jumped from, don't you think?"

Mineko and Sanshirō laughed aloud, but Sanshirō had no idea what kind of place Sappho had jumped from.

"Why don't you try it too?" Mineko said.

"Me? Maybe I should. The water's so dirty, though."

She came away from the edge, and the two began to discuss their errand.

"Are you going to go?" Mineko asked.

"Yes, are you?"

"I don't know, what do you think?"

"Do whatever you like. Why don't I go alone? You can wait here. I'll be right back."

"I wonder . . ."

They could not seem to make up their minds. What was it? Sanshirō asked. Yoshiko explained that she was going to pay a courtesy call to the nurse who had taken care of her in the hospital, as long as it was so near. In Mineko's case no obligation was involved, but she had been thinking about visiting a nurse, too, someone she had become friendly with that summer when a relative was sick.

*

Finally Yoshiko, in her fresh, uncomplicated way, announced that she would be back soon and stepped swiftly down the hill. There was no need to stop her, no reason to go along; the other two simply remained—or, more precisely, were left—behind.

Sanshirō sat down on the boulder again. Mineko was standing. The surface of the muddy pond caught the autumn sun like a mirror. In the pond was a little island with only two trees on it. The green branches of the pine and the pale red of the maple intertwined nicely, as in a miniature tray-garden. Beyond the island, the dense growth of trees on the far side of the pond shone with a dark luster. Mineko pointed toward the shadowy place.

"Do you know what kind of tree that is?"

"That is an oak tree."

Mineko laughed. "So you remember!"

"Is it the nurse I saw you with that day—the one you were going to see just now?"

"Yes."

"She's not the same one as Yoshiko's, is she?"

"No, she's the one who said, 'This is an oak tree.'"

Now it was Sanshirō's turn to laugh. "Right over there is where you were standing with her, holding a fan."

The hill on which they stood jutted into the pond and rose to a considerable height above it. A smaller hill that was in no way connected with this one ran along the bank to the right. From here they could see large pine trees, a corner of "The Mansion," a part of the cloth partition behind the spectators' section of the playing field, and beyond it a smooth stretch of grass.

"Remember how hot it was that day? The hospital was unbearable. I had to go outside for a while. And what were you doing down there?"

"It was the heat. I had just met Sōhachi for the first time. Then I came out and stayed over there for a while in a kind of daze. I don't know, I was feeling a little discouraged."

"From meeting Sōhachi?"

"No, that's not it," he began, looking at Mineko. Then he changed the subject. "Speaking of Sōhachi, he's working hard today, isn't he?"

"Yes, he's even wearing a frock coat. It must be a terrible nuisance for him. The meet goes on all day long."

"Yes, but he looks pretty pleased with himself."

"Sōhachi? Really, Sanshirō!"

"What do you mean?"

"Well, he is certainly not the kind of man to be pleased with himself as the timer of a track meet."

Sanshirō changed the subject again. "He came over to say something to you before, didn't he?"

"At the field?"

"Yes, by the fence," he said, but he wanted to take the question back.

"Yes," she answered and looked steadily at him. Her lower lip began to draw down in a smile, which Sanshirō found too much to endure. He was going to say something to divert the conversation again when Mineko said, "You still haven't answered my postcard."

Embarrassed, he replied, "I will."

Mineko did not say "Please do" or anything else to encourage him. "Do you know the painter Haraguchi?" she asked.

"No, I don't."

"Oh, really?"

"What about him?"

"Oh, nothing. He was at the meet today, sketching everyone. Sōhachi came over to warn us that we had better be careful or Haraguchi would draw caricatures of us."

Mineko sat down next to Sanshirō. He felt like an awful blockhead.

"Won't Yoshiko be going home with her brother after the meet?"

"She couldn't if she wanted to. She lives with me now. Since yesterday."

*

Sanshirō now heard for the first time that Nonomiya's mother had gone home to the country. They had decided that, when that happened, they would move out of the Ōkubo house, Nonomiya would find a room, and Yoshiko would attend school from Mineko's house for the time being.

It was the ease with which Nonomiya had taken this step that surprised Sanshirō the most. If he was going to be so casual about living in a room again, he should not have had a house to begin with. What had he done with all the pans, the rice pot, the buckets, the other household articles? Sanshirō's imagination led him to these irrelevancies, which he decided to keep to himself. Nonomiya's reversion from head of a household to an almost pure student lifestyle was equivalent to his having taken one step back from the family system, and it also gave Sanshirō the personal advantage of shifting his immediate cares to a somewhat greater distance. On the other hand, Yoshiko had gone to live with Mineko ... Sōhachi and Yoshiko were the kind of brother and sister who had to be seeing each other constantly ... As their visits continued, the relationship between Nonomiya and Mineko would gradually take on a new character ... and then who was to say when the time would come for Nonomiya to end the rooming-house life a second time and forever?

Sanshirō carried on his conversation with Mineko while painting this dubious picture of the future in his head. The strain of presenting a normal exterior was beginning to prove painful when, fortunately, Yoshiko came back. The two women talked about going to the track meet again, but this autumn day was swiftly drawing to a close, the sun's decline bringing with it a gradual increase in the chill of the open air. They decided to go home.

Sanshirō thought he would take his leave and return to his rooming house alone, but the three of them moved off together, talking, which gave him no clear opportunity to say goodbye. He felt as if they were pulling him along, and he was perfectly happy to be pulled along. He stuck with them, skirting the edge of the pond, moving past the library toward the Red Gate, which lay in the wrong direction. Nearing the gate, he said to Yoshiko, "I hear your brother has taken a room."

"Yes, he finally did it—fobbing his poor sister off on Mineko. Isn't he terrible?" She said this as though she wanted Sanshirō's sympathy.

He was about to answer when Mineko spoke up in praise of Nonomiya. "A man like Sōhachi is beyond our understanding. He's so far above us, thinking about great things . . ."

Yoshiko listened in silence.

It was all for the sake of research that academics had to keep aloof from life's annoying trivia and content themselves with as uncomplicated an existence as possible, Mineko continued. Finally, it was a mark of greatness that a man like Nonomiya, whose work was known even in foreign countries, should be living in an ordinary student rooming house. The shabbier the rooming house, the more he was to be respected.

Sanshirō left his two companions at the Red Gate. As he turned his steps toward Oiwake, he started thinking. —Mineko was right. The difference between Nonomiya and himself was enormous. He had just arrived from the country. He had just entered the University. He possessed no learning, no discrimination to speak of. It was only natural that he could not command the same respect from Mineko as Nonomiya did. Come to think of it, she might even be laughing at him. When he had said before that he had come to the hill because the track meet bored him, she had asked with a straight face if there was something interesting up there. He had not noticed it then, but she might have been deliberately toying with him. Now, reviewing one by one the things she had said to him, the way she had acted toward him until today, he realized that everything could be given a negative interpretation. Right there in the middle of the street, he blushed scarlet and hung his head. Looking up again, he found Yojirō coming toward him with the student who had spoken at last night's dinner. Yojirō nodded once to him and said nothing. The student removed his hat and bowed.

"Glad you came yesterday. How are things? Don't surrender yourself, now." He laughed and walked on with Yojirō.

7

Yojirō had not been home since yesterday, the old servant woman told Sanshirō in hushed tones. He stood at the kitchen door, thinking, until it finally occurred to her to invite him in. The Professor was in his study, she said, her hands busily washing dishes as she spoke. The Professor must have just finished eating dinner.

Sanshirō went through the sitting room to the hall and down to the Professor's study. The door was open. "Come in here," the Professor barked. Sanshirō crossed the threshold. The Professor was at his desk, his long back hiding his work. Sanshirō knelt on the matted floor by the doorway.

"You must be busy studying," he said politely. The Professor twisted himself around, the shadow of his mustache indistinct and shaggy. Sanshirō thought he looked like the portrait of someone he had seen in a printed photograph.

"Oh, it's you. I thought it was Yojirō. Sorry." He left his seat. On the desk were a writing brush and paper. So he had been writing.

Yojirō had told him once that the Professor often worked on a certain manuscript but that it was something the author alone could understand. "I hope he can turn it into a magnum opus during his lifetime, but if he dies first it'll just be a pile of scrap paper," he had said with a sigh.

"I can leave if you're busy. It's nothing special."

"No, I'm not busy enough to send you away. This is nothing special, either. I don't have to finish it now."

Sanshirō could not find anything to say for the moment. He

thought to himself how good it would be to see things as the Professor saw them; studying would be so easy then.

"Actually, I came to see Yojirō," he said at last.

"Oh, of course. I guess he's been out since yesterday. He wanders off like that now and then. I wish he wouldn't."

"Did something come up?"

"Nothing ever just 'comes up' with Yojirō. He makes them come up. It's a rare sort of idiocy."

All that Sanshirō could say was, "He takes things easy, doesn't he?"

"No, I wish he did take things easy. He can't keep his mind on any one thing. He's like that little stream near Dangozaka: shallow and narrow, the water constantly changing. There's no discipline to what he does. If we go to a temple fair to look at the stalls, he'll have a brainstorm and tell me to buy something crazy like a dwarf pine. Before I can answer him, he's bargained the price down and bought it. I have to admit, though, he always gets a good deal at these flea markets. But no sooner has he spent my money than he's locked up the house in the summer and left the pine inside. When we come back the heat has killed it and turned it bright red. He's like that with everything. I don't know what to do with him."

Sanshirō had recently lent Yojirō twenty yen. Yojirō said he was due to receive a manuscript fee from the *Literary Review* in two weeks, and he wanted the loan until then. His compassion aroused, Sanshirō took five yen from the money order that had just arrived from his mother and gave Yojirō the rest. The money was not due yet, but Hirota's story was making Sanshirō a little uneasy. He could hardly reveal such a thing to the Professor, however, and instead he came to Yojirō's defense.

"Still, Yojirō has enormous respect for you, Professor, and he's going all out for you behind the scenes."

The Professor turned serious. "What do you mean, he's going all out for me?"

Sanshirō had been given strict orders not to tell Professor Hirota about "The Great Darkness" or any of Yojirō's other activities on his behalf. The Professor was sure to get angry if he found out what was going on. They had to keep it quiet while things were still in progress, and when the time came to let him know, Yojirō himself would be the one to tell him. Sanshirō changed the subject.

*

There were many things that brought Sanshirō to the Hirota house. First of all was the unusual way Professor Hirota lived. Indeed, certain aspects of his life were utterly incompatible with Sanshirō's temperament. Thus it was partly curiosity that brought him here: he wanted to study the Professor to find out how one manages to turn out that way. Next was the fact that Hirota's presence made him relax and forget about the competitive way of the world. Nonomiya was like Hirota in having something otherworldly about him, but in Nonomiya's case it seemed that ambitions (albeit otherworldly ambitions) were what kept him aloof from conventional appetites. Thus whenever Sanshirō talked with Nonomiya alone, he would feel that he too must hurry into a full-fledged career and make his contribution to the scholarly world. It was unsettling, irritating. On that score, Hirota was tranquility itself. He taught language in the College, that was all. He had no other accomplishments— a disrespectful thing to say, it was true, but he published no research and was not in the least concerned about it. Therein lay the source of his easy manner, perhaps.

Lately, Sanshirō had become the captive of a woman. He had surrendered himself to her. It would be pleasant enough if they were lovers, but this was an incomprehensible kind of surrender. He did not know if he was being loved or laughed at, whether he should be terrified or contemptuous, whether he should end it or keep going. He was angry and frustrated. There was no one better for him at such times than Hirota. Half an hour with the Professor and all his tensions were gone. To hell with women. It was mainly for this that Sanshirō had come here tonight.

There was a serious contradiction in the third of Sanshirō's reasons for visiting Professor Hirota. He was suffering over Mineko. The thought of Nonomiya with Mineko only increased the suffering. The person who knew Nonomiya best was the Professor, which meant that by coming to see him, the nature of the relationship between Nonomiya and Mineko should become clear to Sanshirō as a matter of course. If their relationship were clarified, Sanshirō would be able to adopt a definite attitude. In spite of all this, Sanshirō had never asked the Professor about them. Tonight, he decided he would give it a try.

"Nonomiya has taken a room, I hear."

"So he tells me."

"I would think that someone who has lived in his own house would hate to move back into a room. I'm surprised Nonomiya could do that."

"Yes, he's oblivious to such things. You can tell by the way he dresses. There's nothing domestic about him. He's very demanding with his research, though."

"Do you think he plans to live there very long?"

"Who knows? Maybe he'll take another house all of a sudden."

"Do you think he plans to take a wife?"

"Maybe so. Why don't you find somebody nice for him?"

Sanshirō forced a smile. He should never have started this.

"And what are your plans?"

"Me? I'm . . ."

"Still too young, of course. You shouldn't have a wife at your age."

"That's what they're pushing me to do back home."

"Who are 'they'?"

"My mother."

"Do you want to do what she says?"

"Not really."

Hirota's teeth appeared below his mustache in a broad smile. They were rather nice teeth. Sanshirō suddenly felt very close to Hirota. The feeling had nothing to do with Mineko, nothing to do with Nonomiya. It was a closeness that transcended any immediate advantage to him and made him ashamed to go on asking these questions.

*

"You ought to listen to your mother," Professor Hirota began. "Young men nowadays are too self-aware, their egos are too strong—unlike the young men of my own day. When I was a student, there wasn't a thing we did that was unrelated to others. It was all for the Emperor, or parents, or the country, or society. Everything was other-centered, which means that all educated men were hypocrites. When society changed, hypocrisy stopped working, as a result of which we started importing self-centeredness into thought and action, and egoism became enormously overdeveloped. Instead of the old hypocrites, now all we have are hypervillains. Have you ever heard the word 'hypervillain' before?"

"No, I haven't."

"That's because I just made it up. Even you are—maybe not—yes, you probably are a hypervillain. Yojirō, of course, is an extreme example. And you know Satomi Mineko. She's a kind of hypervillain. Then there's Nonomiya's sister, an interesting variation in her own way. The only hypervillains we needed in the old days were feudal lords and fathers. Now, with equal rights, everybody wants to be one. Not that it's a bad thing, of course. We all know—take the lid off something that stinks and you find a manure bucket. Tear away the pretty formalities and the bad is out in the open. Formalities are just a bother, so everyone economizes and makes do with the plain stuff. It's actually quite exhilarating—natural ugliness in all its glory. Of course, when there's too much glory, the hypervillains get a little annoyed with each other. When their discomfort reaches a peak, altruism is resurrected. And when that becomes a mere formality and turns sour, egoism comes back. And so on, ad infinitum. That's how we go on living, you might say. That's how we progress. Look at England. Egoism and altruism have been in perfect balance there for centuries. That's why she doesn't move. That's why she doesn't progress. The English are a pitiful lot—they have no Ibsen, no Nietzsche. They're all puffed up like that, but look at them from the outside and you can see them hardening, turning into fossils."

Sanshirō was impressed by all this in a way, but he was a little surprised at how the conversation had switched tracks

and was running full speed in the wrong direction. At last
Hirota, too, became aware of what had happened.

"What were we talking about?"

"Marriage."

"Marriage?"

"Yes, that I ought to listen to my mother . . ."

"Oh yes. That's it. You really ought to listen to your mother,"
he said, grinning, as if to a child. Sanshirō was not angered by
this, however.

"I see what you mean about my generation being hypervillains, but not about yours being hypocrites."

"Look, do you like it when people are kind to you?"

"Yes, I suppose I do."

"Are you sure? I don't. There are times when people are
tremendously kind to me and I hate it."

"When is that?"

"When the formalities *look* kind but kindness itself is not the
person's intention."

"Does that ever happen?"

"Tell me, do you really feel happy when somebody wishes
you a Happy New Year?"

"Oh, well . . ."

"You don't, do you? It's the same when people tell you
they're 'splitting their sides' or 'rolling over' with laughter. Not
one of them is really laughing. Being kind to people is like that.
Some of us do it mechanically. Take my teaching, for example.
My real purpose is to make a living, but the students wouldn't
want to see it that way. Meanwhile, there's Yojirō, the leader
of the hypervillains. He causes me all kinds of trouble, but
he's not malicious. He's actually sort of loveable—like the
Americans, the way they're so brutally frank about money: the
thing itself is their goal. There is nothing as *honest* as an action
taken with the thing itself as the goal, and there is nothing
less hateful than honesty. Restraint was the main thing my
generation was taught, so none of us knows how to approach
things honestly, without *affectation*."

Sanshirō was able to follow the argument this far. The urgent
question confronting him now, however, was not a matter of

general reasoning. He wanted to know whether a very particular individual he had actual dealings with was being honest with him. He thought again about Mineko's behavior toward him, but he could not decide if it had been "affected" or not. Sanshirō began to suspect that his perceptions might be twice as dull as everyone else's.

*

"Oh yes," Hirota said, as if suddenly recalling something. "There's more. Something very odd has come into fashion since the start of this twentieth century of ours, a convoluted tactic of fulfilling the needs of altruism through egoism. Have you come across anybody who does that?"

"Who does what?"

"Here, let me put it differently. It's the use of hypervillainy to practice hypocrisy. You still don't get it, do you? Maybe I'm not explaining it well. —Look. The old-fashioned hypocrite wants, above all, for others to think well of him, right? But there is a type of man just the opposite of this. He will purposely practice hypocrisy when he wants to hurt another's feelings. He will act in such a way that the other person couldn't possibly fail to see how hypocritical he is being. The other person feels bad, of course, and so he accomplishes his purpose. The honesty of conveying one's hypocrisy to the other person for what it is, this *honesty* is the distinguishing feature of the hypervillain. And since all of one's speech and actions appear on the surface to be good, it's a kind of—not a trinity, not three-in-one, but two-in-one. The number of people who can use this technique skillfully seems to have increased greatly in recent years. For a civilized race whose sensibilities have grown extraordinarily acute, this is the best technique for achieving the most refined hypervillainy. It's a barbaric situation when you can't kill someone without spilling blood. Sooner or later, it's going to go out of style."

Professor Hirota spoke like a tour guide describing an old battlefield, putting himself in the position of one who has witnessed the actual events from a distant vantage point. He spoke with the ring of affirmation, evoking the mood of the lecture hall. But it had its effect on Sanshirō, for he could apply Hirota's theory immediately to the woman who filled his thoughts. He set up the standard in his mind and measured everything about her against it. Yet still there was much beyond measurement. The Professor closed his mouth and started blowing the customary philosophical smoke from his nostrils.

Just then, footsteps sounded in the hallway. Someone walked in without knocking and came down the hall. A moment later, Yojirō was kneeling at the door of the study.

"Mr. Haraguchi is here." Yojirō said nothing about his own belated return, perhaps with good reason. To Sanshirō he tendered only a curt nod, and then he went out again.

Haraguchi stepped inside, passing Yojirō at the threshold. He wore a Vandyke and mustache in the French style, had close-cropped hair, and he carried a good deal of fat on him. He looked two or three years older than Nonomiya. His kimono was far handsomer than Professor Hirota's.

"Well, it's been quite a while, hasn't it?" Haraguchi said. "Sasaki has been at my place, and we've been eating and whatnot. He finally dragged me over here."

Haraguchi had an affirmative way of speaking and a voice that naturally brightened the spirits of anyone in his vicinity. Sanshirō had been fairly certain the Haraguchi announced by Yojirō was the painter whose name he had heard on occasion. What a gregarious creature Yojirō was! Sanshirō felt a wave of admiration for the way Yojirō made friends with so many older men. Then he grew stiff. Sanshirō always grew stiff in the presence of his seniors. He interpreted this to be a result of his Kyushu-style education.

Hirota introduced him to Haraguchi. Sanshirō bowed respectfully and received an easy nod in return. After that he listened to the men's conversation without a word.

Haraguchi said that he had only one item of business, and he would take care of that first. He was going to hold a dinner in the near future, and he wanted Hirota to come. It was to be a simple, casual affair. The invitations would go to a limited number of writers and artists and university professors, mostly people who knew each other, so there would be absolutely no need of formality. The purpose would simply be to have dinner together and to exchange edifying literary conversation afterward. That was about all.

He would join them, Professor Hirota answered simply, thus dispensing with Haraguchi's business. The rest of their conversation was much more interesting.

*

"What have you been doing these days?" Professor Hirota asked.

"I'm still singing Itchūbushi.[39] I've already memorized five pieces, some good ones like 'Eight Yoshiwara Scenes in Blossoms and Fall Colors' and 'Koina and Hanbei's Love Suicide at Karasaki.' You ought to give it a try yourself. They tell me it's bad style to sing too loud, though. Itchūbushi was originally performed in small private chambers. But you know me, I'm always loud, and these songs have such intricate melodies I can never get them right. You'll have to hear me sing sometime."

Professor Hirota was smiling. Haraguchi went on, "Bad as I am, though, Satomi Kyōsuke is even worse. He can't get a single tune right. I wonder why—his sister is such a talented girl. The other day he said he couldn't stand it anymore, he was going to quit singing and take up an instrument. Somebody suggested he try Idiot's Delight.[40] They said he'd probably do better banging away on some noisemaker in a shrine festival. It was hilarious."

"They really said that?"

"Really. And Satomi actually said he'd do it if I would. It's not as easy as you'd think, though. There are supposedly eight different styles of Idiot's Delight."

"Why don't you try it? It sounds like something an ordinary human being could manage."

"No, thanks. I'd rather take up the Noh drum.[41] I don't know, when I hear the plop of that little drum, I feel I'm not in the twentieth century anymore. I like that. I mean, how can anything be so delightfully half-witted in times like this? It's great medicine just to stop and think about that. I may be easy-going, but I could never produce a painting like the sound of that drum."

"I'll bet you've never tried."

"I couldn't do it. How could anyone living in Tokyo now paint anything so serene? Of course, it's not only painting—which reminds me, I wanted to do a caricature of Satomi's and Nonomiya's sisters at the track meet the other day, but they ran out on me. I'm planning to do a formal portrait soon and show it in an exhibition."

"Whose portrait?"

"Satomi's sister. The usual Japanese woman has an Utamaro-style[42] or some such face that's all right for woodblock prints but doesn't look good on canvas. Satomi's sister, though, and Nonomiya's could be painted. I'm planning to do a life-size painting of Mineko holding up a round fan and facing into the sunlight with some woods in the background. A Western folding fan would be in bad taste, but a round Japanese fan will be novel and interesting. In any case, I'd better hurry up. She could get married soon, and then I probably couldn't run things my way."

Sanshirō listened to Haraguchi with great interest. When he heard that the painting would have Mineko holding up a fan, he was profoundly moved. Some mysterious, fateful bond must exist between them, he felt.

"That doesn't sound like a very interesting picture to me," Hirota said frankly.

"But that's how she wanted it. When she suggested holding up a fan I thought it would be unusual and agreed to paint it that way. It's not a bad idea. It all depends on how it's done."

"Watch out that you don't make her *too* beautiful. She'll get more marriage proposals than she can handle."

"Good point," Haraguchi laughed. "I'll give it the medium treatment. Speaking of marriage, she's just about that age. Do you know any likely prospects? Satomi has been asking me to keep my eyes open."

"What about you, Haraguchi?"

"Me? I wouldn't mind, but I don't have much standing with her, I'm afraid."

"Why not?"

"I think her brother tells her stories about me. She heard how I stocked up on Japanese food when I went to Europe. I told everybody I was determined to barricade myself in my room in Paris. So Mineko laughed at me and said, 'The minute you got there, you changed your spots.' She's too much for me."

"Mineko won't marry anyone she doesn't want to. And she won't be pushed. The best thing will be to let her stay single until she finds somebody she likes."

"Strictly Western style. Of course, all women will be like that from now on. Nothing wrong with it."

Then Haraguchi and Hirota talked at length about painting. Sanshirō was amazed at how many Western painters' names Professor Hirota knew. Soon it was time for him to leave. As he was searching for his clogs at the back door, the Professor came to the bottom of the stairway. "Hey, Sasaki, come down here a minute," he called.

*

It was cold outside, the sky so high and clear it almost made him wonder where the morning dew would come from. Whenever his hand brushed against the silk of his kimono, that spot of skin felt a chill. He walked down one deserted lane after another and, turning a corner, encountered a roadside fortune-teller. The man held a large, round paper lantern that made him bright red from the waist down. Sanshirō suddenly wanted to buy a fortune, but he suppressed the impulse and let the man pass, taking such care to avoid the red lantern that his shoulder brushed against a cedar fence. A little farther on, he cut across a dark area and came out to Oiwake's main street. There was a noodle shop on the corner. This time Sanshirō followed his impulse and ducked under the curtain in the doorway. He wanted a drink.

There were three College students in the shop. One of them was saying that many professors had begun eating noodles for lunch recently. The delivery boys would come rushing into the school grounds as soon as the noon gun sounded, balancing stacks of baskets and bowls on their shoulders. This particular shop was probably doing a lot of business that way. One of the professors ate boiling hot noodles even in summer. Why would he do such a thing? He probably had a bad stomach. The three students went on like this, referring to their professors by their last name only. One of them mentioned Hirota, which started a discussion about why Hirota was still a bachelor. The opinion was expressed that he probably did not hate women, because he had a nude picture hanging on his office wall. Of course, it was a Western nude, so that didn't prove anything. Perhaps he hated Japanese women? No, he must have been disappointed in love. Maybe that's what made him such an eccentric. Was it true that some beautiful young woman often visited him?

Before long the students began saying what an extraordinary man Hirota was. Sanshirō could not tell why they thought him so extraordinary, but all three of them had read Yojirō's "The Great Darkness" and admitted that the essay was what had started them liking Hirota. There were quotations of some of Yojirō's aphorisms, followed by enthusiastic praise of his style. Who could the mysterious A. Propagule be? In any case, they agreed, he must be someone who knew Hirota very well.

This conversation cleared the air for Sanshirō. He felt new admiration for Yojirō in his decision to write "The Great Darkness." Until now he had doubted that any purpose other than the gratification of Yojirō's ego could be served by the flaunting of his "major" essays in a journal that, by his own admission, sold poorly. But as he listened to these students, Sanshirō was awakened to the power of the printed word. What Yojirō had said was true: writing anything, however modest, was better than not writing at all. This was where men's reputations were made or broken! Sanshirō left the noodle shop overawed at the responsibility of those who wield the pen.

The effect of the sake had worn off by the time Sanshirō reached his lodgings. Everything was so stupid, somehow. He was sitting at his desk, blank, when the maid came upstairs with a fresh kettle and a letter for him. It was from his mother again. He opened it immediately. Today he was overjoyed at the sight of his mother's handwriting.

The letter was a long one, but it had nothing much to say. He was particularly pleased that his mother said nothing about Miwata Omitsu. She had included a strange bit of advice, however.

"You have been cowardly since childhood. This is a terrible disadvantage, and it must make examinations and such very trying for you. You know what a good scholar and middle-school teacher Okitsu Taka is, but every time he takes the qualifying examination the poor man trembles and can never write good answers, so his pay never goes up. He asked a friend of his, a medical school graduate, I think, to make some pills that would stop the trembling, and he took them before the examination, but he trembled just the same. I don't think yours is so bad that you tremble, but you ought to have one of those Tokyo doctors make you something you can take regularly to give you some nerve. It just might work."

Sanshirō found her advice ludicrous, which made it all the more comforting. Mothers were so kind! He stayed up until one o'clock that night writing his mother a long letter. In it was the sentence, "Tokyo is not a very interesting place."

8

This is how Sanshirō came to lend Yojirō money.

At nine o'clock on a rainy evening several days earlier, Yojirō had paid Sanshirō an unexpected visit. The first words from Yojirō's mouth were, "I'm done for."

Sanshirō had never seen him look so pale. At first he thought Yojirō might have been out too long in the chilling autumn storm, but when Yojirō sat down, Sanshirō realized that more was wrong with him than his color. He was in uncharacteristically low spirits.

"Are you sick?"

Yojirō blinked twice, his eyes skittish as a deer's, and answered, "I'm in trouble. I lost some money." With a worried look, he blew two or three streams of smoke from his nostrils.

Sanshirō could not simply wait in silence for Yojirō to explain himself. How much money? Where had he lost it? As soon as the last stream of smoke was gone, Yojirō told the whole story without a break.

He had lost twenty yen. Worst of all, it was someone else's money. When Professor Hirota moved into the house in which he was living the year before, he was unable to pay the entire deposit of three months' rent and borrowed the difference from Nonomiya. This was money that Nonomiya had asked his father to send him from the country to buy Yoshiko a violin. There was, therefore, no pressing deadline by which the money had to be repaid, but the longer it was postponed, the more Yoshiko would be inconvenienced. And in fact she still did not have her violin because Professor Hirota had not returned the money. He would have repaid it if he had been able to, but month followed on month with nothing to spare, and since Hirota was not a man to work for anything beyond his salary, he had simply let it go. Just recently, however, he had at last received the sixty yen due him for grading the College's summer entrance examinations. It was with this that he intended to discharge his obligation, and the task of delivering the money had fallen to Yojirō.

"That's the money I lost. It's unforgivable." Yojirō looked as though he really felt he had done something unforgivable.

"Do you have any idea where you dropped it?"

"Dropped it? I bet it all on the horses."

Sanshirō was astounded. Even indiscretion had its limits, but Yojirō had so overshot them that Sanshirō could not bring himself to admonish him. And besides, Yojirō was so very downcast. Comparing him now with his usual ebullient self, one would have had to conclude that there were two Yojirōs. The contrast was simply too violent, provoking a simultaneous onslaught of amusement and pity that threw Sanshirō—and then Yojirō—into a fit of laughter.

"Oh well," Yojirō said, "I guess it will all work out."

"Does the Professor know?"

"Not yet."

"Nonomiya?"

"Of course not."

"When did you get the money?"

"The first of the month. Just two weeks ago today."

"And when did you bet it on the horses?"

"The day after that."

"And you've just let it go all this time?"

"No, I've been running all over trying to come up with something. If I have to, I can let it go until the end of the month."

"Do you have some money coming in then?"

"The *Literary Review* should be paying me."

Sanshirō stood up and opened his desk drawer. "I've got some money here," he said, looking into the envelope containing his most recent letter from home. "My mother was early this month."

"Dear, sweet Ogawa! A prince among men!" Yojirō responded like a professional Tokyo storyteller, his voice suddenly full of life.

Braving the storm, the two made their way to the main street of Oiwake after ten o'clock and went to the noodle shop on the corner. It was then that Sanshirō learned to drink sake at noodle shops. Both of them drank with pleasure that night. Yojirō paid the check. He was never one to let others pay for him.

*

Nearly ten days later, Yojirō had still not returned the twenty yen. Sanshirō was too honest not to worry about paying the rent. He did not press Yojirō for the money, but he kept wishing that he would do something about it, and soon the end of the month was less than two days away. It never occurred to Sanshirō to hold off paying the rent in case something went wrong. Yojirō would bring the money without fail—no, of course Sanshirō did not have that much confidence in him, but he told himself that Yojirō had at least enough kindness to try to work things out. Hirota had said that Yojirō's mind was always on the move, like shallow water, but if all that movement involved ignoring his responsibilities, Sanshirō was going to be very upset. No, Yojirō couldn't be that bad.

Sanshirō was looking down at the street from his second-story window when Yojirō appeared in the distance, approaching swiftly. He came as far as the house and looked up at Sanshirō.

"You're in?"

Sanshirō, looking down, replied, "I'm in."

This vertical exchange of ridiculous greetings completed, Sanshirō pulled his head in, and Yojirō pounded his way up the stairs.

"I'll bet you've been on the lookout for me and worrying about the rent. I know you. That's why I've been running all over the place. What a stupid business."

"Did you get your money from the *Review*?"

"What money? They don't owe me anything."

"Didn't you tell me they were going to pay you at the end of the month?"

"Did I? You must have misunderstood. I've had everything I'm going to get out of them."

"That's funny. I'm sure you said they'd pay you."

"I said I was going to get an advance, a loan. But they won't give it to me. The bastards don't think I'd pay it back. And it's only twenty yen! I wrote 'The Great Darkness' for them and they still don't trust me. I'm sick of them."

"So you didn't get any money?"

"Not from them. I got it from somebody else. I thought you'd be in trouble if I didn't."

"Oh. Sorry I put you through that."

"But there's a catch. I don't have the money. You have to go and get it."

"Where is it?"

"Well, when the *Review* turned me down I went to see Haraguchi and a few other people, but none of them could manage it for the end of the month. Finally I went to Satomi's. I guess you don't know him. Satomi Kyōsuke. Law graduate. Mineko's brother. Anyway, he was out, so nothing came of that, either. By then I was hungry and didn't feel like walking around on an empty stomach, so I stayed and talked to Mineko."

"Wasn't Yoshiko there?"

"Of course not, it was just after noon and she was at school. Besides, we were in the drawing room, so it wouldn't have made any difference."

"Oh, I see."

"So Mineko agreed to lend you the money."

"Does she have her own money?"

"That I wouldn't know. Anyhow, it's all set. She said she'd do it. And the funny way she has of acting like everybody's big sister, you can relax once she's agreed to go along. There's nothing to worry about, all you have to do is ask politely. But what a shock at the end! She said she had the money but she couldn't give it to *me*. I asked her, 'Don't you trust me?' She said 'No'—and she was smiling! She's too much. I asked if I should send you over and she said yes, she would give it to you. Let her do it any way she likes. Do you think you can go and get it?"

"If I don't go I'll have to wire my mother."

"Forget it. A telegram now would be stupid. Even you can do that much, I'm sure."

"I can do it."

This took care of the twenty yen. Once that had been dispensed with, Yojirō began a report on the Hirota affair.

*

The campaign was making steady progress. Yojirō was visiting concerned students one at a time in their rooming houses whenever he had a chance. Individual discussions were the only way. When a lot of people got together, each one would come up with his own idea just to assert himself. Or else he'd feel slighted and act indifferent. Individual discussions were absolutely the only way. On the other hand, they took time. And money. But if he was going to worry about that, there would be no campaign. Another thing: he was trying not to introduce Professor Hirota's name into the discussions too often. If the others thought this was all for the sake of Hirota and not for the students themselves, everything would fall apart.

This was his technique for advancing the campaign, Yojirō said. Everything had gone well up to now. They had reached the point of convincing everyone that having only Westerners on the faculty was no longer acceptable and that a Japanese must be brought in to teach foreign literature. All they had to do now was hold another large meeting, choose some delegates, and send them to voice the students' desires to the Dean, the President, and others. Of course, the meeting itself was just a formality and could be dispensed with since they knew pretty well which students would be the delegates. All were sympathetic to Professor Hirota. Depending on the progress of the negotiations, they might even bring up the Professor's name.

Yojirō sounded as though he had the world in his grasp. Sanshirō was not a little impressed with his abilities. Yojirō then talked about his having brought Haraguchi to see the Professor the other night.

"You remember how Haraguchi urged the Professor to attend that dinner for literary men." Sanshirō remembered, of course. That, too, had been organized by Yojirō. He had many reasons for doing it, he said, but the most immediate one was that an influential professor in the Department of Literature would be at the dinner. It would be a tremendous advantage to the Professor to bring him and the other man together at this juncture. Eccentric that he was, the Professor did not go out of his way to mix with others. But if Yojirō could arrange suitable opportunities to bring him in contact with people, then—in his own eccentric way—the Professor would associate with them.

"So that's what that was all about! I had no idea. You say you're the organizer, but are all those important men going to come when they get an invitation from you?"

Yojirō turned a somber gaze on Sanshirō. Then, with a sour smile, he looked away. "Don't talk nonsense. It was my idea, but no one's going to know that. I suggested it to Haraguchi and arranged for him to use his influence."

"Oh, I see."

" 'Oh, I see.' I can still smell the farm on you. Anyhow, you ought to go to the dinner yourself. It should be soon now."

"What's the point of me mixing with all those important men? I think I'll skip it."

"There's that farm smell again. The only difference between an important man and a not-so-important man is the order in which they've entered society. You hear that so-and-so has a doctorate or such-and-such is a University graduate, but you meet him and he's like anybody else. They don't go around thinking how 'important' they are. You really ought to come to the dinner. It could do you good in the future."

"Where is it going to be?"

"Probably at the Seiyōken in Ueno."[43]

"I've never been to a place like that. It's going to be expensive, isn't it?"

"Well, maybe two yen each. But don't worry, if you don't have the money, I'll pay for you."

Sanshirō thought of the twenty yen, but strangely enough it no longer seemed funny. Yojirō suggested they go to a restaurant on the Ginza for tempura. "I've got money," he said. What a strange fellow! Sanshirō, who usually went along with

anything, refused this time. Instead, they took a walk. They
stopped in at Okano's Confectionery on the way back, and
Yojirō bought a lot of little chestnut-jam pastries. They were
for the Professor, he said, and he went off clutching a bagful.

*

That night, Sanshirō gave some thought to Yojirō's character.
Was that how you turned out after living in Tokyo for a long
time? Then he thought about going to the Satomi house for a
loan. He was glad enough of the new excuse to see Mineko,
but he didn't like the idea of approaching anyone for money,
hat in hand. It would be a whole new experience for him,
complicated by the fact that the lender was a girl, not an independent person. Perhaps she did have her own money, but if
she were to lend it to Sanshirō in secret, without her brother's
permission, it might later prove to be an embarrassment for
her, if not for him. Knowing Mineko, though, everything might
well have been arranged from the start so as not to become an
embarrassment. In any case, he would go to see her, and if it
looked as though borrowing the money would be unpleasant,
he would refuse it, delay the payment of the rent for a few days,
and have the money sent from home, thus ending the matter.

His thoughts came this far and took a new turn, filling his
head with images of Mineko—her face, her hands, her neckline,
the obi and kimono she wore. His imagination multiplied and
divided them. He thought especially about their meeting
tomorrow. How would she act toward him? What would she
say? He saw ten, twenty different versions of the scene. Sanshirō
had always been like this. Whenever he had to see someone on
business, his imagination would concentrate on how the other
person would act. He never thought about himself—the look
on his own face, the things he would say, his tone of voice—
until afterward. Then he never failed to think about them—
with regret.

Tonight, especially, he had no imagination to spare for himself. He had been having doubts about Mineko. But simply
doubting her would never solve anything. On the other hand,
he had no questions to confront her with, no Gordian knots to

slash. If a solution was necessary for Sanshirō's peace of mind, it involved nothing more than exploiting this chance to see Mineko in order to allow himself one final, precarious judgment based on her behavior toward him. Tomorrow's interview would supply him with indispensable data for that judgment. And so now he tried to imagine what she would be like. The scenes he came up with, however, were always favorable to himself, and as such their accuracy was highly suspect. Each was like a handsome photograph of an ugly place. A photograph might be accurate in every way, but it would never be the same as the indisputably ugly original.

In the end, a pleasant thought occurred to Sanshirō. Mineko had agreed to lend him the twenty yen, but she would not give it to Yojirō. Yojirō might well be untrustworthy when it came to money, but had that been her reason for refusing to give it to him? If not, this meant something very promising for Sanshirō. Her willingness to lend it to him was in itself sufficient indication that she thought well of him, but the fact that she insisted on handing it to him in person . . . He dared to allow himself this much conceit when a new thought struck him. "Isn't she just toying with me again?"

It was enough to make him turn bright red. If someone were to ask him why Mineko would bother toying with him, Sanshirō could not have found an answer. Pressed to think of one, perhaps he could have replied that Mineko was the kind of woman who enjoyed toying with men. It would never have occurred to him, surely, that she did it to punish his conceit, which he believed was caused by Mineko in the first place.

*

With two instructors absent the following day, Sanshirō was relieved of classes for the afternoon. He did not bother going back to his rooming house for lunch, but instead made do with a light snack on the way to Mineko's. He had walked past her house any number of times but had never gone inside. "Satomi Kyōsuke" said the nameplate on the pillar of the tile-roofed gate. What was this Satomi Kyōsuke like? Sanshirō wondered each time he passed by. He had still not met the man.

The central panels of the gate were locked. He entered through the gate's small side door. The distance from the gate to the front door was shorter than he had imagined. Oblong slabs of granite marked the path. The door of handsome, narrow latticework was closed. Sanshirō rang the bell. To the maid who appeared he asked, "Is Miss Mineko at home?" He felt strangely embarrassed. He had never asked for a young woman at the door of her home before, and he found it difficult to do. The maid was unexpectedly grave, almost reverential. She left him at the doorway for a moment, then reappeared, bowed respectfully, and led him to the drawing room, a Western room with heavy curtains. It was rather dark.

"Please wait here. Miss Mineko will be with you shortly." The maid went out. Sanshirō took a seat in the quiet room. The wall in front of him had a small fireplace. Over it was a wide mirror, and in front of that two candlesticks. Sanshirō stood up to look at his reflection between the candlesticks, and sat down again.

Just then a violin sounded in another part of the house. It faded immediately, as though a gust of wind had carried it from somewhere, discarded the sound, and blown it away. Sanshirō felt disappointed. Cradled in the overstuffed chair, he listened intently, wishing for more. But there was no more, and in the space of a minute he forgot about the violin. He looked at the mirror and candlesticks. They had a strangely Western air about them that he associated with Catholicism, though why Catholicism he himself did not know. The violin sounded again. This time some high notes and low notes echoed out two or three times in quick succession before the sound was abruptly cut off. Sanshirō knew nothing about Western music, but he could not believe that this was part of a melody. It was just someone making noises on the violin, sounds that were perfectly suited to his emotions. The random notes had fallen like a handful of freak hailstones from the sky.

Sanshirō moved half-seeing eyes to the mirror, and there stood Mineko. The maid had closed the door, he thought, but now it was open. Mineko was reflected clearly from the chest upward, holding aside the curtain that hung beyond the door.

In the mirror, she looked at Sanshirō. Sanshirō looked at the Mineko in the mirror. She smiled. "Welcome."

Her voice was behind him. Sanshirō had to turn around. The two came face to face. Mineko bowed with the slightest forward movement of her forward-swirling hair. The gesture implied an intimacy that made bowing unnecessary. Sanshirō, however, raised himself from the chair and bent low in formal greeting. Ignoring his bow, she walked around Sanshirō and sat down facing him, her back to the mirror.

"So, you've finally come."

Her tone was as intimate as her little bow. These few words made Sanshirō extremely happy. She wore a kimono of shining silk. Perhaps she had kept him waiting so long in order to change for him? But there was no hint of that in her dignified calm. She sat looking straight at him, saying nothing, a smile about her eyes and lips, and the sight of her filled Sanshirō with a sweet agony. He could not endure being looked at this way, he began to feel, almost from the moment she sat down. He opened his mouth at once in a kind of spasm. "Sasaki . . ."

*

"Yojirō came to see you, I'm sure." Mineko revealed her white teeth. Behind her, to the right and left, the candlesticks were aligned on the mantelpiece. They were oddly shaped pedestals, fashioned of gold. Sanshirō had assumed they were candlesticks; in fact, he did not know what they were. Behind these inscrutable candlesticks was the clear expanse of the mirror. Obstructed by the heavy curtains, the light from the windows did not illuminate the room sufficiently. The cloudy weather added to the gloom. Sanshirō looked at Mineko's white teeth.

"Yojirō did come to see me."

"And what did he say to you?"

"That I should come to see you."

"I thought so. Is that why you came?" She insisted on asking the question.

"Yes." Sanshirō hesitated. "I suppose so."

Mineko concealed her teeth. She rose from her seat, approached the window, and peered outside. "Look how cloudy it is now. It must be cold out."

"No, it's surprisingly warm. There's no wind at all."

"Oh?" She returned to her seat.

"Actually, about the money, Sasaki—"

"I know," she stopped him. Sanshirō did not try to go on. "But what happened to it exactly?"

"One bad bet at the racetrack."

"Oh my!" she exclaimed, but her face showed little surprise. In fact, she was smiling. "What a naughty man," she added. Sanshirō did not attempt a reply. "It must be hard to second-guess a horse race, harder than guessing what's in someone else's mind. Some people wear indexes, too, but you don't even try to guess what's in their minds, you're so easy-going."

"I'm not the one who bet on the horses."

"You're not? Who is?"

"Sasaki."

Mineko laughed aloud. Sanshirō, too, was amused.

"So you didn't need the money after all. How silly!"

"No, I'm the one who needs it, all right."

"Really?"

"Really."

"This is all very strange."

"Yes, I know. So I don't have to borrow it from you."

"Why not? Don't you like the idea?"

"No, I don't mind, but I shouldn't take it from you without telling your brother."

"Why not? It's all right with him."

"Oh, then I guess it's all right. But I don't really have to borrow it. If I write home I can have the money in a week."

"Please don't let me force you . . ."

Mineko grew suddenly distant. It felt as if the woman who had been beside him only a moment ago was standing at the far end of the street. He was sorry he had not taken the money, but now it was too late. He kept his eyes glued on the candlesticks. Sanshirō had never in his life tried to ingratiate himself with anyone. Mineko, too, remained in her distant retreat. After a short time she stood up and peered outside again. "It doesn't look like rain, does it?"

"No, it doesn't," he replied in the same tone.

"I think I'll go out, then," she said, still standing at the window. He interpreted this as a request for him to leave. No, it was not for him that she had changed into shining silk.

"It's time for me to go." He stood up. Mineko saw him to the door.

He stepped down into the hallway and was putting on his shoes when Mineko said from above, "I'll walk with you a little way, if that's all right?"

"If you like," Sanshirō replied, tying his shoelaces.

A moment later she was stepping down to the concrete floor. She leaned close to him and whispered, "Are you angry?" Just then the maid hurried out to see them off.

*

They walked half a block together in silence, Sanshirō thinking all the while about Mineko. Her parents must have raised her to have her own way. And now, as a young woman, she doubtless had more freedom at home than most others and could do anything she pleased. That much was clear if she could walk down the street with him like this without asking anyone's permission. She could do it because she had no parents and because her elder brother, a young man himself, put no restrictions on her. If she were to try this in the country, though, she would not have it so easy. How would Mineko react if someone told her to live like Miwata Omitsu? Tokyo was different from the country, it was wide open, so perhaps most of the women here were like Mineko. He could only imagine what the others were like, but at a distance they did seem to be a little more old-fashioned than Mineko. It occurred to him how right Yojirō had been: she was an Ibsen woman. But was it only her disregard for convention that made her an Ibsen woman, or did it involve her deepest thoughts and feelings? He did not know.

Soon they came to the main street of Hongō. They were walking together, but neither knew where the other was going.

By this time they had turned three corners, doing so each time without a word, as though they had arranged it all beforehand. As they neared the Yonchōme intersection, Mineko asked, "Where are you going?"

"Where are *you* going?"

They glanced at each other. Sanshirō looked very grave. Mineko could not help revealing her white teeth again. "Come with me," she said.

They turned the corner, heading for Kiridōshi. There was a large stone building half a block down on the right-hand side. Mineko stopped when they reached it. She drew a thin passbook and a seal from her obi and held them out to Sanshirō.

"Please," she said.

"Please what?"

"Please take some money out for me with these."

Sanshirō took the passbook from her. In the middle of the cover it said, "Deposit Book," and under that, "Satomi Mineko." Sanshirō stood there looking at her, book and seal in hand.

"Thirty yen," she said, speaking as if to a man used to withdrawing money from the bank every day. Fortunately, while he was still living at home, Sanshirō had often set out for Toyotsu[44] with a bank book. He climbed the stairs at once, opened the door and entered the bank. He presented the book and seal and received the money, but when he came out, Mineko was gone. She had walked a short way down the street toward Kiridōshi. He hurried after her. Catching up, he thrust his hand in his pocket to deliver the money when Mineko asked, "Have you seen the Tanseikai Group's exhibition?"

"Not yet."

"They sent me two complimentary tickets, but so far I haven't found the time. Would you like to go now?"

"I don't mind."

"Let's go, then. The show will be closing soon. I owe it to Mr. Haraguchi to stop in once, at least."

"Did Mr. Haraguchi send you the tickets?"

"Yes. Do you know him?"

"I met him once at the Professor's."

"He's an amusing man, don't you think? He's planning to practice Idiot's Delight."

"I heard him say he wanted to take up the Noh drum. And—"

"And?"

"That he was going to paint your portrait. Is it true?"

"Yes, I'm a high-class model."

Sanshirō was by nature incapable of a clever retort. He could never have topped this. And so he said nothing, even though Mineko seemed to want him to.

*

Again Sanshirō put his hand in his pocket. He pulled out the passbook and seal and handed them to Mineko. The money was supposed to be sandwiched in the book, but Mineko asked, "And the money . . . ?" It was gone. He searched the pocket again and pulled out a handful of worn bills. She did not reach for them.

"Please hold it for me."

Sanshirō felt somewhat put-upon, but he preferred not to argue at a time like this. Besides, they were in the middle of the street. He returned the bills, produced at her suggestion, to the place where he had found them. How strange she was!

Many students passed them on the street. Each one glanced at them without fail as they walked by. A few approaching from the distance stared at them all the way. The road to Ikenohata seemed awfully long to Sanshirō, but not so long that it made him want to take the streetcar. They moved ahead with slow, deliberate steps, and when they reached the museum it was nearly three o'clock.

The building that housed the exhibition had an unusual sign. The name Tanseikai[45]—The Red and Green Society—and the design around the characters were something entirely new to Sanshirō, but new in the sense that one could never see them in Kumamoto, and therefore strange. The paintings inside were even more so. To Sanshirō's eyes the only clear distinction was between oil and watercolor. He did have his likes and dislikes, however. One or two of them he thought he wouldn't mind buying. As far as technical excellence was concerned, however, he understood nothing. And so he said nothing, resigned from the start to his own lack of critical sense.

How about this one? Mineko asked. Yes, how about it. This one is interesting, don't you think? Yes, he supposed it was. He was utterly unresponsive. He might have been one of two things: an idiot who couldn't carry on a conversation, or a man too important to bother. If an idiot, his lack of affectation was charming; if important, his reserve was infuriating.

Many of the paintings were by a brother and sister who had traveled abroad extensively. Their works bore the same surname, and their paintings hung together. Mineko stopped in front of one.

"This must be Venice," she said.

Sanshirō could tell that much. It was so Venetian. He wanted to take a ride in a gondola. *Gondola* was one of his favorite words from College. There was only one way to ride in a gondola: with a woman. The blue water, the tall houses on either side, the inverted reflections of the houses, the bits of red dotting the reflections—Sanshirō viewed them all in silence.

Then Mineko said, "The brother seems to be a much better painter, wouldn't you say?" Sanshirō had no idea what she meant.

"The brother . . . ?"

"The brother painted this one, surely."

"Whose brother?"

Mineko looked at him with a mystified expression. "The sister's paintings are on that side. These are the brother's."

Sanshirō took a step back and turned to look at the other side of the passageway down which they had just come. The many paintings hanging there all showed the same kind of foreign scenes as the ones on this side.

"Someone else did those?"

"You thought they were all by the same person?"

"Yes," he said, and a blank moment followed. Then they looked at each other and laughed.

Mineko opened her eyes wide in mock astonishment. "Really!" she murmured, taking several quick steps ahead. Sanshirō stayed where he was and examined the Venetian canal again. In her flight, Mineko looked around. Sanshirō was not watching her. She came to a halt, staring hard at his profile.

Just then, a loud voice called out, "Mineko!"

*

Both Mineko and Sanshirō turned in the direction of the voice. Outside a door marked "Office" stood Haraguchi. Behind and partially hidden by him was Nonomiya. Mineko looked at the more distant Nonomiya rather than at the one who had called her name. The instant she glanced at him, she moved back to her place beside Sanshirō. Standing so that the others could not see clearly, she leaned close to Sanshirō and whispered something to him. He had no idea what she was saying. He was going to ask her to say it again, but she withdrew to where the two men stood and was already greeting them.

Nonomiya turned to Sanshirō and said, "What a strange companion!"

Before Sanshirō could reply, Mineko said, "We're well matched, don't you think?" Nonomiya said nothing in reply. Instead, he turned on his heels to face a large painting, perhaps six feet high and three feet wide. It was a portrait, and almost all black. So little light fell on the subject's hat and clothing that they could not be distinguished from the background. Only the face shone white in the blackness. It was a wasted face, the flesh of the cheeks sunken.

"This is a copy, isn't it?" Nonomiya said to Haraguchi. At the moment, Haraguchi was intent on explaining something to Mineko. —The exhibition was about to close. The number of visitors had dropped considerably. He himself had been coming to the office every day at first but rarely bothered now. Something had come up today for a change, and he had brought Nonomiya along. What a fortunate coincidence that they should have met here today. As soon as this show was over he would have to begin preparing for the next and would then be very busy. The New Year's show ordinarily opened at cherry blossom time, but some of the other artists wanted it to be a little early, which for him was like having two openings, one right after the other. This would call for desperate efforts with brush and canvas. He definitely wanted to have Mineko's portrait finished by then. It was an imposition, he knew, but would she please go on posing for him straight through to the end of the year? "To make it up to you, I'll hang the picture here."

Only now did Haraguchi turn toward the black painting. Nonomiya had been standing there blankly all that time, looking at the one picture. "How do you like it, the Velazquez? It's a copy, of course, and not a very good one." Haraguchi finally began to explain the painting. Nonomiya no longer had to say anything.

"Who did the copy?" Mineko asked.

"Mitsui. He's really better than this. I don't think much of it," Haraguchi said, stepping back a pace or two. "It was bound to fail. The original was done by a man at the height of his powers."

Haraguchi cocked his head to one side. Sanshirō looked at the bend in his neck. "Have you seen everything?" the painter asked Mineko. He spoke only to Mineko.

"Not yet."

"Why not forget it and come with us to the Seiyōken? I'll buy you a cup of tea. I have to go there anyhow to see the *manager* about our gathering. He's a friend of mine. Now is just the right time for tea. Soon it will be too late for tea, too early for *dinner*, no good for anything. What do you say? Come with us." Haraguchi liked to drop an occasional English expression into his speech.

Mineko looked at Sanshirō. His face said he could go either way. Nonomiya stood outside of the conversation.

"As long as we're here, we might as well see everything, don't you think?" she asked Sanshirō. He said he did.

"Here's an idea, then," Haraguchi went on. "There's a special gallery in back. Fukami's posthumous works are there.[46] Just look at those and come over to the Seiyōken. We'll be waiting for you."

"Thank you very much."

"Now, with Fukami's watercolors, don't look at them the way you'd look at ordinary watercolors. They are his and his alone. You'll find they have some very interesting qualities, but you mustn't think of them as pictures of things. Just look at Fukami's fine personal touch." Leaving these parting instructions, Haraguchi went out with Nonomiya. Mineko thanked him and watched the two men go. Neither of them looked back.

*

Mineko turned and walked into the special gallery with Sanshirō a step behind her. Little light penetrated this far into the museum. Just as Haraguchi had said, nearly all of Fukami's paintings were watercolors. They were arranged on one wall of the long, narrow gallery. What most struck him was their subdued tone. There was little color variety, and those colors the artist had used were pale and low in contrast. They would probably not show up well unless they were in sunlight. More interesting was the brushwork, which revealed no sign of hesitation. Each piece gave the impression of having been done in a single breath. The style was free and easy: that much was clear from the way the pencil lines stood out sharply beneath the colors. The human figures were spare and elongated. They looked to Sanshirō like grain flails. In this collection, too, there was a scene of Venice.

"Here is another Venice," Mineko said, approaching him.

"Yes," he answered, and the name jogged his memory. "What were you saying before?"

"Before?"

"When I was looking at the other Venice."

Again Mineko revealed her white teeth, but she did not speak.

"If it was nothing special, I don't have to know."

"It was nothing special."

Sanshirō continued to look at her oddly. By now it was after four o'clock on this overcast autumn day. The galleries were dark. There were very few people left, and in the special gallery, Sanshirō and Mineko were alone, two shadows in the gloom. She moved away from the painting and stood directly in front of him. "It was Sōhachi. You know . . ."

"Nonomiya?"

"You know."

Mineko's meaning flooded into him like the shattering of a huge wave. "You were toying with Nonomiya?"

"Why should I do such a thing?" Her voice rang with absolute innocence. Sanshirō suddenly lost the courage to say more. He moved off a few steps without a word. She followed, all but clinging to him. "You're not the one I was toying with."

Again Sanshirō came to a halt. He was a tall young man. He looked down at Mineko. "Never mind."

"Why was it so wrong of me?"

"Never mind. It's all right."

Mineko turned her face away. They walked from the gallery together, and as they passed through the door, their shoulders touched. In that instant, Sanshirō thought of the woman on the train. The touch of Mineko's flesh was like a throb of pain in a dream.

"Is it really all right?" Mineko asked in a tiny voice. Two or three other spectators were walking their way.

"Anyhow, let's get out of here," Sanshirō said.

They retrieved their shoes at the door. Stepping outside, they found that it was raining.

"Do you want to go to the Seiyōken?"

Mineko did not answer. They stood in the broad field that stretched away from the museum, their clothes growing damp in the rain. Fortunately the storm had just begun, and it was not violent. Mineko looked across the field and pointed toward the Ueno forest.

"Let's go and stand under the trees."

The rain would probably stop if they waited a little. They crossed the field and stood in the shade of a large cedar. It was not a good tree for warding off the rain, but neither of them moved. They stood there getting wet and cold.

"Sanshirō?"

He was looking at the sky with knitted brows, and he turned this face to Mineko.

"Was it wrong of me, before?"

"It's all right."

"But," she drew closer, "I just wanted to do it, I don't know why. I didn't mean any disrespect to Sōhachi."

Mineko fixed her gaze on Sanshirō. He saw in her eyes an appeal more profound than her words had expressed. "Don't you see?" they were saying, "I did it for you."

"Never mind, it's all right," he said again.

The rain fell more and more heavily. Only the smallest patch was left where the raindrops did not strike. The two of them drew closer together. They stood cowering beneath the tree, shoulders touching.

"Please keep the money," Mineko said through the sound of the rain.

"I'll take it on loan. But only what I need."

"Please, take it all."

9

Sanshirō went to the Seiyōken dinner after much prodding from Yojirō. He wore traditional formal attire that included a black coat of fine raw silk. A letter from his mother explained the making of the coat in great detail. Miwata Omitsu's mother wove the material, and after they had dyed it with the Ogawa family crest, Omitsu did the sewing. He tried it on when the package arrived but, reluctant to wear the Miwata ladies' handiwork, he had left it in the drawer ever since. This was a great waste, according to Yojirō, who badgered Sanshirō to wear it to the dinner, as though he might wear the coat himself if Sanshirō did not. Once Sanshirō relented and tried it on, the coat did not seem so bad.

Sanshirō stood in the doorway of the Seiyōken with Yojirō, dressed in this outfit. It was the proper attire for receiving guests, Yojirō said. Sanshirō had not been expecting to receive guests, however. He had assumed that he himself was a guest. Now he felt like an overdressed doorman. He was sorry he had not worn his student uniform.

The guests began to arrive. Yojirō buttonholed each of them in turn, treating them all like old friends. After each new arrival handed his hat and coat to the valet and passed by the broad flight of stairs to turn into the dark corridor, Yojirō would identify him for Sanshirō. In this way, Sanshirō came to know the faces of many eminent men.

Before long, all the guests had arrived. They numbered close to thirty. Professor Hirota was there. So was Nonomiya—a scientist, to be sure, but fond of art and literature and therefore, according to Yojirō, forced to attend by Haraguchi. Haraguchi himself was there. He had arrived first of all and proceeded to circulate officiously among the guests, exuding charm and fondling his beard.

Soon it was time to be seated. Each man sat where he liked, no one yielding, no one contesting his place. Out of keeping with his usual slowness, Professor Hirota was the first one to the table. Only Yojirō and Sanshirō intentionally sat together, taking seats near the doorway. All of the others found their neighbors by chance.

A critic in a striped formal coat sat between Nonomiya and Professor Hirota. Across the table was one Dr. Shōji, Yojirō's "influential professor in the Department of Literature." He wore a frock coat and was a man of some dignity. His hair, which he wore at more than twice the normal length, seemed to swirl in black eddies beneath the electric lamps, a remarkable contrast to Professor Hirota's close-cropped monk's cut. Haraguchi sat at the far corner, which placed him across from Sanshirō down the length of the table. He wore a suit and had a broad tie of black satin knotted at the collar, with the ends splayed out across his chest. Yojirō informed Sanshirō that all French artists wore that kind of necktie. It looked just like the knot in a man's sash, Sanshirō thought to himself as he sipped spoonfuls of soup.

Soon the conversation started. Yojirō, uncharacteristically quiet, concentrated on his beer. This was an occasion when even he had to practice some restraint, apparently.

"How about a little *de te fabula*?" Sanshirō suggested under his breath.

"Not today," Yojirō answered, turning away to start up a conversation with the man next to him. He complimented the man on a certain essay and said how much he had benefitted from it. This struck Sanshirō as strange, because in his presence Yojirō had torn the thing apart. Yojirō turned back to Sanshirō. "That's a handsome coat. It really becomes you," he said, looking at the white family crests in particular. Just then Haraguchi began to address Nonomiya from his far corner. His loud voice served him well in the distant exchange. Professor Hirota and Dr. Shōji, fearing lest their cross-table conversation interfere with the other dialogue, cut their own discussion short. Everyone else fell silent, too. The gathering had a focal point now for the first time.

*

"Nonomiya, have you completed your experiment on the pressure of light?"

"No, far from it."

"It's real drudgery, isn't it? We artists have to work hard, but yours seems even more strenuous."

"All an artist needs to paint a picture is *inspiration*," Nonomiya said, using the English term. "It's not so easy when you experiment in physics."

"*Inspiration*? Now there's a word that makes me cringe! This summer I heard two old women engaged in a dialogue. They were sharing their 'research' into whether or not the rainy season had ended. The first one was complaining that in the old days a good clap of thunder was sure to end the rainy season but that thunder didn't work anymore. This made the other one mad. She said, 'What are you talking about? A little thunder's not going to do it!' Well, that's how it is in painting nowadays. A little *inspiration*'s not going to do it. What do you say, Tamura? It must be the same for a writer."

A novelist called Tamura was sitting next to Haraguchi. "My only *inspiration* comes from the editors when they hound me for manuscript," he answered, which drew a big laugh. Then Tamura became serious and started asking Nonomiya about his work. Does light have pressure? If so, how does one experiment on it? Nonomiya's answers were interesting.

You make a thin disk about an inch in diameter from mica or some such material, hang it from a quartz thread in a vacuum, and shine the beam of an arc lamp at the surface of the disk at a right angle. Pushed by the beam, the disk moves.

Everyone at the table was listening intently. Sanshirō recalled the time when he had first arrived in Tokyo and had been so startled at the view through the telescope, the view of that tin can which must have contained the device he was hearing about now.

"Yojirō," he whispered, "is there such a thing as a quartz thread?"

Yojirō shook his head. Then Sanshirō asked Nonomiya, "Is there such a thing as a quartz thread?"

"Yes. First you melt powdered quartz in the flame of an oxyhydrogen blowpipe, then stretch it to the right and left with both hands until a fine thread forms."

Sanshirō said only "Oh?" and retreated. The critic in the striped coat sitting beside Nonomiya was the next to speak up.

"We're entirely ignorant when it comes to these things, but what I'd like to know is how you became aware of the problem in the first place."

"It has been a matter of theoretical conjecture since Maxwell, but Lebedev was the first to prove it through experimentation. Now it's reached the stage where someone is using the idea to explain the behavior of comets. The tails ought to be drawn toward the sun, but they're always bent the other way. Perhaps it's because light-pressure blows them back."

The critic seemed greatly impressed. "The idea itself is interesting, I suppose, but what I like about it is that it's big."

"It's not only big," said Professor Hirota. "It's fun because it's harmless."

"And if the idea is wrong, it's even more harmless," Haraguchi said with a laugh.

"No, I'm afraid it's right. The pressure of light is proportionate to the square of the radius, but gravity is proportionate to the cube of the radius, so the smaller a thing is, the less its gravitational pull and the stronger the effect of light pressure on it. If we assume the tail of a comet to be composed of tiny particles, it will obviously have to be blown back away from the sun."

Nonomiya had turned serious, but Haraguchi went on as before. "Now we're paying for the harmlessness with all this calculating. You can't win." This remark restored the beery mood for everyone.

Professor Hirota said, "It looks to me as though a writer of the naturalist school could never be a physicist."

The pairing of physicists with the dominant literary movement excited everyone's interest to no small degree.

*

"What do you mean by that?" asked Nonomiya, the man most
directly concerned. Now Hirota had to explain himself.

"Well, look. It won't do you any good just to open your eyes
and observe nature if you want to test the pressure of light. I
don't see where this fact, 'the pressure of light,' is printed anywhere on nature's menu, do you? You have to go about it
artificially, with quartz threads and vacuums and mica, all these
devices so that the pressure becomes visible to the eye of the
physicist. In other words, physicists are not naturalists."

"But they're not romantics, either," Haraguchi butted in.

"Oh yes they are," Hirota defended himself grandly. "To
place the light and the thing that receives the light in a spatial
relationship that cannot be found in the normal natural world
is something only a romantic would do."

"But once you have put them into that spatial relationship,"
Nonomiya said, "all you do is observe the light's characteristic
pressure, and that much belongs to the naturalist school."

"Then physicists are romantic naturalists," said Dr. Shōji, sitting diagonally opposite Nonomiya, and he offered a comparison: "In literature, that would be someone like Ibsen, I suppose."

"True," said the critic in the striped coat. "Ibsen has as
many devices as Nonomiya, but I doubt if his characters follow
natural laws the way light does."

"That's a good point," Professor Hirota said. "But there is
one thing we ought to keep in mind in the study of man.
Namely, that a human being placed in particular circumstances
has the ability and the right to do just the opposite of what the
circumstances dictate. The trouble is, we have this odd habit of
thinking that men and light both act according to mechanical
laws, which leads to some stunning errors. We set things up to
make a man angry, and he laughs. We try to make him laugh,
and again he does the opposite, he gets angry. Either way,
though, he's still a human being."

Hirota had enlarged the scope of the problem again.

"Well, then, what you're saying is, no matter what a human being does in a particular set of circumstances, he is being natural," said the novelist at the far end of the table.

"That's it," Hirota shot back. "It seems to me that you might create any sort of character in a novel and there would be at least one person in the world just like him. We humans are simply incapable of imagining non-human actions or behavior. It's the writer's fault if we don't believe in his characters as human beings."

The novelist had nothing to say to this. Now it was Dr. Shōji's turn to speak.

"Look at the physicists. Galileo realized that one swing of the lamp in the cathedral took the same time no matter how big the swing; Newton discovered that the apple fell because of gravity. Men like that are dyed-in-the-wool members of the naturalist school."

"If that's what the naturalist school is, I suppose it's all right for literature to have one," Nonomiya said. "Haraguchi, is there a naturalist school of painters?"

"Of course. There was this frightening fellow Courbet. *Vérité vraie.* He accepted only fact. Not that his ideas ran rampant over everything. They were simply recognized as one particular school, which is how it ought to be. It's probably the same with fiction. Isn't that so, Tamura? There must be some writers who prefer symbolism and idealism—men like Moreau or Chavannes."

"There must be," said the novelist beside him.

No one rose to make an after-dinner speech. Only Haraguchi had anything to say. He was intent on criticizing the bronze figure at the top of Kudan.[47] What a terrible thing to inflict on the citizens of Tokyo! How much smarter it would be to put up a bronze image of a beautiful geisha! Yojirō told Sanshirō that Haraguchi did not get along well with the sculptor of the Kudan piece.

The party ended. Outside, the moon was beautiful. Yojirō asked Sanshirō if he thought Professor Hirota had made a good impression on Dr. Shōji. Sanshirō answered that he probably had. Stopping next to a public water tap, Yojirō mentioned that

he had come here for a walk this summer. Feeling the heat, he
was washing himself off when a policeman spotted him and he
ran up Suribachi Hill. Now the two of them climbed Suribachi
Hill to look at the moon.

*

On the way home Yojirō began to make excuses about the
money he owed Sanshirō, but on this fairly cold night with a
clear moon in the sky, money was the farthest thing from
Sanshirō's mind. He could not listen seriously. In any case, he
thought, Yojirō was not going to give it back. Giving it back
was the one thing that Yojirō failed to mention. He concentrated instead on all the reasons why he was unable to do so.
More than what he had to say, however, it was his style that
interested Sanshirō. —Yojirō knew a man who, disappointed
in love, had grown tired of living and had finally resolved to
kill himself. He found drowning unpalatable, throwing himself
into a volcano even worse, and hanging worst of all. So he
bought a gun. Before he had a chance to use it, though, a friend
came to him for a loan. Having no money himself, he turned
the friend down, but the man pleaded for help. All he could do
was lend him the gun. The friend pawned it and kept himself
going. When he had money again, he redeemed the gun and
brought it back. By this time, however, the owner of the gun
no longer felt like dying. In other words, his life had been saved
because someone had come to him for a loan.

"So you see what can happen," Yojirō concluded. To Sanshirō, it was just a funny story, nothing more. He looked up at
the moon and roared with laughter. It didn't matter that Yojirō
would not return the money. He felt good.

"Hey, it's not funny," Yojirō objected. This made Sanshirō
laugh all the more.

"Stop laughing and think about it. You got to borrow the
money from Mineko only because I didn't pay it back to you."

Sanshirō stopped laughing. "So what?"

"So plenty. You're in love with her, aren't you?"

Yojirō knew. Sanshirō grunted and looked up at the moon
again. Now there was a white cloud next to it.

"Have you paid her back?"

"No, I haven't."

"Do her a favor—don't ever pay her back."

Yojirō was so offhand about it. Sanshirō did not answer him, but of course he had no intention of following Yojirō's advice. In fact, after paying twenty yen for his room and board, he had decided to bring the extra ten yen to her the next day and carried it as far as her front gate but had had second thoughts. If he repaid it immediately, it occurred to him, that would be like rejecting her kindness, and he turned back, even if it meant sacrificing an excellent chance to visit her again. At that point something had caused his determination to slacken, and he had broken into the ten yen. Tonight's dinner had come from it, in fact. And not just his own meal, but Yojirō's, too. He had only two or three yen left, and with that he was planning to buy a winter undershirt.

But Sanshirō had made his move some days ago. Concluding that Yojirō would never pay him back, he had written home to request an extra thirty yen. What with the liberal monthly allowance he was receiving, it would not have been enough to say only that he had run short. Never much of a liar, Sanshirō had been hard put to think of a reason for his request. All he could do was explain to his mother that, out of pity, he had made a loan to a friend who had lost some money and was in a bind. As a result, he himself was now in a bind. Would she please send it?

Had she answered promptly, her letter should have arrived before now. Perhaps he would find it in his room tonight.

To be sure, an envelope addressed in his mother's handwriting was waiting on his desk. All of her previous letters had come registered mail, but this one, oddly enough, had arrived bearing an ordinary three-sen stamp. He opened it to find a brief note of a kind she had never written before. It was strictly businesslike, which, from his kind mother, was almost cruel. She had sent the money to Nonomiya's, she said; he should pick it up there. Sanshirō spread out his bedding and went to sleep.

*

He did not go to Nonomiya's the next day, or the day after that. Nor did he hear anything from Nonomiya. A week went by like this. Finally a maid from Nonomiya's rooming house came with a note. "I have something for you from your mother. Come over," it said.

Between classes, Sanshirō descended once again into the cellar of the Science building. He hoped to end the matter in the course of a quick chat, but it did not work out that way. In the room that Nonomiya had occupied alone this summer there were several men with mustaches and several uniformed students. All were pursuing their research with silent intensity, ignoring the sunlit world above their heads. Nonomiya looked busiest of all. Glancing at Sanshirō, who had stuck his head in through the doorway, he approached without a word.

"Some money came for you from home. Come and get it, will you? I don't have it here. And there's something I have to talk to you about."

Would tonight be all right? Sanshirō asked. After giving it some thought, Nonomiya said that it would. Sanshirō left the cellar. As he was going out, he felt a surge of admiration for the great tenacity of scientists. The tin can and the telescope he had seen that summer were standing in the same place.

He saw Yojirō during the next lecture and told him what had happened. Yojirō stared at him incredulously.

"I *told* you not to pay her back. You didn't have to write home. Now your poor old mother's worried, and Sōhachi's going to lecture you. What stupidity!" Yojirō gave no sign of recognition that he had started it all. Sanshirō, too, had forgotten Yojirō's responsibility in the matter. His reply thus carried no hint of blame for Yojirō.

"I wrote home because I don't like the idea of not paying her back."

"*You* might not like it, but Mineko would."

"Why should she?"

His own question rang somewhat false to Sanshirō, but it had no discernible effect on Yojirō. "Why shouldn't she? Why shouldn't I? Suppose I've got some extra money. I'd feel better just letting you keep it than making you pay it back. People like to be kind to other people, as long as they're not put out by it themselves."

Instead of answering him, Sanshirō began taking lecture notes. After he had written a few lines, Yojirō leaned over to him and whispered, "Even I have often lent people money when I've had it, and not one of them ever paid me back. That's why I'm so much fun to be with."

Sanshirō could hardly favor him with a serious reply. After producing a faint smile, he continued moving his pen. Yojirō also settled down and kept his mouth shut until the end of the hour.

The bell rang, and as the two were walking from the lecture hall side by side, Yojirō suddenly asked, "Has she fallen for you?"

The other students came crowding out behind them. Sanshirō was forced to keep silent as they went down the stairs and out of the side door to the open space beside the library. Only there did he turn to Yojirō. "I don't know."

Yojirō stood looking at Sanshirō for a while. "I suppose it's possible not to know," he said. "But even if you did know for certain, could you ever be her *husband*?" He used the English word.

Sanshirō had never considered this before. It had seemed to him that being loved by Mineko was the only qualification a man needed to be her *husband*. Now that it had been put to him like this, he had some doubts. He cocked his head to one side.

"Nonomiya could, I'm sure," Yojirō said.

"Is there something between Nonomiya and her?" Sanshirō's face looked as solemn as if it had been chiseled in stone.

"I don't know." Sanshirō said nothing. "Anyhow, go get your lecture at Nonomiya's." Yojirō flung the words at him and started off toward the pond.

Sanshirō stood rooted to the spot, like a signboard advertising his own stupidity. Yojirō took five or six paces but came back smiling. "Why don't you marry Yoshiko instead?" He dragged Sanshirō away in the direction of the pond, declaring, "That's it! That's it!" Soon the bell rang.

*

Sanshirō left his rooming house for Nonomiya's that evening. It was still early, so he strolled over to Yonchōme to buy a woolen undershirt at a big imported goods store there. The shop boy brought out several different kinds. These Sanshirō stroked and patted, folded and unfolded, without settling on one to buy. He was affecting a lordly air for no good reason when Mineko and Yoshiko happened along in search of perfume. After the initial surprise and greetings, Mineko added a brief expression of thanks to him. She said nothing specific, but Sanshirō knew precisely what she was referring to. The day after he had borrowed her money, Sanshirō had postponed visiting her again to return the extra ten yen and, instead, after waiting two more days, had written her a polite thank-you note.

The letter was an honest expression of the writer's immediate feelings, but of course it was overwritten. Stringing together all the appropriate phrases he could think of, Sanshirō had given passionate voice to his gratitude. Such steam rose from its pages that an innocent bystander could hardly have guessed it to be a letter of thanks for a loan. Aside from its words of gratitude, however, it had nothing to say. And thus, in the natural course of things, gratitude perhaps turned into something more. When Sanshirō dropped his letter into the mailbox, he looked forward to an immediate reply. But his painstakingly wrought epistle went its way to no avail. There had been no opportunity for him to see Mineko until today, and now he could not find it in him to respond to her feeble "Thank you." He held out a large undershirt in both hands and stared at it, wondering if Mineko's coolness could be explained by Yoshiko's presence. It also occurred to him that he was buying this shirt with her money.

The shop boy was pressing him for a decision. The two young women approached, smiling, and helped him with the undershirts. Finally Yoshiko said, "Take this one." Sanshirō took that one. Next it was his turn to advise them on perfume, about which he knew nothing. At random, he picked up a bottle labeled in English, "Heliotrope," and asked "How about this?" Mineko took it immediately. He was sorry he had done that.

Outside, as he was about to leave them, the women started bowing to each other. "I'll see you later," Yoshiko said. "Don't be long," Mineko answered. Yoshiko told him she was on her way to Nonomiya's. This was to be Sanshirō's second twilight stroll with a pretty woman, this time to his own Oiwake neighborhood. The sun was still far from setting.

Sanshirō felt somewhat annoyed, not to be walking with Yoshiko but because he had to go to Nonomiya's with her. He considered returning home and trying it another time. On second thought, though, it might be more convenient to have Yoshiko there for the lecture Yojirō had predicted. Certainly Nonomiya would not be able to deliver a full-blown reprimand from his mother in someone else's presence. Sanshirō might even get away with just picking up the money. A bit of cunning entered into his resolve. "I was on my way to your brother's myself."

"Oh? Are you just going to drop in on him?"

"No, there's something I have to see him about. And you?"

"I have something, too."

They asked the same question and received the same answer, and neither showed any sign of being inconvenienced. As a final precaution, Sanshirō asked if he would be in the way. She replied that he would not at all be in the way. Not only did her words negate his suggestion, her face showed surprise as if to say, "How could you ask such a question?" Sanshirō thought he saw this surprise in her black eyes by the light of a gas lamp from a shop they were passing, but in fact the eyes were merely big and black.

"Did you buy your violin?"

"How did you know about that?"

Sanshirō was hard pressed for an answer. Unconcerned, Yoshiko went right on. "It did me no good to beg. Sōhachi just kept making promises. It took him forever."

Inwardly, Sanshirō blamed neither Nonomiya nor Hirota but Yojirō.

*

The two of them turned off Oiwake's main street into a narrow lane. There were many houses. An oil lamp at each door provided light for the dark alley. Sanshirō and Yoshiko came to a stop in front of one of the lamps. Nonomiya lived at the back of this house.

Nonomiya's new lodgings were only a block or so from Sanshirō's. Sanshirō had visited Nonomiya here two or three times. The scientist lived in a detached two-room cottage that was approached by walking through the main house to the end of a broad corridor, climbing two steps straight ahead, and turning to the left. A spacious neighboring garden came almost to his southern veranda. The place was extraordinarily quiet, both day and night. Sanshirō had been much impressed the first time he saw Nonomiya secluded in his private cottage. No, this return to rooming-house life was not a bad idea at all. That day Nonomiya had stepped down to the corridor and gestured toward the eaves. "Look," he said, "a thatched roof." It was probably one of the few non-tiled roofs left in Tokyo.

This time Sanshirō was here at night and could not see the roof, but modern electric lights were burning inside. He thought of the rustic thatch as soon as he caught sight of the lights, and the contrast seemed amusing to him.

"What an unusual pair of guests! Did you just happen to meet outside?" Nonomiya asked Yoshiko. She corrected his mistaken assumption and added that he ought to buy an undershirt like Sanshirō's. Then she complained that the tone of her new, Japanese-made violin was no good. He had put off buying it for so long, he ought to exchange it for a better one, at least as good as Mineko's. She would content herself with that. She went on whining like this for some time.

Nonomiya did not look especially displeased, but neither did he offer her any sympathy. He went on listening with an occasional "Uh-huh."

Sanshirō meanwhile said nothing. Yoshiko produced a string of absurdities without the least restraint, but to Sanshirō she seemed neither idiotic nor selfish. As he listened to the dialogue she carried on with her brother, he felt as though he had walked out to a broad, sunlit field. He forgot all about the lecture that was due him. Then suddenly Yoshiko treated him to a shock.

"Oh, Sōhachi," she said to her brother, "I almost forgot. I have a message for you from Mineko."

"Oh?"

"Don't act so cool about it. I know how happy it makes you."

Nonomiya's face took on an itchy look. He turned to Sanshirō. "My sister is an idiot, you know."

Sanshirō produced a dutiful smile.

"I am not an idiot. Am I, Sanshirō?"

He smiled again, but inside he was sick of smiling.

"Mineko wants you to take her to one of the Literary Society's[48] drama nights."

"Why doesn't she go with her brother?"

"He's busy."

"Are you going, too?"

"Of course."

Nonomiya turned to Sanshirō again without giving Yoshiko a definite answer. He had called his sister here tonight on serious business, he said, but her pointless chatter was too much for him. Nonomiya went on with scholarly candor. There had been a proposal of marriage for Yoshiko. He had written to his parents, and they had expressed no objection. Now it had become necessary to ascertain Yoshiko's own view of the matter.

Sanshirō replied only that that was very fine. He wanted to settle his own problem and leave here as soon as possible. To that end, he said, "My mother tells me she troubled you with something for me."

"Oh, it's no great trouble." He produced the item in his charge from a desk drawer and handed it to Sanshirō.

*

"Your mother sent me a long letter. She's worried about you. She says you told her you were forced to lend your monthly allowance to a friend, but friend or not, a person shouldn't borrow so freely, or at least ought to pay the loan back. I'm not surprised she would think that; country people are so simple and honest. She also blames you for overdoing it. Here you are, living on money from home and you start lending people twenty yen, thirty yen at a time—you ought to know better. The way she puts it, it sounds as if I'm somehow responsible."

Nonomiya flashed a grin at Sanshirō, whose only response was a somber, "I'm sorry about this."

Nonomiya changed his tone somewhat, as if to imply that he had not been trying to set a young man straight. "Come, now, don't let it bother you. It's nothing. Your mother thinks about money by what it's worth in the country. To her, thirty yen looks like a lot. She says a family of four could feed themselves for half a year on thirty yen. Can that be true?"

Yoshiko burst out laughing. Sanshirō, too, could appreciate the comical side of his mother's letter, but she was by no means making this up. When he saw what a rash thing he had done, he felt a little sorry.

"If that's the case," Nonomiya started calculating, "it comes to five yen a month or one yen, twenty-five sen for each person. Divided by thirty, it's only about four sen a day. Come now, that's too little even in the country."

"What do you have to eat to live that cheaply?" Yoshiko asked in all seriousness. Sanshirō had no time to be feeling sorry. He told them all about life in his home village. One thing he mentioned was the local custom known as "Shrine Retreat." Once a year, Sanshirō's family donated ten yen to the village. Then sixty households sent one man each. The group of sixty would take the day off, gather at the village shrine, and eat and drink from morning until night.

"And that costs only ten yen?" Yoshiko was amazed. Nonomiya's lecture had apparently gone off somewhere. They talked at random for a while, after which Nonomiya returned to the main subject.

"Anyhow, your mother said this. She wants me to find out what's going on and, once I've decided that everything is on the up-and-up, to give you the money. Finally, I'm supposed to report back to her on what I find. But here I've given you the money without asking a thing. Hmm, let's see now . . . you lent the money to Sasaki, didn't you?"

Sanshirō assumed that the story had gone from Mineko, through Yoshiko, to Nonomiya. He felt it odd, however, that neither Yoshiko nor Nonomiya had realized how the money had changed hands many times until it took shape as a violin.

"Yes," he answered, and let it go at that.

"I heard that Sasaki lost his money on the horses."

"True."

Yoshiko laughed out loud again.

"Well, then, I'll think of something to tell your mother. But you had better not make any more of those loans."

Sanshirō replied that he would not. He said goodbye and was getting to his feet when Yoshiko announced that she would be leaving, too.

"We haven't had our talk yet," her brother reminded her.

"That's quite all right," she declared.

"It is not all right."

"Yes it is. I just don't know."

Nonomiya stared at his sister.

She continued, "Don't you see how pointless it is? What can I say when you ask me if I'll marry a total stranger? I don't love him, I don't hate him, I don't know him—literally. I just don't know."

Sanshirō saw now what Yoshiko meant by "I just don't know." He left the brother and sister alone and hurried outside.

*

He emerged from the deserted lane, where door lamps were all that illuminated the darkness. On the main street again, he found the wind blowing, and when he turned north, it struck him full in the face. The wind blew from the direction of his lodgings in rhythmic gusts. Sanshirō thought to himself: through this wind, Nonomiya will be walking soon, accompanying his sister back to Satomi's.

He could still hear the wind even after he had climbed the stairs to his room and sat down on the matted floor. The word "destiny" came to mind whenever he heard the wind blowing like this. He felt like cringing whenever it came howling at him. He had never considered himself a strong man, and now that he thought about it, his destiny since coming to Tokyo had been largely shaped by Yojirō—shaped in a way that put him, to some extent, at the mercy of Yojirō's genial whims. Yojirō was a lovable mischief-maker, he knew, and his destiny would remain in the hands of this lovable mischief-maker for some time to come. The wind never let up. Surely the wind was something greater than Yojirō.

Sanshirō placed the thirty yen from his mother by his pillow. This thirty yen had also been given birth to by a whim of fate. What tasks would it perform? He would bring it back to Mineko, and when she took it, she was certain to fan the flames again. Let her come at me as boldly as she knows how, thought Sanshirō.

With that he fell asleep. It was a sleep too sound for either destiny or Yojirō to touch. He woke to the ringing of a fire bell. There were voices. This was his second Tokyo fire. He pulled a coat on over his sleeping robe and opened the window. The wind had died down considerably, but amidst its ongoing roar, the two-story house across the way looked pitch black, black because the sky behind it was so red.

Sanshirō stared at this redness for a while, enduring the cold. In his mind, destiny shone a brilliant red. He crawled back under the warm covers, and there he forgot about the lives of all those people raging about inside the red destiny.

The next morning, he was an ordinary person again. He put on his uniform, picked up his notebook, and left for school. The one unusual thing this morning was the money, and this he did not forget to put in his pocket. His schedule that day was not a good one, however. It was full until three o'clock. If he went after three, Yoshiko would probably be home from school. The brother he knew only as Satomi Kyōsuke might also be there. He felt quite incapable of returning the money if anyone else was going to be present.

He ran into Yojirō, who picked up where he had left off. "Did you get your lecture last night?"

"No, I wouldn't call it that."

"I thought so. Nonomiya's no fool," he said and went off somewhere.

Sanshirō saw Yojirō in another class two hours later. "Things look very good for Professor Hirota," Yojirō said. Sanshirō asked how far the campaign had advanced. "Don't worry, I'll tell you all about it when we have time. The Professor's been asking for you. You ought to go and see him more often. He's a bachelor, after all. We have to cheer him up. Buy him something next time."

Yojirō gave his orders and disappeared again. He materialized once more in the following class. This time, in the middle of the lecture, something possessed him to pass a white slip of paper to Sanshirō with a telegraphic note: "Received money?" Sanshirō considered writing an answer, but he looked up to find the professor staring straight at him. He crumpled the paper and threw it to the floor. Yojirō had to wait for his answer until class was over.

"Got it. It's right here."

"Good. Are you going to give it back?"

"Of course I am."

"You ought to. The sooner the better."

"I'm going over with it today."

"She might be there if you go late in the afternoon."

"Why? Has she been going out?"

"Has she! She goes out every single day to have her picture painted. It must be pretty much done by now."

"At Haraguchi's?"

"Right."

Sanshirō asked Yojirō for Haraguchi's address.

10

Having heard from Yojirō that Hirota was not well, Sanshirō
came to pay a sick call. He went in through the gate and saw a
pair of shoes in the hallway. Perhaps they were the doctor's.
Walking around to the kitchen door as usual, he found no one.
He wandered in as far as the sitting room. There were voices in
the parlor. Sanshirō stood still, his large cloth bundle dangling
from one hand. It was full of persimmons. He had bought them
in Oiwake in compliance with Yojirō's orders. All of a sudden
there were some heavy thumps and grappling sounds in the
parlor. It had to be a fight. Still holding the cloth bundle, he
shot the sliding door back a foot and glared inside. Professor
Hirota was pinned under a large man in a brown divided skirt.
Straining to lift his face from the mats, Professor Hirota looked
at Sanshirō with a broad grin and said, "Hello there, come in."

The man on top glanced at Sanshirō and continued with the
match. "Sorry, Professor, but try to get up," he said. He seemed
to have the Professor's arms twisted behind his back with the
elbows pinned to the floor beneath his knees. The Professor
replied from underneath that he would never be able to get up.
With that, the man released his grip, lifted his knees, straightened the pleats of his skirt, and sat up on the matted floor. Now
Sanshirō could see what a powerfully built man he was.

The Professor also sat up. "I see what you mean," he said.

"It's a dangerous technique. If you fight it you can break
your arms."

Sanshirō now realized what they had been doing.

"I heard that you were sick, Professor. Are you all right
now?"

"Yes, I'm fine."

Sanshirō untied the cloth bundle and spread the contents of the package between the Professor and his guest.

"I bought you some persimmons."

Professor Hirota went to his study and came back with a pen-knife. Sanshirō brought some knives from the kitchen. The three of them began to eat. Hirota and the unknown man talked incessantly of provincial middle schools—the difficulty of making a living, the student strikes, the man's inability to stay put for long, his extra-curricular teaching of judo, the economies of a colleague who retied old thongs to new wooden clogs, the difficulty of finding work now that he had resigned, and his decision to send his wife home to her parents until a new job turned up.

Spitting out persimmon stones, Sanshirō watched the man's face and started feeling miserable. It was almost as if this man and his present self were of wholly different races. "I wish I could be a student again. The student life is the most carefree in the world." The man repeated this several times. When Sanshirō heard it he wondered vaguely if two or three "carefree" years might be all that were left to him. This was not the light-hearted mood that accompanied eating noodles with Yojirō.

Professor Hirota stood up and went to his study again. He came back holding a book with a dark red cover and dust-blackened edges. "This is the book I told you about the other day, *Hydriotaphia.*[49] Have a look at it if you're bored."

Sanshirō thanked him and took the volume. A passage caught his eye: "But the iniquity of oblivion blindly scattereth her poppy, and deals with the memory of men without distinction to merit of perpetuity."

The Professor was free now to continue his conversation with Dr. Judo. "We hear about the way middle-school teachers and such live, and it all seems terribly sad, but the only ones who really feel sad are the men themselves. That's because modern-day people are fond of facts but they habitually throw out the sentiments that accompany the facts—which is all they can do, because society is pressing in on us so relentlessly we're forced to throw them out. You can see this in the newspaper. Nine out of ten human interest stories are tragedies, but we have nothing to spare, nothing that enables us to feel them as tragedies. We read them only as factual reports. In the newspaper I take I often see the headline, 'So-and-so Many Die,' under which the name, address and cause of death of everyone who has died of unnatural causes that day is listed in small type, one line per person. It's the ultimate in concision and lucidity. There's also a column called 'Burglaries at a Glance,' in which all the burglaries are lumped together so that you can tell literally at a glance what kind of burglaries have been committed where—another great convenience. You have to realize that everything is like this. It's the same with a resignation. To the man concerned, it might be an incident bordering on tragedy, but it's important to face the fact that others don't feel it with the same intensity. You would probably do well to keep this in mind when searching for work."

"Still, Professor," said the judo man, looking serious, "if someone had as much to spare as you, I'd think it would be all right for him to feel things with a *little* intensity." At this, Professor Hirota, Sanshirō, and the man himself all laughed. It seemed as though the man was never going to leave. Sanshirō borrowed the book and went out by the kitchen door.

*

"To subsist in lasting monuments, to live in their productions, to exist in their names and predicament of chimeras, was large satisfaction unto old expectations, and made one part of their Elysiums. But all this is nothing in the metaphysicks of true belief. To live indeed, is to be again ourselves, which being not only an hope, but an evidence in noble believers, 'tis all one to lie in St. Innocent's church-yard, as in the sands of Egypt. Ready to be anything, in the ecstasy of being ever, and as content with six foot as the *moles* of Adrianus."

He read the concluding paragraph of *Hydriotaphia* as he ambled down the street toward Hakusan. According to Professor Hirota, this writer was a famous stylist, and this essay the best example of his style. "That's not *my* opinion, of course," he had laughingly confided. And in fact Sanshirō could not see what was so remarkable about this style. The phrasing was bad, the diction outlandish, the flow of words sluggish. It gave him the feeling of looking at some old temple. In terms of walking distance, it had taken him three or four blocks to read, and still he was not very clear about what it said.

What he had gained from the paragraph wore a patina of age, as if someone had rung the bell of the Great Buddha in Nara[50] and the lingering reverberation had faintly reached his ears in Tokyo. Rather than the meaning of the passage itself, Sanshirō took pleasure in the shadow of sentiment that crept over the meaning. He had never thought keenly about death; his youthful blood was still too warm for that. A fire leapt before his eyes so gigantic that it could singe his brows, and this feeling was his true self. Now he was headed for Hara-guchi's house in Akebono-chō.

A child's funeral procession came toward him. Two men in formal coats were the only mourners. The little coffin was wrapped in a spotless white cloth, a pretty pinwheel attached to its side. The wheel kept turning. Each of its five blades was painted a different color. They blurred into one as the wheel turned. The white coffin moved past him, the pinwheel spinning constantly. He thought it a lovely procession.

Sanshirō had viewed another's writing and another's funeral from a distance. If someone were to come along and suggest that, while he was about it, he should look at Mineko from a distance, he would have been shocked, for his eyes were no longer capable of doing that. First of all, he was not conscious of a distinction between the distant and the not-distant. He knew only that, while he sensed a tranquil beauty in the death of another, there was a kind of anguish beneath the beautiful pleasure he felt from the living Mineko. He would move straight ahead, trying to sweep away this anguish. If he went forward, it seemed, the anguish would leave him. He never dreamed of stepping aside to shed it. Incapable of such a thought, Sanshirō viewed the rites of extinction from afar, as words on a page, and he felt the pathos of early death from a place apart. What should have brought him sadness he viewed with pleasure and a sense of beauty.

When he turned into Akebono-chō, there was a large pine
tree. Yojirō had told him to look for this, but when he reached
the tree, it was the wrong house. There was another pine tree
further on. And one beyond that. There were lots of pines. It
was a nice neighborhood, thought Sanshirō. He passed several
of the trees and turned left. There was a hedge and a handsome
gate. The name plate of this house did in fact say "Haraguchi."
It was a dark strip of wood with convoluted grain, the name
lavishly inscribed on it in green oil paint. The calligraphy was
so ornate that the characters looked more like abstract designs.
Nothing stood between the gate and the front door; it was clean
and fresh. Grass grew on either side of the path.

*

Mineko's wooden clogs were arranged neatly in the hallway. He recognized them because the right and left thongs of
each were different colors. The maid said that Haraguchi was
at work on a painting, but Sanshirō could come in if he liked.
He followed her into the studio. It was a large room, stretching
a long way north and south. On this long floor lay an odd
assortment of items befitting an artist's space. One area was
covered with a rug. Out of proportion to the size of the room,
it seemed less a rug than an elegantly figured, colorful swatch
that had been tossed there as a decoration. The same was true
of the large tiger skin that lay farther on. It did not seem to
have been placed there as a cushion for sitting. Its long tail
stretched out at an angle incongruous to the rug. There was a
large jar that looked as though it had been molded from sand.
Two arrows protruded from its mouth. Between the rows of
gray feathers, the shafts were decorated with shiny gold leaf.
Next to the jar was a suit of armor with overlapping plates
of white and yellow-green. This, thought Sanshirō, was probably what the medieval war tales called *unohana-odoshi*.[51] In
the far corner was something brilliant and eye-catching. It was
a violet robe of wadded silk, with gold thread in the skirt's
lavish embroidery. It had been hung as if for summer airing,
with a cord passed through the short, cylindrical sleeves. This
must be what they call a Genroku.[52] In addition to these objects,

the room had many paintings. The ones on the walls alone came to quite a number, of all sizes. Others with no frames, possibly roughed-out canvases, lay in loose rolls with the edges exposed.

The portrait that was being painted at the moment stood amidst this spread of dazzling colors. The person who was being painted stood against the far wall, holding up a round fan. Shoulders hunched, the man who was doing the painting began to rotate, palette in hand, until he was facing Sanshirō. His teeth clenched a thick pipe.

"Well, look who's here," he said, taking the pipe from his mouth and setting it down on a small, round table where an ashtray and matches lay. Next to the table was a chair.

"Have a seat. This is it," he said, looking toward the unfinished canvas. It was a full six feet high.

Sanshirō said only, "It *is* big, isn't it?"

"Yes, pretty big," said Haraguchi, more to himself than to Sanshirō. He started painting where the hair and background met. Now at last, Sanshirō looked at Mineko. Her white teeth gleamed faintly in the shadow of the fan.

For several minutes everything was silent. The warmth of a stove filled the room. Even outside it was not especially cold today. The wind had died down. A withered tree stood there soundlessly, enveloped by the winter sun. When shown into the studio, Sanshirō had felt as if he were entering a mist. Elbow on the small round table, he gave himself over to this silence more total than night's. Within the silence there was Mineko and there was the image of Mineko gradually taking shape. All that moved was the fat painter's brush. It moved only for the eye; to the ear it was silent. The fat painter also moved at times, but his steps were soundless.

Sealed in silence, Mineko remained utterly still. In her standing pose with the fan held aloft, she was already a picture. As Sanshirō saw it, Haraguchi was not painting Mineko; he was copying a painting of mysterious depth, using all his energy to make an ordinary picture that lacked precisely this depth. And yet, within the silence, the second Mineko was moving ever closer to the first. Sanshirō imagined that between these two

Minekos lay a long, silent time untouched by the sound of the clock. As that time passed by, so quietly the artist himself was unaware of it, the second Mineko would at last catch up. And when the two were on the verge of meeting and melding into one, the river of time would suddenly shift its course and flow into eternity. Haraguchi's brush could go no farther. Sanshirō followed his musings to this point, then came back to himself and glanced at Mineko. She remained motionless, as before. Sanshirō's mind had been on the move in this quiet air without his realizing it. He felt intoxicated. All of a sudden Haraguchi laughed.

*

"All right, I can see you're suffering again."

Without a word, Mineko broke her pose and plopped into the easy chair nearby. Again there was a white flash of teeth. As the sleeve of the upraised arm swept past her face, she looked at Sanshirō. Her glance pierced his brow like a meteor.

Haraguchi walked over to the round table. "How do you like it?" he asked Sanshirō. He struck a match and lit his pipe again. Pressing the large wooden bowl between his fingers, he released two thick puffs of smoke through his mustache, then turned until his rounded back faced Sanshirō again and approached the portrait. He started touching up various parts of the picture at will.

The portrait was unfinished, of course, but the entire canvas had paint on it, and to Sanshirō's unpracticed eye the picture looked quite good. Whether it was in fact a skillful job, he could not tell. Incapable of evaluating technique, Sanshirō had only the feeling that technique produced, and even that seemed to him way off the mark owing to his lack of experience. But he was not wholly oblivious to the effects of art, and at least to that extent he could be said to be a man of refined tastes.

To Sanshirō the painting looked like a single burst of light. The entire canvas seemed to have a powdery overlay of soft, glare-free sunlight. Not even the shadows were black. If anything, they had a touch of pale violet. The painting made Sanshirō feel lighthearted, somehow. It had an exhilarating effect,

like a ride in a swift riverboat. And yet there was something
calm and settled about it, too. It was not disturbing, certainly
in no way bitter or sharp or heavy. It was very much like
Haraguchi himself, thought Sanshirō. Just then Haraguchi
spoke up, manipulating the brush almost casually.

"Here's an interesting story, Ogawa. A fellow I know got fed
up with his wife and asked her for a divorce. She refused. 'Fate
brought me to this house,' she said. 'Even though you may be
tired of me, I will never leave.'"

At that point Haraguchi stepped back from the canvas to
view the results of his brushwork. Then he spoke to Mineko.
"I do wish you had put on summer clothes for me. I'm having
a terrible time with the kimono. I'm doing it all by guesswork,
and I think I've been a little too bold."

"It's all my fault," said Mineko.

Haraguchi approached the canvas again without answering
her. "Well, anyhow, since his wife was too firmly planted to
think of leaving, my friend said to her, 'Don't go if you don't
want to. Stay as long as you like. I'll go.' —Mineko, could you
stand up a second, please? No, don't worry about the fan, just
stand up. That's it. Thanks. —So the wife said, 'How can I stay
if you leave? Who'll support me?' My friend told her, 'Don't
worry, you can always find a man who will marry into the
family and take your—my—name.'"

"What happened after that?" Sanshirō asked.

Haraguchi seemed to think the rest of the story was not
worth telling. "Nothing happened. It's just that you've got to
think twice before you get married. It means the end of your
freedom—freedom to separate, freedom to get together with
someone else. Look at Professor Hirota, look at Nonomiya,
look at Satomi Kyōsuke, and look at me—all bachelors. When
women come up in the world, lots of men stay single. As a basic
rule of society, women ought to advance only to the degree that
you don't produce bachelors."

"My brother is going to be married very soon, you know,"
Mineko broke in.

"He is? What's going to happen to you?"

"I don't know."

Sanshirō looked at Mineko. Mineko looked back at Sanshirō and smiled. Only Haraguchi was facing the portrait, and when he spoke it was mostly to himself: " 'I don't know,' she says. 'I don't know.' Oh well . . ." He started painting again.

*

Sanshirō took this opportunity to leave the table and approach Mineko. She had flung herself down, too exhausted to care about appearances, her lusterless head of hair drooping against the chair back, her throat arched prominently from the collar of her under-kimono. The pretty lining of her coat, which lay on the chairback, was visible above her swirling hairdo.

Sanshirō had the thirty yen in his breast pocket. This money represented some inexplicable thing that existed between them—or at least he believed that it did. Because of this belief he had thought about returning the money but had never done it. It was also because of this belief that he was trying now to return the money once and for all. When he had given it back, they would either drift apart for lack of this mutual concern, or they would grow closer in spite of it. —Normal people might find Sanshirō a bit superstitious.

"Mineko."

"Yes?"

She looked up at him without moving her face. Only her eyes moved. They slowed to a stop when they were looking directly at him. He could see that she was tired.

"As long as I've found you here, let me give this back." He loosened a button and thrust his hand into his jacket.

"What is it?"

Her tone, as before, betrayed no emotion. Hand still thrust inside his jacket, Sanshirō wondered what he should do.

"The money," he said at last.

"What can I do with it here?"

She was looking up at him. She did not reach out or change her position. Her face stayed motionless. He did not understand this woman. He did not understand her question. Just then a voice behind him said, "It won't be long now. How about it?"

He turned to find Haraguchi facing them. A brush between

his fingers, he tugged at the neat triangle of his beard and smiled. Mineko grasped the arms of the chair and sat up very straight.

"Will this take long?" Sanshirō asked softly.

"Another hour," she answered just as quietly. Sanshirō went back to the round table. Mineko resumed her pose. Haraguchi lit his pipe again, and again his brush began to move.

Turning his back to Sanshirō, he said, "Ogawa, look at Mineko's eyes."

Sanshirō did as he was told. Mineko lowered the fan and broke her pose. She turned to look through the window at the garden.

"No, you can't move now. I've just started."

"Why did you have to say that?"

She faced front again.

Haraguchi explained, "I'm not making fun of you. I have something to tell Ogawa."

"What is it?"

"Just listen. Come, stand the way you were. That's it. Elbow a little more this way. Now, as I was saying, Ogawa, do you think the eyes I've painted have the same expression as our actual model's here?"

"I don't know, really. But when you paint someone like this over a long period of time, do the eyes keep the same expression day after day?"

"No, they change, of course. And it's not just the model. The painter's mood changes every day, too. There really ought to be several portraits when you're through, but we can't have that. The strange thing is that you end up with one fairly coherent painting. Think about it."

Haraguchi was manipulating the brush all the while he talked. He kept looking at Mineko, too. Sanshirō witnessed in awe this simultaneous functioning of Haraguchi's faculties.

*

"When I work on a painting day after day like this, each day's work accumulates, and soon the picture takes on a certain mood. So even if I come back from someplace in a different mood, once I walk into the studio and face the picture, I can get right into it because the mood of the picture takes over. The same thing happens to Mineko. If you just leave her to be her natural self, different stimuli are bound to give her different expressions. But the reason this has no great effect on the painting is that her pose, say, and the clutter in here—the drum, the armor, the tigerskin—naturally come to draw out one particular expression, and the habit of it becomes strong enough after a while to suppress any other expression, so that I can fairly well go on painting the look in the eyes as is. Now, I keep using the word 'expression' but—"

Haraguchi suddenly broke off. He seemed to have come to something difficult. He took two steps back and started intently comparing Mineko and the picture.

"Mineko, is something wrong?"

"No, nothing."

It was inconceivable that this answer had come from her mouth, she kept her pose unbroken with such perfect stillness.

"I keep using the word 'expression,'" Haraguchi went on, "but an artist doesn't paint what's inside, he doesn't paint the heart. He paints what the heart puts on display. As long as he observes everything in the display case, he can tell what's locked up in the safe. Or we can assume that much, I suppose. A painter has to resign himself to the fact that anything he can't see on display is beyond the scope of his responsibility. That's why we paint only the flesh. Whatever flesh an artist paints, if it hasn't got the spirit in it, it's dead, it simply has no validity as a painting. Now take Mineko's eyes, for example. When I paint them, I'm not trying to make a picture of her heart, I'm just painting them as eyes. I'm painting these eyes because I like them. I'm painting everything I see about them— the shape, the shadow in the fold of the lids, the depth of the pupils—leaving nothing out. And as a result, almost by accident, a kind of expression takes shape. If it doesn't, it means I mixed the colors badly or I got the shape wrong, one or the other, because that color and that shape are themselves a kind of expression."

Again Haraguchi took two steps back, comparing Mineko

with the picture. "Something is wrong today, I'm sure. You must be tired. If you are, let's quit. Are you?"

"No."

Haraguchi walked up to the canvas again. "Now, let me tell you why I picked Mineko's eyes. You find a beauty in Western art, and no matter who's painted her, she has big eyes. They all have these funny-looking big eyes. In Japanese art, though, women always have narrow eyes, from images of Kannon down to comic masks and Noh masks, and especially the beauties in ukiyo-e prints.[53] They all have elephant eyes. Why should standards of beauty be so different in East and West? It seems strange at first, but actually it's very simple. Big eyes are the only thing they have in the West, so an aesthetic selection takes place among the big-eyed ones. All we have in Japan are whale eyes. Pierre Loti made fun of them in *Madame Chrysanthème*.[54] 'How do they ever open those things?' he said. You see, it's the nature of the country. There is no way for an aesthetic appreciation of big eyes to develop where materials are so scarce. Our ideal came from among narrow eyes, where there was so much freedom of choice, and we see it prized in artists like Utamaro and Sukenobu. As nice and Japanese as they look to us, though, narrow eyes look terrible in Western style painting. People think you've painted a blind woman. On the other hand, we don't have anybody who looks like Raphael's Madonna, and if we did, nobody would consider her Japanese. That, finally, is how I came to put Mineko through all this. —Just a little while longer, Mineko."

She did not answer. She stood absolutely motionless.

*

Sanshirō found the painter's remarks very interesting. If only he had come there specifically to hear them, he felt, their interest would have been vastly increased. The focus of his attention, however, was neither Haraguchi's conversation nor Haraguchi's painting. It was concentrated, of course, on the standing figure of Mineko. He heard everything the painter had to say, but his eyes never left Mineko. To him, her pose looked like a natural process caught in its most beautiful moment and

rendered immobile. There was lasting solace in her unchang-
ingness. But Haraguchi had suddenly turned his head and asked
her if there were something wrong. Sanshirō felt almost terrified, as though the painter had informed him that the means of
keeping this changeable beauty unchanged had spent itself.

Now that Haraguchi mentioned it, Sanshirō noticed there
might indeed be something wrong with Mineko. Her color was
bad, the glow was gone. The corners of her eyes revealed an
unbearable languor. Sanshirō lost the sense of comfort this
living portrait had given him, and at that moment the thought
struck him—perhaps he himself was the cause. An intense personal stimulus overtook Sanshirō's heart in that instant. The
communal emotion of regret for passing beauty vanished from
him without a trace. So great was his influence over her! With
this new awareness, Sanshirō became conscious of his entire
being. But was the influence to his advantage or his disadvantage? This was a question as yet unanswered.

Haraguchi laid his brush aside at last. "Let's stop now," he
said. "We'll never get anything done today."

Mineko dropped the fan to the floor where she stood. She
picked up her coat from the chair and while putting it on walked
over to Haraguchi and Sanshirō.

"You're tired today," Haraguchi said.

"Am I?" She straightened the coat and fastened the front tie.

"Actually, I'm tired too. Let's try again tomorrow when we
have a little more energy. Have a cup of tea now—don't run
off."

It was a while yet before evening. But she would be on her
way, Mineko said, there was something she had to do. Sanshirō
also pointedly turned down Haraguchi's invitation to stay, and
he left with Mineko. Given Japanese social customs, no amount
of planning could have presented him with such a perfect opportunity, and he meant to exploit it, to stay with her as long as
possible. He invited Mineko to take a stroll with him through
this quiet neighborhood, where there were relatively few
passersby. She was surprisingly unreceptive to the idea, however, and headed straight down the hedge-lined road to the
main thoroughfare.

Walking beside her, Sanshirō said, "Haraguchi was right, wasn't he? You are feeling out of sorts today."

"Am I?" she said again, as she had replied to Haraguchi. Sanshirō had never known Mineko to be overly talkative. A phrase or two was all she ever needed. And yet in Sanshirō's ears these simple utterances produced a kind of profound resonance. There was a tone to her speech that was all but impossible to find in others. Sanshirō stood in awe of it. He marveled at it.

When she said "Am I?" Mineko had turned part way toward Sanshirō and looked at him from the corner of her eye. A halo seemed to overlay the eye, which had a lukewarm feeling to it that he had never seen before. The cheek, too, was somewhat pale.

"You look a little pale, I think."

"Do I?"

They took several steps without speaking. Sanshirō wanted desperately to tear away the thin, curtain-like thing that hung between them, but he knew no words that would rend the fabric. He refused to speak the syrupy phrases they used in novels. The social usages of young men and women might permit it, but his personal sense of taste did not. He was hoping for the impossible—not only hoping, but struggling to devise a way to attain it as he walked along.

*

Finally it was Mineko who spoke. "Did you have some business with Mr. Haraguchi today?"

"No, none."

"You just came for a visit, then?"

"No, that's not it, either."

"Well, then, why did you come?"

Sanshirō seized the moment. "I came to see you."

He felt he had said everything he could possibly say. Mineko went on in a tone that betrayed no emotion, the tone that always had an intoxicating effect on Sanshirō. "I could hardly take the money from you there."

He was crushed. They took several more steps without

speaking. Then Sanshirō said all at once, "I didn't come to give you the money."

Mineko did not reply immediately. When she spoke, her voice was soft. "I don't need the money, either. You keep it."

Sanshirō could endure this no longer. "I came because I wanted to see you," he said, searching for her eyes.

She would not look at him. He heard a tiny sigh escape her lips. "The money is . . ."

"The damned money . . ."

Both left unfinished sentences hanging in the air. They walked on another half block. This time she spoke. "What did you think when you saw Haraguchi's portrait?"

There were so many ways he could answer this, Sanshirō walked a little while without replying.

"Weren't you surprised at how quickly he was completing it?"

"I was," he said, but the idea had not occurred to him. Now that he thought about it, only a month had gone by since Haraguchi visited Professor Hirota's and revealed his desire to paint Mineko, and his request to her at the museum had come even later than that. Unenlightened in the ways of art, Sanshirō found it all but impossible to imagine how much time it took to do a painting of that size. Now that Mineko had called his attention to it, he felt that the painting was indeed being completed too quickly. "When did he start working on it?"

"He started painting in earnest only a short while ago. But I had him doing a little bit at a time from before."

"When was 'before'?"

"You should be able to guess from my outfit."

Sanshirō recalled at once that hot summer day long ago when he had first seen Mineko at the pond.

"Heavens, you *must* remember. You were squatting under the oak tree."

"You were standing on the hill, holding up a fan."

"Just like in the picture."

"Yes, just like in the picture."

They looked at each other. A little farther on, they would reach the top of Hakusan Hill.

A rickshaw came dashing toward them from that direction. The passenger was wearing a black hat and gold-rimmed glasses. The glow of his complexion was obvious even at this distance. From the moment the rickshaw entered his field of vision, Sanshirō felt that the young gentleman passenger was staring at Mineko. The rickshaw stopped just ahead of them. Sanshirō watched the young man deftly thrust aside the blanket on his knees and spring down from the footboard. He was a handsome, well-built man, tall and slim with a long face, and though clean-shaven, he was thoroughly masculine.

"You were so late, I came to get you." He stood directly in front of Mineko. He looked down at her, smiling.

"Oh, thank you." She was smiling, too, as she returned his glance, but she immediately turned to Sanshirō.

"Who is this?" the young man asked.

"Ogawa Sanshirō of the University," she said.

The man tipped his hat to Sanshirō.

"Let's hurry. Your brother is waiting, too."

As it happened, they were standing at the corner where Sanshirō was to turn for Oiwake. He had still not returned the money when they parted.

11

Yojirō was circulating through the school, selling tickets to the Literary Society's forthcoming drama nights. After two or three days, he seemed to have palmed tickets off on just about everyone he knew. That much accomplished, he concentrated on people he did not know. He generally caught them in the hallway, and once he had them he would never let go. He nearly always got them to buy in the end. There were times, however, when the bell would ring in the middle of his pitch, and the customer would escape. To explain these mishaps, Yojirō relied on Mencius. "The opportunity of time has not been vouchsafed me," he would say.[55] He had a similar pronouncement for those occasions when his adversary managed to put him off with smiles: "The compliance of man has not been afforded me." Once, he caught a professor who had just emerged from the men's room and was still wiping his hands. "Not now," he protested and disappeared into the library. For this, Yojirō had no pronouncement. He simply watched the professor running off and informed Sanshirō, "The man has intestinal catarrh, I'm sure of it."

—How many tickets was Yojirō supposed to sell?

—As many as he could.

—Wasn't there any danger of selling more tickets than there were seats?

—Yes, there was some danger of that.

—Then wouldn't there be trouble after the tickets were sold?

—No, not at all, Yojirō explained with a perfectly straight face. Many people bought tickets out of sheer obligation, unforeseen events would keep others from attending, and there would be a little intestinal catarrh in the works, too.

Sanshirō watched how Yojirō sold his tickets. He took money on the spot from those who gave it to him, and to students who did not he gave the tickets anyway. He handed out enough tickets this way to worry his more timid companion, who asked if Yojirō would receive the money later. Of course not, Yojirō answered. It was more profitable overall to sell a lot sloppily than a few carefully. He compared this to the London *Times*'s method of selling encyclopedias in Japan.[56] The comparison sounded impressive enough, but it still left Sanshirō feeling uneasy. When he cautioned Yojirō, he received an interesting answer.

"I'll have you know that I am dealing with students of Tokyo Imperial University!"

"Maybe they are students, but most of them are just as easy-going about money as you are."

"Don't be stupid. The Literary Society is not going to have anything to say about people who don't pay in good faith. They're going to be in the red no matter how many tickets they sell."

"Is that your opinion or the Society's?"

"It is my opinion, of course, as well as the Society's," came Yojirō's expedient reply.

If one were to believe Yojirō, only an idiot would miss the performance. He held forth on the subject until his listeners began to feel like idiots themselves. But was he doing this to sell tickets? Or because he actually had faith in the show? Or simply to lift his own spirits and those of his listeners and ultimately the spirits of the performance, thus making the air of the world in general as lively as possible? This was a distinction that eluded his customers. And so, despite his success in making them feel like idiots, Yojirō was unable to influence them very much.

He spoke first on the tremendous efforts of the actors in rehearsal. If what he said was true, most of them would be worn out before the day of the show. Then he talked about the scenery, which he said was extraordinary. He made it sound as though the Society had recruited all the talented young artists in Tokyo and had encouraged each of them to devote his special skills to it. Next he talked about the costumes. They were historically authentic in every detail. Then he talked about the plays. They were all new works and all delightful. He had any number of topics in addition.

Yojirō said he had sent complimentary tickets to Professor Hirota and Haraguchi, and he had gotten the Nonomiyas and Satomis to buy the most expensive seats. Everything was going well. Sanshirō offered Yojirō his best wishes for the show's success.

*

Yojirō showed up at Sanshirō's room that night a changed man. He sat stiffly at the charcoal brazier complaining of the cold. More than the cold was bothering him, however, judging from the look on his face. At first he hunched over the brazier, warming his hands, but eventually he put his hands inside his kimono. Sanshirō moved the oil lamp from one end of his desk to the other, hoping to lend some brightness to Yojirō's countenance. But with his chin buried in his chest, the black burr of Yojirō's close-cropped head was the only part of him to catch the light. The lamp made no difference. What was wrong? Sanshirō asked. Yojirō raised his head and looked at the lamp.

"Don't they have electricity in this house yet?" His question had nothing to do with the look on his face.

"Not yet. They're planning to get it soon, though. Oil lamps are too dim for much of anything."

But Yojirō seemed to have forgotten all about lamps even while Sanshirō was answering him.

"Something terrible has happened, Ogawa."

"What is it?"

Yojirō produced some wrinkled newspapers from the breast of his kimono. There were two papers folded together. He peeled one off, refolded it, and thrust it toward Sanshirō. "Read this." His fingertip lay where Sanshirō was to read. Sanshirō moved closer to the lamp. The headline said, "University Literature Department."

Heretofore, said the article, administrators of the University's programs in Foreign Literature had assigned all courses to foreign instructors. But now, at long last, in response to the march of time and the demands of many students, the lectures of a Japanese were to be recognized among the compulsory courses. A search for an appropriate individual had been underway for some time, and the announcement of a decision in favor of one Mr. So-and-so was to be made shortly. This particular man was an outstanding scholar who, until recently, had been studying abroad under orders from the government, and his appointment was no doubt most fitting.

"So, Professor Hirota didn't make it?" Sanshirō turned to Yojirō, who was still looking at the newspaper. "Is this definite?"

"I'm afraid so." Yojirō cocked his head to one side. "I thought it was just about a sure thing, but we bungled it. Of course, I had heard the other fellow was pushing hard for it, too."

"But this is still a rumor, after all. You can't be sure until they finally make it public."

"If that were the only thing, it wouldn't matter, of course. It has nothing to do with the Professor. But . . ." He refolded the other paper and pointed to the headline as he placed it in front of Sanshirō.

This article started out saying much the same thing as the first one and could hardly be expected to make a new impression on Sanshirō. When he came to the next part, however, Sanshirō was astonished. Professor Hirota, it said, was an unscrupulous schemer. He had been a language teacher for ten years, utterly unknown, a mediocrity, but no sooner had he heard that the University was due to appoint a Japanese professor of foreign literature than he began a furtive campaign on his own behalf and disseminated propaganda leaflets among the students. Moreover, he had urged a protégé of his to write an essay called "The Great Darkness" for one of the little magazines. It had appeared under the pseudonym "A. Propagule," but in fact the

author was known to be an habitué of the Hirota house,
a student in the Faculty of Letters by the name of Ogawa
Sanshirō. And so the article concluded.

Sanshirō looked questioningly at Yojirō. Yojirō was already
looking at Sanshirō. For a while, they said nothing. Finally,
Sanshirō spoke. "This is bad."

The note of resentment in his voice was meant for Yojirō,
but Yojirō had other things on his mind. "What do you think
of it?" he asked.

"What do you mean, what do I think of it?"

"I'm sure the newspaper just published a letter to the editor
as is. No reporter dug it out. Stuff like this comes to the *Literary
Review*'s readers' column all the time. That's what a readers'
column is, after all—a pile of crimes. Look into most of the
stories, and they're a pack of lies. Some are lies on the face of
it. And why do you think people print such stupidity, eh? The
motive is always some personal advantage. So whenever I was
in charge of the readers' column I threw most of the ugly ones
into the wastebasket. That's just what this article is. It comes
from the other guy's campaign."

                                          *

"Why does it have my name and not yours?"

"That's what I was wondering," said Yojirō, and then he
attempted an explanation. "Maybe it's because you're a regular
student while I'm just a special student."

To Sanshirō, this was no explanation at all. It did nothing to
soften the blow.

"Instead of that Propagule nonsense, I should have signed it
'Sasaki Yojirō' for all to see. There's not another man alive who
could have written that essay!"

Yojirō was serious, as though Sanshirō had usurped his
copyright.

Sanshirō was finding this ridiculous. "Have you told the
Professor?" he asked.

"Ah, that's the trouble. It doesn't matter who the real author
of 'The Great Darkness' is, but as long as it reflects on the
Professor's character, I have to tell him. You know what he's

like: before, I could have said I didn't know a thing, that it was probably a mistake, that an essay had appeared in a magazine under a pseudonym, that he needn't worry about it because it was written by an admirer of his. He'd have said 'Oh?' and that would have been the end of it. But not the way things are now. I'll have to confess my responsibility. If things had worked out, I would have felt good doing my part anonymously, but now that I've failed, I'd never feel right keeping quiet. I'm the one who started it all. I'm the one who got that good, innocent man into this mess. And now I'm damned if I'll just stand idly by and watch what happens. Strict questions of right and wrong aside, I feel sorry for him. It hurts me to see this happen to him."

For the first time, Sanshirō felt Yojirō to be an admirable man. "Do you think he saw the newspaper?"

"It wasn't in the paper we take. That's why I didn't know about it. But the Professor reads other papers at school, and even if he didn't see it, somebody would be sure to tell him."

"So he probably knows by now."

"Of course he knows."

"He hasn't said anything to you?"

"Not a word. But then, I haven't had time for a decent talk with him lately. I've been running all over the place with that drama thing—and I'm fed up with that, too! I ought to quit. Who cares if a bunch of idiots smear themselves with makeup and put on a show?"

"The Professor's going to blow up when you tell him."

"I suppose he will. I can't help that. But I'm *so* sorry I had to stick my nose in and give him this to worry about, a man like that, without vices. He doesn't drink, he doesn't smo—"

Yojirō cut himself short. A month's worth of the Professor's philosophical smoke would make a prodigious cloud. "He does smoke a lot, but that's all he does. He doesn't fish or play Go, he has no family life to enjoy. That's the worst thing. He ought to have a wife and kids. He's such an ascetic."

Yojirō folded his arms. "For once I put a little effort into trying to cheer him up, and look what happens. You ought to do him a favor and drop over."

"Do him a favor! I share some of the responsibility too, you know. I'll go and apologize."

"You've got nothing to apologize for."

"All right. I'll go and explain things."

Yojirō left after that. Sanshirō crawled into bed and lay there, tossing and turning. It was easier to fall asleep at home in Fukuoka. Here, there were so many stimuli: false news reports, Professor Hirota, Mineko, the handsome young man who came and took her away.

*

It was after midnight when he finally fell asleep. Waking at the usual time next morning was truly painful. He met another Faculty of Letters student in the lavatory, someone he knew only by sight. From the fellow's perfunctory "Good morning," Sanshirō sensed he had read the article. He did avoid the subject, however, and Sanshirō volunteered no excuses.

As the warm fragrance of his morning broth reached him, Sanshirō found a letter from his mother. It looked like another long one. After he had pulled on his divided skirt—it was too much bother to change into Western clothes—he thrust the letter into the breast of his kimono and went out. Everything gleamed with a light frost.

He came to the main thoroughfare. Practically all those he saw walking there were students, all heading in the same direction, and all in a hurry. The cold street was full of the vitality of young men. In the midst of this he saw the long shadow of Professor Hirota in a gray tweed overcoat. His stride made the Professor an anachronism in these youthful ranks. It was so much slacker than that of the others around him. The Professor's shadow disappeared through the College gate. Inside was a large pine tree, its branches spread out like a giant's umbrella blocking the front door. When Sanshirō passed the gate the Professor's shadow had vanished. The only things out front were the pine tree and the clock tower above it. This clock always had the wrong time—if it was running at all.

As he glanced in through the gate, Sanshirō twice muttered the word *hydriotaphia*. Of all the foreign words he had learned thus far, *hydriotaphia* was one of the longest and one of the hardest. He still did not know what it meant. He was planning to ask Professor Hirota. Yojirō had guessed that it was something like *de te fabula*, but Sanshirō saw an enormous difference between the two. *De te fabula* was a phrase that called for dancing. Just to learn *hydriotaphia* was a time-consuming effort, and saying it twice caused one's pace to slacken. It sounded like a word the ancients had devised for Professor Hirota's personal use.

At school, Sanshirō felt as though everyone's attention was fixed on him as the author of "The Great Darkness." He tried waiting outside for class to start, but it was too cold. He stayed in the corridor. Between classes, he read his mother's letter.

Come home this winter vacation, it said, much like the orders she used to send him when he was at school in Kumamoto. Once, a telegram had arrived at the start of a vacation telling him to come home right away. Shocked to think that his mother might be ill, he had rushed back to Fukuoka. She was overjoyed to see him in one piece. What was this all about? he wanted to know. She said he seemed to be taking forever to come home, so she had asked an oracle of the Inari Shrine. It told her he had already left Kumamoto, which made her fear that something had happened to him on the way. Recalling the incident, Sanshirō wondered if he had been the victim of another oracle, but the letter said nothing about Inari. It did have a note squeezed between the lines saying that Miwata Omitsu was looking forward to seeing him, too. Omitsu had left girls' school in Toyotsu and was living at home again. His mother had asked Omitsu to sew him a quilted robe, which should be arriving soon in the mail. Kakuzō, the carpenter, had lost ninety-eight yen gambling in the hills. Her report of this incident was very detailed, and he skimmed it. Apparently three men had come to see Kakuzō about buying a hill that he owned. He lost the money while showing them around the property. At home, he told his wife he had no idea when the money was taken. She guessed that he had been chloroformed, and Kakuzō said he did remember some kind of smell, but everyone in the village thought he had been cheated at gambling. His mother concluded with the moral of the story: if something like this could happen in the country, then he had better watch his step in Tokyo.

As he was rolling up his mother's long letter, Yojirō walked over to him and said, "Aha, a woman's hand!" His spirits had improved since last night if he was making jokes.

"Don't be stupid, it's from my mother," Sanshirō answered with a touch of annoyance. He returned the letter in its envelope to the breast of his kimono.

"Are you sure it's not from a certain Miss Satomi?"

"No, it is not."

"Say, have you heard about Miss Satomi?"

"Heard what?"

Just then a student came to tell Yojirō that someone was waiting on the floor below to buy a ticket to the play. Yojirō hurried downstairs.

*

With that, Yojirō disappeared. Sanshirō badly wanted to catch hold of him, but Yojirō was not coming back. There was nothing for Sanshirō to do but throw himself into taking notes. When the lectures ended, he went to Professor Hirota's, as he had promised to do the night before.

The house was as quiet as ever. The Professor was stretched out in the sitting room, asleep. Was he not feeling well? Sanshirō asked the old servant. No, that was not it, she replied. He had told her that he was sleepy from staying up late the night before, and he had lain down as soon as he came home from school. A small quilt lay on top of his long frame. Again Sanshirō questioned the maid in soft tones: what had kept him up so late? The Professor always stayed up late, she said, but last night, instead of studying, he had had a long talk with Yojirō. Now that Yojirō had taken the place of studying, Sanshirō no longer had an explanation for the Professor's nap, but at least he could be sure that Yojirō had had his talk with the Professor. He wanted to ask what sort of scolding Yojirō had received, but the maid could not be expected to know that. He had lost any chance of finding out when he let Yojirō slip from his grasp at school. Yojirō had probably gotten off lightly, though, judging from his good spirits. But then the workings of Yojirō's mind were forever beyond Sanshirō, and he could not imagine what had actually happened.

Sanshirō sat down in front of the charcoal brazier. The iron kettle was ringing. The maid withdrew to her room. Sanshirō sat cross-legged, warming his hands over the kettle and waiting for the Professor to wake up. He was sound asleep. Sanshirō enjoyed the tranquil mood. He tapped the kettle with his fingernails. He poured himself a cup of hot water, blew across it a few times, and drank it down. The Professor lay facing the other way. His hair was exceedingly short; he had probably had it cut just a few days ago. The tip of his heavy mustache was visible. Sanshirō could not see his nose from here, but the steady sound of his breathing was clearly audible. He was sleeping peacefully.

Sanshirō opened *Hydriotaphia*, which he had brought to give back to the Professor. He sampled a few passages at random but understood very little. There was something about throwing flowers into the grave. It said the Romans "affected" the rose. He did not know what that meant, but he supposed you could translate it something like "to be fond of" them. The Greeks used the "amaranthus," it said. This was not clear, either, but it must have been the name of a flower. A little farther on, the text became completely unintelligible. He took his eyes from the page and looked at the Professor, who was still asleep. Why had the Professor lent him such a difficult book? And why, though he could not understand it, did this book arouse his curiosity so? He decided in the end that Professor Hirota was himself *hydriotaphia*.

At that point Professor Hirota woke up. He raised his head and looked at Sanshirō. "When did you get here?" he asked. Sanshirō urged him to go back to sleep. In fact, he was not at all bored.

"No, I'm getting up," he said, and did so. He started blowing more philosophical smoke. It emerged in shafts in the silence.

"Thanks for the book. I'm returning it."

"Oh, did you read it?"

"Yes, but I didn't understand it. To begin with, I don't understand the title."

"*Hydriotaphia.*"

"What does it mean?"

"I don't know myself. I suppose it's Greek."

Sanshirō lost the courage to ask any more. The Professor yawned. "Mmm, I was tired. That was a nice nap. I had an interesting dream."

It was about a girl, he said. Sanshirō expected him to go on with the dream, but instead the Professor invited him to the public bath. They went out carrying towels.

*

After bathing they mounted a scale in the dressing room and measured their heights. Professor Hirota was five feet seven inches, Sanshirō only five feet five.

"Maybe you'll grow some more."

"No, that's it for me. I've been the same for three years."

"I wonder."

The Professor still thought of him as very much a child, it seemed. When they got back to the house, the Professor invited him to stay and chat if he had nothing to do. He opened the door to his study and stepped in. Sanshirō followed. In any case, it was his duty to take care of that one outstanding piece of business.

"I guess Yojirō hasn't come home yet," Sanshirō began.

"I think he said he'd be late today. He's been running around a lot on drama business. It's impossible to tell whether he enjoys helping out or he just likes running around."

"He's a kind person, that's for sure."

"I suppose there's some kindness in what he aims to do, but his brain is not made for kindness, so he doesn't do much good with it. At first glance, he seems to know what he's doing— knows all too well what he's doing—but in the end he loses track of what he was doing it for, so it all falls apart. I just leave him alone, though, because he won't change, no matter what I say. He was born into the world to do mischief."

Sanshirō felt there must be some way to defend Yojirō, but he was faced now with an unfortunate case in point. He changed the subject. "Did you see the article in the paper?"

"Yes, I did."

"Was that the first you had heard of all that?"

"It was."

"It must have been a shock."

"A shock? Well, I suppose to some extent it was a shock. But I know what life is like, so I don't shock as easily as a younger man."

"It must have been upsetting."

"I suppose, to some extent, it was upsetting. But not everyone who has lived in this world as long as I have would accept that article as the truth. So again, I'm not upset as easily as a younger man. Yojirō was spouting a lot of nonsense about setting things straight—he'd ask a friend of his on the newspaper to have the true story printed, he'd find out who sent it in and get even with him, he'd feature a rebuttal in his own magazine—but if you have to go to all that trouble, it would be better not to stick your nose in to begin with."

"He did it all for you, Professor. He didn't mean any harm."

"No, of course he didn't mean any harm. But don't you see? If a man starts a campaign on my behalf without consulting me, he's just toying with my existence. Think how much better off you'd be to have your existence ignored. At least your reputation wouldn't suffer!"

Sanshirō had no way to respond to this.

"And that asinine thing he wrote, 'The Great Darkness'—the paper said you wrote it, but Sasaki tells me it was really him."

"That's right."

"Sasaki confessed last night. You're the one who ought to be upset. Sasaki's the only man alive who could write such idiocy. I read it. It's like some big Salvation Army drum, without substance or dignity. You'd think it was written to put people off. It's calculated from beginning to end. Anyone with a little common sense can see the author has an ulterior motive. No wonder they thought I had a protégé of mine write the thing.

When I read it, I could see the newspaper article wasn't so far-fetched after all."

*

With that, Professor Hirota stopped talking and began to blow the usual smoke from his nose. According to Yojirō, you could tell the Professor's mood by the way the smoke emerged. When it streamed out thick and straight, his philosophy had attained its ultimate height, and when it crumbled out slowly, he was serene in spirit—which meant there was some danger of his unleashing his wit on you. When the smoke lingered beneath his nose and seemed loath to part from his mustache, he was in a meditative frame of mind, or else he was feeling poetic inspiration. Most terrifying of all were the whirlpools at the nostrils, which meant he was going to drag you over the coals. Since the source of this information was Yojirō, Sanshirō did not take it seriously. But given the nature of the occasion, he carefully noted the forms in which the smoke emerged. He discovered none of the clear-cut types that Yojirō had mentioned. Instead, all of the characteristics seemed to be there at once.

Several moments went by, during which Sanshirō refrained from speaking, as though intimidated. The Professor began again. "Anyhow, it's over, so let's forget about it. Sasaki apologized for everything last night, and I suppose he's his old self again today, flying around. It won't do any good to criticize him behind his back. He's out selling tickets as if nothing had happened. Let's talk about something more interesting."

"Yes, let's."

"I had an interesting dream while I was napping. I suddenly met a girl I'd seen only once before in my life. This may sound like something from a novel, but it will be more fun than talking about newspaper articles."

"Yes. What kind of girl?"

"A pretty little thing, maybe twelve or thirteen. She had a mole on her face."

Sanshirō was a bit disappointed when he heard her age.

"When did you first see her?"

"Twenty years ago."

This, too, came as a surprise.

"It's amazing you knew who she was."

"This was a dream. You know these things in dreams. And because it was a dream, it didn't matter that it was mysterious. I was walking through a big forest, I guess, wearing that faded summer suit of mine and that old hat. Ah, I remember—some complicated thoughts were going through my head. The laws of the universe are all unchanging, but all things in the universe governed by the laws inevitably change. Thus, the laws must exist independently of the things. Now that I'm awake, it sounds pretty silly, but in my dream I was walking along in the forest, thinking seriously about this kind of thing, when I suddenly met her. We didn't walk up to each other; she was standing there, up ahead, very still. She had the same face as before, the same clothing, the same hairdo, and of course the mole. She was still twelve or thirteen, exactly as I had seen her twenty years before. 'You haven't changed at all,' I said to her, and she said, 'You're so much older than you were!' Then I asked her, 'Why haven't you changed?' and she said, 'Because the year I had this face, the month I wore these clothes, and the day I had my hair like this is my favorite time of all.' 'What time is that?' I asked her. 'The day we met twenty years ago,' she said. I wondered to myself, 'Then why have I aged like this?' and she told me, 'Because you wanted to go on changing, moving toward something more and more beautiful.' Then I said to her, 'You are a painting,' and she said, 'You are a poem.'"

Sanshirō asked, "What happened after that?"

"After that, you came."

"It wasn't a dream that you saw her twenty years ago, was it? That actually happened."

"Yes, that's what's interesting."

"Where did you see her?"

The Professor's nostrils started smoking again. He stared at the smoke and said nothing for a while. Then he continued.

*

"The promulgation of the Constitution took place in 1889, the twenty-second year of Meiji. The Minister of Education, Mori Arinori, was assassinated before he was to leave for the ceremonies.[57] You wouldn't remember. Let's see, how old are you? Yes, you were still an infant. I was in College. A number of us were ordered to participate in the funeral procession. We left school with rifles on our shoulders, thinking we would be marching to the cemetery. But that wasn't it. The gym instructor took us over to Takebashiuchi and lined us up along the street. We were supposed to 'accompany' the Minister's coffin to the cemetery by standing there. It amounted to nothing more than watching the funeral go by. I can still remember how cold it was. The soles of our feet hurt from standing still. The fellow next to me kept looking at my nose and saying how red it was. Finally, the procession came, and I guess it was a long one. An endless number of rickshaws and carriages went past us in the cold. In one of them was the little girl. I'm trying to bring back the scene, but it's too hazy, I can't form a clear picture of it. I do remember the girl, though. Even she has become less distinct as the years have passed, and now I rarely think of her. Until I saw her in my dream today, I had forgotten all about her. But back then the image was so clear, it was practically burned into my brain. Strange . . ."

"And you never saw her again?"

"No, never."

"Then you don't know anything about her?"

"No, of course not."

"Didn't you try to find out who she was?"

"No."

"And is that why you . . ." Sanshirō could not go on.

"Why I what?"

"Why you never married?"

The Professor burst out laughing. "I'm hardly such a romantic! I'm a far more prosaic character than you."

"But you would have married her if you could have, isn't that true?"

"Well . . ." he said and, after thinking about it, "Yes, I suppose I would have married her."

A look of pity crossed Sanshirō's face. When he saw this, the Professor went on. "If you're going to say I was forced to remain single because of that, it means the girl turned me into a cripple. But some people are born matrimonial cripples. They are simply incapable of marrying. Others can't marry for one reason or another."

"Are there so many things that prevent people from marrying?"

The Professor looked at Sanshirō steadily through the smoke.

"You know that Hamlet didn't want to marry. Maybe there was only one Hamlet, but there are lots of people like him."

"For example . . . ?"

"For example," the Professor began and stopped. The smoke was pouring out of him. "For example, let's suppose there's a young man. His father died early and he has been raised by his mother. Then his mother falls ill and when she is about to die she tells him to go to a certain man, that this man will take care of him. The son has never met the man, has never even heard of him. He asks his mother what this is all about. She doesn't say anything. He presses for an answer and in a feeble voice she tells him that the man is his real father. —This is just a story, but suppose there were a son with a mother like that. Don't you think he would lose all faith in marriage?"

"There couldn't be many people like that."

"No, not many, but there are some."

"You're not one of them, Professor, are you?"

The Professor laughed. Then he asked, "Your mother is still living, isn't she?"

"Yes."

"And your father?"

"He's dead."

"My own mother died the year after the promulgation of the Constitution."

12

The weather was relatively cold when the Literary Society presented its four nights of drama. The old year was drawing to a close and the new lay just in sight, not quite three weeks away. The men of the marketplace felt the holiday rush; the year-end balancing of the books fell on the heads of the poor. In the midst of this, the drama nights welcomed the more comfortably off, the men of leisure, those who saw no difference between the old year and the new.

And of these there were many, men and women, mostly young. On the first day, Yojirō proclaimed their great success to Sanshirō and told him to bring Professor Hirota along for the second day's show. Their tickets were for different performances, Sanshirō objected. Yes, of course, Yojirō answered, but the Professor would never go on his own; Sanshirō must stop by and lure him out. He agreed to do so.

He went in the evening and found the Professor seated at his low desk on the matted floor, a large book spread open in the glow of the lamp. When Sanshirō invited him out, the Professor smiled faintly and shook his head. It was the sort of thing a little boy might do, but to Sanshirō it seemed typical of a scholar. Perhaps he found a certain dignity in the silent gesture. Sanshirō bent over, looking blankly at the Professor. Hirota felt sorry he had turned him down. "If you're going, I'll walk with you as far as the theater."

They went out, the Professor wearing a black cape. He seemed to have his arms folded under the cape, but Sanshirō could not be sure. The sky hung low. It was the kind of cold night when the stars are not visible.

"Looks like rain," the Professor said.

"I hope not, for their sake."

"Yes, it would be awkward for going in and out of the theater. But Japanese theaters are a bother even when the weather is good: you have to check your shoes at the door. Plus, there's no ventilation, the place fills up with tobacco smoke, you get a headache—it's a wonder people stick it out."

"Maybe so, but they certainly couldn't have it outdoors."

"Local Shinto dancing is always done outdoors, even in cold weather."

That was beside the point, thought Sanshirō, foregoing a reply.

"To me, outdoors is best. I'd like to see a beautiful play, breathing beautiful air beneath a lovely sky, when it's neither too hot nor too cold. Then you could have a play as pure and simple as the transparent air."

"Your dream would be like that, Professor, if it were made into a play."

"Do you know about Greek theater?"

"Not much. They performed outdoors, didn't they?"

"That they did. In broad daylight. It must have been a joy. The seats were natural stone, a theater in the grand manner. I'd like to take old Yojirō there and let him have a look. It would do him good."

He was starting in on Yojirō again. Funny, because right about now Yojirō was in his element, racing around inside the cramped theater, ostentatiously lending his assistance to all he deemed in need. And even funnier would be Yojirō's plaint if Sanshirō showed up without the Professor: "He really didn't come! I wish he would come and see something like this once in a while. It would do him good. But he never listens to me, damn it!"

The Professor went on to describe the construction of a Greek theater in detail. Sanshirō learned the meaning of *theatron, orchêstra, skênê* and *proskênion.* He learned that, according to some German or other, the theater in Athens could seat 17,000. And that was on the small side. The largest seated 50,000. He learned that there were two kinds of tickets used: ivory and lead. Both were fashioned into something like medallions, with embossed or carved designs. The Professor even knew the price of admission. One day's performance cost twelve sen, a full three-day program thirty-five sen. Sanshirō was still expressing his admiration for the Professor's knowledge when they came to the door of the theater.

The place glowed with electric lights. People were streaming into the entrance. The activity here surpassed even Yojirō's description.

"Why not come in, Professor, now that you've walked this far?"

"No, not me."

He went off into the darkness again.

*

Sanshirō stood watching the Professor's receding shadow, but then he saw more rickshaws arriving and their passengers rushing inside as if they resented the time it took to check their shoes. Sanshirō, too, hurried—was in effect pushed—into the theater.

At the entrance stood four or five men with nothing to do. One in formal dress took his ticket. Sanshirō glanced across the man's shoulder into the hall. In an instant the space became very broad—and very bright. He almost wanted to shade his eyes as he was led to his seat. Fitting himself into his narrow allotted space, he scanned his surroundings. His eyes danced after the colors that these assembled human beings had brought with them. This was not simply because he kept his eyes moving but because the colors attached to the numberless human beings all moved, moved ceaselessly, each independent of the others, within the great enclosure.

On stage, the action had already begun. All the characters wore the shoes and headgear of ancient Japanese nobility.[58] A long palanquin was carried on. Someone in the middle of the stage forced it to a halt. When the men lowered the palanquin, yet another character emerged from it. He drew his sword and began dueling with the ones who had stopped the palanquin. Sanshirō had no idea what was going on. Yojirō had told him the story, but he had not paid much attention, assuming that it would be clear enough when he saw the play. Now, however, the meaning eluded him. He remembered only the name of the Great Minister Iruka. Which of them could be Iruka? he wondered. Soon he despaired of ever finding out and decided to watch the entire stage as a manifestation of Iruka. After a while the headgear, the boots, the narrow-sleeved robes, even the language began to seem Iruka-esque. In fact, Sanshirō had no very precise idea of who Iruka was to begin with. His study of Japanese history was itself a thing of the distant past, and Iruka, who figured in the most ancient part, he had forgotten entirely. Perhaps he had lived in the reign of Empress Suiko? Though it might just as well have been Emperor Kinmei. It was neither Ōjin nor Shōmu, of that he felt certain. Sanshirō was simply in an Iruka mood. That was quite enough for watching the play, he decided, looking at the vaguely Chinese-style costumes and scenery. The plot, however, he did not understand in the least. Eventually, the curtain fell.

A little before the play ended, the man next to Sanshirō said to the man next to him that the actors all spoke as if they were having a nice family chat in the living room; they were utterly undisciplined. His neighbor responded with the criticism that none of the actors knew how to stand still; they were all fidgeting. The two men knew the actors' names. Sanshirō listened closely to their conversation. Both men were handsomely dressed. He thought they must be famous. He felt certain, however, that if he could let Yojirō hear their remarks, he would disagree with them. Just then, a man in the rear shouted his approval like some Kabuki claque.[59] The two men looked around. After that they stopped talking. Then the curtain fell.

Here and there, spectators left their seats. From the stage ramp to the exit, a great milling of people began. Sanshirō raised himself slightly and, in this uneasy crouch, looked all around. There was no sign of the one he had hoped to see here. He had done his best during the performance to hunt her out. When that had failed, he had counted on finding her between plays, and now he was a little disappointed. All he could do was face front again.

The two next to him appeared to be men of broad acquaintance. Turning right and left, they produced a steady stream
of famous names—over there was so-and-so, over here was
such-and-such. They exchanged bows across the hall with one
or two. Thanks to them, Sanshirō learned who were the wives
of a few famous men. One was a recent bride whom Sanshirō's
neighbor was also seeing for the first time, apparently; he went
to the trouble of wiping his glasses and looked at her, saying,
"Oh yes, oh yes."

Just then Yojirō came scurrying across the front of the cur-
tained stage, stopping about two-thirds of the way toward
Sanshirō's end. He bent over slightly and started talking into
the audience. Sanshirō followed his line of vision—and there,
several yards directly ahead of Yojirō, was Mineko in profile.

*

The man next to her had his back to Sanshirō, who kept wishing
that something would cause the man to look in his direction.
Almost in response, the man stood up, probably tired of sitting
cross-legged in the matted box. He sat on the low railing and
looked all around the theater. It was then that Sanshirō recognized the broad forehead and large eyes of Nonomiya Sōhachi.
As Nonomiya stood up, Sanshirō caught sight of Yoshiko
behind Mineko. He tried to ascertain if there was anyone else
in the party, but the audience was packed together so tightly that,
from this distance, everyone in the front of the theater might as
well have been with them. Mineko and Yojirō appeared to be
exchanging remarks from time to time. Nonomiya also seemed
to contribute an occasional word or two.

Suddenly Haraguchi came out through the curtain. He stood
next to Yojirō and stared into the audience. He, too, was probably moving his mouth. Nonomiya nodded as if in a signal, and
Haraguchi slapped Yojirō on the back. Yojirō spun around
and, diving under the curtain, disappeared. Haraguchi came
down from the stage and made his way through the crowd to
Nonomiya, who straightened up and let him go by. Haraguchi
plunged into the crowd and disappeared somewhere near
Mineko and Yoshiko.

Sanshirō, who had been watching every movement of this group with far greater interest than he had experienced in watching the play, suddenly felt envious of this Haraguchi style of doing things. It had never occurred to him that one could approach people in such a convenient way. Perhaps he ought to try imitating Haraguchi? But the very consciousness that it would be an imitation destroyed whatever courage he might have had to try. Further restrained by the unlikelihood of there being any space left into which he might wedge himself, Sanshirō stayed where he was.

Soon the curtain rose again and *Hamlet* started. Once, at Professor Hirota's, Sanshirō had seen a photograph of a famous Western actor dressed as Hamlet. The Hamlet that appeared before him now was in much the same costume as that one. The faces, too, were similar. Both had brows knit in anguish.

The movements of this Hamlet were wonderfully nimble. He moved grandly across the stage and imparted grand movement to the others. This was vastly different from Iruka's restrained Noh style.[60] Especially when he stood in the middle of the stage, stretching his arms out wide or glaring at the sky, he aroused such excitement that the spectators were conscious of nothing but him.

The dialogue, however, was in Japanese, translated Japanese, Japanese spoken with exaggerated intonations, unusual rhythms. It poured forth so fluently at times it seemed almost too eloquent. It was in a fine literary style, but it was not moving. Sanshirō wished that Hamlet would say something a little more characteristically Japanese. Where he expected him to say, "Mother, you must not do that. It is an affront to Father's memory," Hamlet would suddenly bring in Apollo or someone and smooth things over. Meanwhile, both mother and son looked ready to burst into tears. Sanshirō was only dimly aware of the inconsistency, however. The courage to pronounce the thing absurd was not forthcoming.

And so, whenever he tired of *Hamlet*, he would look at Mineko, and whenever Mineko was hidden behind someone, he would look at *Hamlet*. When Hamlet told Ophelia, "Get thee to a nunnery," Sanshirō thought of Professor Hirota. No one like Hamlet could possibly marry, the Professor had said, which seemed true enough when you lingered over the poetry in the book, but on stage it seemed that Hamlet might just as well marry. After careful consideration, Sanshirō concluded that this was because the line "Get thee to a nunnery" was no good. The proof of this was that even after Hamlet had said it to Ophelia, you didn't feel sorry for her.

The curtain came down again. Mineko and Yoshiko went out, and Sanshirō followed their lead. When he reached the corridor, he saw them farther down, talking to a man who stood half inside the door that opened into the corridor from the left-hand seats. Sanshirō drew back as soon as he saw the man's profile. Instead of returning to his seat, he reclaimed his shoes and left the theater.

*

The night, in its true form, was dark. Passing beyond this place illuminated by the power of men, he thought he could feel an occasional drop of rain. The wind sighed in the trees. Sanshirō hurried back to his room.

The rain came late at night. Listening to it in bed, Sanshirō made "Get thee to a nunnery" into a pillar and wandered round and round it. Professor Hirota might also be awake. What kind of pillar would he be embracing? And Yojirō—Yojirō was sure to be out cold, buried in his great darkness.

Sanshirō ran a slight fever the next day. His head felt so heavy he stayed in his futon, sitting up amid the still-spread-out bedding to eat his lunch. After another nap, he woke perspiring, his mind in a fog. At that point Yojirō charged in. He had not seen Sanshirō at the theater last night or in class this morning. What was wrong? Sanshirō thanked him for coming.

"But I was there last night. I was there. I saw you come onto the stage and talk to Mineko out in the audience."

Sanshirō was feeling a little dizzy. Once he started talking, the words slipped out of him. Yojirō pressed his hand to Sanshirō's forehead. "You've got a real fever. You need some medicine. This is a bad cold."

"The theater was too hot and too bright, and outside all of

a sudden it was too cold and too dark. It's not good for you."

"Maybe it's not good for you, but there's nothing you can do about it."

"Maybe there's nothing you can do about it, but it's still not good for you."

Sanshirō spoke in ever shorter snatches, and while Yojirō was humoring him, he fell asleep. He opened his eyes again an hour later.

"You're still here?" he said when he saw Yojirō. Now he was his normal self. Yojirō asked how he was feeling. He said only that he felt heavy in the head.

"Must be a cold."

"Must be a cold."

They agreed on that point. A moment later, Sanshirō said, "Remember, the other day, you asked me if I had heard about Mineko?"

"Mineko? Where?"

"At school."

"At school? When?"

Yojirō could not seem to remember. Sanshirō had to go into detail.

"Oh, sure, I might have mentioned something like that to you," Yojirō said. Sanshirō found him highly irresponsible. Yojirō himself had a twinge of conscience and did his best to recall the day for his friend. Finally he said, "Maybe this was it. Maybe I was going to tell you that Mineko is getting married."

"Is it definite?"

"It was when I heard it. I'm not sure."

"Nonomiya?"

"No, it's not Nonomiya."

"Then it must be . . ." he started to say, and stopped.

"Do you know who it is?"

"No," he declared.

Yojirō moved a little closer to him. "I don't understand exactly, but something weird is going on. I guess it'll be a while before we know what it is."

Sanshirō wished that Yojirō would come out with the weird something, but Yojirō blithely kept his view of the situation—

and the weirdness—to himself. Sanshirō stood it as long as he could, but finally he demanded that Yojirō tell him every last thing he knew about Mineko. Yojirō laughed. And then— perhaps to comfort Sanshirō—he turned the subject in a wholly new direction.

*

"You're crazy to fall in love with a woman like Mineko. It's hopeless. First of all, she's the same age as you. Women don't go for men their own age anymore, not since O-Shichi,[61] the greengrocer's daughter."

Sanshirō kept silent, but he had no idea what Yojirō was talking about.

"Now, let me tell you why. Put a twenty-year-old man and a twenty-year-old woman side by side, and what have you got? She has the upper hand in everything, and he looks like a fool. No woman wants to marry a man she can't respect—except maybe a woman who thinks she's the greatest thing in the world. She *has* to marry an inferior man or live single. You've heard how often that happens with rich girls and such. They're happy enough to get married but they end up looking down on their husbands. Well, Mineko is a lot better than that. She would never marry a man she can't respect. Anyone who thinks he's going to marry her had better realize that—which is why guys like you and me don't qualify to be her husband."

So Sanshirō ended up in the same camp as Yojirō. Still, he remained silent.

"Look at it this way. Both of us are way ahead of Mineko. Right now. You and me. Just the way we are. But she won't be able to see that until another five or six years go by. Of course she's not going to sit around waiting that long, so you've got as much chance of getting together with her as a horse and cow in heat."

Yojirō chuckled to himself over that one. "Think about it. Another five or six years and there'll be way better women than Mineko. The women outnumber the men in Japan even now.[62] It's no use catching a cold and running a fever over one of them. I mean, there's a world full of women out there: it's not worth the worry. Tell you the truth, I've got a few myself, but one of them was giving me so much trouble I told her I had to go to Nagasaki on official business."

"What are you talking about?"

"What do you mean, what am I talking about? A woman of mine."

Sanshirō was astonished.

"Well, she's not the kind of woman you've ever gotten close to. Anyhow, I told her I had to go to Nagasaki for a bacteria test and I wouldn't be able to see her for a while. But she said she'd bring me some apples when she came to the station to see me off. I didn't know *what* to do!"

Sanshirō was more and more astonished, but he managed to ask, "So what happened to her?"

"I don't know. She was probably waiting at the station with her apples."

"You rat! How could you do such a rotten thing?"

"Yes, I know it was rotten and she didn't deserve it, but I didn't know what else to do. Fate just kept things moving that way, one small step at a time. Actually, I was a 'medical student' from early on."

"Why did you have to lie to her?"

"I don't know, it just sort of happened. It got me in trouble one time, though. She got sick and asked me to examine her."

Sanshirō was beginning to see the humor in all this.

"I looked at her tongue and tapped her chest and gave her this phony doctor act. So far so good, but then she asked if I could give her a thorough examination in the hospital."

Sanshirō finally burst out laughing.

"So don't worry. These things happen all the time," Yojirō concluded. Sanshirō had no idea what that was supposed to mean, but he was feeling happy now.

Yojirō chose this moment to explain the "weird something" about Mineko. Both Yoshiko and Mineko, he said, had received proposals of marriage. That in itself was nothing special, but it was apparently the same man in both cases. That was what was weird.

Sanshirō, too, found it somewhat mystifying, but the Yoshiko part, at least, was true. He had heard it with his own ears. He might have been confusing Mineko's with Yoshiko's, but Mineko's marriage was no lie, either, it seemed. He wanted to know the facts, and since Yojirō was here, it was Yojirō he asked for them. Yojirō agreed without hesitation. He would have Yoshiko pay a sick call, he said, and Sanshirō could ask her directly. An excellent solution.

"So you'll have to take your medicine and wait here in bed."

"I will, I will—even if my cold clears up."

They laughed and Yojirō went out. On the way home he arranged for a neighborhood doctor to visit Sanshirō.

*

The doctor came that evening. Sanshirō was a little flustered at first, never having received a doctor by himself before, but the man wasted no time in taking his pulse, and this calmed him down. The doctor was a polite young man. Sanshirō thought he must be a medical assistant. Within five minutes his illness was diagnosed as influenza. He was ordered to take a single dose of medicine that night and avoid drafts.

Much of the heavy feeling in his head was gone when he awoke the next day. Lying in bed, he felt practically normal. Away from the pillow, however, he was unsteady. The maid came and said the room smelled of fever. Sanshirō ate nothing, but lay looking at the ceiling. He dozed off now and then. He had clearly surrendered himself to fever and exhaustion. While he remained in their power, unresisting, drifting between sleep and wakefulness, he found a certain pleasure in submitting to nature. This was, he decided, because his illness was a minor one.

When four hours, then five hours had gone by, he began to feel the tedium. He tossed back and forth. Outside, it was a lovely day. The sun moved shadows slowly across the shoji's translucent paper. Sparrows chirped. Sanshirō hoped that Yojirō would come again today.

The maid slid back the shoji and announced the arrival of a lady guest. He had not been expecting Yoshiko to come this soon. Yojirō had done his job with typical dispatch. Sanshirō lay in bed, eyes fixed on the open doorway, when at last a tall figure appeared at the threshold. She was wearing a purple divided skirt today. Standing in the hallway, she seemed a little hesitant to enter. Sanshirō raised his shoulders from the mattress and said, "Come in."

Yoshiko closed the shoji and sat down near his pillow. The small room was a jumble and seemed all the more cramped for not having been cleaned this morning.

"Don't bother to get up," she said to him. Sanshirō rested his head on the pillow again. As far as he could tell, he was calm.

"It must smell bad in here."

"Yes, a little," she answered, but her face expressed no discomfort. "Do you have a fever? What's wrong with you? Has the doctor been to see you?"

"The doctor came last night. He said it's influenza."

"Yojirō came early this morning and told me to make a sick call. He said he didn't know what you had but that it looked serious. Mineko and I were both shocked."

Yojirō had been stretching the truth again. He might even be said to have lured Yoshiko out under false pretenses. Sanshirō was too good not to feel bad about this. He thanked her for her concern. Yoshiko untied a cloth wrapper from a basket of mandarin oranges.

"Mineko suggested I buy these on the way," she said frankly. He could not be sure whose gift it was. He thanked Yoshiko and let it go at that.

"Mineko was supposed to come too, but she's a bit busy these days. She sends her regards."

"Has something special come up to make her busy?"

"Yes, something very special." Her large black eyes fell on Sanshirō where he lay, head propped on his pillow. He looked up at her pale forehead and thought of the time, long ago, when he had first met her in the hospital. Even now, she appeared languid and, at the same time, vivacious. She brought to Sanshirō's sickbed a total comfort in which he could place his trust.

"Shall I peel an orange for you?"

She drew a fruit from the mass of green leaves. In his thirst, he drank deeply of the sweet dew, its fragrance overflowing.

"I'm sure they're delicious. They're from Mineko."

"I've had enough."

She brought a white handkerchief from her sleeve and wiped her hands.

"Yoshiko, whatever happened to that marriage proposal?"

"Nothing. That was the end of it."

"I've heard there was one for Mineko too."

"Yes, it's all settled."

"Who is the man?"

"The one who asked for me! Isn't it funny! He's a friend of Mineko's brother. Soon I'll be living in a house with my brother again. I can hardly stay at the Satomis' after Mineko is gone."

"Won't you be getting married?"

"I will, if there's a man I want to marry." She wrapped the subject up neatly with a hearty laugh. There was no one she wanted to marry now, that was certain.

*

Sanshirō stayed in bed four more days. On the fifth he risked a bath and looked at himself in the mirror. Not bad, for a corpse. The sight spurred him on to the barber's.

The next day was Sunday. After breakfast he dressed to ward off the cold, with two undershirts and an overcoat, and went to Mineko's. Yoshiko was in the hallway, preparing to step down into her sandals. She was about to leave for her brother's, she said. Mineko was out. He accompanied Yoshiko as far as the street.

"Have you recovered completely?"

"Yes, I'm fine now, thanks. I was hoping to see . . ."

"Kyōsuke?"

"No, Mineko."

"She's gone to church."

This was the first he had heard of Mineko's being a church-goer. He asked Yoshiko for directions as they parted. Turning three corners, he came out in front of the church. Sanshirō had never had anything to do with the "Jesus religion," had never seen the inside of a church. He stood out front and looked at the building. He read the placard announcing the sermon. He walked back and forth beside the iron fence, and sometimes he leaned against it. He was determined to wait there until Mineko came out.

Eventually he heard singing. This must be what they call a hymn, he thought. It was something that happened inside high, sealed windows. Judging from the volume, there were a good many people singing. Mineko's must be one of the voices he was hearing now. Sanshirō listened closely. The singing stopped. The wind blew. Sanshirō turned up the collar of his overcoat. One of Mineko's clouds appeared in the sky.

Once, he had looked at the autumn sky with Mineko. That had been upstairs at Professor Hirota's. Once, he had sat by a little stream in the fields. He had not been alone that time, either. Stray sheep. Stray sheep. The cloud had taken the form of a sheep.

Suddenly the church door opened. People came out, returning from Paradise to the fleeting world of men. Mineko was fourth from the last. She wore a striped, ankle-length coat. Her head was bowed as she came down the front stairway. She seemed to be feeling the cold. With her shoulders hunched and her hands clasped before her, she was doing her best to minimize contact with the outside world. Mineko maintained this air of rising to nothing until she reached the gate. As if only then aware of the rush of the street, she looked up. The dark image of the cap in Sanshirō's hand registered in her eyes. The two young people moved together by the sermon placard.

"Is something the matter?"

"I just dropped by your house."

"Oh? Well, let's go back there."

She began to turn away. She wore the same low clogs she always wore. Instead of following her, Sanshirō edged against the church fence.

"I just wanted to see you here for a minute. I've been waiting for you to come out."

"You should have come inside. You must have been cold."

"I was."

"Is your cold all better now? You could have a relapse if you're not careful. You still look a little pale."

He did not answer, but instead took a small packet wrapped in writing paper from his overcoat pocket.

"It's the money I borrowed from you. Thanks very much. I've been meaning to give it back for a long time now. Sorry I let it go."

Mineko glanced at Sanshirō, but she took the packet without protest. Once it was in her hand, though, she simply looked at it. Sanshirō looked at it too. For a few moments, they said nothing. Finally, Mineko spoke. "Are you sure you don't need this?"

"No, I had it sent from home a while ago for this very reason. Please take it."

"I see. Well then, I will."

She put the packet in the breast of her coat. When she withdrew her hand, she was holding a white handkerchief. She pressed it to her face, looking at Sanshirō. She might have been inhaling something in the cloth. All at once, she held it out. The handkerchief came before Sanshirō's face. A sharp fragrance poured from it.

"Heliotrope," she said softly.

Sanshirō jerked his head back. The bottle of Heliotrope. The evening in Yonchōme. Stray sheep. Stray sheep. In the sky, the high sun shone bright and clear.

"I heard you're getting married."

Mineko dropped the handkerchief into her sleeve. "You know?" she said, narrowing her softly creased eyelids to look at Sanshirō. She had placed him at a distance, her eyes were telling him, but now she was sorrier about that than she ought to be. The concern did not show in her brows, however, which maintained an undeniable calm. Sanshirō's tongue became glued to the roof of his mouth.

After she had looked at him for a time, Mineko released an almost inaudible sigh. And finally, touching a slender hand to her rich eyebrows, she murmured, "For I acknowledge my transgressions, and my sin is ever before me."[63]

She spoke almost too softly to be heard, but Sanshirō heard

her distinctly. It was thus that Sanshirō and Mineko parted.
When he came back to his room, he found a telegram from his
mother. "When do you leave?" it said.

13

Haraguchi's painting was finished. The Tanseikai hung it on the main wall of one gallery. In front of the painting they set a long bench. It was for resting. It was also for looking at the painting. It was for both rest and appreciation. The Tanseikai thus catered for the convenience of the many spectators who would linger by this major work. This was special treatment. It was, they said, because the painting was a special accomplishment. Some said it was because the title attracted people's notice. A few said it was because of the woman in the picture. One or two of the Tanseikai members explained that it was simply because the painting was so big. And big it certainly was. In its new, six-inch-wide gold frame, it looked big enough to be taken for a whole new painting.

Haraguchi stopped in the day before the opening to inspect his work. He sat on the bench and looked at it for a long time, smoking his pipe. Finally, he sprang to his feet and made a careful circuit of the show. Then he returned to the bench and smoked a second leisurely pipeful.

Crowds gathered before "Woman in Forest" from the day the show opened. The bench turned out to be a useless ornament— although tired spectators would sit there in order *not* to see the picture. But even while they rested, some exchanged views on "Woman in Forest."

Mineko's husband brought her to the show on the second day. Haraguchi was their guide. When they came to "Woman in Forest," Haraguchi looked at the couple and asked, "How do you like it?"

"Excellent," the husband said, fixing his gaze on it from behind his glasses. "This standing pose holding up the round fan is especially fine. The eye of a professional *does* see things differently after all. Who else could have thought of this? The light on the face is beautifully done. The contrast between shadow and sunlight is distinct. The face alone is full of extraordinarily interesting modulations."

"I'm afraid I can't take credit for it," Haraguchi said. "The subject herself wanted it this way."

"Thank you very much," Mineko said.

"And let me thank you," Haraguchi answered.

Mineko's husband looked very pleased to hear that the idea for the picture had been his wife's. The thanks he expressed were the most gracious of all.

After midday on the first Saturday following the opening, Professor Hirota, Nonomiya, Yojirō and Sanshirō all came to the exhibition together. Leaving the rest for later, the four of them went straight in to see "Woman in Forest."

"That's it, that's it," said Yojirō.

A crowd stood in front of the painting. Sanshirō hesitated for a moment in the doorway. Nonomiya calmly strolled in.

Sanshirō glanced at the painting once from behind the crowd, and turned away. He leaned against the bench, waiting for the others.

"What a big, beautiful painting!" Yojirō exclaimed.

"Haraguchi tells me he wants you to buy it," Professor Hirota said to him.

"I'm not the one . . ." he started to say until he noticed Sanshirō leaning against the bench, scowling.

"His use of color is very stylish. It's rather chic." This was Nonomiya's critical opinion. Professor Hirota then offered his.

"It's almost too cleverly done. Now I see why he confessed he could never do a painting that plops like a drum."

"Plops like a drum? What kind of painting is that?" Nonomiya asked.

"One that's pleasantly half-witted like the plop of a little Noh drum. An interesting sort of painting."

The two of them laughed. They discussed only technique, but Yojirō had his own view. "Nobody could paint Mineko looking pleasantly half-witted."

Nonomiya shoved his hand in his pocket, looking for a pencil with which to mark the catalogue. Instead he came out with a printed card. It was an invitation to Mineko's wedding reception. Nonomiya and Professor Hirota had gone in their frock coats. Sanshirō had found an invitation on his desk the day he came back to Tokyo. The wedding had already taken place.

Nonomiya tore the invitation apart and threw it on the floor. Soon he and Professor Hirota became involved in criticizing the other paintings.

Yojirō moved closer to Sanshirō. "How do you like 'Woman in Forest'?"

"The title is no good."

"What should it be, then?"

Sanshirō did not answer him, but to himself he muttered over and over, "Stray sheep. Stray sheep."

Notes

1. *moxibustion scars*: A procedure used in traditional Chinese medicine, as practiced in Japan, sometimes performed with acupuncture, wherein bits of dried moxa (Japanese *mogusa*, or mugwort) are burned on the skin to stimulate the circulation in certain key locations of the body.

2. *Kyushu... homesick*: It is the second day of Sanshirō's three-day trip from Kyushu, the southernmost of Japan's four main islands, to Tokyo, 730 miles away. See Translator's Note for more on this tiring itinerary.

3. *during the War*: The Russo-Japanese War (1904–05), fought to determine which of the two imperial powers would dominate parts of Manchuria and Korea, cost Japan over 100,000 fighting men's lives as they took such strategic Russian-occupied ports in Manchuria as Port Arthur and Da-lien (Dairen in Japanese).

4. *college*: Sanshirō has graduated from one of five national colleges (or higher schools: *kōtō gakkō*) by way of which the exclusively male-educated elite prepared to enter one of three imperial universities, Tokyo Imperial University being the premier institution. Kyushu Imperial University would not be founded until 1910.

5. *electric lights*: A modern luxury in 1907, when most Japanese homes still used oil lamps.

6. *Fukuoka Prefecture*: See Translator's Note for information on this partially fictional address in northern Kyushu.

7. *Kumamoto*: A major city in the middle of Kyushu, site of the Fifth National College.

8. *Shiki's*: Masaoka Shiki (1867–1902), the modern haiku master, was a great friend of Sōseki's. See Chronology.

9. *straddling the fence ... fallen asleep there*: More literally, "He had taken a nap on Hora-ga-tōge." In the Battle of Yamazaki in 1582, one general was thought to have lingered on top of a

mountain pass (Hora-ga-tōge), waiting to see which side would be stronger before committing his forces. Sanshirō has gone one better and fallen asleep in the midst of his indecision.

10. *Meiji*: Period in Japanese history from 1868 to 1912. See Chronology.

11. *beam of light*: Sōseki based his description of Nonomiya's laboratory on that of a former student and literary disciple of his, the physicist Terada Torahiko (1878–1935), who did not want his own current work described in fiction and instead verbally summarized for Sōseki an experiment on the pressure of light by the American physicist Ernest Fox Nichols (1869–1924) that he was just reading. Terada later wrote how impressed he was with Sōseki's accuracy, based on a single hearing.

12. *Hongō*: One of Tokyo's fifteen wards at the time (now part of Bunkyō Ward), best known for the presence of Tokyo Imperial University. Most of the novel is set in Hongō around the University in such neighborhoods as Oiwake (where Sanshirō lives), Nishikatamachi, and Masago-chō.

13. *The Mansion*: The central campus of Tokyo Imperial University was built on the former estate of the great Maeda feudal lords of the Edo Period. The pond was a major feature of its ornamental garden, and the hilltop mansion was converted to serve as a faculty conference center. The Red Gate, frequently mentioned in the novel, was (and is) another relic of the Maeda estate.

14. *noon gun*: A cannon fired at noon in the imperial palace grounds every day from 1871 to 1929.

15. *Uraga*: The small port town into which Commodore Matthew Perry sailed in 1853, demanding that Japan open its doors to trade with the United States. See Chronology.

16. *old horse . . . Napoleon III*: In the fall of 1867, just a few months before the last Tokugawa Shōgun was overthrown, Napoleon III (r. 1852–71) presented him with twenty-six Arabian horses, one of which was said to have been kept at Tokyo's Ueno Zoo until 1894, so the rumor about the "old horse" could well have been true.

17. *letter to his mother*: Sanshirō writes in the modern colloquial style (*genbun-itchi*), more appropriate to friends and family than the traditional epistolary style (*sōrōbun*), still used in formal correspondence in Sōseki's day.

18. *Shōnosuke's latest doings*: Stage name of Toyotake Yone (*c.*1889), an actual female balladeer (*musume gidayū*) popular around the time of the novel.

19. *Professor Koizumi Yakumo*: The Japanese name of Lafcadio
    Hearn (1850–1904). See Translator's Note.
20. *Yonchōme*: The "fourth block" of the University's Hongō Ward
    included the northwest corner of the busy intersection through
    which the streetcars passed, although the stop itself officially
    belonged to the "third block" (Sanchōme) across the street. This
    was the most commercially active area near the University, but
    anyone seeking entertainment was likely to come to the inter-
    section to travel to more interesting areas such as the two
    mentioned here, Shinbashi and Nihonbashi.
21. *Kiharadana ... Kosan*: Kiharadana (or Kiharatei) was an actual
    variety theater at the time, and Kosan (1856–1930) and En'yū
    (1849–1907) were actual storytellers.
22. *fifty-five yen a month*: The average monthly income of a low-level
    civil servant at the time was 29 yen, while 50 yen was a middle-
    class average, and Sōseki had to hold three teaching jobs in 1906
    to earn up to 155 yen to support his extended family. At 200
    yen per month as the *Asahi* newspaper's staff novelist, he was
    considered handsomely paid.
23. *chrysanthemum doll show ... Dangozaka*: "Dangozaka, 'Dump-
    ling Slope,' just north of the university in Hongō, was a famous
    chrysanthemum center" (Edward Seidensticker, *Low City, High
    City* (New York: Knopf, 1983), p. 131) where, from Edo times,
    an annual display was held of large dolls clothed in chrysan-
    themums and posed to portray characters and scenes from the
    kabuki stage. The practice was abandoned for the first decade of
    Meiji but revived in 1878.
24. *new baron*: The Japanese government created a new peerage
    system in 1884, with "baron" (*danshaku*) the most widely held
    rank.
25. *lighthouse*: Yojirō is not being clairvoyant. He is referring to a
    well-known Japanese proverb for missing what is close at hand
    while focusing on what is far away, "It's darkest beneath the
    lamp," in which the word for "lamp" is synonymous with the
    word for "lighthouse," the meaning Sōseki uses here.
26. *Meiji 18*: 1885. This assumes that the novel is set in Meiji 40
    (1907) and that Sanshirō's age is calculated in the traditional
    Japanese manner, according to which a baby is counted as one
    year old in the year it is born and becomes a year older each New
    Year's day. See Translator's Note on the novel's chronology.
27. *those slim pipes*: The traditional Japanese tobacco pipe, or *kiseru*,
    usually consists of a slim, straight bamboo tube with a metal

mouthpiece and tiny metal bowl that burns the tobacco a pinch at a time.

28. *Chinese literary references*: Yojirō quotes briefly from "Fu Studies South of the City" by the poet Han Yu (768–824). See Stephen Owen, *The Poetry of Meng Chiao and Han Yü* (New Haven and London: Yale University Press, 1975), pp. 271–5. Han Yu's encouragement of learning sounds ironic coming from Yojirō's lips.

29. *Burning House of worldly suffering*: A well-known Buddhist image.

30. *History of Intellectual Development*: Sōseki owned a heavily marked-up copy of John Beattie Crozier's 1897 book by that title.

31. *moving pictures*: First shown to large audiences as a foreign import in Japan in 1897. The first Japanese films were shown in 1899, and by 1908 Tokyo had perhaps a dozen theaters.

32. *attack of the Soga Brothers*: Story based on an actual event of 1193. Brothers Gorō and Jūrō avenged the death of their father, who was a retainer of General Minamoto no Yoritomo (1147–99), *de facto* ruler of the country.

33. *Yōrō waterfall*: From a traditional tale of filial piety in which a young man scoops life-giving liquor for his father from a stream.

34. *A. Propagule*: Yojirō uses a haiku poet's playful pseudonym, "Reiyoshi," which literally means "propagule," i.e., plant material used for propagation, but which puns self-deprecatingly on the word *reiyo*'s meaning of "tiny remnant," or "remainder". As a young man hoping to germinate a new age of creative ferment, he probably would have preferred the former reading.

35. *the beach at Tago-no-ura*: celebrated in poetry for its view of Mount Fuji.

36. *red sake, a cheap local brew*: Made only in the Kumamoto area, red sake contains wood ash and other additives and preservatives that impart a reddish hue to the otherwise clear rice wine.

37. *De te fabula*: Odd fragment of a phrase from Horace's *Satires*, "*de te fabula narratur*," meaning, "the story is told of you," from a longer line meaning, "What are you laughing at? Change the name, and the story [of greed] might just as well be about you."

38. *Anglo-Japanese Alliance*: Treaty concluded in 1902 intended to limit the advance of Russia into East Asia. Abrogated in 1922.

39. *Itchūbushi*: A genteel style of narrative singing, concentrating on mournful scenes from kabuki and other dramatic traditions, with

the accompaniment of the three-stringed *shamisen*, originated by Miyako Itchū (1650–1724) and still practiced today.

40. *Idiot's Delight*: *Baka-bayashi* is Tokyo shrine festival music, performed with drums, bells and flutes.

41. *Noh drum*: Cords control the tautness of the leather head of the small hand drum used in the Noh theatre since medieval times. When the player releases the tension at the moment of striking the drum, it gives off a pleasant hollow plop rather than a sharp crack.

42. *Utamaro-style*: Kitagawa Utamaro (1753–1806), woodblock print artist.

43. *Seiyōken in Ueno*: The capacious Ueno Park branch of a famous Western restaurant originally founded in 1872.

44. *Toyotsu*: An actual village a short distance from the model for Sanshirō's Masaki Village.

45. *Tanseikai*: "Tansei," meaning "red and green," suggests the colors used in painting and is itself a synonym for "painting." According to art historian Haga Tōru, the fictional society here called Tanseikai was probably modeled on an actual organization known as the Pacific Painting Society (Taiheiyō Gakai), the sixth exhibition of which was held in June 1908, featuring over 200 works by "brother and sister" Western-style artists Yoshida Hiroshi (1876–1950) and Fujio (1887–1987), including scenes of Venice. Hiroshi had been adopted into the Yoshida family, and became Fujio's husband in 1907 or 1908.

46. *Fukami's ... works are there*: Fictional artist thought to be modeled on the recently deceased Western-style painter, Asai Chū (1856–1907).

47. *bronze figure at the top of Kudan*: Japan's famous (and internationally infamous) Yasukuni Shrine, dedicated to the spirits of the country's war dead, is situated at the top of a long hill known as Kudan Slope. There, in 1893, Tokyo's first bronze statue was unveiled, a memorial to Ōmura Masujirō (1825–69), a founder of Japan's modern army, who was assassinated by reactionary samurai for his overly Western views. At the time that *Sanshirō* was being serialized in 1908, the sculptor of the piece, Ōkuma Ujihiro (1856–1934), an influential member of the Ministry of Education's Committee for the Judging of Art, was at the center of a widely reported clash between conservative and progressive forces in the Tokyo art world. An outspoken critic of government meddling in aesthetic affairs, Sōseki was no doubt using Haraguchi to poke fun at Ōkuma.

48. *the Literary Society's*: Founded in 1906 to promote the moderniz-
    ation of Japan's literature, drama, fine arts, education, and even
    religion, the Literary Society (Bungei Kyōkai) soon narrowed its
    focus to drama and gave rise to many key developments in
    modern Japanese professional drama and the performance of
    translated Western drama by the time it disbanded in 1913.

49. *Hydriotaphia*: Sir Thomas Browne (1605–82), *Hydriotaphia,*
    Urne-Buriall: or, a Discourse of the Sepulchrall Urns Lately
    Found in Norfolk (1658).

50. *bell of the Great Buddha in Nara*: The Tōdaji temple, first built
    in the eighth century, houses a huge bronze image of Buddha
    and a giant bell. It is located in the ancient capital city of Nara,
    over 300 miles west of Tokyo.

51. *unohana-odoshi*: The protective plates of samurai armor were
    held together with elaborately woven colored thread "bindings"
    (*odoshi*), distinguished by color (*unohana*, or deutzia, combined
    white and yellowish green).

52. *Genroku*: A style of robe popular in the Genroku Period (1688–
    1704) and again at the time of the novel.

53. *Kannon*: The Buddhist bodhisattva of compassion, Kannon
    (Chinese Guanyin, Sanskrit Avalokitesvara) is usually depicted
    as a female. *Ukiyo-e prints*: Woodblock prints of everyday life,
    beautiful women, actors, etc., flourished in Japan from the seven-
    teenth to the nineteenth centuries. Two representative artists are
    named below in the paragraph: Kitagawa Utamaro (1753–1806)
    and Nishikawa Sukenobu (1671–1751).

54. *Pierre Loti . . . Madame Chrysanthème*: The writer (1850–1923)
    published his novel in 1887.

55. *The opportunity of time . . . he would say*: Here and in the
    next quotation, Yojirō is playing with phraseology familiar to
    educated Japanese of Sōseki's day from the Chinese philosopher
    Meng-tzu or Mencius (*c.*371–*c.*289 BC). The passage in question
    reads as follows in a classic English translation: "Mencius said,
    'Opportunities of time vouchsafed by Heaven are not equal to
    advantages of situation afforded by the Earth, and advantages
    of situation afforded by the Earth are not equal to the union
    arising from the accord of men.'" See James Legge, *The Chinese*
    Classics, 5 vols (Oxford: Clarendon Press, 1895), vol. 2, p. 208.

56. *selling encyclopedias in Japan*: In 1902, the London *Times*
    contracted with Tokyo's Maruzen book store to sell the ninth
    edition of the *Encyclopedia Britannica* in Japan, delivering all
    twenty-five volumes upon receipt of a 5-yen down payment

and accepting the remaining 190 yen in monthly installments of ten yen.

57. *Minister of Education . . . ceremonies*: See Translator's Note and Chronology. Sanshirō would have been in his fifth year at the time, Hirota in his twenty-third (or twenty-second by Western count).

58. *ancient Japanese nobility*: Sōseki attended the Literary Society's second performance series on 22 November 1907, which included Sugitani Daisui's (1874–1915) *Daigokuden* ("Great Hall") on the assassination of Minister Soga no Iruka in 645, and five acts from *Hamlet*, the full text of which was not performed in Japan until 1911.

59. *Kabuki claque*: It was (and is) customary for audience members—or theater staff seated among the audience—to shout their support for the star players in a Kabuki performance. The elevated "stage ramp" mentioned in the next paragraph is a standard Kabuki theater fixture, running perpendicular to the stage, left of center, which enabled actors to make dramatic entrances and exits through the audience. The audience here is seated in matted four-person boxes, separated by low railings, as in a traditional theater.

60. *restrained Noh style*: Developed largely in the fourteenth and fifteenth centuries, Noh (or Nō) survives as a form of masked theater noted for its restrained aesthetics and slow, stately pace.

61. *O-Shichi*: The fifteen-year-old daughter of a greengrocer, O-Shichi is thought to have fallen in love with a temple acolyte her age whom she met when she and her family were taking shelter in a temple after a fire in the Oiwake district of Edo (where Sanshirō lives) late in 1682. Convinced that arson would be the only way to meet him again, she was caught attempting to start a fire and executed in 1683. The story was retold, with many variations, in drama and fiction. See, for example, "The Greengrocer's Daughter with a Bundle of Love" in Ihara Saikaku, *Five Women Who Loved Love*, trans. Wm. Theodore DeBarry (Rutland: Charles E. Tuttle Co., 1956), pp. 157–94.

62. *The women outnumber the men . . . even now*: In fact, women of marriageable age did outnumber their male counterparts in Japan at this time.

63. *For I acknowledge my transgressions . . . sin is ever before me*: From Psalm 51.